Bunty Avieson was born and raised in Victoria. She spent twenty years as a journalist working on newspapers and magazines in Australia and overseas. Bunty spent three years on newspapers in Fleet Street before returning to Australia where she became Editor of *Woman's Day* then Editorial Director of *New Idea*. She is also a Williamson Fellow.

In 2000 Bunty took up fiction writing full-time. *Apartment 255* is her first novel. She lives in Sydney.

buntyavieson@bigpond.com

APARTMENT 255

BUNTY AVIESON

MACMILLAN

Pan Macmillan Australia

First published 2001 in Macmillan by Pan Macmillan Australia Pty Limited
St Martins Tower, 31 Market Street, Sydney

National Library of Australia
Cataloguing-in-Publication Data:

Avieson, Bunty.

Apartment 255.

ISBN 0 7329 1100 1.

I. Title.

A823.3

Typeset in Palatino 11.5/13.5 by Post Pre-press Group
Printed in Australia by McPherson's Printing Group
Author photograph: Sydney Freelance Agency

For my best friend Anna

ACKNOWLEDGEMENTS

With thanks to Linda Smith for all her help, Selwa Anthony and Cate Paterson for their faith in me, Bob Muscat, Ian Miekle and Clem Martin for their support, Kate Grant for use of her dining room, the person, whom I can't name, for their expertise on bugging procedures, my sister Christine Ronaldson for her advice on hospital procedures and Mal Watson for his love and enthusiasm.

CHAPTER 1

They say I am mad. I'm not. I'm just very, very smart. Too smart for them. I scored so well on their silly little tests they want to publish my results in a journal. Huh! Don't I get a say in that? Don't I own the copyright in my own madness? They were particularly impressed with my problem-solving abilities, they said. Ironic really, considering that's what got me in here.

They remind me of laboratory mice, scuttling around in their white coats. Why can't they wear red coats or overalls? That's what I want to know. I asked that the other day but they wouldn't answer me. Just smiled. They don't answer questions, they ask them and then they don't listen to your answers. They write them down, but they don't listen. They should. They might learn something.

The front door was heavy frosted glass with a rusty lock that made it hard to open. Ginny Hawthorne watched patiently as the Grey Suit struggled with the key, jiggling it this way then that. His smooth, steady patter continued uninterrupted.

'. . . built in the 1960s . . . a landmark in Elizabeth Bay.

1

Boats on the harbour still use the beacon on the roof for navigation.'

One final click and he had it. He chortled, a thin insincere sound that barely left his mouth. He held open the door. Ginny ducked under his outstretched arm, wincing at his aftershave.

Once she was inside it took a moment for her eyes to adjust to the gloom. The foyer was dimly lit and rather dingy, with grey-fleck carpet and beige walls. It may have been an architectural trendsetter in its day, but that was thirty-five years ago.

The Suit still hadn't drawn breath as he continued his sales pitch, extolling the virtues of the building. He spoke carefully and precisely, enunciating each syllable and looking sideways at Ginny, to gauge the effect.

'. . . most of the fifty-six apartments have been renovated and re-renovated, on average every seven years . . .'

Clearly no-one had bothered with the foyer. It was grey on grey. One forlorn potted palm struggled in a corner. A bank of letterboxes lined a wall, junk mail collecting on the floor beneath them in a messy puddle. A noticeboard hung next to them with memos about garbage days pinned next to a Neighbourhood Watch notice about car thefts in the area. Ginny took it all in with one withering glance. This really wasn't suitable. Not at all. She followed Suit past the lift and up the narrow stairs to the second floor. His socks were the same shade of dark grey as his highly polished brogues. She watched as the cuff of each leg rode up a little with each step, then bounced back onto the heel of his shoe.

They walked along an open-air corridor with a magnificent view of the Harbour Bridge. Ginny could just make out the top of a couple of the Opera House's distinctive white sails, peeking through high-rise apartment buildings. Suit stopped at Apartment 255 and sorted through his bunch of keys.

'From your kitchen you can see the Harbour Bridge and your lounge room looks out across Rushcutters Bay. It's a million-dollar view,' he said with a flourish.

He stood back dramatically with a smile so smug and triumphant Ginny wanted to turn and flee, just out of spite. She willed herself to hate whatever she saw.

As she stepped inside her first impression was of baby blue. The walls were baby blue, the carpet faded blue, even the doors and cupboards were painted glossy baby blue. It made her feel nauseous. A corridor led into a vast empty lounge room with floor-to-ceiling glass doors opening onto a small balcony. The bay sparkled in the sunlight. Dozens of yachts were moored in neat rows, their halyards tinkling on their masts. It was breathtaking.

Ginny stepped out onto the balcony. The harbour was bustling with traffic, water taxis, ferries, sailing boats, all going about their Saturday morning business. In front was Rushcutters Bay, home to some of Sydney's most expensive boats. Surrounding the pretty little bay were dozens of apartment blocks, built at different times in different colours and styles. Suit pointed out the Cruising Yacht Club, asking if she was interested in sailing.

Ginny was hearing but not listening. It took her a moment to realise his tone had changed. She knew he was expecting some sort of response from her. She had said almost nothing since Suit had introduced himself outside as the real estate agent, as if he could have been anything else. Everything about him irritated Ginny.

'I'm sorry?' she asked politely, wishing he would fall backwards over the balcony.

He repeated the question.

'No, I don't sail,' she said flatly, trying to get her tone just right – rude enough to silence him but not so rude as to make further business uncomfortable. In spite of herself she liked what she saw.

'Is that Toft Monks?' she asked, pointing to a huge building with rows and rows of balconies facing her.

'Yes, one of Sydney's most expensive properties,' he replied, studying her from beneath his heavy-lidded eyes. She had small neat features with beautiful almond-shaped, grey-blue eyes. Her face was pretty but in profile there was little softness. It was angular and stern. His eyes darted furtively down from her face. They took in the small swell of her breasts under the crisp white shirt then darted back to her face. Ginny continued to stare at the buildings. She seemed oblivious of him so he quickly glanced at her breasts again. He liked breasts. He imagined what Ginny's would look like naked, small and deliciously pert. Ginny ignored him even though she was aware of his eyes roaming over her body, sizing her up.

He moved down her body, taking in her jeans, firm around her bottom, her navy blue cardigan skimming her waist. She turned quickly to him, smiling innocently as his eyes travelled back to her face. He looked stricken, caught out.

'Gotcha,' she thought. She smiled thinly and turned back to the block of apartments facing her. Her eyes roamed over the twelve storeys. Each floor had three balconies facing her and long expanses of glass windows. They were just forty metres away, close enough to throw a ball.

'It's a very exclusive block but their view is not as good as yours. You block the Bridge from them but they see directly north. I manage a couple of apartments in there, too.'

Ginny's eyes narrowed as she counted up to the second floor. She followed the line of windows and balconies. Outside the corner apartment a man sat at a table, reading a newspaper in the morning sun. She dismissed him, moving along the windows to the middle apartment. The balcony was empty, the doors closed and the huge windows on either side were solid blocks of impenetrable darkness. The next balcony's doors were open. A surfboard leaned against a chair. She could see children moving about inside. Her eyes were drawn back to the empty balcony with its closed doors. It looked like a face, blank and expressionless, as if asleep, all life temporarily suspended.

Suit moved inside, explaining about the two double bedrooms but Ginny didn't hear him. She continued to stare at the closed balcony doors and the shuttered windows. She felt a delicious tremor work its way up her body.

'I'll take it,' she said, breaking into a delighted giggle that started as a squeak, then swelled and rose, becoming shriller and louder. Suit was startled. The unrestrained laughter seemed so out of keeping with this slim, mousy, snooty woman. There was something unnerving about that laughter that caused a ripple of unease to run along the hairs of his scalp. But even more shocking, he hadn't shown her any of the other rooms. She hadn't seen the built-in robes in both the bedrooms or the Miele appliances in the kitchen, with its cleverly hidden combination washing machine and dryer. She hadn't even seen the spa.

Suit looked at her gently heaving shoulders and neat buttocks. She had a tiny waist he was sure he could circle with his hands. He thought how much he would like to try.

'Do you have a . . . domestic partner?' he inquired.

What on earth was he talking about, thought Ginny. 'A what?'

He cleared his throat nervously. 'Will you be sharing the apartment with someone else? A boyfriend?' he asked, flashing what he hoped was his most winning smile.

Ginny looked at his brown wavy hair, slicked back behind his ears, his heavy-lidded eyes and his baby-soft skin that looked like it would bruise if she touched it. Visions of his flabby white bottom and fat paunch running through the apartment flashed before her and she suppressed a shudder. She returned his winning smile.

'I'm sure Isabel and I will be very happy here,' she said sweetly.

Suit looked crestfallen.

Ginny turned back to the view. A shadow crossed her blue-grey eyes, her expression was inscrutable. She stared intently at the closed balcony doors on the second floor of Toft Monks, enjoying little electric shocks of excitement and anticipation. The beginning of a plan was coming into focus. It was vague and unformed at the moment but she could feel it, tugging at her, rising up inside her, empowering her.

★

A few days later Ginny heaved her shopping bags up the stairs to her new apartment. She felt a thrill of happiness as she took in the view. It was breathtaking on sunny days with the sun sparkling on the water. Days like today were equally beautiful. The sky was dark purple, angry with the coming storm. She put down her bags and opened the balcony doors wide to let in the fresh salty air. She breathed it in deeply. She unpacked her shopping – a window mop, three boxes of reflective, copper-tinted window tint, a Stanley knife, a plastic bucket and Windex.

While the storm raged about her, she scrubbed and wiped the windows and balcony doors of the lounge room and her bedroom, which all looked directly across to the apartments of Toft Monks. When every skerrick of dirt was gone she wet the windows and applied the window tint, slicing around the edges with the Stanley knife. Using the window mop she pressed out the air bubbles, leaving a smooth transparent film across the glass.

Ginny stood on the balcony buffeted by wind and rain and tried to look back into her windows. Instead of seeing into her bedroom, the apartment lights from Toft Monks twinkled back at her. She looked into her balcony doors and saw her own reflection smiling triumphantly.

'Well, Isabel, what do you think of that?' she said aloud to the cat perched on top of an unopened crate. Isabel stared back glassily. Isabel had been dead for nearly three years.

CHAPTER 2

Sarah Cowley inhaled deeply, held her breath and blew out the candles. The others at the table clapped and cheered, adding to the noise in the rowdy Thai restaurant. Sarah picked up the knife and hesitated, thinking about her wish, then plunged the knife deep into the rich chocolate. Before she hit the bottom her friend Kate took the knife from her and sliced the cake into generous pieces.

The rest of the table thought this was what they were there for, an early celebration of Sarah's twenty-eighth birthday. Only Sarah and her boyfriend Tom knew otherwise. Sarah looked happily about the table at the people she loved most in the world. Kate, a cabaret singer had arrived dressed head-to-toe in leopard skin, bearing a huge stuffed, boldly printed Versace cushion. It was so expensive, so decadent and just so Kate, thought Sarah. She was a diva in the making, flamboyant and gregarious, with enough energy and charisma to turn any room into a stage with herself firmly – and loudly – in the spotlight. And underneath it all she had a heart the size of Texas.

Sarah's oldest friend Ginny was there, smiling tightly. Sarah felt a rush of sympathy. Ginny had just returned from a week in Perth where she had been sorting out her late aunt's estate. Even though Ginny hadn't been close to her aunt, she had been Ginny's last living relative and Sarah worried for her friend. How lonely she must feel, thought Sarah. And to make matters worse she was sitting next to Tom's best mate, Marty. Sarah could see by Ginny's thin-lipped smile and tense shoulders that she was not enjoying their conversation. Sarah assumed he would be making various ill-informed comments about the slaughter of rabbits. It was a topic they could never agree on. Ginny was a vet and Marty came from a long line of farmers. They should have had so much in common, but they didn't. Or at least Ginny didn't. She endured Marty, whom she dismissed as a redneck country bumpkin while he assumed they got on famously. If anyone had asked him, he would have said he and Ginny were great friends, but Sarah knew Ginny didn't share the sentiment.

Sarah's workmate Anne was there with her husband John. They had hired their first babysitter to look after their two-month-old baby and were enjoying themselves enormously. Sarah noticed that Anne had removed her dainty black sandal during the first course and propped her foot in John's lap. She obviously thought that the tablecloth covered them both but Sarah had seen the wandering foot when she dropped her napkin and had kept a bemused eye on the lusty looks that continued to pass between them. She wished she was sitting opposite Tom. She missed his big beefy presence, but he was at the other end of the table laughing along with Thelma, his gregarious mother. No party would be complete without Thel. She was an artist in her late forties, who looked like she was in her thirties, wore her jet black hair in two loose braids and told the most outrageous stories about her hippie days. She was completely devoted to Tom, having brought him up as a single mum since he was a young child, carting him around artist colonies and hippie communes, wherever she could find work and cheap accommodation. Sarah adored her.

Sarah's own parents lived in Singapore and had little to do with their only daughter. Thel had immediately recognised the loneliness of the 20-year-old girl and happily adopted her since the day Tom, then a struggling university student, had brought her home nearly eight years ago. Sarah had virtually moved into Thel's home, in the New South Wales coastal town of Kiama, during the university holidays.

Tom looked at Sarah and she gave him what he called 'the look'. It could mean an assortment of things. Can we go home now? Who's the blonde you're talking to? I miss you. Tonight it meant 'I'm ready'. Tom finished up his conversation with Thel and gestured to the restaurant owner, who had been hovering nearby waiting for the sign. The owner appeared beside Sarah with a tray of glasses and bottles of champagne.

Tom moved to the end of the table and stood by Sarah's chair, placing an arm over her shoulder. Sarah looked up at him, smiling happily. The rest of the people at the table gradually stopped their conversations and looked at Tom.

He stood still and cleared his throat.

'I know you all think you are here to celebrate Sarah's birthday . . . well you're not. That's not until next week. Tonight is special for another reason.'

Tom grinned around the table while the waiter handed each guest a glass of champagne. Marty gallantly handed his on to Ginny. He had been irritating her so much she couldn't bear to look at him and accepted it with a distant nod.

Tom squeezed Sarah's shoulder.

'We have an announcement! We thought about writing it in the sky, taking a full page advertisement in the newspaper but finally agreed that what is most important to us is sharing it with you guys. So, here you are.'

Tom paused for effect.

'Sarah and I have decided to get married.'

There were gasps of surprise and delight around the table. Anne burst into tears. Marty thumped the table. Thel laughed with joy, leaping to her feet.

'Sarah, I am so pleased,' she said, squeezing both of Sarah's hands between her own. 'I've looked forward to this day for a long, long time. You are already part of my little family, this just makes it official for the rest of the world.'

It was what Sarah needed to hear. Deep inside, beneath the confident, capable face that she showed to the world, she yearned for a place in a loving family.

The group raised their glasses and toasted Tom and Sarah. It wasn't really a surprise. They were so right together. They matched each other in so many ways. Only Ginny's enthusiasm was a little reserved. She clapped and smiled along with everyone else but her smile was stretched and her face started to ache with the strain.

Ginny watched Tom who was grinning foolishly at Sarah, looking as if he had just discovered her all over again. Ginny felt her heart ache. Sarah had charisma. There was no doubt about it. She had a special quality that made you watch her. She wasn't classically beautiful. Her hair was a mass of unruly curls. Her mouth was overwide, dominating her face. But it was an animated face, constantly changing and rearranging itself into a myriad of expressions. Her voice, like her very presence, bubbled. It caught your attention and echoed in your head long after she had stopped speaking.

There was an invisible thread between Sarah and Tom. Ginny felt it whenever she was around them. She was aware of it even when they were in a crowded room. They were like a pair of birds, flying together, mirroring each other's movements, then flying apart, sweeping and dipping and gliding in the air currents. Individual entities but tied together with an invisible thread. The bitterness welled inside Ginny.

Anne started to tell the story of Sarah as a young girl, obsessed by garden gnomes. Ginny had heard it a thousand times before and it annoyed her every time.

'She used to steal garden gnomes from lawns in the neighbourhood, bring them home and repaint them,' explained Anne. 'If they originally had red britches and a yellow shirt she would repaint them with blue britches and a green shirt, or whatever. Then, weeks later, when they were all freshly painted she would sneak in and return them to their original positions in the gardens.'

'But why?' asked Marty, the only one at the table who hadn't heard the story before.

'Because she thought they were unloved,' said Tom tenderly. 'She only picked gnomes that needed a new coat of paint.'

Thel nodded along throughout the story. It all made perfect sense to her.

'But what did the owners think when they found their family gnome had changed colours?' asked Marty, shaking his head.

Ginny steeled herself to be further irritated.

'I have absolutely no idea,' replied Sarah. 'Perhaps they thought he had changed clothes.'

Marty looked confused.

Tom laughed.

'Not everything Sarah does makes sense,' he said. 'At boarding school the teachers were always finding half-painted gnomes hidden in Sarah's shoe cupboard. They threatened to expel her if she didn't stop. Isn't that right, Sarah?'

Sarah groaned.

'Oh, Ginny, do you remember Mrs Venn? She grounded me for a week. I was stuck in that awful place, not allowed to go anywhere but from my bedroom to the classroom. I thought I would die. That was the weekend you all went off to the planetarium.'

Everyone at the table looked at Ginny as she nodded and laughed along. She remembered it well. A few times she had gone with Sarah, creeping out with her to return the gnomes to suburban gardens in the area. It had been the height of adventure for the two of them, who were closetted away from the world at the exclusive girls' school in Sydney's eastern suburbs. Ginny's face was the picture of jolly humour as she joined in the merriment over Sarah's childhood folly, but inside she seethed.

Sarah looked happily about her, warmed by the alcohol, the occasion and being surrounded by the people who meant most to her in the world. She basked in their affection. Ginny looked around the same table but the faces she saw were those of fawning sycophants. She never understood why but that's how she felt people behaved around Sarah. They just loved her. Ginny, who felt like an outsider in most social situations, found it intensely threatening. She never stopped to analyse the way she felt around Sarah. She had spent a lifetime wallpapering over the misconceptions of her psyche, each layer binding her more tightly to her distorted view of herself and the world.

Ginny believed everything had been handed to Sarah on a silver plate. At senior school Ginny had to work like a dog to get the grades she needed to become a vet. Sarah had sailed through doing a minimum of work, which didn't interfere with her socialising, but still managed to finish in the top ten per cent of the state and secured a spot in the journalism faculty at university. It was so unfair, but so typical.

Ginny saw herself as the quiet achiever, strong and navy blue. But beside Sarah she felt beige. Sarah sapped her colour, her lifeblood. Her energy could be overpowering and Ginny was constantly struggling to assert herself.

Once they had been innocent giggling schoolgirls together, spending hours sharing their important 11-year-old secrets. Then, when they hit puberty, a subtle battle had begun. Ginny had become intensely competitive, measuring her own progress and achievements against the progress and achievements of Sarah. It was a competition she couldn't win, except in her own mind, where *she* was master of the universe. She saw Sarah through a veil of self-delusion, perceiving every success and kindness as further evidence that Sarah was really weak and vain and skilfully managing to fool the world. Only she, Ginny, seemed to be able to see through Sarah to the truth.

To Ginny it seemed that Sarah had been adored since she was born and Ginny despised her for that. She also despised

Sarah because she was smart and appeared so confident. Sarah had it all so easy, Ginny thought. And it was so bitterly unfair.

It had been fine when they were young. Ginny had been happy to follow along in Sarah's wake. She lacked confidence herself and admired Sarah's easy grace and poise. She had been flattered that someone as popular as Sarah had chosen Ginny to be her special friend. But as they moved into womanhood, the dynamic had shifted and that's when Ginny's adoration had soured. It curdled inside her. She wore affection like a mask, but Ginny's own inner world was different. It was a rich private place where Ginny ruled. It was a place Ginny had retreated to a long time ago and she allowed no-one inside, not even for a glimpse.

Sarah cared deeply for Ginny. She worried about her friend. She sensed the deep-rooted unhappiness that lay at her core. Sarah did feel she was blessed. She did have everything. But she also carried with her her own insecurities, a range of emotional baggage that would fill an airport carousel. Being sent off to Kilvonia Ladies' College on the other side of the world from her parents when she was just ten years old had created inside her a deep loneliness that neither her professional success nor Tom could ever erase.

Like Ginny, Sarah wasn't given to introspection. But unlike Ginny she had a basically kind heart. She would never set out to hurt anyone else. When she felt unsure and intimidated she had developed a way of switching off her own feelings to focus on someone else. As long as she had someone else to worry about she could avoid facing herself. It worked beautifully. Focussing on other people's problems usually pushed her own to the background where they lost their intensity and power. It was part of the reason people naturally gravitated toward her. They sensed her genuine interest in them.

Sarah made sure she included Ginny in everything she and Tom did, and worried that if she didn't ask her out she would wither away in her apartment with just her stuffed cat for company. When Sarah looked at the forthright, attractive

13

young woman sitting at the table she still saw the wild-eyed, scared 11-year-old girl who had appeared one evening in the boarding school dining room. She had looked like a little doll, petite and neat in her starched new uniform. The class bully had immediately locked onto Ginny, sensing her unease, hissing loudly so everyone could hear, 'Check out the new girl, what a loser.' Sarah's heart had turned over at the look of bewilderment on Ginny's face.

Back then Sarah had instinctively reached out to the timid young girl. Ginny had been almost disbelieving when Sarah had loudly invited her to join her table. As the weeks progressed they spent every moment together and Ginny was so proud to be friends with the most popular girl at school. But as they grew older Ginny grew tired of living in Sarah's shadow. She resented the role she felt she had been cast. She wanted more. She was tired of being a bit part in Sarah's fabulous life. She wanted to *feel* the confidence, the adoration, and have the fun. And she wanted Tom. More than anything in the world, she wanted Tom. She wanted to see the love in his eyes when he looked at her. Not the friendly, good-natured affection she saw now, but the desire and hunger that was palpable when he looked at Sarah. She wanted to feel his desire, his passion.

She felt it was her right. Sarah could have any man she wanted. Ginny wanted only one.

Ginny's love for Tom had twisted inside her over the years. It crystallised the resentment she felt for Sarah and that resentment had festered, growing like a malignant tumour. Ginny was powerless to walk away. She had to beat Sarah to reclaim her sense of self.

They were an unlikely duo, their lives inexorably entwined. Ginny was locked in an unholy war that existed entirely in her own head. Sarah was equally trapped by her own blind loyalty. To her Ginny was still the scared and vulnerable little girl she had rescued from the school bully. Ginny needed her. Their friends knew – albeit instinctively – how it worked.

When Sarah organised a birthday party for Ginny, they all came armed with smiles and champagne. When they threw dinner parties at home they would include Ginny. But the relationships never took on a life of their own, independent of Sarah. Kate would never think to call Ginny and arrange lunch. And John and Anne wouldn't have invited Ginny to their baby's christening if Sarah hadn't first suggested it. Sarah and Ginny were mostly a package. You wanted Sarah, you got Ginny thrown in.

But, unbeknown to anyone at the table that night, Ginny had decided to change the script. Things were going to be different from now on. She had been thinking while she was in Perth. From behind her champagne glass she watched Sarah sparkle and shine among her friends and family, blissfully ignorant of the years of repressed venom Ginny was about to unleash.

Tom and Sarah's table was still celebrating at midnight as the Thai restaurant owners started to clear away the other tables. No-one was in any mood to leave and the owners were happy for them to stay as long as they liked. Sarah finished her umpteenth glass of champagne and feeling quite giddy, made her way to the ladies toilet. She passed the kitchen, smiling her greetings to the Thai owner. He was stocky and fit with a broad grin.

'Good evening, Miss Sarah. Congratulations to you and Tom,' he said with a faint bow. 'May you be very happy together for many, many years.'

Sarah was touched by his sincerity.

'Thank you, Sawar. The food was delicious as always,' she said, or, at least it was what she tried to say. Her voice was slurred and unintelligible. She giggled and shrugged. Sawar smiled. Sarah and Tom often came to dinner there and he liked the friendly young couple. He was happy they chose his restaurant for their momentous announcement. He had taken special care tonight, giving them the best table, overlooking the floodlit courtyard. He and his wife Liam had been excited all night, watching discreetly what was happening at their table, waiting for Tom to give them the nod.

As soon as Sarah left the table Tom leaned across to Ginny.

'Ginny, could you do me a favour?' he whispered.

Ginny nodded immediately.

'I'm surprising Sarah with a weekend in the Blue Mountains. We will be away for three days and I know Sarah will fret about the goldfish and the plants. Please, could you drop in and look after things?'

'Tom, you are so sweet. Of course I will,' said Ginny.

Tom slipped a spare key to her under the table.

'Thanks, Ginny. I want to take her away for a romantic break.'

Ginny felt an electric current pass up her arm as Tom's warm fingers grazed her palm. She held them for just a moment. The key was warm from Tom's pocket and Ginny clutched it, smiling happily.

As Sarah emerged from the cubicle she could still hear her rowdy table. Tom was laughing loudly, his deep baritone sounding masculine and sexy. Kate was firing up and launching into her favourite country and western song, 'Delta Dawn'. It was going to be a long night. She splashed cold water on her face and pinched her cheeks. She could hear Tom and Marty erupt into another round of raucous laughter as the women of the table joined Kate singing *'Delta Dawn, what's that flower you have on, could it be a faded rose from days gone by . . .'* Sarah reapplied lipstick, pouting at her reflection. *'. . . And did I hear you say, he was a meetin' you here today . . . to take you . . . to his mansion in the skyyyyy . . .'* She was back at the table in time for the final chorus. She wouldn't have missed it for anything. Kate, resplendent in her leopard skin, and Thel, braids flying, were on top of their chairs belting it out, while Sawar and his wife looked on in bemusement.

'I said he's going to take you . . . yeah, he's going to take you . . . and you and you and you . . .'

CHAPTER 3

There's something going on. I don't know what it is. No-one will talk to me. Everyone is talking in urgent whispers. They think I don't notice. But I do. I notice everything. I have seen the way Sister Johns looks when Dr Hubert comes around, like some lovesick twit, and how she fights with that other nurse to join him on his rounds.

But it's something else. I can smell it. Dr Hubert's been asking some funny questions during our little talks. What's he up to?

He writes it all down, with that scratchy fountain pen on that frighteningly white, white paper. Whatever I say or don't say, or think, goes into that folder. I know which drawer he keeps me in, in that big grey filing cabinet that looks like a slick, glossy whale, perched on its flippers. I'm in the chest cavity.

'Sarah, this is gorgeous,' Kate said, looking around her with interest.

The party, minus Thel, had staggered drunkenly down the street to Tom and Sarah's new apartment in the very upmarket Toft Monks, one of Elizabeth Bay's most famous buildings. The fresh air went some way towards sobering them up but they were still merry and charged with energy.

'Isn't it stunning?' agreed Ginny. 'Come and see the view, Kate.'

Outside, the evening was warm and still, a beautiful Sydney night. The sky was filled with stars. The only sound was the gentle tinkling of halyards on boat masts and the distant sound of laughter and music from a cruising party boat.

Ginny pointed out the lights of Taronga Park Zoo across the harbour.

'You can't see the Bridge because of that building,' Ginny said gesturing to the high-rise apartment block opposite.

Kate was uncomfortably aware of how close Ginny was. The large balcony was empty but Ginny stood next to Kate, her arm against Kate's. Kate shifted her weight onto her back foot and eased herself imperceptibly away.

'God, it's ugly,' continued Kate. 'It looks like something out of the eastern bloc. Moscow is filled with apartment blocks that look just like that – ugly.'

Ginny leaned towards Kate. Her shoulder rubbed against Kate's shoulder. She was so close Kate could smell the alcohol on her breath.

'But the beauty of living inside an ugly building like that would be that you wouldn't notice it. You would only see out, to the view. It's the other people, like the people who live here, who have to put up with its ugliness,' said Ginny.

Kate knew Ginny was looking at her, expecting some sort of reply. Her face was a short distance from her own. Kate nodded, unable to turn her head and meet Ginny's gaze. She felt herself tense. Ginny always had this effect on her. She always stood too close, crashing through that invisible comfort zone that Kate felt was her own inviolate body space. It wasn't that Ginny was overly intimate. She was just intrusive. She didn't seem to recognise people's natural boundaries.

'My father shared that same philosophy,' said Tom, stepping onto the balcony, his booming voice making Ginny jump. 'When we were kids he used to buy the ugliest cars second-hand because they were cheaper. He had a bright orange Holden and then, when he had driven that into the ground, a lime-green Ford. No-one else would buy them because the colours were so awful but Dad figured he didn't have to look at them. He was in the car looking out, at all the nice white or red or navy-blue cars with their shiny chrome.'

Kate was relieved Tom had appeared. It meant she could extricate herself from Ginny.

'I'll just go and see how that Versace cushion looks on your couch,' she said, sliding past Ginny.

Ginny didn't notice her leave. She was aware only of Tom.

'You know in all the years I've known you that is the first time I have heard you mention your father,' said Ginny. Her face softened as she looked up at Tom. 'You don't talk about him much, do you?'

It was a calculated understatement. Tom *never* spoke of his father. Ginny felt a rush of warmth, standing on the darkened balcony, drinking in his nearness.

'Well, I guess there hasn't been much to say. He left us when I was eight, took off for Sydney and I haven't seen him since. But, funnily enough, I got a message at the newspaper from him the other day. He had read something I wrote and realised I was living in Sydney. He wants to catch up.'

'How wonderful,' enthused Ginny.

'That's what Sarah said.'

'You're not so sure?'

Tom breathed in deeply, leaning forward on the railing. The merriment of the night had loosened his tongue. He wasn't the kind of man to share his innermost feelings, except perhaps with Sarah.

'I don't know. It's been so long,' he said slowly, looking across the harbour. 'What if I don't like him? What if he doesn't like me?'

'I doubt that, Tom,' said Ginny softly.

'Hey, it's possible,' said Tom with a grin. 'Unlikely, but possible. And then there's all those other questions like, for starters, why did he leave, why didn't he keep in touch? Why now?'

Ginny pictured Tom as a small, tousle-haired boy, bewildered by his adult world. She ached for him. She had her own painful childhood memories that she kept locked away in a secret place. She leaned on the railing, her arm comfortably, companionably, against Tom's bare, muscular arm. She warmed to his body heat.

'What does Thel say?' she said carefully, desperate to say the right thing and not break the mood.

'I haven't told her. It would upset her. We don't talk about him, at all. We haven't talked about him since he left. It was pretty rough for her then, bringing up a son on her own. I don't want to upset her.'

Sarah's voice interrupted them. She called them inside for coffee, shattering the moment. Tom moved inside and reluctantly Ginny followed. Ginny watched as Sarah heaped three teaspoons of sugar into her coffee.

'Why do you have to have so much sugar?' commented Ginny, happy to find a focus for her annoyance.

'Oh, yes, Sarah likes her sugar,' said Tom. His tone was soft and suggestive and he was looking at Sarah in a way that made Ginny hurt inside.

'You know I do,' said Sarah, stirring it into her coffee slowly and seductively. 'It's a pity you *don't* like sugar.'

'Oh, no, I don't like sugar myself. I can't stand the stuff. But I like for *you* to have sugar,' replied Tom.

Ginny felt uncomfortable and she wasn't sure why. There was something passing between them that she didn't understand. They seemed oblivious of the others in the room. Their banter was tender and intimate and the look passing between them was laden with sexual innuendo. She wondered what private meaning sugar held for them. Sarah happily shared much of her and Tom's relationship with Ginny. But there was a point where Sarah would smile serenely, as if she held a delicious secret, and she would draw a veil over the conversation.

Sarah continued to smile at Tom. She knew he was remembering the first night they had made love. They had had dinner at an Italian restaurant and, as the night wore on, the realisation that this would be the night she would give herself to him had dawned on her slowly, tantalising her and filling her body with a languid ease. Every mouthful and every gesture had become a form of foreplay. Tom had ordered coffee and had been surprised as she placed three sugar cubes in her cup.

'You like sugar,' he had said to her then, eight years ago. When she nodded, he had taken a sugar cube out of the bowl and held it to her lips. He had continued to hold it, while she licked and nibbled the cube. It was almost unbearably sensual and she had felt herself surrendering to him there and then.

Sarah brought herself back to the present. She turned to her friend, suddenly self-conscious as she became aware of Ginny's eyes on her.

She had heard snatches of Tom's conversation with Ginny on the balcony.

'So what do you think, Ginny? Doesn't it seem kind of exciting to discover you have a dad who you haven't seen since you were a child?'

Sarah was instantly sorry she had spoken. She knew Ginny's own upbringing was a deep-rooted source of pain for her. Her parents had died when she was a baby and she had been brought up by an aunt in Perth until she was eleven, when the aunt had sent her off to boarding school in Sydney. Sarah, being separated from her own parents, had under-stood her anguish. The aunt, who clearly hadn't wanted the young girl, had set up a trust fund to pay her way and then wiped her hands of her. Ginny never spoke of those early years.

When Sarah's parents had jetted in to Sydney a few times a year to see their daughter, Sarah had always included Ginny in their outings. Her parents, constantly distracted though they were by their own lives, had always made Ginny wel-come. Sarah saw the look of pain on Ginny's face.

'Well, I think that's entirely up to Tom,' replied Ginny evenly. 'Your relationship with your parents can be very per-sonal. I don't think anyone can tell anyone else how to handle such things.'

Ginny curled herself into an armchair. She had a knack of folding herself into a compact package, taking up the smallest amount of space possible. Sarah watched her shrink and chastised herself for being so insensitive. The poor girl had just come back from burying her only relative. Sarah moved the topic back to Tom, trying to recapture the light mood.

'Well, I can't imagine not being at least curious. Tom, don't you even want to see him? I know I do. It might give me some idea of what you will look like in twenty years, whether it's worth my while hanging around or whether I should get out now. I want to know if he's bald, with a beer belly and no teeth.'

Ginny looked disapproving. 'Sarah, how could you be so flippant?'

Sarah laughed and wrapped her arms protectively around Tom. 'I'm sorry, darling,' she purred. 'I've had far too much champagne and that was insensitive of me. I promise I'll love you whether you lose your hair and your teeth or not.'

Ginny looked away, closing her ears to the sound of the kiss she knew was coming. From where she was sitting she could see across the water to her own balcony, dark and closed and silent, as if it held secrets of its own.

A few nights later Ginny sat in the darkness, her winged armchair pulled up to her bedroom window. She sat perfectly still, barely breathing. Her eyes were fixed, staring through a pair of high-powered binoculars. Her elbows were propped on the armrests, holding the binoculars steady. The remains of her dinner sat neglected on the floor.

A cockroach in the bathroom, scenting food, made its way along the edge of the tiles. It was huge, the size of Ginny's little finger, with wings that helped it fly short distances when it was in danger. It crossed the bathroom floor, hesitated at the carpet in the doorway, then edged slowly along the skirting board, stopping every few millimetres, twitching its antennae, then darting forward.

Ginny was oblivious of everything around her, her body taut and focussed on what she could see through the eyeglasses. Forty metres away Sarah held a delicate pale-peach satin nightgown against her body. It had slender ribbons for straps. Sarah was laughing. Ginny could see Tom leaning against the bookshelves as he smiled at Sarah, enjoying her delight. Sarah opened a second box and removed tissue paper. She spread it open and pulled out a matching peach satin wrap. She jumped up and wrapped herself around Tom, hugging and kissing him all over his head and face. Ginny groaned aloud. The cockroach, just centimetres from her unfinished dinner, froze, its senses alert. Sarah picked up the nightgown and wrap and disappeared out of the room. Ginny moved the binoculars along to the next window. Sarah tore off her clothes, kicking them aside as they fell. She looked fragile and ethereal in the subdued light of the bedside lamp. Ginny watched her strip with intense fascination. She pulled the satin nightgown over her head. It fell luxuriously around her thighs, moulding itself against her slender body as she moved. Sarah smiled at her reflection in the full-length mirror. She draped the wrap around her shoulders. It had transparent chiffon sleeves, each with a band of peach-coloured feathers around the edge. Sarah tied the sash, a peach-coloured pompom on each end. It was divinely decadent. Ginny had never seen anything like it. Sarah let the wrap hang loosely, tossing it off one shoulder with voluptuous abandon. She swirled in front of the mirror, fluffing her hair and pouting, then floated across the floor and out of sight.

Ginny moved the binoculars back to Tom. He pursed his lips as Sarah came into view. She stood in front of him, twirling provocatively. He reached for her but she pirouetted away, teasing him playfully with the pompoms. He chased her around the sofa, tearing off his shirt and tossing it behind him. Sarah stayed one step ahead, ducking and diving as he reached for her. Tom strode over the sofa, knocking it to the ground as he did so. He caught the hem of Sarah's wrap and dragged her to him. She stopped struggling and melted into his arms. Gently Tom laid her on the carpet.

Ginny watched as Sarah wrapped her hands around his neck. Ginny could have wept at the sight of Tom's broad bare back, with its well defined muscles. Ginny dropped the binoculars. They landed with a soft thud on the cockroach, severing its legs. She lunged for the telephone beside her bed and dialled their number. Juggling the phone in one hand she picked up the binoculars, not noticing the dying cockroach, and put them to her eyes. She listened to the phone ring. It rang and rang. She watched as Sarah and Tom continued writhing on the floor. 'Answer the bloody phone,' she hissed. 'Answer the bloody phone,' she repeated, more loudly, a note of hysteria creeping into her voice.

Sarah gently pushed Tom away. Smiling and blowing him kisses she crawled over to the telephone. Ginny heard her voice, soft and breathy. 'Hello?'

'Sarah, I hope I haven't disturbed you. It's Ginny.'

'Ginny. Hi. No, of course not. We were just watching TV.'

Ginny watched as Sarah grimaced at Tom and mouthed the word Ginny.

'I phoned to check you got your present. I left it with the doorman.'

'Yes, I did. He gave it to me tonight. Thanks, Ginny, I've always wanted an espresso machine. But it must have cost you a fortune. You shouldn't have spent so much.'

'Oh, you deserve it. I know how much you like your coffee. And this way I can be guaranteed of a decent cappuccino when I come over.'

'Well, I can certainly promise you that.'

Tom stretched over, kissed Sarah on the top of her head and disappeared into the kitchen.

'Did you get home okay the other night, after you left here? We were all so pissed I didn't really think about it till the next morning. Then I was awfully worried. I'm sure it's not safe to walk around Elizabeth Bay at that time of night.'

Not worried enough to call, thought Ginny.

'Yes, I was fine. It's not far at all. I was home before you turned out the lights.'

Ginny flinched as she said it. *How would I know that?* But Sarah didn't seem to notice.

'When do we get to see your new place? You're awfully mysterious about it.'

'No, I'm not. It's just a shocking mess at the moment, with boxes everywhere. As soon as I'm settled and have had it painted I'll have you both over, I promise.'

Tom reappeared in the kitchen doorway, opening a can of beer.

'Did you have a nice day at work?'

'Yes, everyone has been really lovely. I can't remember when I've had such a good birthday. And they are all delighted about our engagement. The girls in the newsroom want to throw me an office tea, whatever that is.'

Tom righted the sofa and turned on the TV. He switched channels until he found the football. He sat back on the sofa, put his feet on the table and propped a cushion behind his neck.

'Do you suppose it means you get presents to go in a home office?' suggested Ginny.

Sarah laughed. 'I sincerely hope not. I'd prefer sexy lingerie.'

'Well, all the best,' said Ginny, smiling at the sight of Tom's absorption in the television.

'You too. Thanks for the call. See you soon.'

After they hung up, Ginny settled back with the binoculars. The injured cockroach limped, unseen, under her bed to slowly die. Ginny's eyes remained glued to the window opposite. She saw Sarah try to speak to Tom. He answered her, keeping his face turned to the TV. He was completely engrossed in what was happening on the screen. Sarah gave up and walked into the kitchen.

With a triumphant smile, Ginny lowered the binoculars.

'Tee hee,' she said aloud.

CHAPTER 4

All day Ginny had tingled with excitement and anticipation. She could hardly keep her mind on the tasks at hand. A splint for a puppy. The owner, a young girl of about eight, had accidentally trodden on one of its tiny toes and broken it. She sat sobbing in the waiting room with her mother while Ginny bandaged the toe to a couple of splints the size of matchsticks. A local woman had brought in her small terrier, which the family had imaginatively named Dog, for a check-up. Dog was thirteen years old and incontinent. There wasn't much Ginny could do. Dog's kidneys had packed it in. Ginny reassured the owner as best she could and gave her some salt tablets, which wouldn't do much for Dog but at least made the owner feel better.

Ginny had offered to stay back late and tend to a sickly Rottweiler, which pleased Dr Black, who was keen to leave early. After she had given medication instructions to the Rottweiler's owner she locked the surgery doors. Her heart was racing as she pulled down the blinds. She opened the medicine cupboard and took out three huge earthenware jars filled with white powder. She read the labels carefully. She knew what she was after. Dr Black had a formidable reputation among racehorse owners. While Ginny was left in the city surgery to tend to the myriad of family pets that were brought in, Dr Black spent most of his time in the outer suburbs tending racehorses. Ginny was left in charge of the books, ordering new equipment as it was needed and re-ordering drugs from the suppliers who dropped by each fortnight.

Ginny wanted a particular steroid, a synthetic form of testosterone, which she knew Dr Black used on racehorses suffering hormonal deficiencies. She found it. Limondol. She carefully measured out two cups and put them in a small glass jar. She put the lid back on the earthenware jar, shaking it to aerate the contents, which looked considerably less but Ginny was confident Dr Black wouldn't notice. He expected Ginny to keep track of things like that. She popped the smaller jar into her handbag and wiped all the surfaces clean.

As Ginny locked the security grille she noticed a kitten eyeing her from a distance.

'Miaow,' it called plaintively, its green eyes glinting in the darkened street. Ginny looked with pity at the skinny kitten. It was a tortoiseshell, all orange and black swirls with a snowy white underbelly. She dropped to her knees and held out her hand.

'Hello, little kitty,' she crooned. She stayed perfectly still, making soothing noises, gaining the kitten's trust. The kitten came closer and sniffed Ginny's hand. She smelled of domestic dogs and cats. Interesting smells. The kitten entwined itself around Ginny's legs, purring. She could feel the kitten's bones through its fur. Its coat was shiny and not matted but it clearly hadn't eaten for days.

'You poor little thing. Don't you have a home to go to?'

The kitten purred in response.

It followed Ginny to her car and when she opened the door, leapt inside. Ginny thought for a moment. Its eyes were healthy, its fur looked pretty good. It obviously hadn't been living on the streets for long. She climbed in and shut the

27

door. It was a precarious ride, the kitten sitting up attentively on the passenger seat, swaying as Ginny turned corners. They arrived at Tom and Sarah's apartment. Ginny slid out of the car seat, juggling her handbag and a bunch of fresh flowers, and carefully blocking the kitten from escaping.

'I won't be long. Behave yourself,' she told the kitten.

She let herself into Tom and Sarah's apartment just as the sun was setting behind Ginny's own apartment. A vibrant red glow of the lights in the city reflected from the windows of the neighbouring apartment blocks, making them appear to be on fire.

It was just how Ginny felt. On fire. Alive.

'Hello,' she called out. 'Hellooooo.'

The apartment was quiet. Ginny laughed aloud, feeling wicked and powerful. She walked around the deserted flat. Sarah's birthday flowers were drooping on the dining table. She moved into the bedroom. The faint smell of Sarah's perfume hung in the air. Ginny wrinkled her nostrils with distaste. She never wore perfume herself. She hated it, the artificiality of it, just like she hated aftershave and air freshener. To her they all smelled wrong.

The bed, a magnificent wrought-iron four-poster, was covered with a white lace bedspread and white lace pillows of all shapes. Ginny's eyes skimmed over it, even though she willed herself not to look at it. The room disturbed her. The bed, the smells, Tom's navy bathrobe hanging on the back of the door. She had been inside the bedroom once before. Sarah had taken her in to show her an expensive new suit and Ginny had sat on the bed watching while Sarah tried it on for her approval. Of course, Sarah had looked gorgeous and, of course, Ginny had told her so. Ginny had felt uncomfortable then too. She remembered that close smell, the intimate sight of Tom's discarded clothes on the chair and, while Sarah had modelled the outfit for her, Ginny had been consumed with the thought that she was sitting on the exact spot where Tom made love to Sarah.

A photograph of Sarah, smiling, her hair blowing about

her face, sat framed on a bedside table. Ginny curled her lip. No doubt Sarah put it there. What vanity.

Ginny felt the bitterness well inside her. Any doubts she had were smothered under its weight.

In the kitchen she hunted through the cupboards and found the sugar bowl. It had a screw top to discourage the cockroaches and ants. She set it down beside the new coffee maker with a small smile of delight that her gift was clearly being used. She took the jar of white powder from her handbag and sprinkled some of the contents inside. She looked at her hands. They were perfectly still. She was trembling inside but she knew her hands wouldn't betray her. They were the hands of a skilled surgeon.

The steroid powder was much finer than the sugar. Using a teaspoon, she mixed it around until it was indistinguishable from the sugar. She opened the pantry and took out a paisley tin marked 'Sugar'. She tipped the remainder of the white powder into the tin, stirred it up and then inspected it carefully. Dissatisfied, she took out a serving spoon and stirred vigorously. When she was sure the powder wasn't visible, she carefully washed the spoon under hot water, dried it on her jeans and put it back in the drawer. She replaced the sugar tin, turning the label around to the front just as it had been when she opened the pantry.

Then Ginny fed the fish. She sprinkled the food on the surface, watching for a moment as they realised it was there and swam hungrily towards it. She enjoyed being in the apartment on her own. Everywhere she looked she could see evidence of Tom. She could almost imagine him sitting in the kitchen chatting to her while she worked. She threw out the dying flowers and replaced them with a fresh bunch. Flowers for Tom. She watered the plants, Tom's plants.

She bustled about, humming to herself, remembering the first time she had laid eyes on him. It had been the day of her twentieth birthday and he had taken a seat opposite her at the University Café. He was tall and solid, with piercing blue eyes and a shock of unruly blond hair. He had asked her if the seat was taken. She had looked up at him and found herself unable to speak. He had smiled, a sort of shy, lopsided grin that touched something deep inside her. She had been too shocked to speak and just stared at him dumbly. He kept smiling and when she still didn't speak he sat down. He was wearing a rumpled denim shirt. Ginny could hardly take her eyes off him. He was just twenty-two and oozed maleness. Ginny had had little contact with men and was completely at a loss as to what to say.

She had never had a boyfriend or a lover. Her experience with the opposite sex had been limited to just two clumsy, and unhappy, episodes.

The first was at fifteen when she was invited along to see a movie with Sarah and her boyfriend Craig and Craig's best friend Howie. Howie was a handsome, funny 16-year-old Jewish boy from Edgecliff who Ginny found entertaining. She was quite chuffed when they sat down and Howie immediately put his arm along the back of her seat, just like Craig had with Sarah. When the hero of the movie had taken the leading lady into his arms Ginny quite liked the way Howie stroked her bare shoulder. It suited the mood so perfectly. But when suddenly he planted his lips over hers and tried to stick his tongue in her mouth she was so shocked she had fled the cinema. Sarah had laughed when she told her, then been all concerned when she realised how upset Ginny was. Ginny had resented Sarah intensely and that day a tiny seed had been planted.

Her second experience came a few months later at a party that she and Sarah had snuck out of the school grounds to attend. They had arrived just as a round of spin the bottle was starting. Ewen was a neat, good-looking blond boy with gold wire-rimmed glasses. He was a maths whiz, whom Ginny had met at dancing classes. He had been quite determined when he invited Ginny to join in the game. Ginny had been so surprised she had said yes. Ewen led her into the darkened lounge room, lit only by a freestanding lamp covered with a red scarf. In the lurid red glow eight others gathered in a circle on the floor.

Ginny was relieved to see Sarah join the group, giggling at something Craig was saying in her ear.

For Ginny the anticipation was almost unbearable as each player took it in turns to spin the empty wine bottle. Nervous laughter would erupt as the bottle ended its spin, pointing at one of the teenagers. Ginny was relieved that for the first few rounds the bottle had pointed away from her. The kisses started out chaste, just a peck on the lips. Then it had been Ewen's turn. He looked Ginny in the eye and winked, then picked up the bottle and spun it. But Ewen didn't remove his hand, deliberately guiding it to its stop, pointing directly at Ginny. She felt a mixture of embarrassment and excitement. Ewen stood up and – ignoring the cries of 'You cheated' – strode confidently across the circle to Ginny. He held out his hand to help her to her feet. Ginny felt her cheeks grow hot as he took her in his arms and bent her backwards. He planted his lips hard against hers. This time the tongue wasn't such a shock and Ginny was quite delighted when she felt it probing in her mouth. The warmth of his mouth and his tongue filled her senses. The kiss seemed to last forever and Ginny gave herself up to it completely, revelling in the new sensations.

When finally Ewen released her she felt quite giddy. It took her a moment to realise the roar in her ears wasn't the blood racing through her arteries but her friends erupting in raucous, ribald laughter. She stumbled and they cheered more loudly. One wag called out 'Ewen's got a hard-on' and another added 'So's Ginny!' They all roared with laughter and Ginny felt instantly shamed. She couldn't meet anyone's eyes. She hated to be the centre of attention. She hated even to be noticed. And to be mocked in this way was the ultimate humiliation. She had no quick rejoinder, no smart, sassy comeback. Her confidence plummeted. She felt once again the outsider and fled to the bathroom. Sarah rushed after her but Ginny couldn't face her. She felt wretched as she sat in the cold bathroom, ignoring her friend's concerned voice outside the locked door. Her friends were high on adolescent hormones and alcohol, and the next day no-one really remembered Ginny's public moment. But Ginny did. Ginny's budding sexuality took a beating that night and it wasn't until Tom strode into her life five years later that she again felt the stirrings of desire.

The day that Tom took a seat opposite her, something in Ginny came alive. Tom settled down with his books and tray of food and they ate their meals in silence. The café was busy and noisy with students and teachers filling their trays and finding seats, but no-one came near their table. Ginny felt she and Tom were surrounded by a bubble of energy that excluded the rest of the world. She was acutely aware of Tom's hands, as they handled the cutlery, slicing the food and forking it into his mouth. He had strong, square hands with short, neat fingernails. He chewed slowly and thoughtfully. Ginny wondered what he was thinking. She imagined he was as aware of her as she was of him. She basked in the thought, squaring her shoulders and preening ever so slightly. She felt a charge in the air.

It was to be the first of many such encounters. The good-looking young man, she discovered from the sticker on his book, was Tom Wilson, a third-year journalism student, majoring in politics. He ate at the café every Tuesday and Thursday. So Ginny did too. She worked out what time his class finished and made sure she came into the café just after he had taken a seat. Then she would sit where she could see him. She was never quite confident enough to sit opposite him but always sat nearby, in his line of sight. She was far too shy to strike up a conversation. Instead, as she ate, she would enjoy wonderful conversations in her head, where she was witty and charming and he was attentive and interested. It went on for the whole year. While the rest of the students made lifelong friends, started relationships, broke up and partied, Ginny was busy with her studies, content to enjoy her imaginary affair with Tom.

Every Tuesday and Thursday Ginny would sit in her classes watching the clock on the wall above her tutor's head as the hand inched its way to 12.30 pm. The last ten minutes were excruciating as she would anticipate the café and seeing her Tom, as she had come to think of him, for their twice-weekly date. She would bite her lip anxiously as she wondered if he would be alone and whether this would be the day their relationship moved along and they spoke. She imagined he was shy like her and that he was taking it slowly, because he respected her and wanted their love to develop slowly.

So it came as something of a surprise when Sarah dragged her along to a party to celebrate the end-of-year exams and Tom was there. Ginny had never imagined seeing him outside their café. He was easily the best-looking man in the room, leaning casually against a door, a beer in his hand. Ginny spotted him and felt a nervous rush. She immediately bolted to the bathroom. Her head was spinning. It was Tom. He was here. Every centimetre of that gorgeous man was out there in the hallway. He hadn't seen her, Ginny was confident of that. What would he do when he saw her? Her mind raced. Of course it was inevitable. They were meant to be together. It was fate. She looked in the mirror and noted her reflection. She looked pretty good. Sarah had talked her into borrowing a low-cut blue chiffon shirt. It was far sexier than anything Ginny owned. It accentuated her grey-blue eyes, deepening the colour of them. She pulled the neckline higher, feeling self-conscious and exposed. Then she pushed it a bit lower, and a bit lower, revealing just a hint of cleavage. She felt reckless. She felt sexy.

When Ginny walked out the bathroom door into the hallway crowded with university students, drinking and yelling over the loud music, she was beautiful. One man smiled invitingly at her but she sailed past him, on her way to be with the man she loved and who she was confident loved her. The timing was so right. Everything about this night was so perfect.

She moved slowly along the hallway, past couples chatting and flirting. She laughed with good humour when a man knocked into her. She didn't recognise anyone but she didn't care. There was only one person she wanted to see – and he was just seconds away. Ginny felt elated, on heat. Her pulse throbbed and her abdomen ached but not in a painful way. It was delicious.

She manoeuvred her way through the throng towards Tom. The crowd parted and she could see him. He was half turned from her, listening attentively to someone in the next room. He was wearing the same crumpled blue shirt he wore to university. Ginny knew all his shirts and this was her favourite. He looked like a rugged cowboy when he wore it with the faded denim jeans and cowboy boots she knew so well.

He tipped his head back and laughed, a deep rich baritone that resonated within Ginny. It was such a contagious sound. She laughed too as she drew level with him. She stood in front of him, looking up expectantly into his handsome face, her eyes aglow with happiness. He was still laughing as he turned his head towards her. He looked down into her upturned face, his eyes piercing her heart. She felt a rush of warmth flood her being, starting in the pit of her stomach and spreading through every cell.

'Ginny, there you are,' said a voice from inside the room.

It took Ginny a moment to recognise someone else was talking to her and another moment still to register that it was Sarah. With aching slowness Ginny wrenched her eyes from Tom. Sarah was standing next to him, leaning against the same doorway, her shoulder intimately close to Tom's.

'Ginny, meet Tom. He's lucky to be alive. Someone drove into the back of him as he parked out the front and then they took off.'

Tom laughed again.

'Tom, this is my best friend Ginny. She doesn't drive so it couldn't have been her.'

Tom put out his hand to shake Ginny's.

'Pleased to meet you, Ginny. And I'm glad it wasn't you.'

Ginny grasped Tom's warm hand. She started to speak but Sarah continued.

'Tom figures it was most likely someone coming to the

same party but that they chickened out after driving into him and took off. He's half expecting them to come back and quietly slip into the party,' said Sarah.

'Yes, and when they do I'll be ready for them,' said Tom in mock seriousness.

Ginny struggled to find something amusing to add. She stood there, her smile fixed on her face. It was an awkward moment. Tom and Sarah looked at her expectantly.

'Nice to meet you, Tom,' she finally stammered. She looked into Tom's face, searching for a flash of recognition. '*It's me, Tom. Ginny from the café*,' she screamed silently inside. He smiled politely, but she knew with a stab of heartbreaking certainty that he didn't recognise her. He turned back to Sarah.

'I'll bet it's that bloke over there with the green jumper,' said Sarah, tilting her head towards a bespectacled man in a loudly striped, mostly lime-green jumper.

'Why him?' asked Tom.

'I reckon he was blinded by his own jumper and ploughed straight into you.'

Ginny laughed along with the cosy twosome, feeling cold fingers of jealousy clutching at her heart. She couldn't join in their banter, didn't know how to. The confidence she had felt just minutes before dissolved and again she felt the outsider. She smiled wanly as Sarah prattled on and Tom turned his whole attention back to her.

Sarah was animated and funny. Ginny felt her own personality ebb away, draining into a puddle at her feet.

It came as no surprise then when days later Sarah had told her she was head over heels in love with a new man – Tom. At the party he had asked for her telephone number. He had taken her to the movies. They had parked outside her house and talked until the early hours of the morning. They had *so* much in common, Sarah had breathlessly informed Ginny. And ever the interested friend Ginny had listened to her gush, each word another icy dagger through her heart.

That summer Tom and Sarah fell in love. And Ginny had a ringside seat to watch. Her own love for Tom also grew. He was so decent, so kind. Before, when albeit unknown to Tom, Ginny had imagined their deep, sharing lunches, he had remained a shadowy image, reflecting back the Ginny that she wanted to be. But over the years he was with Sarah, Ginny got to know the real Tom, his humour, his gentleness, his kindness. He was a strong man with deep passions, but his love for Sarah was tender and he wore it unself-consciously. But in Ginny's own private world, she had never stopped seeing him as her Tom. That was just how it was meant to be.

The kitten was curled up asleep on the passenger seat when Ginny returned to the car. She had no trouble smuggling it, curled trustingly in her arms, into her apartment block. Once inside, the kitten leapt to life, sniffing around the furniture and boxes, eyeing off Isabel from a distance. Ginny laughed and introduced them.

'Isabel, meet Kitty.'

Tom carried the bags through the door. Sarah followed with a box of fresh fruit and vegetables that they had bought from road stalls along the way home. She stopped at the lounge room.

'Tom, look, Ginny has left fresh flowers. Isn't she thoughtful?'

Sarah dumped her box on the kitchen table and walked over to admire the bright bunch of red gerberas on the coffee table.

'Aren't they lovely. She really is sweet. I must ring and thank her.'

She looked into the aquarium. 'And the fish look happy.'

'What did you expect? She is more than qualified to shake some fish food into a fish tank,' said Tom.

Sarah laughed.

'I wonder what she did for the weekend. I hope she went out. She spends far too much time on her own. Are you sure there aren't any nice single men in your office who might like to meet her?'

'Forget it, Sarah. We're not playing matchmaker.'

'Why not?'

'Because if it goes wrong we end up stuck in the middle.'

'What could go wrong? She's smart, attractive, down to earth, loyal. She'd be a great catch for any man.'

'Yes, she would. But that's not for us to organise. She's smart enough to find her own match.'

'Yes, but what's wrong with just putting a few in front of her? For all you know the guy sitting next to you at work could be her Mr Right. And if we don't ensure that they meet each other they may never know. Would you like a coffee?'

'Yes, please. The guy who sits beside me has been divorced twice and is devoted to his job. He burps and farts. Ginny would never be interested in him. He's a dill and really that's being kind. Newspaper offices are notorious for their broken relationships. She's far more likely to find someone who interests her in her own job.'

Sarah poured boiling water into two large ceramic mugs. She made Tom's coffee strong, black and without sugar. Into her own mug she poured a dollop of skim milk and added three teaspoons of sugar. It was her one indulgence. She would read every label in the supermarket searching for stray fat molecules. But she liked her coffee hot, strong and very sweet. She stirred the sugar thoroughly and took a sip. The caffeine and sugar hit her bloodstream and gave her a rush. It felt good.

'I just feel sorry for her. I'm sure she must be lonely. I'd love to see her fall in love. She's never really had a proper boyfriend.'

'Stop worrying about her. She seems perfectly happy with her life, so why not let her be? She'll meet someone when the time is right.'

Sarah sipped her coffee thoughtfully. 'I guess so. It's just I'm so happy that I have you and you're so wonderful, I'd like to see her as happy.'

'What about Marty?' suggested Tom.

Tom had been mates with Marty since school. After they had graduated Tom had gone to university in Sydney and Marty had moved out to the country to an agricultural college. Recently Marty had moved back to the city, taking a job in the government's agricultural department. He was an affable man with a hearty sense of humour.

Sarah looked at Tom with amusement. 'For this country's top investigative reporter, you don't notice much, do you?' she said.

Tom looked bewildered.

Just forty metres away Ginny sat at her window, studying Sarah's thoughtful face through her binoculars as she cradled her coffee mug. She tried to imagine what they were saying to each other. She followed every gesture, every movement, trying to will herself into the room.

In the kitchen Kitty thumped her paw down on a cockroach, severing its spine. She toyed with its limp body, tossing it in the air playfully. Yachts returned home to their moorings in Rushcutters Bay, the sailors exhilarated from a day of racing on the harbour. The sun dropped behind the city buildings as Sarah downed the last of her coffee and Ginny watched.

CHAPTER 5

How come those birds can sit on the electricity wires? Can't they read the signs? Maybe that's why they have those red feet. It's red rubber for insulation.

Why don't dogs ever get tired? That kid has been throwing him that stick for half an hour, at least. I'm getting tired just watching. I'd like to organise a cartel of loons and take it in turns to toss the stick till the dog dropped. I might suggest that in our next group session. If I'm awake for it. He's trying me on new fog pills. Stelazine. Supposed to be just like Valium but different. Doesn't want me to get addicted to Valium. Ha. That's a joke. The only one addicted to me taking Valium is him. Makes me manageable, he says. Tears apart my soul, I say.

Sarah was in a bad mood when she got home from work. She had fought with a researcher and it had thrown her off balance so they had to do five takes of her stand-up. It made Sarah feel foolish, and she was sure the cameraman thought she was an idiot as she struggled with the simple sentences for the fifth time. She had felt edgy all day. Tom poured her a glass of wine as soon as she walked in and as soon as she tasted it she decided she didn't want it. She tried to explain to Tom about her fight with the researcher and became annoyed when he just shrugged.

'Don't let it get to you, Sarah,' he had said, summing up his own non-confrontational attitude to the working world.

Sarah felt stung.

Then when they watched the news, her story hadn't made it to air at all. Feeling like a complete failure she flounced off to have a bath. By the time she reappeared Tom had cooked dinner and she felt guilty for being so bad tempered.

'How was your day?' she asked, as he placed her dinner before her.

Tom had spent the day in court following a protracted murder trial. As a senior feature writer on the country's only national newspaper he had the luxury of spending weeks on a single article. It almost seemed an indulgence to Sarah who as a TV news reporter was supposed to churn out stories every working day.

She listened patiently as Tom explained the intricacies of the court trial. Suddenly, he changed the subject.

'I'm having lunch with Hal on Saturday,' he blurted.

Sarah had been wondering when Tom would bring up his father again. It had been a couple of weeks since he had phoned Tom, out of the blue. Tom hadn't mentioned him for more than a week but Sarah knew he had been thinking about him. He had been sleeping badly, tossing and turning and calling out in the night.

'Do you want me to come?' Sarah asked.

'No, but thank you for the offer. We're meeting at a pub in North Sydney.'

Sarah looked at him anxiously. 'Are you okay about that? Do you want to see him?'

'Yes and no. But ultimately, yes.'

Tom took the dinner plates into the kitchen, effectively ending the conversation. Sarah followed him. 'I must say you seem awfully calm about this.'

Tom kept his back to her and continued rinsing the plates. 'Do I?' he said.

'Well, yes,' said Sarah.

Tom shrugged.

After dinner they cuddled up together in front of the TV with a video and coffee.

It was a thriller and both paid little attention to the plot, each consumed with their troubled thoughts. Tom was straining to recall his father's features. He remembered his father's woody aroma, a mixture of tobacco, eucalyptus oil and automotive grease. And he could remember the feel of his father's brushed cotton shirts against his cheek. But he couldn't picture his father's face and it disturbed him deeply. He had no photographs of his father and his mother had certainly hidden away, or more likely destroyed, any she might have had.

Tom thought about his father's hands. They were huge and wide with scars and bumps. His nails were chipped and dirty. They were workman's hands. He looked at his own hands. His fingers were big and wide. The only bump he had was a writing bump on his middle finger. He remembered his dad in his workshop, hunched over the bench, always fixing something. But when he tried to picture his father's face it was blurry and indistinct. It hovered in Tom's memory but he couldn't quite grasp it.

Sarah was restless and fidgety. In her mind she went over her argument with the researcher, touching it up here and there to make herself feel better. Tomorrow she would admit she had overreacted but right now she was still smarting. She felt heavy and bloated. She disentangled herself from Tom and went into the bathroom. She slumped her shoulders, lifted her shirt and looked with disgust at the profile of the tiny mound of her belly. The tension of the day, all her old feelings of inadequacy, not being able to measure up to the impossible ideal she held for herself, welled up inside her. She felt angry and out of sorts.

She turned to the porcelain bowl and lifted the seat. She steadied herself then, placing two fingers in her mouth, she pushed them until they tickled the back of her throat. She felt a moment of discomfort then her throat started to convulse. The spasm started in her throat and worked its way down her oesophagus. She started to dry retch and then working her throat muscles brought up a sludge of undigested dinner and red wine into the bowl.

Beads of sweat formed on her forehead and at the back of her neck. She felt the gastric juices burn the lining of her throat. She tried not to breathe through her nose. She looked at the dark brown sludge in the bowl. Her throat muscles worked involuntarily, trying to keep the rest of the contents of her stomach down. Sarah shoved her fingers back down her throat and felt her stomach heave again.

When the final spasm passed she wiped the sweat from her face and the back of her neck with toilet paper, tossed it into the toilet and pressed the button. She unlocked the bathroom door and caught her reflection in the mirror. Her face, framed by a mass of corkscrew curls, was as white as the tiles.

She was filled with self-loathing. It had been so long since she had felt the need to do that. She was in control of her life now. Or she thought she was. She felt edgy now, had for the past few days. It was building inside her and the urge to purge had returned, too strong to ignore. She felt disgust at her own emotions. She wasn't going back to that again. She was better now. Just this time. But never again.

Tom watched her as she walked back into the room. She sat at the other end of the couch, staring intently at the TV.

'What did I miss?'

'Sarah, what have you been doing?' he asked suspiciously.

'Nothing. I went to the toilet. Is that all right?' Sarah replied, not meeting Tom's eyes.

'Sarah, you said you wouldn't do that any more. Why do you do that?'

'I didn't do anything,' she snapped. 'I just went to the toilet. Give me a break.'

Tom shook his head wearily. 'I don't understand you.'

'There is nothing to understand. I went to the toilet. End of story.' Sarah's tone was icy and final.

Tom felt inadequate. 'I love you, Sarah,' he said quietly.

'And I love you too. Now can we finish the movie?'

Both slept badly that night. Sarah was cold and kept waking with a draft down her back. She followed Tom across the bed, seeking his warmth, but he kept pushing her away. He was hot and kept throwing off the blankets.

Sarah was up early and cycled around the park. She had energy to burn. She brought Tom croissants and the morning papers in bed. She opened the curtains to a beautiful sunny day. They lay in bed watching the sun-speckled boats on the harbour, their spinnakers billowing in a stiff breeze. They read the papers, then they loved each other, lazily and with much tenderness, rolling over the newspapers so that Sarah ended up with newsprint on her buttocks.

Tom admired the row of gleaming Harley Davidson motorcycles as he parked outside the hotel. He stopped to look at them, taking a moment to quieten his agitation. He was reluctant to go inside, apprehensive about what he might find in there. He felt as if he were about to have a mirror held up to some facet of himself and he wasn't sure that it was a part that he would like. In his working life he liked to be completely prepared. He always knew as much about his subject as was possible before he walked into a room. But he was uncomfortably aware that there was no preparation he could do for this meeting.

He stopped and looked at a beautifully maintained Fat Boy, wide and low to the ground, its chrome handlebars reflecting the sunlight. Tom superimposed over the bike a vision from his childhood. It was fifth grade and Mr Barkley was telling him to hold out his hand. Mr Barkley administered six hard stinging slaps with the leather strap. Tom had stood and watched angry red welts rise on his palm. He remembered the searing pain and how badly he wanted to cry but he had held fast, drawing on reserves he didn't know he had. He had pushed all his emotion down and looked up unflinchingly at Mr Barkley. It was the most sobering moment of his young life. Tom drew on that memory whenever he needed courage. He took a deep breath, squared his shoulders and strode confidently into the main bar.

The hotel was old and unrenovated, one of the few inner-city hotels still to be gentrified. It was busy but subdued inside. A few old-timers at the bar, drinking solemnly. A group of bikers in leather vests and jeans played pool. A TV screen showed the day's races from around the country. Tom took a seat and ordered a beer from the barmaid. He looked around him, wondering if the grey-haired bloke staring intently at the TV screen could be Hal. No, too old.

The bar door opened and a man came in. His tall, imposing frame was silhouetted against the bright sunshine outside. He nodded to the men playing pool and they nodded back. He walked over and stood at the bar next to Tom.

'Gidday,' he said stiffly.

'Gidday,' replied Tom.

They sized each other up awkwardly.

Tom saw a fit, wiry-looking man in faded black jeans with a denim shirt and black leather vest. His face was lined with deep crevices on each side of a full sensuous mouth. He had a shock of white hair, neatly trimmed. His eyes were deep blue, the colour of Tom's. He was a stranger and yet he looked familiar. Tom felt a sneaking sense of relief.

Hal looked Tom over, taking in his vivid blue eyes, blond curly hair and lopsided grin. There was no mistaking whose son he was. Hal smiled shyly. Tom slid off the bar stool and stood in front of his father. Their eyes were level. Hal held out his hand to Tom. It was warm, dry and leathery.

Tom felt his own hand grasped in a firm handshake.

'I've been thinking about this for such a long time and now that you are here I don't know what to say.'

Hal's voice was deep and gravelly. It echoed along the walls of Tom's memory.

44

'I don't know what to say either. I know I'm pleased to see you, Dad,' replied Tom. It sounded awkward and the word hung in the air between them.

'Call me Hal, mate. Everyone does.'

Hal wanted to know all about Tom's life and he listened patiently as Tom stumbled through it, not knowing what to say or where to start. He talked of his job on the newspaper.

'Sounds like you've done pretty well for yourself. What else? Are you married?'

Tom explained about Sarah, how they had met at university.

Hal watched his face soften as he spoke of her. 'She sounds like a nice lady,' he said.

'I'd love you to meet her,' said Tom. 'She wanted to come today but I thought it was better if she didn't.'

'That's right. We've got a lot of catching up to do.'

The barmaid kept the beers coming as Tom and Hal skirted around each other. Their conversation was peppered with awkward silences. Tom's mind was full of questions that he didn't know how to articulate. He desperately wanted this man's approval.

Tom needn't have worried. Hal liked him before he walked in the door. He remembered him as a feisty eight-year-old boy, full of mischief. Hal had loved that eight-year-old boy, and carried the memory with him wherever he had travelled in the past twenty-two years. Whoever Tom had become, Hal had no doubt he would love him too. But Hal was equally anxious that Tom might not approve of him. He didn't know what to expect. Perhaps Tom was an angry young man, bitter that his father had walked out on him and his mother. And so they skirted around each other, self-conscious and wary, yet wanting to open up.

Hal talked about his Harley Davidson dealership and the bike chapter he ran in North Sydney.

'I remember your motorbikes, Hal,' said Tom, drawing on his memory's deepest recesses. 'I remember you used to lift me up onto the petrol tank and wheel me up the driveway.'

Hal was chuffed. 'You remember that? I would have taken you on the road but your mother would never let me.'

It was the first time Tom's mother had come into the conversation and Tom was attentive for what would follow. He waited for Hal to ask about her, but he didn't. Hal swiftly moved the conversation back to motorbikes.

The opening was gone and Tom, who made his living from manoeuvring conversations where he wanted them to go, was at a loss as to how to get it back there. They talked about football, politics and which Sydney petrol station sold the cheapest petrol. They compared hands, holding their palms against each other and both were delighted when they were a perfect match. Hal's hands were covered in the scars and bumps that Tom remembered but his nails were neat and clean. Tom pulled up his shirtsleeves and showed Hal a scar on his elbow. He had fallen over playing footy, not long before Hal left, and he remembered Hal gently cleaning the wound and telling him he could cry if he wanted to.

The tears filled Hal's eyes as Tom spoke. He made no effort to brush them away. 'I don't remember that,' he said softly. 'But thank you for giving me back that memory.'

As the afternoon wore on they ate meat pies, played pool with the bikers and ended up half slumped over each other at the bar. The evening trade started to pour through the doors and they said their farewells, slapping each other on the back like old war buddies. Hal embraced Tom in a smothering bear hug and then he was gone.

By the time Tom stumbled into the flat Sarah was hysterical. Her hands shook from all the caffeine she had drunk while she stared out the window imagining him wrapped around an electricity pole or stabbed in a bar room brawl.

'You could have telephoned,' she sobbed into his chest.

Tom smoothed her hair, crooning softly how he loved his Sare Bear. His eyes were bleary and his words came out thickly.

Sarah led him to the couch. She removed his boots, then went to make him a coffee.

When she came back Tom was snoring, his mouth gaping open and spittle running down his chin.

★

Sarah and Ginny met at 10 am at the beauty salon in Oxford Street for their monthly appointment. Sarah wanted a deluxe facial which included half an hour of massage. Ginny told Sarah she was having her legs waxed. It was partly true. Ginny had a problem with excess body hair. Dark curly hair, the texture of steel wool, stretched down beyond her bikini line to the top of her thighs. It was a source of great embarrassment to her and one of the reasons she was too shy to go swimming. Every month she had electrolysis to kill the roots.

Venetia, the beautician, was an attractive, petite blonde of about twenty, who probably never had a stray hair in her life. Venetia assured Ginny yet again that her stray hairs would be all gone in another six months, never to return. She led Ginny through to the booth next to Sarah. Ginny could hear Sarah chatting through the thin plasterboard that separated them.

Ginny stripped down to her briefs and lay on the vinyl bed. Venetia attached the electrodes to the needle and inserted it in a hair follicle on Ginny's thigh. On the other side of the partition Sarah was chatting about the lovely weekend she and Tom had spent at the Blue Mountains. Her lilting voice carried over the thin wall, as Ginny lay helpless on the bed.

'So it's still hot and lusty?' asked Sarah's beautician.

'I am desperate for him,' replied Sarah. 'He is the sexiest man alive, I swear. He asked me to marry him.'

The other woman congratulated Sarah and cooed over the engagement ring.

'We bought it in a beautiful little antique shop in Leura. It's rose gold. The woman said she knew the owner and she had been happily married for sixty-two years. Can you believe that?'

'Well that should bring you luck,' said the other woman.

They chatted happily about wedding plans.

'We haven't set a date but probably around September when the weather is nice but not too hot.'

Venetia pressed the foot pedal, sending a stinging current

down the probe into Ginny's hair follicle. Ginny flinched and clenched her teeth.

'How long have you been together?'

'Since uni,' sighed Sarah. 'We have just moved into a new apartment in Elizabeth Bay. It's beautiful. Lots of Sundays in bed admiring the harbour view.'

The two women laughed heartily.

Venetia moved the needle to a new follicle and pressed the pedal. Ginny's face contorted with pain. Venetia noticed and adjusted the dial, reducing the current.

'Sorry. You're not so good today?' she asked Ginny. 'Are you tired? PMT?'

Ginny nodded weakly.

Sarah made little moaning noises of contentment as her beautician worked on her neck muscles.

'I just had a birthday and Tom gave me the most gorgeous negligee and wrap. It is like something out of a thirties Hollywood movie.'

'Lucky you. The last present my boyfriend gave me was a sandwich maker because he likes toasted sandwiches when he watches the footy.'

Ginny listened to the women laugh and giggle and prattle on. She envied their easy camaraderie. Sarah could talk to anyone about anything. It infuriated Ginny.

'Why can't anyone see how spoiled she is, how vain and self-centred she is?' thought Ginny angrily, as Venetia silently pressed the pedal again.

When they both were finally finished they walked together down Oxford Street, Ginny's face a mask. Sarah walked fast, as if she were in a hurry to get somewhere but Ginny knew they had hours to browse and stop for coffee. It was their monthly ritual. They strode up Oxford Street until Sarah spotted an orange shirt she liked in a shop window. She pulled Ginny inside where it was cool and empty, with only a few dozen designer items displayed on rods on the walls. It all looked horribly intimidating to Ginny, and difficult. Skirts with uneven hems, jumpers with large slashes across the chest – Ginny would never even look at such things. She wouldn't know how to wear them. The shop assistant pointedly ignored them as she applied bright yellow nail polish behind the counter. Sarah stood in front of her.

'Excuse me,' she said for the second time, her voice rising slightly.

The shop assistant looked up, boredom radiating from every pore. She arched one eyebrow.

'If it's not too much trouble, may I see the orange shirt in the window, please,' said Sarah with exaggerated patience.

The girl set aside her nail polish with obvious irritation, put both hands carefully on the counter, fingers splayed to keep them apart and looked at Sarah.

'What orange shirt?' she asked.

Sarah turned and pointed to the sole item in the window. It was vivid orange with a high mandarin collar and slashed sleeves.

'*That* orange shirt,' she replied.

The sales assistant glanced in the direction Sarah was pointing. 'Oh *that*,' she replied, turning back to Sarah. 'That's not orange. It's goldfish.'

Sarah was too stunned to speak.

The girl resumed applying her nail polish. Her message was clear. You have been dismissed. You are not worth talking to. Ginny was agog at her rudeness and desperate to get out of there. But Sarah was having none of it.

'Oh, it's *goldfish*, is it?' she asked, her tone icy.

The girl ignored her.

'Well aren't you the rude little madam,' said Sarah angrily. 'What's your name?'

The girl looked confused. She hadn't expected this.

'Your name,' repeated Sarah ominously.

'What's it to you?' the girl asked. She still looked sullen and disdainful but there was a new wariness in her expression.

'I want to know the name of the rude little tart with the tacky yellow nail polish so I can tell Jom why I didn't buy his orange shirt,' said Sarah.

49

Ginny wondered who Jom was.

'My *friend* Jom,' continued Sarah.

Ginny had never heard Sarah mention a friend called Jom.

'It's Jane, Jane Smith,' said the girl with a sneer.

'Somehow I don't think so,' replied Sarah archly. 'But no matter. I'm sure Jom will remember who was running his shop and insulting his customers today.' She turned on her heel.

'It has been such a *pleasure* meeting you,' she said before slamming the heavy glass door. It rattled dangerously behind her. Ginny had been forgotten and with a meek smile at the assistant, who was now glowering at Sarah's retreating back, she followed her friend outside. Sarah was seething when they sat down at a nearby café.

'Can you believe that? I'm so angry. She should be sacked.'

Ginny was elated. Admittedly she had been shocked by the girl's rudeness. She had seen attitude in trendy shops before, it was part of the reason why she never went into them, but never quite so blatant as that. But what interested Ginny was Sarah's reaction. Mild-mannered, always understanding, friend-to-everyone Sarah. While Sarah vented her rage over the girl's rudeness, Ginny replayed the scene in her mind. It was glorious to see the look of dislike on the girl's face as she had sized up Sarah then turn into a look of pure loathing when Sarah had attacked her. It was balm to Ginny's soul. And Sarah's angry reactions had been so *good*. In all the years Ginny had known Sarah, she had never seen her react like that. She was usually insufferably poised.

'Who is Jom?' asked Ginny.

Sarah looked at her friend and started to laugh. 'I have no idea. His name is written on the front of the shop as proprietor. I saw it when we walked in.'

Ginny laughed too. She had been holding in all her joy and delight and now she gave it full rein. It made Sarah laugh harder. The two friends laughed until they had tears pouring down their faces. They couldn't stop, nor did they want to. It was the sort of laughing fit they had had frequently when they were schoolmates. In those days they had doubled over laughing at something silly. It hadn't taken much to set them off. It felt good to laugh like that. It was such a release of tension. Finally it subsided. Ginny composed herself first. Wiping her eyes and smoothing her hair, she looked across at her friend. Sarah had mascara smeared across her cheeks and her eyes were red and bleary.

'I haven't laughed like that in years,' said Sarah.

'Nor have I,' agreed Ginny.

'God, it feels good,' said Sarah, smiling fondly across the table at her friend.

The waitress interrupted them to take their order. When they were alone again Sarah turned to Ginny.

'How was Perth?' she asked.

Ginny's face changed instantly, her smile replaced with the tense, thin-lipped look she had worn all night at Sarah's birthday. 'Fine,' she said.

It was obvious she was lying. Sarah wondered how to draw her out. 'Did you sort out your aunt's affairs?'

Ginny would not be drawn. She would not discuss her trip to Perth with Sarah. It had been a difficult time for her and, as was Ginny's way, she would internalise her pain. She changed the subject. 'So did Tom meet his dad?'

'Yes,' said Sarah. 'They had lunch together. It sounds like it went pretty well. He said Hal is into motorbikes. He has a bike shop in North Sydney. Tom thinks that's pretty cool.'

'Has he remarried?' asked Ginny.

'That's exactly what I asked,' laughed Sarah. 'Tom doesn't think so. He said he didn't mention anybody so Tom assumes not.'

'You mean Tom didn't ask?'

'No. Don't you love it? That would have been my first question. But according to Tom they didn't talk about things like that. They didn't talk about Thel at all. Tom says her name didn't even come up. Can you believe that?'

This was familiar ground for the two friends. They had often discussed the difference between the way women, namely Sarah, went about things and the way men, namely Tom, did. It was a constant cause of fascination for Sarah and of course anything to do with Tom was of interest to Ginny. She would listen avidly to Sarah's anecdotes about life with Tom. It was a double-edged sword for Ginny. She ached for the intimacy of the life Sarah described and through encouraging Sarah to share all the details she was able to live vicariously and feed her own fantasies. But it also brought up her overwhelming feelings of jealousy. She felt its white heat burn inside her.

'Men are weird,' replied Ginny, playing her part, knowing the expected response.

'Hal says he wants to meet me,' said Sarah, looking worried.

Ginny shifted in her seat. Sarah had to bring it back to Sarah. It was always about Sarah, she thought nastily. Ginny wasn't interested in Sarah and how she fitted into this new family arrangement. She wanted to know about Tom – how he felt, what it meant to him, what he and his father had said to each other. But Ginny knew her role, the concerned friend, understanding and empathetic.

'Oh, how scary. Are you going to?' she asked.

'I suppose so, eventually,' said Sarah. 'Tom is going on a ride with him next weekend but I'm not invited. He is going to ride on the back of Hal's bike. It's a charity ride. All these bikers take toys that they have collected to a park on Pittwater where they give them to underprivileged kids and have a fete.'

'I didn't know bikers did things like that,' said Ginny.

'Me neither. Hal reckons they get about forty bikers along.'

'Wow.'

'I know, amazing isn't it?'

'So what else did Tom say about this cool guy Hal?'

'Not much. He was so hung-over when I left this morning it hurt him to talk. I hope to get the rest out of him tonight.'

The waitress arrived with their order and Sarah heaped three teaspoons of sugar into her coffee.

'How much coffee do you drink, Sarah?'

'Too much, but I love it. I love the rush it gives me. I don't think I could function without my morning cup and then my mid-morning coffee and pretty much every one after that. I get headaches if I don't have a cup.'

Ginny looked thoughtful. 'I was reading a report from America. They say that caffeine is actually good for you. I know everyone has been saying too much is bad for you but according to this report it actually helps protect you from disease. Brazilians, who drink the most, have virtually no heart disease and no blood disease.'

'Really?' said Sarah.

Ginny nodded. She had been planning this conversation for weeks, looking forward to the right time to drop it casually into the conversation. 'Yes, and what's more, it actually helps burn up calories.' She knew her friend well enough to know her triggers.

'Really,' said Sarah, suddenly very interested.

'Well, have you ever seen a fat Brazilian?' asked Ginny.

They erupted in laughter.

'Ginny, you are my oldest and kindest friend and I love you dearly, particularly now I know I can have as much coffee as I like and it's actually doing me good.'

Ginny lifted her cup to conceal her triumphant smile. 'Thank you, Sarah. The feeling is entirely mutual.'

The café was crowded and a young waitress squeezed past some people waiting for a table. She hoisted a tray of steaming focaccias and coffee above her head. It was an accident waiting to happen. As the waitress drew level with Sarah and Ginny's booth, she lost her footing on the uneven floor and the tray slipped. Ginny saw what was coming but her reflexes were too slow. The focaccias tipped sideways off the plate, knocking the coffee, which spilled onto Sarah. It was only a drop, but it landed on Sarah's bare arm. Sarah leapt to her feet in shock. Her face, which had been relaxed and smiling, instantly turned purple with rage as she turned on the waitress.

'*You stupid idiot!*' she screamed, stunning the crowd at the café into silence.

The girl was stricken. Sarah loomed over her, her face contorted in uncontrolled fury. Ginny watched in horror as Sarah shoved the girl against a seated diner.

'YOU BLOODY FOOL!'

The girl scrambled in an attempt not to fall and the diner put out his arm to steady her. She was frozen in fright and the man rose slowly, blocking her from Sarah, his eyes fixed on Sarah's white face. 'I think that's quite enough,' he said.

He wasn't a tall man but his demeanour was formidable. His tone was like steel. Sarah stood toe to toe with him, unflinching, as she angled her head so he had a view straight up her nose. The diners watched in embarrassed but fascinated silence as Sarah glared at the man. The only sound was the hissing of the cappuccino machine and muffled noises of clanging plates from the kitchen. The waitress burst into tears and fled.

'Come on, Ginny, we are out of here. I wouldn't stay in this cockroach hole for another minute,' spat Sarah.

Ginny left money on the table, gathered up Sarah's bags and scuttled out of the booth. Displaying all the righteous indignation and fury she felt, Sarah turned on her heel, haughtily dismissing the stares and whispers of the other café patrons and followed Ginny out. She stalked down Oxford Street elbowing shoppers out of her way, with Ginny scurrying behind to keep up.

Ginny stared through her binoculars. She felt elated. If she hadn't seen it for herself she would never have believed it. 'That, Kitty, is what is known colloquially as "a roid rage",' she said, rocking backwards and forwards and chuckling. She could see Tom sitting on the couch and Sarah moving about in the lounge room. They were deep in serious conversation. She wondered what they were saying. Was Sarah telling Tom about what a witch she had been, what a spectacle she had made of herself? Or was Tom talking about Hal and was Sarah

54

making wildly inappropriate comments? Poor Tom. How confused he must be feeling. Her eyes strained as she willed herself to follow what they were saying. It was no use.

Frustrated, she undressed and went to bed. She opened a book she had borrowed from the library on a whim many months ago. It was way past its return date but it was just too good to give back. Ginny had no intention of returning it. It fell open at the chapter headed 'Steroid Abuse by Women Bodybuilders'. She could almost recite the text by heart, she had read it so many times before. She read it again for pure enjoyment.

An anabolic steroid is basically synthetic testosterone, a hormone that differentiates men. While no-one is suggesting it makes women men, the effect it has on the female body is called virilisation.

'Isn't that a lovely word?' Ginny said to Kitty as the cat curled contentedly into her lap. 'Virilisation.' Ginny repeated it, enunciating every syllable of the word. 'Vir-il-is-ation.'

She continued reading.

Most notable side effects are a deepening of the voice, and increased and excessive hair growth on the arms, legs, back, chest and pubic region.

'Oh, Kitty, how gross. I wonder if that is happening to our Sarah.'

Other side effects can be a reduction of breast size. They become 'plate-like'. More symptoms include bad breath and sweating with strong body odour, since steroids are excreted through the lungs and sweat glands. Steroids are also excreted through the skin which can lead to severe acne, mainly on the chest and back. Growth of the nose and jaw have been reported, as has male-pattern baldness.

'Oh, Kitty, I like the sound of that. Male-pattern baldness. I wonder what Sarah would look like bald. Tee hee.'

Indications suggest steroid use in women leads to severe menstrual problems. As with male anabolic steroid users, they can make women irritable and cranky. 'Roid rage is more commonly associated with males but that's probably because so many more males take them.

The rest of the chapter was a series of case studies describing violent episodes that had been attributed to roid rages. One man went berserk, killing his wife with a dumbbell then attacking the neighbour who barged into the house after hearing the screams. Ginny felt her eyes grow heavy. She folded the corner of the page and put the book aside for another time. With a contented smile she drifted off to sleep.

CHAPTER 6

It was a quiet day. Dr Black was in the surgery so Ginny took a long lunch. She walked briskly to the local shopping centre, taking great, long strides. She wasn't in a hurry but she walked everywhere like that – fast, with her head thrust forward, as if her brain should get there first. She bought herself a sandwich and sat in the courtyard, by the fountain. It wasn't running. It had been broken for months and the council hadn't bothered to fix it, but she liked to eat her lunch by the still pond. It was calming.

She looked at the paved brickwork and felt a stirring of unease. It was a basket-weave pattern, quite complex, but worrying. It reminded her of something, something scary, but she wasn't sure what. It nagged at a memory so long buried the merest hint of it resurfacing sent waves of terror through her. Some of the bricks seemed to hover above the others. But when she looked directly at them, they retreated and the others seemed to hover. Ginny brought her hand up in front of her and tried to focus on it, sending the bricks away. She looked at her short, slim fingers. They looked so white, not at all like her hand. And hovering on the periphery of her vision she could see the bricks looming, swelling and retreating.

Ginny felt the panic rising in her. She looked up at the sky then bolted for the shopping centre. Her feet found the grey concrete and she kept walking, her heart clutching painfully. Neon awnings covered the sky and she started to relax. Her breathing slowed and she allowed her eyes to look down. She saw the grey concrete and felt relief wash over her. Her hands were clammy and she wiped them on her jeans.

She leaned against a shop to catch her breath and stared at the window display. It was an electronics shop. She looked at the mobile telephones laid out, all on sale, the tape recorders and microphones. She had been wrestling with a tricky problem for a few days and something was coming into focus. If she could just figure it out. On a whim she went inside. An hour later she emerged, laden with shopping bags. She walked back to the surgery, the terror of the courtyard forgotten. Her step was lighter and a small smile played about her lips.

Sarah looked in horror at the red patch on her chin. More pimples. There were three new ones, angry and red. She applied foundation, smearing it thickly across the offending patch, then patted it with a sponge to make it look natural. It didn't. She looked pasty and decidedly unnatural. There was a knock at the bathroom door.

'Sarah, are you going to be much longer? I'm running late,' called Tom.

'All right, all right,' snapped Sarah. She had slept badly and been up for an hour already, drinking strong coffee and reading the morning newspapers.

She had showered thinking she could get into work early but the sight that greeted her in the mirror had exacerbated her anxiety and she had spent fruitless minutes trying to make herself look what she considered half decent. She patted some blush over the foundation, hoping to give her pasty face some natural colour. She inspected her reflection. She looked like a garish clown. She took a tissue and wiped away most of it. She had bags under her eyes and her hair felt like straw. She looked awful.

'Sarah, it's eight-thirty. We are both going to be late. Please,' pleaded Tom.

Sarah flung open the door and glared at him. 'For God's sake,' she growled as she swept past him to the kitchen. She wasted a further five minutes hunting for her keys, which were on the floor, under the kitchen table.

She drove to work in a fury, her foot alternating between the accelerator and the brake pedal. On the approach to the Harbour Bridge a woman in a Volvo tried to move in front of her and Sarah deliberately blocked her. 'Why should I let you in?' she muttered under her breath. The woman, neatly coiffed, in her impeccably new car, annoyed Sarah for no reason at all and when she pulled in behind her, Sarah slammed on her brakes. The woman braked too, screeching her tyres and narrowly avoiding driving into the back of her. Sarah smiled with satisfaction then sped off.

She was twenty minutes late when she walked into the TV newsroom. The news director stared at her as she tried to creep past him to her desk.

'You're late again,' he barked.

Sarah knew there was no point making excuses. Bob McKenzie ran his newsroom with an iron determination. He was short and squat with a flabby beer belly and a receding bottom. He wore his trousers belted tightly under his stomach and they hung loosely behind. His temper was legendary. Sarah had borne the brunt of it a lot recently – two weeks ago because she had missed a story that a reporter from a rival news channel had succeeded in getting and twice last week because she was late. He was starting to lose patience with her and she knew it.

Sarah mumbled an apology, hoping she could get away before his temper took hold. But McKenzie's nostrils flared. He had Sarah in his line of fire this morning and it wasn't going to be so easy.

'What's that on your chin?' he asked.

Sarah kept her face averted, aware of the pimples throbbing painfully on her face. He kept staring, sizing her up like a piece of rancid meat.

'You look awful. Have you been partying all night? Doing drugs? Well you look like shit. How are we supposed to send you out looking like that? You would scare the kiddies. I don't know what's going on with you, Sarah, but get your act together or you are out. There is a queue all the way to the Harbour Bridge of people just itching to do your job. If you don't appreciate this gig, there are a hundred others who would give their eye teeth for such an opportunity . . . '

Sarah had heard this speech before. The same lines, the same threats. It was legendary McKenzie. He never commented on how the men looked. But for the women in the newsroom, it was suits with short skirts, no trousers, *never* trousers, and impeccable grooming. The message was clear. The men had to be smart. The girls had to be sex on legs. There was nothing she could say. She knew the rules. And she knew she looked awful.

'You can do foreign today.'

Sarah was flattened. It meant sitting in the editing suite cutting stories that came in from the overseas bureaus. All that would go to air of her tonight would be her voice.

'But, Bob, I've been chasing the firebug story all week . . .'

'I warned you. Now it's too late. The Premier's giving a press conference in five minutes and I've already sent someone else.'

'But, I . . .'

'I'm not interested, Sarah,' said McKenzie in a tone that left no room for argument. 'There was an earthquake in Korea last night and we have lots of footage. Get down to the editing room. Now,' he added menacingly.

The yellow phone on his desk rang and he lunged for it, knocking coffee over his desk. His face looked like thunder but his tone was moderate and calm as he spoke to his own boss. He had forgotten Sarah. She was dismissed. Sarah felt deflated. She bit her lip and headed for the ladies toilet. Once inside the cubicle she burst into tears. The mascara coursed down her cheeks, leaving black train tracks in her foundation. 'I'm too old to have pimples,' she sobbed.

She looked at her sad face in the mirror. What was wrong with her? Her skin was dry, the fine lines around her eyes were deeply etched. Her face was blotchy and red, between the pimples. She looked ghastly. And that was nothing compared to how she felt. She felt on the edge of hysteria, like she wanted to cry and throw up and kick a cat, but she didn't know which one to do first. She felt a tingling in her groin and wondered what dreadful gynaecological ailment she might have.

Maybe she should go home. Tell McKenzie she had the flu. But she couldn't face him. She'd have to stick it out.

Sarah calmed down by lunchtime. A couple of cups of strong coffee and her head cleared so she could be civil to the tape editor and get the job done. He was a nice man. Gentle and friendly. She liked sitting in the darkness with him, poring over all the film footage, arranging it into a package that would tell a story. By the time she got home she had a headache, her whole body was sore and the tingling in her groin was starting to cause her real concern. She dreaded the thought she might be pregnant. She pushed it aside. She was only just overdue. Too soon for alarm.

She took a coffee and the mail onto the balcony where the sight of the boats soothed her jangled nerves. A postcard from friends holidaying in Bali had arrived. The picture showed a beautiful stretch of snow-white sand and crystal-clear azure water. Sarah stared at it dreamily. Maybe she and Tom could go there, soon. She felt she badly needed a holiday.

Ginny sat on the floor of her living room, open boxes and discarded shopping bags strewn across the carpet. She had a book on electronics, a printout from an internet site and a tray of tools.

The man in the electronics shop had been so helpful,

explaining how to connect a carphone to a regular power supply. Then he had helped her out with a tiny microphone, so small she kept dropping it off the shop counter and losing it on the floor.

There was just one thing he had been unable to help her with which had sent her searching the net when Dr Black supposed she was updating stock on the office computer. Finally she found what she was looking for on a rogue internet site entitled 'Bugging Procedures of the FBI – What They Won't Tell You'. Ginny had read everything on the site then dropped back to the electronics store in the afternoon to buy a telephone answering machine.

She sat comparing the circuit board of the answering machine to the computer printout. Kitty circled her playfully, leaping onto the bubble wrap and tossing it in the air. This was painstaking work and Ginny knew she had to be accurate. Ignoring Kitty's wails, she locked her in the bedroom. It was nearly 10 pm when she finished, exhausted but satisfied.

Tom was late home and Sarah was in bed reading when she heard his key in the lock. She listened to him dump his briefcase on the kitchen table and felt a tremor of irritation. Why couldn't he put it in the study? She would be making breakfast there in the morning and it was annoying to have to always move his things out of the way.

He came into the bedroom, hanging his suit jacket on the door handle. He looked exhausted. 'Sorry I'm late. Are you okay?' he asked, dropping onto the bed.

'Yes. Why are you so late?' asked Sarah.

'I told you I wouldn't be home for dinner, but I didn't expect to be this late. I had to finish my piece on the juror. God, I'm exhausted.'

'Are you happy with it, your story?' asked Sarah.

Tom started peeling off his tie as he explained what he had written and why. Sarah took in little of what he was saying.

She watched him drop his clothes piece by piece on the floor. He pulled back his side of the bed and started to climb in.

'Do you think you could put those in the laundry basket?' asked Sarah.

'Sarah, I'm too tired. I'll do it in the morning,' replied Tom snuggling up to her. His feet were cold and insistent.

'If you had any respect for me you would pick up your dirty clothes and put them in the laundry basket,' said Sarah coldly.

Tom looked at her. 'Are you angry with me?' he asked.

'No, I'm not angry with you. I just think it would be nice if you would put your dirty clothes away instead of leaving them for me to pick up. I'm not your mother.'

Sarah's shoulders were rigid and her tone brittle.

Tom considered this for a moment then got out of bed, picked up his clothes and dumped them, one by one with exaggerated slowness, in the cane laundry basket behind the bedroom door.

'There,' he said sarcastically. 'Happy?'

'I would be happy if you would also pick up that blue rugby jumper on the floor. You may not have noticed it, but it has been there since last weekend.'

'Sarah, I plan to wear it tomorrow. Don't be difficult. I'm tired and I just want to go to sleep.'

Sarah leaped out of bed. She was shaking uncontrollably. It was as though Tom had pressed some unseen button. 'I'm sick of living like this. You have no respect for me. You treat me like some geisha girl, here to pick up after you.' The frustration poured from Sarah as she stood in the centre of the room, her fists clenched with impotent fury. 'You leave your hairs in the basin after you shave. You never take out the garbage. What kind of man doesn't take out the garbage? And when, when, may I ask have you ever bought toilet paper?'

Tom was perplexed. He opened his mouth to speak, not sure what he was going to say, but Sarah continued her torrent, a catalogue of imagined slights, misdemeanours and outright insults that Tom had heaped on her over their years together.

'You are so goddamned lazy. You lie around on that couch all weekend watching the football. We never go anywhere. When did you last take me out to dinner? And I don't mean for my birthday or Sawar's restaurant, I mean a really nice restaurant where you have to book a table and it's not BYO.' Sarah glared at Tom, challenging him with every fibre of her being.

'Sarah,' he said softly. 'What has gotten into you?'

He wondered if she was premenstrual. If so, this was a doozy. He bit his tongue and looked at her in complete bewilderment.

'Why . . . are . . . you . . . so . . . angry?' he asked, articulating each word.

Sarah faltered. The question hung between them. Why was she so angry? And she was, violently angry. She had never felt so angry in all her life. She didn't know what to say, how to respond. She opened her mouth to speak, then closed it again, swallowing hard.

As Tom watched, she crumpled. Her face, her shoulders. She shrank before him. Tom felt his own anger and frustration melt away. He moved slowly over to Sarah and took her in his arms. She collapsed against him, her anger spent. He could feel her heart beating frantically against his chest. He cradled her gently.

'It's okay, Sarah,' he crooned. 'It's okay.'

A week later Ginny let herself into Tom and Sarah's apartment. They had never bothered to get the key back from her. But then, why would they? In Ginny they had the perfect lackey. They could go away on a whim and leave her to tend to their fish and plants. It wasn't like *she* ever went away for a romantic weekend. It was 7 pm and she figured she had only four hours. They were having dinner with friends an hour's drive away. If they had too much to drink they would stay the night but Ginny knew she couldn't count on that. She would have to be gone by 11 pm at the latest.

She walked quickly into the living room, dropping a plastic shopping bag that contained everything she would need. She drew the curtains before she took out her torch. She found the mains switch in the cupboard by the front door and turned off the power. Then she fetched the stepladder from behind the kitchen door and placed it in a corner of the living room, directly under the manhole. It was painted the same cream as the ceiling. It blended so beautifully no-one would know it was there. But Ginny knew. She had climbed up there when Tom and Sarah had moved in. Tom had helped push her through the hole then stood below passing her boxes. While Ginny crawled among the cobwebs doing the dirty work, Sarah unwrapped ornaments and laid them out, calling out to Tom to admire her flair for decorating. But Tom, bless him, had refused to move from below the manhole. As long as Ginny was up there he had stayed below where she could see him.

Ginny tossed the plastic bag through the opening and then hoisted herself through. She wasn't the least bit scared of spiders, never had been. She had kept some very large, hairy tarantulas as pets when she was a child. But she still would have liked to see the top of Tom's curly head below her. She flashed the torch about her. There were boxes of books, shoeboxes of cutlery and oddments, a couple of directors chairs and Tom's scuba gear in an open yellow plastic crate. Ginny remembered how she and Tom had heaved that through. God it was heavy. The space, created by the false ceiling, was exactly how Ginny remembered it. About a metre high with crossbeams covered in sheet plaster. Ginny wondered if anyone had been here since the day they moved in. Tom's broad shoulders wouldn't fit through the opening and Sarah's fear of spiders and discomfort would prevent her from even sliding open the cover.

Ginny's torchlight searched along the wall until it fell on the electricity junction box. She crawled along on her stomach, dragging her shopping bag with her, being careful to stay on the crossbeams, just like Tom had told her. She unwrapped her purchases from the electronics store – rubber gloves, a transformer that would convert 240 volts to twelve volts, a hands-free carphone that ran on twelve volts, a roll of gaffer tape and two metres of cable attached to a tiny microphone the size of a thumbnail.

It was slow, painstaking work but Ginny was diligent. She slit the wires in the junction box and attached the transformer cable. Then she plugged it into the cradle for the carphone. She stretched the phone away, concealing the cable in the insulation batts to a point behind some boxes. She buried the phone in its cradle beside a pink insulation batt. It was hot in the small cavity and Ginny could feel the beads of sweat forming on her top lip and in her cleavage. She wiped her face on her arm. She plugged the microphone into the phone and stretched the cord along the batts to a downlight, positioned directly above the sofa. She taped the microphone to the downlight. Ginny crawled back to the telephone and flicked a switch, selecting the silent option. She didn't want it ringing loudly, waking everyone up.

Then came the most crucial part of the operation, the part that excited Ginny the most – connecting the auto-answer device she had removed from the telephone answering machine, to the carphone cradle. Ginny felt the tension build inside her. She held her breath and connected the wires. With a little click, it was done. It had worked when she tested it in her lounge room so there was no reason why it wouldn't work now. But still she felt anxious. She patted the batts back into place.

Ginny collected all her gear and shone the torch around. The junction box was the only thing that looked different. It had an extra wire, a new clean black one, coming out from it, but it would take a practised eye to recognise that. Nothing else seemed amiss. Ginny let herself down the manhole. She slid the cover across, carefully matching up the lines of dust that had collected.

Ginny turned on the mains switch, half expecting the circuit to short, but when she flicked the wall switch, the ceiling light burst into life. She laughed with relief. She returned the stepladder to its spot behind the kitchen door and noticed the microwave clock, flashing 12.00 at her.

'Damn,' she thought. 'All the digital clocks will be out.'

This was something she hadn't anticipated. She could go about the apartment resetting them all – the bedside clock, the video, but what if she missed one and she didn't know what time the alarms were set for? Better to leave them. Tom and Sarah would just think they had had a power surge. It happened all the time.

Ginny picked up her shopping bag and turned out the light.

She moved across to open the curtains and stood for a moment looking back at her own, dark apartment. It stood out from the others. The windows were like mirrors, reflecting the lights of the building. She could see Arthur next door watching TV with his dinner on his lap.

Ginny looked at her watch. It was only 9.45. She was reluctant to leave. She walked into the bedroom and opened the closet door. It smelled of Sarah. She opened another door. More Sarah. She noticed a rugby jumper on the floor. She lifted it to her face and breathed in Tom's sweat. It smelled so good. Ginny lay back on the bed, burying her nose in Tom's pillow. It was intoxicating. She opened her eyes and saw Sarah's smiling face. Her face darkened and she slammed down the photo. The glass jolted but didn't break. Ginny snuggled back into the bed, Tom's jumper scrunched against her cheek. She lay like that for what seemed like eternity, drinking in his scent, imagining him lying there with her, wanting her, kissing her, loving her.

She arched her back and rolled languidly over, her thighs pressed closely together, letting the tension build. She moved her hands slowly over her body, imagining they were Tom's strong hands, lovingly caressing her curves. She moaned with pleasure.

With a heavy sigh she picked herself up, folded the jumper with infinite care and placed it lovingly on the chair.

She gathered her bag to her and walked towards the front door. She was almost at the front door with one foot poised in midair when she heard a scratching. It took her a moment to realise what it was. With a lurching feeling of dread she heard Sarah giggling.

'Give it to me.'

That was Tom. They were home. They were on the other side of that door and about to walk in.

Ginny looked about her in panic. The kitchen clock flashed 12.00 at her. What could she do? How could she explain being here? She couldn't. She looked for somewhere to hide. Tom had the key in the lock. Ginny fled to the bathroom. She stood behind the door, her knees pressed against the toilet bowl. She heard the front door open. Muffled sounds. They were kissing. Hungry, passionate kisses. Ginny was trapped. What if they came in here? She heard a zip being undone. She looked across at the shower cubicle. She silently slipped off her shoes and held them carefully in her hand. Then with aching slowness, she placed one foot gently in front of the other and moved soundlessly across the floor. She stepped into the cubicle, willing herself not to slip, and leaned back behind the curtain.

Ginny heard a thud as the phone crashed to the floor. Tom swore and Sarah giggled. They were drunk. Ginny eased the heavy plastic shower curtain up off the rail and inched it closed. She stood, barely breathing, her eyes staring wildly through the closed curtain into the darkness when the ceiling light burst into life. It was as though the sun had exploded in front of her, momentarily blinding her. She gasped involuntarily as Sarah called out: 'Don't start without me.'

Sarah shut the door and sat down heavily on the toilet. Ginny squeezed her eyes shut, just like when she was a child and had believed that if she couldn't see anyone no-one could see her. Ginny heard a sound like running water, then the flushing of the toilet. Sarah slid open the cabinet and started brushing her teeth. The bathroom door opened and Ginny heard Tom's voice.

'What is my Sare Bear up to?'

Sarah's reply was thick and indistinct, her voice muffled by toothpaste.

Ginny clutched her shopping bag to her and pressed herself against the shower taps, trying to blend into the wall. Her heart was pounding like a trapped bird in her chest.

Sarah rinsed her mouth. Ginny could hear more kisses. Panting. She dared not move a muscle. Every nerve fibre was stretched painfully. She opened her eyes. Tom and Sarah were blurred into one image through the heavy plastic shower curtain. They were so close. She could reach out and touch them. Or, she realised with horror, they could reach out and touch her. Ginny stayed perfectly still in the shadowed cubicle, watching with fascinated revulsion as Tom peeled off Sarah's dress and flung it against the curtain. It hung suspended for one agonising moment, in front of Ginny's face, then slid to the floor.

Ginny could feel their heat, the rising passion. Tom moved down Sarah's body as she moaned and writhed with pleasure. Sarah gave little gasps of ecstasy. Ginny clutched her bag against her, the torch digging painfully into the soft flesh of her breasts and bringing tears to her eyes.

Sarah started to whimper, faster and louder, until she was almost sobbing. She arched her back and gave one final, heaving sigh of infinite, exquisite delight.

'Oh, Tom,' breathed Sarah, as the tears coursed silently down Ginny's face.

Tom lifted Sarah over his shoulders and carried her out of the bathroom. Ginny could hear the bedsprings creaking as they continued their lovemaking. She slipped to her knees on the cold, damp tiles, her shoulders heaving with silent, wracking sobs. She stayed that way till long after the noises had stopped and a heavy silence fell over the apartment.

Ginny waited still longer, then, finally, made her way carefully out of the bathroom. In the foyer she nearly tripped over Sarah's handbag. She carefully and quietly opened the front door. It created a draft that tugged at the bedroom curtains and they billowed inward. Sarah stirred in her sleep and snuggled closer to Tom, backing her bottom into his lap, into what he called her little chair. Instinctively he tightened his arms about her as Ginny gently pulled the door closed.

CHAPTER 7

He told me today I had hit my plimsoll. What the flying fuck is that? A worn-out sneaker? Where does he get these from? He just announced it today as if it was the most natural thing in the world. He loves using wheelbarrow words that no-one else understands, then explains them to you like he is the only person in the world with a brain and you are an idiot. Wouldn't give him the satisfaction. Ha. I got a dictionary and looked it up. Plimsoll mark – a nautical expression designating the line placed around the hull of a ship to indicate how heavily it may be safely loaded and retain enough surplus buoyancy to withstand the added stress of storms. So now I'm an unseaworthy boat.

I've got to get out of here. They are sending me mad.

Sarah stretched luxuriously in the bed. She felt liquid from her toes to her scalp. She listened to Tom singing in the shower. It was a silly TV advertising jingle but he sang it like grand opera. Sarah smiled happily as she recalled their night of lovemaking. She arched her back and pointed her toes.

She noticed her photograph lying face down. Frowning, she reached over and set it upright. The bedside clock was flashing at her. 'Power surge,' she thought, but she was too happy to let it annoy her this morning. She spotted Tom's navy jumper, neatly folded on the chair and smiled to herself. When did he do that? She felt a surge of tenderness. He really was the most wonderful man.

Tom came into the bedroom, a towel around his waist and his trim, naked torso glistening with droplets of water.

'Are we shopping today?' he asked.

Tom had no intention of joining Sarah in the supermarket queue but he figured once he got there, he could find some excuse to head to the hardware store and be finished just in time to meet her at the car.

It was their regular fortnightly ritual. He would suggest shopping, feign interest all the way to the shopping centre, then at the last minute – just as they approached the super-market entrance – he would suddenly remember something he needed urgently from Bill's Hardware and go off to spend half an hour chatting about drill bits and widgets to Bill.

Sarah was well aware she would be shopping alone and it suited her. She preferred shopping on her own. She liked to read every label before she bought anything, ever on the look-out for a stray fat molecule. She knew she was obsessive but she tried to keep her obsession from Tom. She kissed him, slowly and deliberately.

'I'm quite fond of you, you know?' she told him as she headed off to the shower.

Tom dried himself and dressed. He looked for his rugby jumper on the floor, where he knew he had left it, but it was gone. He called out to Sarah.

'Where's my blue jumper?'

He hoped she hadn't taken it on herself to wash it. He would be annoyed if she had. She knew it was his favourite jumper and he liked to wear it on weekends. And after Sarah's outburst the week before, he was now all too aware that its position on the floor had become some kind of barometer of their relationship.

He spotted it folded neatly on the chair and smiled to himself.

Sarah reappeared.

'Did you want me?'

'Just to tell you that I think you are wonderful.'

They smiled stupidly at each other.

'We're in love again, aren't we?' said Sarah.

'Always have been,' said Tom.

Ginny picked up the binoculars. There was no-one home. The apartment was deserted. They must be out shopping. She dialled Sarah's number, just to be sure, and hung up when the answering machine picked up the call.

Ginny connected her new mobile telephone to the amplifier and the speaker in her bedroom. She dialled the carphone, concealed in the ceiling. It rang twice in Ginny's ear then the line clicked open. Ginny felt excitement surge through her. She was in . . . in their apartment, in their lives. Now she wouldn't miss a thing. She lay back and looked at the ceiling and waited for them to come home. Kitty was curled up asleep on the bed.

A currawong flew onto the windowsill. It looked in the window, seeing only a currawong looking back. It cocked its head, puzzled, then tried to peck at the other bird. Its beak hit the glass. Frightened, it flew off.

Ginny counted the fleur-de-lis loops that circled the ceiling. She lost count halfway through and started again. How long could they be? She looked across the bay at the pretty white boats, heading out for a day on the harbour. Ginny hated boats. She liked them to look at but didn't ever want to go on one again. The motion made her seasick. She hated the feeling of the water beneath her feet, moving, uncontrollable, unsteady, unpredictable. Ginny liked her life ordered.

She had gone out on a boat just once in her life. She hadn't really wanted to. Boats had never interested her, but Tom had a mate with a new boat and they had invited her along. It was about two years ago. Sarah had been in her element, standing on deck, arm draped over Tom's shoulder, calling him captain. She had looked gorgeous, wearing navy blue and white. Ginny had started to feel ill as soon as she was on board. The combination of Sarah poring over Tom and the motion of the boat had made her nauseous. She had thrown up all over the anchor, coiled neatly in its hatch. Tom had been so understanding, throwing buckets of water over it and making light of the dreadful smell that had lingered all day. Sarah hadn't been very helpful, thought Ginny, leaving the messy stuff to Tom.

'Wouldn't want to mess up your yachtie look, would we sweetie,' thought Ginny nastily. She looked across at their quiet balcony. Where the hell are you? Buying more chocolate for greedy guts Sarah no doubt. Or coffee. Oooh yes, we don't want you to run out of coffee now, do we? Ginny wished they had left a radio on, or the television, anything so she could check how well her system worked.

The answering machine. Of course. Their answering machine was turned up loudly so they could screen their calls when they didn't want to be disturbed.

Excited and chastising herself for not thinking of it sooner, Ginny picked up her bedside phone and dialled Sarah's number. She jumped as the ringing sounded from the speaker in the corner and filled her bedroom. Then Sarah's lilting voice floated through the room.

'Hi, this is Sarah. Tom and I can't take your call at the moment but if you leave a message we'll call you right back. Have a lovely day.'

Ginny bounced on the bed with excitement. She held Kitty's paw aloft and gave her a high five then punched the air like Rocky.

Sarah couldn't sleep. The bedside clock read 5.00. Tom snored heartily beside her. Sarah gently nudged him with her foot, then harder. He slept on, oblivious. She tossed and turned for another five minutes, then got up. She made a coffee and took it out onto the balcony. The bay looked eerie, bathed in mist. She could just make out the apartment building opposite. The harbour was engulfed in fog. The only sound was the muffled foghorns of the distant ferries, already at work. Sarah was restless. She decided to go for a bike ride. She dressed in the dark, being careful not to wake Tom. He snored on happily. She felt annoyed. She hunted around in her shoe cupboard for her running shoes, dropping one loudly, hoping he might stir. She watched him as she tied her laces, propping one foot on the bed, near his legs. His mouth was open, his chin disappearing in the folds of his neck. A stream of spittle dribbled down his cheek. He gasped with each inward breath then chortled and grunted with each outward breath. She marvelled that he didn't wake himself.

Sarah headed for Centennial Park. Few cars were on the road at that hour. They loomed out of the mist and were gone. The streetlights cast a ghostly halo. It was nearly dawn and the sky was filling with flocks of plump fruit bats leaving the fig trees, where they had spent the night feeding, to return to the Botanic Gardens, where they would spend the daylight hours upside down in the trees, their wings cloaked about them as they slept. Sarah rode through the gates, building up to a comfortable rhythm. The park seemed deserted. The huge fig trees – hundreds of years old – formed a menacing canopy above her head as they emerged from the mist. An ethereal figure jogged past. He was swallowed up by the fog almost as soon as he appeared. Sarah started to feel nervous. Perhaps this wasn't such a good idea at this early hour. She had covered enough police stories to know what went on in this park at night. People were just coming home from clubs and parties and God knew what else. For them it was still night.

Sarah could hear noises behind her. The leaves rustled as she rode over them, then rustled again not far behind her. She looked over her shoulder. She could see a bike headlight behind her, its light refracting in the water droplets of the mist. Sarah increased her speed. She was powering along and could feel the strain in her calf muscles. She looked behind her. The bike was keeping pace. She couldn't see the rider. Fingers of fear clutched her heart. He was a madman, chasing her. Paranoia overtook her sense of reason. A rush of adrenaline pushed Sarah's aching legs onwards. An exit gate loomed in front of her. She hurtled through, over the kerb and onto the road. The unexpected drop jolted her and she gasped as it travelled up her spine. A car appeared suddenly from nowhere, saw her at the last moment and swerved violently, missing her by millimetres. Sarah felt the air rush past her and struggled to keep control of her bike. She veered across the road, mounted the kerb and landed with a dull thud sitting upright against a tree.

A twisted root rammed against her coccyx. She lay still as the world swam about her. She started to moan. She sat up. A spot low down on her back hurt. She stretched her legs, then her arms. Everything seemed to be working.

She looked after the car and yelled angrily: 'Thanks, mate, I'm fine.'

Then she burst into tears, loud howling sobs that wracked her whole body.

Sarah limped in the door, her T-shirt torn, scratches on her arm. She appeared in the doorway of the bedroom. Tom was sound asleep. Sarah whimpered and crawled over the bed to him.

'Tom,' she wailed. 'Tom.'

Tom stirred. 'Sarah, what's wrong?'

He took in her dishevelled appearance and felt his heart lurch.

'Whatever has happened to you? Where have you been?'

'I fell off my bike. I was being chased and then this man deliberately drove into me on the road.' Sarah collapsed sobbing onto Tom's chest.

'Are you okay? Are you hurt?' He was instantly awake and alert.

'No,' wailed Sarah.

Tom inspected her bleeding elbow. It was minor. She had a few shallow scratches on her cheek, but otherwise she looked okay. Her T-shirt was torn and dirty. She reeked of sweat.

'Who chased you? Who hit you?'

Sarah gave a highly colourful version of events. As she told her story it sounded weak to her own ears so she exaggerated it. Her voice had an unfamiliar ring of hysteria that worried Tom. He decided probably half of what she told him was true. Once he realised there was no danger and there had been no mugging, he was annoyed at being woken.

'Sarah, it's barely 6 am, what were you doing out so early anyway?'

'I couldn't sleep so I went for a ride,' she sobbed.

Tom looked at her with disbelief. 'In Centennial Park? Are you mad?'

'Don't be angry with me. Lots of people go there before work for a jog.'

Tom wasn't angry. He was tired and wished he could go back into the cosy world of sleep. He tried to ignore the stench of body odour that was assailing his nostrils.

'Not without a trained Doberman. Sarah, honestly, sometimes you do the stupidest things.'

'Thanks for your concern, Tom,' said Sarah coldly, slamming the bedroom door as she stalked off to the shower.

Ginny heard the door slam and rolled over in bed giggling to herself. She didn't mind being woken so early. Her eyes were dancing, like a little girl with a new toy. Kitty was curled up, a tight, warm furball against her back. Ginny climbed out of bed, flung the bedclothes over her and padded naked to the front door to collect the morning's newspaper. In the kitchen she poured herself a glass of orange juice and a fresh saucer of cream for Kitty. She took her juice and Kitty's cream back to bed with the newspaper. Kitty was unimpressed at being covered in the bedclothes and stood on all fours wailing at her.

Ginny opened the curtains to radiant sunshine and climbed back into bed, placing the saucer carefully on the crumpled bed in front of Kitty. Kitty ignored it and cuddled up to Ginny's bare thigh. Ginny looked down her naked body at the bundle of black, white and ginger fur, a startling contrast against her own mass of dark pubic hair. She looked at the front page. The sun warmed her naked body. Kitty snuggled contentedly against her thigh, nudging gently with one paw, then the other. She purred happily. Ginny could feel the vibrations radiating throughout her body, travelling along each nerve. She shifted her hips. Kitty continued to pummel her gently. It reminded Ginny of her aunt kneading dough. It was soothing, with a hypnotic rhythm.

Ginny scooped a dollop of cream onto her fingers and offered it to Kitty. She lapped at it, her tongue soft but abrasive. Ginny shifted her hips a bit further. Kitty pummelled her pubic bone. It sent waves of pleasure up Ginny's body. Ginny scooped another dollop of cream and dropped it amongst her own curly black hair. Kitty lapped at it hungrily, her tongue darting in and out, seeking more. Ginny spread her legs a little further apart and tipped all the cream over her crotch. It dripped through her hair, down her thighs. Kitty lapped at it, sending out ripples of pure bliss. Ginny felt a warmth emanate throughout her body. 'Tom,' she moaned softly, as she abandoned herself to rolling waves of pleasure.

CHAPTER 8

The empty yachts, sails tied down and fastened for the night, swayed gently, their masts nodding to each other like wise old men. The water shimmered, different currents clashing and changing directions. The high-rise towers reflected the setting sun brightly, blindingly before the sun moved on.

Ginny arrived home juggling bags of groceries. She set them down on the kitchen bench, opened the pantry and removed two heavy-bottomed crystal glasses.

'I think we both need a scotch,' she said. Her eyes were unnaturally bright, the pupils dilated.

She fetched the bottle and splashed liquid into the glasses. She put one down on the coffee table and took the other back into the kitchen, placing it on the bench while she rummaged in the fridge.

'I hope you like Thai noodles,' she called, laying out vegetables, strips of lean beef and noodles by the wok. She set about chopping and slicing, humming to herself.

'I'll just change out of these clothes,' she called.'Make yourself comfortable.'

Ginny opened the cupboard and removed a long black satin sheath. She slipped out of her jeans and jumper. She unhooked her bra, fumbling clumsily in her excitement, and pulled the sheath over her head. It fell about her body in sensuous folds, lightly skimming her breasts and hips. In the bathroom she brushed her hair, smiling seductively in the mirror and pouting at her reflection. She applied bold red lipstick and heavy black mascara. She felt wanton as she floated back into the kitchen, her movements graceful and sensuous.

'Your glass is empty. Let me get you another,' she called, picking up the bottle and gliding across the room. She topped up the untouched glass on the coffee table then looked across at the twinkling lights. Kitty watched her with bemusement.

'That's Toft Monks,' she said. 'I don't suppose you've ever seen it from this angle.'

Ginny returned to the kitchen. She bustled about happily, tossing the vegetables in the wok, adding a dash of oyster sauce and a hint more soy with a flourish.

She climbed the stepladder in the pantry and pulled down a canteen of silver cutlery. It had been a present from her aunt in Perth when she turned twenty-one. It had been such a shock when Ginny received it. She had not had contact with her aunt since the day when, as a bewildered eleven year old, she had climbed the stairs to the plane bound for Sydney and boarding school where she was supposed to be turned into a refined young lady. Ginny had never used the cutlery. It represented many things to her, all of them unhappy. But tonight she wanted the best for her special guest. She laid two places at the dining table, with two wine glasses of fine-cut crystal. In the centre she placed a lit candle. She served dinner on two large white plates.

'Please come and sit down,' she said to the empty apartment.

Ginny took her place at the head of the table, pouring herself a glass of wine. The flickering candlelight cast a muted glow over her face, softening her angular features. Kitty, attracted by the interesting smells of cooked food, moved under the table, being careful to keep clear of Ginny's legs.

Ginny ate with her head cocked to one side as she chewed, nodding occasionally toward the empty chair at the other end of the table.

She swallowed and replied '. . . oh, Tom, how kind of you to say so . . . Really, I'm flattered . . . It's just a stir-fry, but I'm glad you like it . . . Tom, you are sweet . . . Of course I will.'

Kitty leapt up onto the empty chair, expecting to be shooed away.

'Oh, Tom,' Ginny breathed, rolling the name around her mouth sensually, like a sweet. Kitty, pretending not to be interested in the food, raised her hind leg, examined it carefully then, ignoring Ginny, started to lick her fur. She was tense, wary, expecting to be reprimanded. But Ginny was in another world.

'Do you remember the Nosherie Café at Sydney University, Tom?' asked Ginny.

Kitty placed a tentative paw on the table and waited. Ginny continued chatting, absorbed in her imaginary conversation. Kitty moved up on her hind legs, taking her weight on her front paws. Her nose was just centimetres from the plate. Delicious aromas of meat juices and other smells wafted across Kitty's palate. She licked her lips in anticipation.

'That was the first time I ever saw you.'

Kitty nibbled delicately at the pile of food. She extricated the beef expertly with her tongue, swallowed it and searched around for some more. When she had eaten up all the beef she sniffed at the noodles, trying to find something else of interest. The faint hint of beef juices mingled with soy was only slightly appealing. She sampled it then turned her noise up in disdain. She resumed cleaning her fur.

Ginny raised her wine glass in a toast. 'To the future . . . our future,' she said, looking unseeingly through Kitty.

'If you play your cards right you can be my onion,' Tom told Sarah when he came home, exhausted but happy. He'd spent the day with his father. They had ridden out to Kangaroo Valley, enjoyed a pub lunch, then taken the scenic route home.

Sarah was standing in the centre of the lounge room wearing bicycle shorts and a singlet, a can of soup in each hand. She squatted on her heels, bringing the cans of soup to chest level, then lowered her arms and slowly straightened up.

'What does that mean? What is an onion?' she asked.

'That's what they call the bikers' molls.'

'An onion?'

Tom nodded, following her face as it rose and fell with each squat.

'Why an onion?'

'They say it brings tears to your eyes when she takes off her clothes.'

'What? That's awful,' said Sarah dropping the soup cans onto the carpet. She stared at Tom.

'Yes, well, bikers' molls aren't known for their hygiene.'

Sarah was feeling a little sensitive on the topic of body odour. In the past few days Tom had twice suggested she might like to shower before bed. He had never been so picky before about the way she smelled. He used to nuzzle into her neck and tell her he loved the way she smelled. She felt he was deliberately finding fault with her. Here he was having another dig about body odour. She felt the anger rise.

'Tom, that's terrible. One afternoon with a bunch of bikies and you're talking like the club president of the Hells Angels. Is this what Hal is teaching you?'

Immediately Tom felt contrite. He knew body odour had become a sensitive topic between them. He had tried to broach it carefully with Sarah but he had been clumsy. He wasn't a particularly fastidious man but lately Sarah's personal hygiene had caused him some concern. She hadn't seemed to notice but, damn it, he had. They shared their lives, their dreams and their bodily fluids. He didn't think it unreasonable to mention something so intimate with the woman who shared his life and his bed.

He saw the defensiveness in Sarah's eyes and reached out

to her but she pushed him away. Scowling she lifted her left leg and placed it on the back of the couch. She leaned forward, placing her head on her knee.

'Sarah, it wasn't like that at all. I'm just teasing you. Hal is actually a very urbane guy. Anyway, you can decide for yourself. I've invited him for dinner next weekend.'

Sarah lifted her head. 'Hal's coming here for dinner?'

'Yes. Is that okay?'

Sarah looked horrified. The sensitive topic of body odour was forgotten. The prospect of meeting Tom's long-lost father was far more threatening.

'Well, sure, of course it's okay,' she said, trying to conceal her feelings. 'I just don't know what I'm going to talk to him about. I don't know anything about motorbikes.'

Tom hugged her to him, trying not to react to the smell of her sweat.

'Sarah, you will charm him. And he will charm you. Don't worry about that. He is very laid back. You will love him. Trust me.'

Sarah smiled back weakly. She wasn't so sure. She felt antsy and uptight. She wanted to get into a hot bath and not talk to anybody. And she wanted to get on her bike and ride and ride until the breath left her body. She wanted to do both right now.

'You smell all greasy,' she said to Tom. 'Why don't you have a shower while I make dinner? I planned a special night so be quick.'

She actually didn't feel so loving now. She felt cranky. She was spoiling for a fight and she knew it. She tried to remember her good intentions for a special dinner. It had seemed such a good idea this afternoon.

'Go and have a shower, Tom,' she said, forcing a gentle tone that she didn't feel. 'I'll cook dinner.'

As soon as the bathroom door shut she raced around, laying the table with a candle and flowers, then she flung off her clothes and dressed in the beautiful peach-coloured negligee and wrap. When Tom reappeared from the bathroom she was draped on the couch. Next to her on the table were two glasses and a bottle of French champagne in a wine bucket.

'What have we here?' he asked.

Sarah rolled languidly over on the couch, allowing the wrap to slip seductively off one shoulder, as she picked up the champagne.

'Champagne, darling?'

For a moment Tom thought he must have forgotten an anniversary.

'What's all this for?' he said, sitting down, taking one of Sarah's feet between his hands, and gently massaging it.

'This,' said Sarah, handing him a glass of champagne, 'is to say sorry for being such a brat lately. I know I have been really difficult to live with and I want to say I'm sorry. I've had some problems at work and I guess I've been taking them out on you. I've cooked a special dinner to say I love you and I am really sorry.'

Sarah said it and meant it. She had been feeling so confused lately. She felt she was riding an emotional roller-coaster and her only point of reference was Tom. One minute she loved him, the next she hated him, but throughout it he was there, holding her tightly at night, stroking her hair and making a little chair for her to snuggle into.

Tom smiled and raised his glass in a toast.

'To my Sare Bear.'

'So you forgive me then?' asked Sarah. Her voice was genuine and pleading and Tom's heart went out to her.

'Nothing to forgive.'

Sarah smiled, secure in his love. 'I don't know why you put up with me,' she said. 'You deserve a medal.'

Tom looked at her thoughtfully. He didn't want to break the mood or disturb the happy equilibrium but he was worried and this was obviously the best opportunity he had had to broach the subject.

'Sarah,' he said, gently massaging her foot. 'You still throw up, don't you?'

Sarah looked at Tom, her eyes wide and round. 'Darling,

no,' she said, her voice tinged with just the right shade of indignant disbelief.

'I haven't done that since, God, I don't know when.' Sarah ran her eyes along the ceiling as she tried to recall a time. 'I haven't done that since I last saw the doctor and what was that, six years ago? I have no need to now, darling. How can I convince you? I'm happy, I'm in control. My only problem is I don't get to the gym as often as I should and that makes me ratty. I seem to have energy to burn so I'm going to try and get more exercise. How about running with me in the mornings?'

Tom looked at her closely. He knew that she could lie. Bulimics could be devious when they were threatened. The behaviour of a bulimic was not rational. It came from a deep ache. And they would behave irrationally to feed that ache. To try to stop a bulimic, in the grip of the disease, from making themselves throw up, was futile. They had to stop themselves. They had to beat that ache. It indicated a deep insecurity. Sarah was so confident on the outside but in so many ways she was terribly vulnerable, always worried she wasn't measuring up. Tom looked at Sarah and wondered, again, what went on inside her head. It didn't matter how much in love they might be, or how close, you could never really know what was going on inside someone else's head.

He had no way of knowing whether she was throwing up again. And if he did know, what did it matter? There was absolutely nothing he could do. That was the tragedy of loving a bulimic. They had been down this path before. He shrugged inwardly. She sounded convincing.

'I'm turning over a new leaf, starting tonight,' continued Sarah. 'No more temper tantrums, more exercise, more sleep and more of you . . .'

Sarah knelt astride Tom, the peach negligee hitched up around her thighs. She pulled aside Tom's dressing gown as she lowered herself onto his lap. She kissed him hard on the mouth. As her passion rose, she pinched his nipples hard. He cried out in pain and she suddenly thrust him inside her with one brutal movement. Sarah was ferocious and unrelenting, riding him like a wild animal, her face twisted and strained as if in pain. Tom tensed beneath her, then came in one long, shuddering climax. Sarah moaned and writhed violently, tears spilling onto her cheeks and landing softly on Tom's chest. He opened his eyes and watched her contorted face as she threw herself off the edge and came with a wild, blood-curdling scream that filled the room, bouncing off the cream walls and out through the open balcony doors, losing its potency as it rolled across the bay.

Tom looked at Sarah in amazement. Their lovemaking had never been quite like that. In fact he wasn't sure that what they had just done had been lovemaking. It had been hard, urgent and ferocious. He felt as if he had been taken, albeit willingly, but it had been her show and he was just a passive partner. He thought again how completely unpredictable was this woman he loved. This was a side of her he hadn't seen. But, he decided, he quite liked it.

Ginny lowered her binoculars. She sat in the darkened bed-room, rocking herself backwards and forwards as the scream reverberated around her walls. Her thin arms wrapped around her legs, holding them tightly against her thundering heart. She put her thumb in her mouth and sucked it, stroking the bridge of her nose with her index finger. Gradually her heart stopped its frantic beating and her muscles loosened. She stayed sitting there in the dark corner. The only sign she was alive was a tic beneath her wildly staring eyes.

Ginny couldn't sleep. It was 4 am. The only sound was a distant, intermittent rumble. She turned up the volume switch on the amplifier that sat in the centre of her bedroom. It looked incongruous, a large shiny black box with wire mesh covering one side, dominating the room. Tom's snores floated out of the speaker. They were deep and guttural, reassuring jungle sounds. With each intake of breath, Ginny's bedroom seemed to swell and breathe. Then there was silence. Tom would breathe again and Ginny imagined the room stretching and growing, like a womb surrounding her, enveloping her, keeping her safe. Her breathing slowed to match his snores and she drifted off to sleep.

Sarah slowly opened her eyes. It was 4.02 am and Tom was snoring again. Too much champagne. He was lying on his back, his mouth wide open, one leg flung across Sarah. Sarah gently nudged him with her foot. He slept on. Sarah nudged him again, harder. Tom spluttered and rolled towards her, his face just millimetres from hers. Sarah stayed perfectly still, not wanting to wake him. The dark night was impenetrable but she could feel his breath on her face. It smelled of fermented alcohol and mint toothpaste. It was warm and sweet.

Sarah pondered the notion that the air she was breathing was what he had just exhaled and, as she exhaled, he breathed in her air. It seemed almost unbearably intimate. She leaned forward in the darkness and kissed him gently on the lips. He grunted, then rolled away, turning his back to her. She looked through the darkness at him and waited. After a few moments he backed his bottom into her, grunting softly. Sarah smiled inwardly and wrapped herself around him, pushing her breasts into his back and circling an arm around his waist. Tom stroked her hand absently, making contented noises in his sleep.

Ginny put her bag down in the kitchen and saw the dead cockroach, lying where Kitty had finally abandoned it, with its feet pointed upwards, on the cold white linoleum floor. A mass of ants swarmed around its prone body, branching off in one neat line that disappeared under the dishwasher. As Ginny looked closer she noticed the ants passing each other in single file as if on an imaginary bridge. She watched in fascination as the cockroach trembled, then moved an almost imperceptible distance, lifted, tugged and pushed by dozens of ants. They were a fraction of its size, but a thousand times smarter and stronger. Ginny placed a teaspoon on the floor, beside the cockroach. She placed another below it, fixing its position. In the bedroom she looked at the speaker and listened. Someone was in Sarah and Tom's kitchen. Saucepans clanked and cupboard doors opened and closed. Ginny cranked up the volume. She could hear Sarah chatting to herself. 'Skim the cream from the top of the coconut milk,' then 'Oh shit.'

Ginny unpacked her groceries.

Sarah swore loudly again.

Ginny smiled to herself.

'Having a rough day, Sare Bear?' she said loudly and laughed.

Ginny stepped over the cockroach and the spoons, catching snatches of Tom's voice.

'What can I do to help?' Tom was asking.

'You can lay the table. I've bought new candles, the candlesticks are in the crystal cabinet and we'll use the good crystal wine glasses.'

Ginny could tell from Sarah's tone she was stressed. They must be expecting company. Ginny felt a ripple of hurt that she hadn't been invited.

'It smells good. What are we having?' asked Tom.

'Don't touch anything, Tom. It's all delicately balanced,' said Sarah. 'It's green chicken curry with jasmine rice and a tomato, cucumber and basil salad.'

'Sounds great. What's for dessert?'

Ginny fed Kitty as she listened. There was silence. What's for dessert, Sare Bear?

'Oh Tom,' said Sarah, sounding aghast.

'What's wrong?'

'I forgot dessert. I, I – oh no.'

'Have we got any ice cream or chocolate or tinned fruit? Anything?'

'Oh God. I was in such a flap over the chicken curry I completely forgot.'

Ginny listened as Sarah slammed cupboard doors.

'Nothing. Sorry, Tom. We'll just have to skip dessert.'

Ginny winced at Sarah's whining tone.

Then Tom spoke. 'Sarah, how could you? You know how important this is to me. Don't we even have any cheese?'

Tom sounded tense. It wasn't like him to be snappy. Ginny moved closer to the speaker to listen.

'No, Tom, we don't.' Sarah's voice had a steely edge to it. 'Maybe if you did the supermarket shopping every now and then we might have the things you want but right now, no, we don't happen to have any cheese. Or fruit. Or chocolate. Nothing. But don't you dare give me a hard time. I've gone to a lot of trouble with this curry. You've done nothing towards this dinner for your father.'

Ginny laughed. Of course, this was the night Tom's father was coming for dinner. No wonder Sarah was in such a flap. And obviously Tom was stressed too.

'I'll go to the corner store and buy something. We can't not have dessert.'

'You can't go out now.' Sarah sounded on the verge of complete panic. 'He'll be here any minute. The table isn't laid and it would be rude if you weren't here to greet him.'

'Bloody hell, Sarah. Was it too much to ask? You only had to cook dinner for three.'

Ginny picked up the binoculars and watched as Tom came into view laying the table. He was standing almost directly under the microphone and she could hear his tense breathing.

'Bloody hell,' he muttered. 'Why leave it to her? You're an idiot, Tom. If you want something done, you've got to do it yourself. You know that.'

Sarah continued to bang saucepans and cupboards loudly, angrily, in the kitchen.

Ginny was suddenly in a tearing hurry. She carefully disconnected the telephone in her bedroom from the amplifier.

Holding the mobile phone to her ear, she slipped quietly out of her flat.

They both jumped when the door buzzer rang. Tom dumped the last of the cutlery onto the table. Sarah dropped a saucepan lid, sending it crashing to the floor. She looked at Tom and he looked at her.

'Well, answer it,' hissed Sarah.

Tom picked up the telephone intercom: 'Take the lift to the second floor, Hal.'

Tom hung up the telephone and looked around the room.

'It's Hal,' he said. Sarah feigned shock.

'Don't we have any nuts or dips to have with a drink?' asked Tom.

'I don't know, Tom. Do we? Did you buy any?' replied Sarah archly.

'I've had a busy week, Sarah. I left it for you to do.'

'Well, I had a busy week too.'

They stood glaring at each other.

'Great. Just great,' said Tom, turning away. 'No appetisers, no dessert.'

There was a knock at the door.

Sarah stood by Tom's side as he opened it.

They stood together, smiling a united welcome. Hal walked through the door, greeting Sarah awkwardly with a kiss on her cheek. He handed Tom half-a-dozen stubbies of beer and a bottle of red wine and strode into the room.

'What a lovely view,' he said.

'Sarah, show Hal the view while I fix us some drinks. Hal, beer?'

'Thanks, mate, that would be fine.'

Sarah led Hal onto the balcony. It was a warm and humid night. The air was thick and heavy and cloying. It sat on their bare skin like a warm, wet towel. The stars were hidden behind a layer of dense cloud.

Hal was dressed simply in jeans, cowboy boots and a

freshly ironed white shirt. Sarah was fascinated by him. He didn't look like Tom but there was an expression on his face that was hauntingly like Tom. His eyes were the same vivid blue. His wide sensual mouth wasn't really like Tom's and yet the way he smiled definitely was Tom. She pointed out the various landmarks and Hal found his bearings.

'How long have you lived in Sydney?' she asked.

Hal laughed. It was deep and resonant. Just like Tom's laugh. Sarah tried not to stare. 'About fourteen years. And I've never tired of it. It's a breathtakingly beautiful city, or at least it is if you can afford a view. A fabulous view like this.'

'Yes, but it's not the real Sydney, is it?' asked Sarah. 'I mean, it's the postcard view of Sydney. Not what the majority of Sydneysiders live with, out there in the western suburbs. The harbour is what the tourists in the expensive hotels get to see as well as a handful of privileged Sydneysiders.'

Hal didn't say anything. He looked across the water to the Manly ferry making its way across the harbour.

Sarah continued. 'But I think everyone who has grown up in Sydney, no matter what part, would consider the Harbour Bridge and the Opera House, and indeed the whole harbour, as theirs, part of their individual heritage. Whether they see it every day or not. Don't you?'

Hal smiled and looked like Tom again.

'Do you think the Harbour Bridge and the Opera House are the heart of Sydney?' asked Hal.

Sarah, wishing she hadn't started this, shook her head.

'No, but I think they are at the geographical heart of Sydney,' replied Sarah.

'Well, physically speaking, the geographical heart of Sydney is closer to Parramatta,' said Hal. 'But I think I know what you are trying to say. To Sydneysiders the Harbour Bridge *is* Sydney and the Opera House, whether they ever go to a production there or not, *is* Sydney. Is that what you mean?'

Sarah nodded. She didn't really know what she had meant. She was just trying to keep the conversation going. She had no idea what to talk to this tall, imposing stranger about, but when faced with social silences, she would rush in to fill them, talking about anything and everything, whatever popped into her head. And after she had launched in, while all around her people were taking it slowly, she would feel foolish and wonder what she was talking about.

She was relieved when Tom appeared with the drinks. He handed them out then draped his arm casually around Sarah's shoulder. Their fight was forgotten. She felt a rush of affection for him.

'I don't see a helmet, Hal. Did you not ride over?'

Hal shook his head. He looked Tom directly in the eye, Sarah noticed. Not many people could do that. Tom was unusually tall.

'No. I never ride when I'm drinking.'

The two men sipped at their drinks and Sarah was overcome again by the silence.

'It's easy to see you're Tom's father,' she burst in.

Tom and Hal both looked at her. Their faces shared the same questioning expression, eyebrows raised slightly, head cocked to one side.

Sarah laughed. 'You're both so tall. Hal, you are the first person I've ever seen who is able to look Tom in the eye.'

Hal and Tom puffed out their chests and drew themselves up to their full height.

Ginny, telephone glued to her ear, listened to this exchange.

'Do you want a bag for that?' the woman was asking her. Ginny could tell by her tone that she was repeating the question.

'I'm sorry. Yes, please. In a bag,' she said covering the mouthpiece.

Ginny watched her place the cake box in a plastic shopping bag and hand it over the counter to her. The woman glared her disapproval at the mobile phone.

'I said, that will be thirty-two dollars.'

Ginny paid her while juggling the phone, not wanting to miss a moment of Sarah's discomfort.

By the time Ginny arrived at Toft Monks, Tom, Sarah and Hal had sat down for dinner and Ginny's shoulder was aching from supporting the phone to her ear as she drove. She locked the phone in the glovebox and carefully removed the cake box from the shopping bag. Outside, she rang the door-bell marked T. Wilson and S. Cowley.

Sarah's breathy voice sounded over the intercom.

'Hi, it's Ginny. I've got something for you. Can I come up?'

'Sure,' said Sarah, sounding flustered.

Sarah looked pleased to see Ginny and ushered her into the room.

'Ginny, how lovely of you to drop by. Please come in.'

Ginny smiled across the room at Tom then hesitated as she noticed Hal.

'I'm sorry, I didn't know you had company,' she said, pausing at the doorway.

'It's okay, Ginny. Come on in and meet my dad,' said Tom.

Shyly Ginny moved across to greet Hal. He pushed back his chair and Ginny found herself looking up into a pair of beautiful sparkling blue eyes just like Tom's. Hal held his napkin in front of him and smiled awkwardly.

'I'm sorry to disturb you in the middle of dinner,' said Ginny. 'I just wanted to drop off this cake. It was given to me by a woman at work. I performed a miracle on her little dog and she wanted to say thank you. Unfortunately I'm not much into chocolate cake so I thought you guys might like it.'

Tom looked at Ginny with a mixture of amazement and delight.

Ginny felt her face grow hot under his admiring gaze. She knew she was blushing and hoped no-one would notice.

'We'd love it, wouldn't we, Sarah?' said Tom.

'We sure would,' agreed Sarah, taking the box gratefully.

'Will you stay for dinner, Ginny?'

'Oh, I couldn't,' said Ginny, hesitating for just the right amount of time.

'Of course you could,' said Hal, gallantly pulling back a chair.

Tom fetched another glass, Sarah served another meal and Ginny joined the little party. Her palms were clammy with nerves and excitement. This was such an important night for Tom and she was going to be part of it. She wouldn't miss a thing. She smiled warmly at Hal as he filled her glass. He really had the most beautiful eyes. She took a big gulp of wine and then another. It made her feel giddy.

Hal leaned forward and asked about her miracle. Ginny explained about the little dog's asthmatic wheeze and how it was having trouble climbing the owner's back stairs. Hal listened attentively, his eyes following every expression on Ginny's face. Tom and Sarah listened too. Ginny was acutely aware of Sarah at the head of the table, silent except for murmuring noises of encouragement. Ginny didn't often talk about her work to them. Sarah usually did most of the talking. But tonight Sarah was looking to her for help. Ginny warmed to the attention and explained about the lung operation she had performed on the little dog's lungs. In fact Dr Black had performed the painstakingly difficult microsurgery and she had assisted him – administering the anaesthetic, handing across each instrument as it was needed and stemming the blood flow while Dr Black sewed up the wound. But other than that minor detail, Ginny accurately described the operation that had taken place on Mrs Ronaldson's ageing Pekinese that afternoon in the surgery.

Hal was fascinated. 'How could you perform such a delicate operation on something so tiny?' he asked.

Ginny explained about the huge magnifying glass that was held in position above the animal throughout the operation. She explained about cauterising tiny wounds, anaesthetising small animals. To demonstrate the point she talked of the huge hydraulic tables they used for horses, strapping them as they stood to the side of the table, anaesthetising them, then swivelling the table.

They all looked at her uncomprehendingly.

94

'Imagine trying to lift an unconscious horse onto an operating table,' she said.

Hal shook his head. 'I must admit, it never occurred to me,' he said.

'Before hydraulic tables vets used to operate on horses on the ground. Once the horse lay down, asleep, they would lay out their instruments and get down on their hands and knees. Can't have been very comfortable. But I'll bet the floors in their surgeries were pretty clean.'

'How similar is veterinary surgery to surgery on humans?' asked Tom.

'Very and not at all,' replied Ginny. 'The basics of hygiene and the principles of anatomy are the same but that's about where it stops. Animals have organs that we don't have and different muscle groups. They use their muscles differently and the ratio between organs varies from animal to animal. The difference between treating a guinea pig's heart and a racing horse's lung would be the same as the differences between a human and a cat. Then there are differences within species. Like dogs. A German Shepherd is prone to different diseases from a poodle.'

'Yes, of course,' nodded Hal.

Sarah cleared away the plates and disappeared into the kitchen. Ginny didn't follow her. She had the spotlight and she was blossoming under the attention. She didn't feel beige at all.

'My poor old mutt has been having a bit of trouble,' said Hal. 'Laddie. He's a border collie cross. Been with me for about fourteen years. He's lost his bounce. I don't know what it is.'

'Could be old age, Hal,' suggested Tom.

'Perhaps you could let the expert speak,' replied Hal, smiling at Ginny.

He didn't really look like Tom, thought Ginny, except when he smiled his face lit up with that same expression of joy and delight. Ginny looked at Tom. His expression mirrored his father's. It was like the sun beaming at her in stereo. Ginny basked in its warmth.

'Sounds to me like he may be chronologically challenged,' she said with a mischievous grin. 'Of course, I'd have to examine him to be sure.'

Hal looked confused.

'She's telling you he's old,' explained Tom.

Hal's confusion cleared and he laughed. It was a loud and relaxed laugh, full of power that swelled and filled the room. Tom joined in, his own hearty chuckle blending in perfect harmony. Ginny smiled coquettishly from one to the other.

'Really, why don't you let me take a look at him? Old age may not be curable but the ailments of old age certainly are. It could be something as simple as cataracts. Blurred vision will rob a dog of any age of his confidence. A problem with hearing will do the same. Of course, it could be canine Alzheimer's, which isn't curable. But bring him in and I'll have a look.'

Hal looked relieved. Tom looked delighted. And when Sarah reappeared she kept smiling at Ginny.

After dessert Ginny decided she had starred enough and cleared away the cake plates. Sarah followed her to the kitchen.

'Thanks, Ginny. You are a lifesaver. We were having such a boring time till you arrived. Who'd have thought you would save the day?'

Sarah looked aghast as soon as the words escaped her mouth.

'Sorry, Ginny. I didn't mean that quite the way it sounded.'

Ginny smiled benignly. It would take more than a comment from Sarah to dent her happiness tonight. 'That's all right. I have been having a lovely evening.'

'You don't have to see his silly old dog. I mean it was nice of you to be polite but don't feel that you have to.'

'Well, I can't very well back out now, Sarah, can I? Anyway, he obviously loves his old dog. I'd be happy to take a look at him.'

'Well, if you're sure,' said Sarah.

'It's what I do all day, Sarah, look at sick animals, see if I can help them. That's my job. I'm a vet.'

'Yes, yes, I suppose,' said Sarah.

Ginny could see Sarah had lost interest in the vet talk. She wasn't at all herself tonight.

'So, what do you think of Hal?' asked Sarah. 'He doesn't look much like Tom, and yet, when he smiles and laughs he does. Sometimes there is an expression in his eyes. It's quite unsettling.'

Ginny started to speak, keen to share her observations of the similarities and differences between the two men, but Sarah continued, not noticing her friend's sudden keenness to talk.

'He's older than I expected, more urbane too. When Tom said he was a biker I just expected a Hells Angel. He's not at all like that. Just goes to show you shouldn't make judgements about people, I suppose. So that's my new father-in-law. A new member of the family.'

Sarah sounded so proprietorial that Ginny felt resentment burn at the back of her throat. She recognised its bitter taste and tried to swallow it away. It stayed, a persistent lump. She reached for the sugar bowl. She noticed it was nearly empty and asked Sarah where she kept her sugar to refill it. Sarah gestured vaguely towards the food cupboard.

'I'm so glad you dropped by, Ginny. I hadn't organised a dessert. It was a lovely cake. Really. But more than that, thank God, you came and talked about your work. You lost me a bit with the details of the operations. Bit gruesome. But very interesting. Hal is hard work, don't you think? I couldn't think what to talk to him about. Imagine that. Me stuck for words.'

Ginny poured the last of the sugar in the canister into the sugar bowl, carefully scraping the fine dust from the sides of the canister.

'You're out of sugar, Sarah. You'll need to buy more.'

CHAPTER 9

Ever tried to open your veins with a plastic knife, pulling that pathetic excuse for a serrated edge across your wrists? They don't cut vegetables, much less meat. That's all we're allowed. No steel cutlery, no pins, not even a brooch or belt buckle. They think we'll try to kill ourselves. Or, worse still, try to carve each other up. Then there would really be trouble. Loon kills loon. I don't want to die. And I don't want to kill anyone else either. Not in my nature, I keep telling them that. But I did try once, I know. I didn't really mean it. Not really. But they won't let me forget.

Ginny felt uneasy. She was tense and feeling as if something was about to happen. It was like that heightening of the senses before the climax of a movie, that moment when she realised she was holding her breath. She would let it out and try to relax her shoulders but it didn't ever help. She always still felt scared. That's how Ginny felt but she didn't understand why. It was like there was something in the air. It was all around her. She stood on her balcony and looked across the bay at the sun sparkling on the water and shivered involuntarily.

She couldn't see the huge storm that was approaching, but she could sense it. It was rolling across the Tasman Sea, sucking up the energy in its path, swelling and growing, increasing its power and might as it charged towards Elizabeth Bay. It was still nearly an hour away but the atmospheric pressure was building and the air was alive with electricity. Ginny's nerves felt sharp and raw. She saw Kitty pacing on the back of the couch looking out at her. Kitty sensed the change in energy and was agitated too.

Ginny stared across at Toft Monks. Sarah and Tom's balcony was like a closed face. It was 8 pm and they should have been home from work by now. Ginny felt her irritation grow. Her moods, her thoughts, her whole being, revolved around Sarah and Tom. She no longer had a life of her own. She was completely consumed by what went on inside that four-room apartment at Toft Monks.

Her days at the vet were an interruption. Shopping for food was an interruption. Anything that took her away from her apartment, her binoculars and the loud speaker was an interruption. Every waking moment her senses were strained toward that apartment. When Sarah and Tom were home she listened and watched their every movement, their every word. She took notes, writing the minutiae of their lives down in a big spiral-bound notebook.

She had different headings on different pages: 'Fights', 'Possibilities' and 'Tom's dad'. The section she added to most, writing away furiously with a tight, satisfied smile, was 'Bitch', where she recorded her observations of Sarah and what Ginny considered her unreasonable behaviour. A simple friendly discussion between Sarah and Tom about who had last used the TV remote control, the sort of discussion that went on amiably in homes across the country every evening, would be recorded under the 'Bitch' heading as a further example of Sarah's lies and callous manipulation of Tom.

Indeed, Tom and Sarah would have been astounded to read

their lives as perceived by their secret observer. They would have struggled to recognise either of themselves in Ginny's record of their lives. Even though it was an extraordinarily detailed and accurate record of what went on in the supposed privacy of their own apartment, Ginny's spiral-bound notebook actually revealed very little of them and an awful lot about her own warped and malicious sense of reality.

The storm continued to roll towards Elizabeth Bay. Ginny glanced again at Toft Monks. Lights were on in half the apartments as people went about their evening rituals, cooking dinner, settling down in front of the television, but Tom and Sarah's windows stayed stubbornly dark. Ginny sighed and bent down to pet Kitty.

'Where are they, Kitty? Do you know?' she murmured, tickling her under the chin.

Kitty tossed her head. She wasn't interested right now, thank you.

Ginny did another restless lap of her small apartment. She peered into the fishbowl. The water was a bit murky. Probably should clean it in the next few days.

'How are you little fishy?' she said putting her face close to the glass. 'You look like I feel – bored. Want to come for a swim?' Ginny picked up the bowl, smiling as the startled fish rocked in the suddenly choppy water.

She turned up the speaker in her bedroom, so she would know the minute her prey arrived home. The sound of static bounced around the walls of the apartment. It was a piercing hiss that added to Kitty's agitation but satisfied Ginny. She placed the fishbowl in the washbasin. As she ran the bath she stripped off her clothes. She was small-boned and slight and very, very pale. She slowly lowered herself into the bath, holding the fishbowl tightly to her chest. As the water settled she placed the bowl on her stomach, being careful to keep the rim just above water level.

The fish was an exotic bubble-eyed fish from South America. It had small gold and black spots on a squat white body, with huge fluid-filled pouches under each eye, which looked to Ginny like swollen blisters. Every time she looked at it she felt the urge to pierce the pouches with a needle. It was the same curiosity she had about animals ever since she was a child and it was the reason she had wanted to become a vet. She didn't really love animals in the way the other students in her university class had. She was intrigued by their unique bodily functions, their differences, their variety and how each species differed so dramatically from humans and then from every other animal species. She saw the whole animal kingdom as one huge puzzle and it appealed to her intellect to unravel how it all worked, to find connections. She loved dissecting them, poking around inside their little bodies, discovering their intriguing little organs. Most people found the bubble-eyed fish grotesque but to Ginny its uniqueness made it terribly appealing.

Ginny watched it swim, the pouches bouncing around with each swish of its tail. She sighed and settled languidly into the bath. Her mind emptied of thoughts. Her tension dissolved into the water, into the fishbowl. She imagined what the fish might be experiencing. As the fish's world expanded, so did Ginny's. She lost sense of her body and felt as if she was floating. The fish swam round and round, rhythmically, hypnotically. It was energised. Ginny lost herself in its movement, dozing in the space somewhere between daydreaming and falling asleep.

The storm rolled into Elizabeth Bay, hitting the roofs of the homes with hailstones the size of huge marbles. Within seconds of the first few hundred hailstones hitting their roofs, residents were outside moving their cars undercover, or tying towels and old blankets to car roofs and bonnets. People walking home from bus-stops and railway stations huddled together under bus shelters and shop awnings. Across the parks the homeless men and women gathered up their garbage bags of belongings and cardboard beds and piled into the public toilets where they sat tightly together.

The storm passed in a matter of minutes, venting its fury on Elizabeth Bay then diminishing as it rolled on across the rest of the city. By the time it reached Blacktown on the city's western edges and headed towards the Blue Mountains it was just a quick rainshower. The residents of Elizabeth Bay breathed a collective sigh of relief as it passed and went back to their Monday-night business. Those at home moved away from their windows and turned back to the TV. The people huddling together in the bus shelters and under awnings shook themselves off and moved apart, suddenly conscious of their personal space. The homeless stayed huddled together in the toilets, enjoying the break in their otherwise bleak routine, and happily sharing their cheap plonk and cigarettes. They knew the police would leave them alone and the workers from the Sydney City Mission would be along soon with hot soup and offers of a bed at one of the city shelters.

Ginny, dozing mindlessly in the bath, heard the hail and short burst of rain that followed but it blended with the static and the dripping bath tap and became part of the foggy dreamworld in which she floated. She remained lost in her reverie, unaware of the fury raging outside.

When she finally stirred she was surprised by how much her mood had improved. The air was fresher. The oppressive feeling of her apartment had lifted. Humming to herself, she dressed and put her fish back on its table in the lounge room.

She looked across at Toft Monks. Tom and Sarah's apartment was still in darkness. But through the static she heard a very welcome sound. The click of their front door opening.

'About bloody time,' she muttered to Kitty, and raced excitedly into her bedroom.

'I'm soaked,' announced Sarah, her booming laugh reverberating around the walls of Ginny's room.

She sounded exalted and Ginny's heart tightened. She picked up the binoculars in time to see Sarah and Tom falling over each other as they peeled off their wet clothes, throwing them at each other as they raced to the bathroom. She continued to watch as the sound of the shower running filled her apartment. She could see steam spilling out the open doorway as Tom and Sarah showered noisily, laughing and splashing.

Ginny's relaxed mood evaporated in an instant. She threw down the binoculars angrily. They missed the bed and thudded onto the floor. When she bent to pick them up Ginny saw the body of a dead cockroach, lying feet up, under her bed. She picked it up with her thumb and forefinger and carried it into the lounge room where she dropped it into the fishbowl. The cockroach sank slowly to the bottom. The bubble-eyed fish swam furiously about the bowl, startled by its new visitor.

'Eat that,' said Ginny nastily.

Sarah stretched out on the couch, wearing a fluffy white bathrobe with her wet hair wrapped in a towel. She had a large notepad on her lap, a pen in one hand and a mug of coffee in the other. Tom sat at the other end of the couch, wearing his favourite rugby jumper and a pair of sloppy track pants, massaging her feet in his lap.

Sarah moaned. 'That is so good.' She watched Tom's face, absorbed in his task. He felt her eyes on him and smiled back, his eyes soft and content.

'What are you going to do about Hal and your mum?' she asked. 'You want both of them to be there, don't you?'

Tom sighed.

'Yes, of course I do. But I can't imagine how Thel will feel about it. She has no idea I've been seeing Hal. I just can't think how she will feel.'

'Tom,' said Sarah gently, 'don't you think it's time you did tell her that you've been seeing Hal? You have every right to see him. He's your father. She will understand that. And the sooner you tell her the sooner she can get used to the idea that he will be at the wedding and she will have to deal with him.'

'Sarah, I know that. Really I do. I just keep going over it and over it in my head. I can't remember the last time Thel and I even had a conversation about him. It's not like his name comes up and I could just casually add that I've been seeing him. She has not mentioned his name to me in – I don't know – ten years. And I can't even tell you why. She's never said anything bad about him, ever. And I can't remember her telling me that it was too painful for her to talk about. It's just something I've known all my life. I have absolutely no idea what happened between them but it is a source of enormous pain to her. She hasn't told me that but I know. I've always known. It's unspoken but clear as a bell.'

'Well, maybe it's not still painful for her, Tom. I mean, how would you know if you haven't spoken about it in ten years? She may be well and truly over it for all you know.'

Tom was thoughtful as he looked at Sarah. 'Sarah, there are some things that people just don't talk about because they are so painful.' He chose his words carefully. 'In any close relationship you develop a knowledge, an understanding, of what hurts people and just how far you can go. And when you love someone I think it makes you doubly sensitive. You want to help but you also don't want to blunder in and say the wrong thing.'

Sarah started to twirl a strand of hair around her finger.

Tom watched her closely.

'I think there are areas of our relationship which we don't talk about because they are too sensitive.'

Sarah squirmed uncomfortably.

Tom continued. 'I'd like to talk about them. I think it might help. What do you think?'

Sarah looked out across the bay at the building opposite. Tom watched as a myriad of expressions flashed across her face. He knew there was an internal struggle going on. She was debating something within herself. He barely dared breathe. Sarah stopped twisting her hair and looked him squarely in the face. She searched his eyes.

'I think I love you and I want to marry you,' she said quietly but with total conviction. 'I want to spend the rest of my life being with you, going to sleep in your little chair. I know I've been tired and grumpy lately but that's not because I don't love you or that I don't think this marriage is the right and best thing for us. I'm just under a lot of pressure at work. But it's nothing deeper than that.'

Sarah climbed forward over the notepad to get to Tom. She took his face in her hands. 'I promise you, darling.'

'Oh, Sarah,' said Tom. 'Are you sure? Is there anything you want to talk about with me? Anything else that might be worrying you?'

'No, darling. I feel stronger and happier than I have ever been. And that's because of you. You make me feel so special. You make me feel strong. I know you love me. I don't doubt it for a moment. And I can't tell you how wonderful and confident that makes me feel. I am so lucky. Sometimes it scares me. I wake up in the night scared that I'm too happy. I'm using up all my happiness quota now and it can't possibly last. What right do I have to be this happy when all around me are people who aren't half as lucky? Who do I thank for this? And what can I do to make sure it lasts? I love that you worry about me but please relax. I'm fine. Really. We need to concentrate on you. How are we going to get your parents and my parents to our wedding and find a way that we can all enjoy it?'

Tom listened to her words and listened to her tone. He knew Sarah about as well as anybody could know another human being. She sounded happy and relaxed, just like the girl he had fallen in love with and spent the past eight years with. He knew she loved him. There didn't seem to be anything else to say. He allowed himself to be reassured.

'All right Sarah. Back to the problem at hand. How am I going to do this? What do I say to Thel?'

Sarah breathed out slowly, consciously relaxing her muscles. That was close. She resolved, yet again, to make it the truth. She happily moved the conversation back to the wedding.

'I think you should go and see her, alone, without me, and just tell her. Tell her how it happened. It's not like you sought him out. He found you. He recognised your byline in the newspaper and rang you at the office. You met him for a drink and have seen a bit of him since.'

Tom nodded thoughtfully. 'For the past twenty years it's been just Thel and me. I don't want to hurt her.'

'I think you are selling your mum short, Tom. I can't imagine Thel being angry about anything you did that made you happy.'

'It's not about her getting angry. It's about bringing it up for her again, but I know you're right. I have to do it.'

'Okay, well, you go and see Thel this weekend and talk to her. That's one problem solved. Now who else in your family would you like to invite?'

They spent the next few hours writing their wedding invitation list. It was a slow but happy process as they explained their relationships with and feelings about each person as their name was added to the list. Sarah learned more about Tom's family – his aunts and cousins and his much-loved Uncle Bill – than she had ever heard before. And Sarah in turn revealed more about her own family.

'Will your parents come, do you think?' asked Tom carefully.

Sarah looked out across the bay. She twirled a strand of hair around her finger, tugging it gently. She pulled it and released it, allowing it to hurt just a little.

'I don't know. They haven't been home to Australia for years now. I don't think Daddy is up to travelling. Mother's last letter said he made it down to his club and back and that was about it.'

'Would your mother come on her own?'

Sarah made a face. 'Mother wouldn't go anywhere without Daddy.'

Tom had met Sarah's parents a handful of times over the years, during their infrequent visits to Sydney to see their only daughter. He remembered her mother Geraldine as a slim, brittle woman with too much make-up and a forced laugh. She had a peculiar way of relating to Sarah that made Tom uncomfortable. Tom's expectations of motherhood were based around Thel, Thel the earth mother with the huge, open heart. Geraldine was as far from that as Tom could ever have imagined.

She was constantly pushing Sarah to the front, as if she

expected her to perform. Sarah was unable to sit silently for too long without risking her mother's disapproval. Silence meant boring and in Geraldine's eyes that was the worst sin a person could commit, particularly a woman. She demanded gaiety. On more than a few occasions Tom had had to bite his tongue when he felt overcome by the urge to intercede on Sarah's behalf.

Around Geraldine, Tom noticed how Sarah's natural exuberance became forced. He didn't like that. Tom had never said so to Sarah but privately he wondered if Geraldine actually disliked her daughter. Whenever Tom had gently probed into their relationship Sarah had always been dismissive.

'Oh that's just Geraldine,' she would say airily and Tom felt forced to leave it at that.

Her father, Gus, he had liked. He was a tall gruff man, a man's man, and Tom related to him easily. Gus was a retired diplomat who had been stationed in various countries throughout their early married life. They had liked the climate and pampered life of the expatriates in Singapore and so had stayed on there for the past twenty years. They had sent Sarah to school in Sydney when she was ten because they believed they would eventually return there. That was what they had said. Tom wondered if Geraldine had other reasons for not wanting to have her beautiful daughter around.

Geraldine appeared to be acutely competitive around other women. After some time Tom had realised that her attitude might have some justification. Gus, Tom noticed, had quite an eye for the ladies. He would flirt with all the waitresses, whenever Geraldine'e eagle eye wasn't focussed intently on him.

Tom wondered how Sarah really felt. 'Would it worry you if they didn't come?' he asked.

Sarah heard the concern in Tom's voice. Knowing this man loved her and wanted to make a family with her seemed to make everything all right.

'Not as long as you are there,' she replied.

Tom wasn't convinced but he let it pass. Perhaps now wasn't

the time. He looked closely at her. She had stopped tugging at her hair and was smiling brightly at him.

'I suppose you want Marty as your best man?' asked Sarah.

'Yup,' said Tom. 'Of course.'

'Poor Ginny,' sighed Sarah. 'That means they will be partners all night.'

'What's wrong with that?' asked Tom. 'They are great friends.'

'Oh, Tom, you don't really think that, do you? Ginny can't stand Marty.'

Tom's eyes widened. 'You're joking. Since when?'

'They have never got on. Ginny puts up with him but she doesn't actually like him. Haven't you ever noticed?'

'Well, no, I haven't. I'm sure you're imagining it. Do you want Ginny as your bridesmaid?'

'Of course. She's my oldest and dearest friend.'

'Well then, she will just have to put up with him for another night.'

That night, as Tom lay in bed watching Sarah sleep, he felt the uneasiness return. There was something, he couldn't put his finger on it, but he knew something was going on in that head of hers. There had always been a part of Sarah that Tom couldn't reach, a private place where she wouldn't allow him to go, and he had long ago come to accept that. He believed her parents had a lot to answer for.

Whatever was worrying Sarah wasn't about him or them, but about her. He believed everyone was entitled to their secrets. He had a few of his own that he chose not to share. He still carried scars from his childhood – the shock and pain when his father had left so suddenly. In the early days with Sarah it had taken him a while to fully trust her, to trust that she would hang around. He had worked through that but he knew he carried his own share of insecurities that he couldn't always articulate and often didn't want to.

But something didn't feel right. He sensed it. He sighed and moved closer to Sarah, wrapping his tall body around hers. Sarah automatically snuggled back into him and pushed her bottom into his lap. Tom stroked her shoulders. He felt the muscles along her arms. The biceps, even at rest, were well defined. Tom moved his hand down and gently felt Sarah's stomach. He was surprised by how taut the muscles were across her abdomen. Sarah moaned in her sleep. Tom tightened his arms about her trying to quell his growing apprehension.

Sarah tossed and turned for most of the night. As she slept her subconscious tried to release some of the emotional pressure that was building and that she managed to suppress during her waking hours. The result was bone-shaking nightmares, the sort she hadn't had for years. She was small and alone in a vast empty space, hiding under a table. There was nothing around her but empty, blinding white space and the overpowering stench of fear. She crouched under the table, feeling vulnerable and exposed, filled with unspeakable terror. She woke shaking at 5 am, her body wet with sweat. She didn't remember the dream, just its sour aftertaste. Her heart was racing and pumping the last of the adrenaline around her body.

When she woke she was instantly alert. Tom was snoring loudly beside her. He was flat on his back, spread-eagled across most of the bed. His chest rose and fell in time with the low growl that burst forth intermittently from his open mouth.

He was making quite a noise but Sarah knew instinctively that wasn't what had woken her. She tried to remember what she had been dreaming, but it was wispy and abstract. The more she tried to grasp it, the further it receded.

A full moon shone brightly through the open curtains, filling the room with pale light. The room was stuffy and hot and Sarah felt she couldn't breathe. It was useless trying to go back to sleep. She padded barefoot into the kitchen to make herself a cup of coffee. As she poured the boiling water into the cup she noticed her hands were shaking.

She was completely unnerved. She opened the balcony

door wide to let in some fresh air. She stepped out onto the balcony and looked across Rushcutters Bay, sparkling silver with the light of the full moon. As her eyes adjusted, she was able to see clearly the boats in the harbour and the outline of neighbouring buildings. The light cast by the moon was surreal, making the view almost two-tone, dark grey and silvery white. There was the merest hint of colour.

She looked across at the apartment building opposite. It was so ugly. She wished it wasn't there and she could see the Harbour Bridge. She thought the Bridge must look beautiful in this ethereal light. Something caught her eye on a balcony. A movement. Who else could be up at this hour? she wondered. But they were gone, if indeed they had been there at all. It was just a sudden blur then an empty balcony. But Sarah felt comforted. She wasn't the only person in the world awake at this unfriendly hour.

Tom's snores *had* woken Ginny. The loud, rhythmic growl had filled her bedroom, terrifying Kitty and awakening in Ginny an unbearable yearning. Ginny had slipped on her dressing gown and ventured onto the balcony, looking longingly across to where she knew Tom slept. She didn't dare go onto her balcony in daylight, afraid of being seen. But tonight she was drawn to him, needing to feel as close to him as she could.

She had been startled to see an outline appear in the shadows of Sarah and Tom's balcony. At first she had thought it was Tom, sharing her yearning, knowing she was there, and answering her call. She felt like a siren as she stood, buffeted gently by the fresh breeze, calling silently across to her imaginary lover. When the dark shape moved into the moonlight Ginny realised it was Sarah. She carefully and slowly withdrew back into her own apartment, sliding the tinted glass door shut, feeling safe again sealed inside her own cell.

★

Sarah waited till dawn broke at 5.40 am before heading out for a run. She powered through the park, pushing her body harder and harder. She wanted to feel it burn. By the time the clock radio by their bed burst to life at 7 am she was showered and reading the newspapers in the kitchen. She felt strong and powerful, ready to take on the world. She assumed it was the endorphins kicking in from her run and resolved to do more exercise. She felt so good.

Tom frowned when he found her. 'Have you been running again?' he asked.

'Yup,' said Sarah. 'And I feel great.'

Tom didn't look happy. He sat down opposite Sarah and helped himself to coffee.

'Do you think you may be overdoing the exercise?'

There, it was out in the open. Tom didn't want a fight but he wanted to know what was going on. He could feel Sarah slipping away, retreating inside her own head. It had happened before and he was going to make damn sure it didn't happen again. He was paying attention this time. And he wanted her to know it.

Sarah stared him down.

'No, I don't think so,' she replied. 'I think it's good for me. Frankly, I think you could do with a bit more exercise.'

Tom refused to take the bait. 'You don't think you are becoming – obsessive?'

Tom chose the word carefully. It sounded innocent enough but it carried a special resonance for them both, within the context of their relationship. There was a time, six years ago, when that word had been bandied about a lot. The word sat between them, taking them back to that raw and painful time.

'No, I don't,' replied Sarah. 'I know what you are getting at and may I say I think you are an arsehole.'

Tom considered this new information. 'I see. Well, I guess there's nothing more to say then.'

They sat in silence. It was uncomfortable but neither wanted to walk away. Part of Sarah did want to talk to Tom, to express the emotions spilling about inside her. But she was frightened. It would mean going back to that dark, malevolent place where she had no bearings. She couldn't risk going back there. It was too scary. And she could feel Tom coming too close. She felt threatened.

Tom sat staring at Sarah. He wanted her to see him, to feel him, there, right in front of her face. 'I'm not going away,' was his silent message.

The only sound in the apartment was the chipmunk voice of the breakfast announcer, shrill and distant, floating to them from the bedroom.

They both listened, without comprehending, as he read out the newspaper headlines of the day. It was soothing, in a domestic, grounding kind of way. The heat of the tension between them eased slightly.

Finally Tom spoke. 'The car needs re-registering,' he said.

Sarah looked up. 'Does it?'

Sarah paid the bills for the couple. It had just evolved that way. Tom was often away researching stories and Sarah had said she was happy to do it, to assume responsibility for the day-to-day running of their lives. It was unusual for her not to have been on top of something as simple as the car registration. The Roads and Traffic Authority sent out a reminder notice weeks in advance.

'I guess I must have forgotten it.'

'It runs out on Sunday,' said Tom.

Sarah twirled a strand of hair around her finger.

'Do you think you could pay it this week, Sarah?'

'Yes, of course. I'll send a cheque today.'

'You will have to. It will take them a while to process it and send out a new sticker. Perhaps you should go in to the RTA and pay it over the counter.'

Sarah felt annoyed. Why was it always her responsibility? What had seemed an act of love, as their lives became entwined, was now a burden.

'And when would I have time to do that? Perhaps you could make time in your busy day to take care of it. You could go into the RTA and stand in the queue.'

Tom sighed. 'Sarah, you know I am working on a big story right now. I will most probably have to go to Canberra for a few days at the end of the week to talk to some people. I think I've convinced the body builder who killed his wife in a steroid rage to talk to me.'

Sarah wasn't interested. She resented what she saw as the unspoken assumption that his work was more important than her own, his time far more valuable than hers, so she should be the one to waste it standing in a queue.

'Fine, Tom, let me do it. Your time is *far* too important to be spent on such trifles.'

Tom held his tongue. She was spoiling for a fight and he wasn't in the mood. He was running out of patience.

'As long as they get the cheque we are registered and legal,' he replied. 'It should be fine if you just make sure you send it today.'

Sarah downed the last of her coffee and went to get dressed. She left for work without kissing Tom goodbye. He was shaving when she left and he came out of the bathroom to an empty apartment.

Ginny opened her notebook at the page headed 'Bitch'. With a happy little smile she recorded Tom and Sarah's conversation. She wrote the word 'arsehole' in capitals, each letter at different angles to the other. It was the writing of an angry child.

CHAPTER 10

Ginny was excited all morning. So excited she could hardly concentrate on her work. Hal had arranged to bring in Laddie at 11 am. Ginny had told Dr Black he was a friend and would he mind if she saw to him. Dr Black, himself distracted by the forthcoming start of the horseracing carnival, his busiest time, was only too happy to have one thing less to do. They didn't have a full book of appointments but he had a lot of reports to finish ready for the weekend and he hoped to get out to visit some stables on the outskirts of Sydney.

'If you need me, just holler,' he had told her.

The receptionist, Annie, had been told to alert Ginny as soon as Hal arrived.

Annie was surprised by Ginny's excitement. While Dr Black had been too preoccupied to notice, Annie hadn't been. She noticed everything.

'Is he a friend of yours?' she asked innocently, but with just enough emphasis on the word friend to let Ginny know she knew something was up.

Ginny was such a closed person. Annie had often wondered

about her. She was pretty enough, though Annie thought she could have done more with herself. She didn't wear make-up and wasn't the least bit interested in fashion. That alone, in Annie's book, made Ginny strange.

Annie was nineteen and spent every cent she earned buying fashion magazines. On her salary she couldn't afford what she saw on the glossy pages, but she loved to sew and would create her own versions of whatever caught her eye. She wasn't particularly good at sewing so she often looked thrown together. But somehow with her youth and bravado, she managed to carry it off.

Today she was trying out a hot pink sarong skirt with a lopsided hem, which she had run up the night before, and a wildly clashing orange bolero, stretched tightly across her ample bust. Her hair was streaked with electric blue highlights.

'How do I look?' she had asked Ginny that morning, more for her own entertainment than because she cared what the older girl thought.

Ginny always felt uncomfortable around Annie. She was so saucy it unsettled her. Ginny knew she was being teased and it annoyed her.

'Like a clothesline that has fallen over,' said Ginny. 'Just tell me when he gets here.'

Annie poked her tongue out as the doors to the inner sanctum swung closed behind Ginny.

When Hal did arrive, ten minutes early, with Laddie on a leash, Annie chose to forget her instructions and sat him down where she could get a good look at him. She set aside her pile of typing and eyed him up and down. She took in the washed-out denim jeans, the cowboy boots and the leather vest over the white singlet. Pretty good for his age, she thought. Handsome, though a bit older than she would have expected for Ginny. Nice blue eyes. Muscly arms.

'You're a friend of our Ginny's?' she said to him innocently.

'Yes,' replied Hal, petting Laddie who was unsettled by the smells of the other animals.

'Aaaaah,' she said.

Hal ignored the invitation to elaborate. He devoted all his attention to his dog, holding him gently by the scruff of the neck and whispering soothing words.

Annie pressed on. 'Been friends long?'

Hal looked up. He hadn't really noticed Annie when he came in and said who he was. He took in her blue streaked hair, the heavy make-up and sassy tone.

'Laddie and I have been together for fourteen years,' he said slowly and deliberately. He wasn't rude but he made his point.

Reluctantly Annie turned back to her typing. They could have each other, she thought to herself. What a boring pair. Usually she offered customers a drink or pointed out the pile of magazines, *Pet Monthly*, *Racehorse News* and *Dogue*. But if he didn't want to be friendly, well he was on his own. He could just wait till Madame came and got him.

At ten past eleven Ginny, dressed in a white coat with a stethoscope around her neck, came to check at reception and was annoyed to find Hal and Laddie sitting there patiently waiting.

She shot Annie a withering look, which Annie ignored, and welcomed Hal. He rose to greet her and she noticed, with disappointment, how he looked less like Tom in the daylight. Then he smiled and it was like looking at Tom again – sparkling blue eyes and a warm, open smile that invited you to trust him. She felt herself grow warm and realised she was blushing. Annie noticed too and raised an eyebrow. This was just too interesting.

'Ginny, your *friend* is here,' she said pointedly.

Ignoring her, Ginny led Hal and Laddie through the swinging doors into a consulting room. Hal and Ginny helped Laddie onto the table.

'He's a border collie cross?' asked Ginny.

'Yes, crossed with a labrador,' said Hal.

'How old?'

'I've had him fourteen years,' said Hal, stroking Laddie's head with affection. He held the dog steady, looking all the time into his eyes to comfort him. Ginny was touched by how much Hal obviously cared for the old dog.

Laddie was well and truly past his prime. His black coat was no longer glossy and his white underbelly was yellowing with clumps of bare patches. His eyes showed a little build-up of mucus in the corners. Nevertheless, they were bright and focussed. He seemed to have no problem seeing. Ginny ruled out cataracts.

Laddie stood patiently while Ginny inspected him. She pressed her fingers gently but expertly on his major organs looking for swelling and tenderness. Everything seemed fine. She listened to his heart. There was the faint sign of tachycardia, a slightly fast heartbeat, but nothing unusual for his age. She believed Dr Black would have been impressed. She was conducting the examination just as he would have done. Ginny moved down to the legs. She tenderly lifted up a hind paw. On the underside was a rash. It was red and angry.

'Is he urinating normally?' asked Ginny.

'Um, no,' said Hal. 'He's always been really good about going outside. I've got a doggy door and he lets himself in and out. But lately he's been wetting himself while he sleeps.'

'Aaaah,' said Ginny, sounding much like Dr Black did when he was coming close to a diagnosis. 'Can you get him to lie down?'

Hal patted Laddie, gently pushing him down on the table. Laddie was tired of standing and needed little encouragement. He curled up on his side, tucking his hind paws beneath him. He looked up at Hal with big trusting brown eyes. Ginny looked at him thoughtfully.

'Is that how he sleeps?'

'Well, yes, I think so,' said Hal.

Ginny straightened up and smiled.

'It's not serious, Hal,' she said. 'I think your Laddie has nappy rash. Or the canine equivalent.'

Hal looked confused and Ginny laughed.

'He is getting old,' she told him gently. 'He's becoming a bit incontinent and when he urinates in his sleep the acid in his urine is burning the tender skin on his paw. Walking is causing him a lot of pain. That's why he has lost his bounce. I can give you some cream for the rash, which should clear it up in a few days, and at night I'm afraid you will have to put a nappy on him.'

Hal looked relieved.

'But, Hal, please understand, he is old.'

Hal nodded. 'I know. It breaks my heart but I know I'll lose him one of these days.'

Ginny wouldn't let Hal pay. Annie watched with conspicuous amusement as she waved away his cheque book.

'Can I at least take you to lunch?' said Hal.

Ginny was thrilled.

They arranged to meet at a café down the street in a few minutes.

'Shall I charge that consultation to you?' asked Annie after Hal had gone.

'No,' said Ginny. 'There will be no charge at all. Dr Black has said that is fine. Thank you, Annie.'

Annie made a big production of tearing up the account.

'It would help me if you had told me that before I wrote it up,' she said grumpily. 'It's not like I don't have anything better to do. Anybody would think I just sat here waiting for more work . . .' She was still complaining as Ginny took her bag and cardigan and closed the door behind her.

Ginny forgot Annie instantly. It was warm and sunny outside. A perfect summer day. Ginny hurried along to meet Hal. She found him sitting contentedly in the sun at an outdoor table with Laddie tied to his chair. He stood up as she arrived, towering over her as he pulled out her chair.

They talked about Laddie and how Hal had found him as a stray pup and taken him home. Ginny talked about Kitty and the other strays she had collected along the way. She thought of Isobel, the first pet she had truly loved, and started to tell Hal about taxidermy and how it still comforted her to have Isobel there at home with her. Laddie's time couldn't be too far off and Ginny thought Hal might like to have him stuffed.

Hal was horrified and Ginny was instantly sorry she had spoken.

'It's just something to think about,' she finished lamely. She wasn't sure what horrified Hal – the idea of Laddie dying, the taxidermy or the combination of the two.

The waitress arrived to take their order and Ginny and Hal settled back in silence.

Ginny tried to move the conversation to safer ground. She broached the topic that she wanted to find out about.

'Tom tells me he has only just been reunited with you,' she said. 'That must be very strange for you both.'

Hal smiled that Tom smile. 'I've rediscovered my son. He seems a fine young man. I'm very proud, although I can't take any of the credit. Sarah said you are her oldest friend so I guess you've known Tom for some time too.'

It was on the tip of Ginny's tongue to say she had known him first, before Sarah, but she stopped herself. 'I see a lot of Tom. He is one of my closest friends too,' said Ginny. 'He is a fine man. You *should* be proud of him.'

Hal nodded as he chewed.

'How old was he when you last saw him?' asked Ginny.

'He had just had his eighth birthday. He was a good kid even then. I knew he would be in safe hands. Do you know Thel, Tom's mother?'

Ginny nodded.

'She's a pretty amazing lady. I knew she'd bring up Tom to be a decent lad. Lord knows I couldn't give him any sort of stable life. And that's what a kid needs.'

Ginny wondered what had happened between Hal and Thel but didn't feel it was her business to ask. 'What have you been doing in the past twenty or so years?' she asked instead.

'Oh, lots of different things. I worked for a while on a fishing trawler up north, spent time on the oil rigs, travelled a lot around Australia. Spent time in Papua New Guinea. Then about fourteen years ago I came to Sydney. I've always had motorbikes so decided it was time to be my own boss and bought out the motorcycle dealership.

'I didn't know Tom was living in Sydney until I read a story he wrote. I'd often thought about him, wondered how he had turned out. But I had long since lost contact with his mother. When I rang the newspaper I thought it was a long shot that it would be the same Tom Wilson, Tom Wilson my son. But it was.'

'It must have been pretty amazing to see him again,' said Ginny.

'It was. I remembered him as an eight-year-old kid and instead I had this fully grown man in front of me. It was quite disconcerting, but good. He looked kind of . . . familiar, you know?'

'Tom was really pleased that you rang,' said Ginny, remembering the look on Tom's face when they were standing close together on the balcony.

'Yeah, so am I. We've got a lot of catching up to do. But I don't feel like there's any hurry. I've got my son back and that's enough. And I'm delighted that he has such a wonderful girl in Sarah, and such nice friends.'

Ginny flinched when he mentioned Sarah. It took her a moment to realise he had been paying her a compliment too. She smiled at him, looking happily into his sparkling blue eyes. Ginny revelled in the attention. 'Perhaps you could take me out on your bike one day,' she said.

'Sure. Anytime you like,' replied Hal easily.

'How about this weekend?' suggested Ginny, her heart racing.

'Okay, this weekend it is. I shut the shop at twelve so we could go for a ride after that.'

'Okay,' said Ginny. 'Saturday it is. You can pick me up from work just after twelve.'

Ginny was humming when she walked back inside the door to the vet practice. Even Annie's scowling face couldn't affect her mood.

'I've got a date with Tom's dad, Tom's dad, Tom's dad,' she was singing to herself under her breath.

Dr Black had left for the day. He had gone to visit some of

his racehorses and that left Ginny to clean up the consulting rooms, prepare whatever would be needed for the next day and lock up.

'Why don't you leave the rest of that typing till tomorrow,' she said kindly to Annie. 'It's much too nice a day for you to be in here.'

Annie was surprised. Ginny being kind? Caring? What next? A girlie chat about boys? Annie wasn't about to hang around for that. She had places to go and people to meet. Always. 'Thanks, Ginny. See you tomorrow.' She was out the door in an instant.

Ginny locked the door after Annie left and pulled down the blinds. She turned on the answering machine and let herself into Dr Black's medicine cupboard. The Limondol was standing among the row of earthenware jars. Its level had dropped since she was last there, which was a good thing. Dr Black had been using it and was unlikely to notice that more had gone. Ginny scooped as much as she dared into a smaller jar, then popped it into her handbag.

'I've got a date with Tom's dad, Tom's dad, Tom's dad, oh I've got a date with Tom's dad . . .' she sang loudly and happily as she cleaned up the last of the mess in the consulting room.

Ginny arrived at Toft Monks just after 7 pm. Kate and Anne were already there. Tom was out of town for a few days and Sarah had invited them all over for dinner.

'Sit down, Sarah,' said Ginny. 'I know where the glasses are. I can help myself to wine.'

Sarah rejoined her friends in the living room where Kate was in full flight mimicking the director of her new show. She minced around the living room, waving her arms and pouting.

'*Dahhhling*, it has to have more *emotion*. You must make me cry . . .' Kate was saying in an exaggerated camp tone.

Ginny held her handbag tightly to her as she entered the kitchen. She looked at the pantry and deliberated. She wondered how long she might have before she could be interrupted. She wavered then decided she should wait. She put her handbag down carefully on the kitchen bench, took a wine glass from the cupboard and opened the fridge. She took the half-empty bottle with her into the living room.

'Anyone for a top-up?' she asked, smiling at the circle of women.

They all nodded as Kate continued with her story.

'So I did what *any* half-talented singer with an *ounce* of self-respect would do,' said Kate. She stopped for effect. The women looked at her expectantly. Kate loved to work an audience, no matter its size. 'I threw the chair at him.' Kate laughed triumphantly at the shocked faces around her. '*That* made him cry!'

'Oh, Kate, you didn't,' gasped Anne.

'I most certainly did. More emotion! How *dare* he. What does he want, Celine Dion? Huh! The chair hit him on the arm. Which is a pity as I was aiming at his head. He burst into floods of tears. Threw a complete hissy fit and ran sobbing from the stage. I mean *really*. I can't be expected to work with such *amateurs*.'

Kate looked outraged and indignant and the women stared at her, wide-eyed and transfixed. Kate looked at their faces and burst out laughing. The diva was gone in an instant and it was their old mate Kate again.

'Okay, maybe I didn't exactly *throw* the chair . . .'

The girls laughed and chatted, opened more wine, talked about Anne giving up work to care for the baby, Sarah's tough boss McKenzie and everything in between. When Sarah got up to serve dinner Ginny followed her into the kitchen, propping herself on the bench close to her handbag in case an opportunity arose.

'So why is Tom in Canberra?' she asked as casually as she could. She was always self-conscious saying Tom's name out loud to anyone else. That simple word carried so much meaning for her she didn't trust her voice to sound normal.

Sarah, noticing nothing unusual, answered happily. 'He's

working on a story on drug abuse among athletes,' she said. 'He's gone to Canberra to visit the Australian Institute of Sport to interview some of the coaches. It's a follow-up to see what is happening at the world competition level since all the promises that were made after the Sydney Olympics.'

Ginny felt a cold chill along the nerve endings beneath her skin. 'Really. How interesting?' she said, suddenly wary. She wanted to know more but was unsure how to elicit information from Sarah without sounding too interested in the subject.

'Oh, it is really interesting,' agreed Sarah. 'You remember how much bad press the Americans got? Their achievements were completely overshadowed by the drug scandal. The way everybody spoke then you would assume they were going to clean it up starting right from the top.

'Well what Tom is discovering is that while that may be so at the top there are still athletes who are using steroids to train. It hasn't been stamped out, just pushed even further underground.'

Ginny remembered the drug scandal of the 2000 Olympics. Living in Sydney at the time it was impossible not to know all about it. The media had been full of stories about the American team, the Romanians and the doping scandals. She had read a lot about steroid abuse and its effects at that time. In fact, she had devoured everything she could, subscribing to body-building magazines, borrowing books from the library and searching the internet for more information. She had developed quite an interest in it.

It was an article Ginny found on the web describing the side effects of anabolic steroids that had particularly interested her. Then she had gone to the library and taken out every book she could find on the subject. She knew about steroids, of course, from her vet training. But the effects on the human body were really quite interesting. The side effects were horrendous. Body builders and sportspeople were often so obsessive that they were willing to put up with them to achieve their goals.

The information had set Ginny thinking. What would happen to someone who wasn't an athlete, who didn't know they were taking steroids, if their body started to react differently? She was fascinated in particular by the pent-up aggression that was a regular by-product of steroid abuse. It was the sort of experiment that appealed to Ginny. In vet school she loved opening up animals to see how they worked inside, attaching electrodes to the muscles and stimulating them to react. She was as close to being happy as she had ever felt when she was working away in the science lab stimulating dead animals at her whim. Being so in control made her feel omnipotent, something she never felt in daily life. The idea of being able to do that to a living person was compelling. Oh yes, Ginny knew a lot of about steroid abuse and the scandal of the Sydney Olympics.

'How interesting,' she said again, as she helped Sarah carry the dinner plates into the living room.

Anne had overheard the last of their conversation and was interested. She had covered her share of drug abuse stories during the Olympics. Ginny sat quietly in her seat, feeling self-conscious and trying to shrink back into the fabric of the chair, as Sarah repeated the content of Tom's story to Kate and Anne. Sarah prattled on, speaking fast, her words tumbling over each other. Her eyes were unnaturally bright and she had large grey circles under her eyes. Anne stopped listening to what she was saying, instead noticing the way she was saying it. Sarah came to an abrupt halt in mid-sentence.

'Tom would kill me if he thought I was talking about a story he is working on,' said Sarah. 'Please keep it to yourselves. Or I'll have to shoot you all.'

The girls all agreed it was not for further discussion and Ginny took the opportunity to steer the conversation to a safer topic. She told Sarah she had seen Hal. Ginny delighted in the feeling that she knew more about Tom's dad than Sarah.

'He brought in his dog Laddie to see me,' said Ginny.

Sarah was keen to know all and Ginny savoured the

124

moment. She explained the problem with Laddie, casually adding that Hal was taking her for a motorbike ride on the weekend.

'That's great,' said Sarah. A raft of possibilities occurred to her. Ginny and Hal. Now that was unexpected. But it had definite potential.

'Tom and I were planning to meet Anne and John for a barbecue at Palm Beach on Saturday. If you are heading in that direction you should pop in.'

'Yes, you must,' said Anne, feeling lukewarm about Ginny but enthusiastic to meet this Hal that they were all talking about. Palm Beach was a beautiful, rugged ocean beach about an hour's drive from the city. It had once been a quiet beachside village but being so close to the city, the old weatherboard homes had been demolished to make way for substantial holiday homes where the rich liked to spend their time. Large modern houses had taken over all the clifftop blocks with their extensive ocean views. Anne and John were renovating an Edwardian villa at the not so fashionable end of the suburb.

Ginny liked the idea. Another opportunity to share time with Tom and, she thought with a delicious thrill, as Hal's date.

'I'll see what Hal thinks,' she promised.

Anne watched Ginny. There was something about her that was unsettling, or at least more so than usual, she thought. Anne had long suspected that Ginny had a crush on Tom. She noticed the way Ginny's face lit up when she spoke to him. And whenever he wasn't around it seemed to Anne that Ginny always seemed to bring the conversation back to Tom. The idea of Ginny seeing Tom's new-found dad sounded a warning bell to Anne. There was something unhealthy about it. Anne couldn't put her finger on why that should trouble her. It just did. She didn't like it.

Anne thought about mentioning it to Sarah but dismissed the idea. She had tried to talk to Sarah about Ginny before, but Sarah just didn't get it. She could see no bad in her childhood friend. 'Oh that's just Ginny,' she would say.

Anne watched Sarah. There was something about her manner that seemed brittle, Anne didn't like that either. She didn't appear to be a happy bride, looking forward to her wedding day. She had bags under her eyes and she seemed uptight, testy. Not like the bubbly, easygoing girl Anne knew so well. There was an edge to her tonight. A sharpness. It was probably just that Tom was away, thought Anne. Sarah always hated it when he was away.

But still . . . Anne felt a tremor of unease.

The women returned to admiring Sarah's ring and she started to explain its history. Ginny leapt up, offering to make coffee. Anne helped her clear the plates but Ginny insisted she sit back down. She was a new mum and Ginny declared she deserved to be waited on for a change. Anne was touched at her concern. She had never warmed to Ginny but maybe she was too hard on her, she thought. Ginny was just eccentric but really, her heart was in the right place. Anne resolved to be nicer to her.

Once Ginny was alone in the kitchen she wasted no time. Quickly and efficiently she emptied the contents of her jar into the sugar canister, carefully stirring it around and screwing the lid back on. She reappeared in the living room with a tray, and watched with satisfaction as Sarah heaped three teaspoons of sugar into her coffee. Anne asked for the sugar bowl and Ginny felt a moment of concern.

'Is that wise when you are breast feeding?' she asked.

'Oh Ginny, you don't know much about having a baby, do you?' replied Anne with a smile.

To Ginny she sounded superior and smug. Ginny shrugged and passed her the sugar bowl.

'Help yourself,' she said, smiling back at her.

On the way home from Canberra Tom took a detour to the coastal resort town of Kiama. Thel lived in a rambling old weatherboard a few kilometres out of town. The house was in the hills and surrounded by an airy, open verandah with views of the rugged ocean coastline. Thel spent hours on the verandah absorbed in the play of light and mood, which she would try to capture on canvas. She was sitting on the verandah on her favourite old torn leather couch, two glasses and an open bottle of wine on the floor beside her, when Tom parked the car. Her thick black hair was piled on top of her head with a pen and a pencil poked through it to keep it in place.

'You look tired, honey,' she said as she hugged Tom. 'And skinny. Doesn't my favourite daughter-in-law-to-be ever feed you?'

'Not like you, Mum,' replied Tom.

It was a traditional, affectionate Thel-and-Tom greeting. Thel was making fun of herself, her mothering. It was a parody of how she thought mothers were meant to behave. Tom always played along, calling her 'Mum' just for the purposes of the exercise. Tom sat on the floor, putting a cushion against one of the solid verandah posts and accepted a glass of wine.

'Here's to my two favourite people getting hitched,' Thel said, raising her glass in toast.

It was a superb 1998 Vasse Felix Merlot from Western Australia. Quite rare. Thel knew her wines and had been keeping this one for a special occasion.

Tom swirled the heavy red liquid around his glass, sniffed it appreciatively then took a small sip. He savoured the flavours, rich and deep.

'Magnificent,' he said.

Thel nodded with pleasure. 'Isn't she a beauty?'

Thel and Tom sat comfortably together, enjoying the superb wine as the sun set behind them and they looked out across the Pacific Ocean.

'We have had so many wonderful times here, haven't we? You, me and Sarah. I think you know how I feel about your girl,' said Thel.

Tom nodded. Sitting on the verandah as the day seeped

away reminded him of many happy times. Thel often had an assortment of people staying in her rambling home – they came and went as they pleased. But always the day ended there on the verandah, with whoever was around, drinking wine and watching the ocean.

'She's got a good heart. And a good head. And she's a bit mad. All my favourite things.'

Tom laughed. Thel and Sarah had clicked from the start. He hadn't realised quite how well they had clicked until he came home from surfing one afternoon, only a few days after introducing his mother and his girlfriend, to find them rolling about on the kitchen floor, clutching their sides in hysterics.

Tom had been flabbergasted at the sight of them, tears streaming down their faces as they tried to explain what they found so incredibly amusing. They had been incapable of speaking, bursting into new fits of laughter at each new attempt. Tom had laughed along with them, not knowing why, except that their childish joy had been so contagious. Finally he had understood that whatever had so tickled Sarah and Thel was under the tea towel on the bench.

Tom pulled it back and was stupefied at the sight of a freshly baked penis made from what appeared to be puff pastry. The look of bewilderment on his face sent the women into more peals of laughter. Tom had finally given up, taking himself off to shower while the women in his life continued to roll about on the floor.

Tom marvelled at how the two women complemented each other. Sarah loved to cook while he didn't think Thel had ever opened an oven door. But Thel had an earthy sense of humour and loved to create. Unleash the two of them in the kitchen and this was the result.

He reminded his mother of that afternoon.

Thel laughed.

'We had so much fun baking that. I can't remember what started us off. I think Sarah had asked if I minded if she cooked something for dinner. I think she had figured out that it was the only way she was likely to get fed. She went to the local milkbar, which as you know doesn't have the biggest range of food, and came home with a roll of puff pastry so, voila. We baked puff pastry.'

Tom and Thel reminisced some more as a gentle breeze wafted across the Pacific Ocean, rustling the leaves around them.

Tom thought it was time to broach the topic that had brought him home to his mother. He was nervous but knew the best way was just to come out with it.

'A month ago, out of the blue, I had a call from Hal,' he said.

At mention of the name Thel stiffened. It was almost imperceptible, a slight setting of her shoulders, a tightness about her mouth, which would have gone unnoticed except that Tom was so attuned, looking for any sign of a reaction.

'He had seen my name in the paper and wondered if it was me, so he rang.'

Thel stared out at the reflection of the half moon on the sea. She didn't seem inclined to speak so Tom continued.

'We caught up for a drink and I've seen him a few times now.'

Tom wondered what was going through his mother's head.

'How do you feel about that, Thel?'

Thel took a long time to answer. 'How is he?' she asked at last.

'He seems great,' replied Tom. 'He owns a motorbike store in North Sydney.'

Thel nodded. 'Has he remarried?' she asked.

'No.'

'I see.'

Thel disappeared inside to get another bottle of wine. She was gone quite a while and Tom wondered if he should go after her. He knew he was reopening a very personal wound. He wished he didn't have to have this conversation but at the same time he wanted to. All his life he had carried with him a lot of questions that he had never felt able to ask. Hal had answered some of them, just by meeting him, but that had also left him with more questions.

Thel reappeared with more wine and a plate of stuffed olives, dips and bread.

'I'm sorry if I have upset you,' said Tom.

'Oh, you don't have to worry about that. It's just a bit of a shock. I wasn't sure if he was still alive. I haven't spoken to him in many years. I wondered what happened to him. So he is living in Sydney. How does he look? Is he well?'

'He looks good,' said Tom. 'Actually we look kind of alike.'

Thel smiled at her son.

'Yes, you do. You get your height from him. Your eyes. Even your smile. It's always reminded me of your father.'

Tom thought how wistful she sounded. It had never occurred to him that by looking at him, she would be reminded of Hal.

'That must have been tough for you at times,' he ventured.

'Oh, not really. Your father was a very handsome man. I was glad you took after him. You got my sense of humour, though. And my creativity. And my legs. All in all, a good combination.'

Tom couldn't see Thel's face but he recognised her flippant and breezy tone, which most likely meant she was avoiding the issue. It was her way. If something disagreeable presented itself, she would try to find something about it she could like and would then concentrate on that. She had dealt with Tom's school principal whenever he was in trouble in the same way. When Tom had been caught spray-painting graffiti on the school shelter sheds, Thel had applauded his use of colour.

'I would like to invite him to the wedding,' said Tom.

'Of course. You must,' replied Thel. 'Oh, I see. You are worried your parents will misbehave. Start throwing plates and airing the family linen. We won't embarrass you with nasty scenes. Is that what is worrying you?'

Tom tried to keep her on track. 'No, of course not. I just don't want you to be hurt.'

'Have I told you how proud of you I am, how much I actually like you? Forget that you're my son. I just really like you.'

'Yes, Thel, you have told me that, repeatedly,' said Tom.

'I have?' said Thel vaguely. 'Well good. It's important you should know.'

'I don't want it to be uncomfortable for you at the wedding,' continued Tom. 'I guess I'm asking for you to help me here. I don't know why you and Hal split up. I don't know if you hate each other, though he certainly doesn't seem to hate you. I only know that he is a topic you and I have never discussed. But I don't even know why that is. Why have we never talked about it?'

Thel looked steadily at her son, the smile fading from her face. 'I don't know how to explain it to you. I guess that's why I've never tried. I don't think of it as being any of your business. What happened between your father and me is between us. It's personal. I don't think I owe you any explanation.' Her tone was no longer flippant. She was calm and measured. Tom watched the wall go up. Whatever he wanted to know, Thel wasn't going to be the one to tell him. She simply would not discuss it.

'What about Sarah's parents? Now that you know this side of the family will behave, what's happening with the other side?'

'Her father is too sick to travel,' replied Tom.

'And her mother?'

Tom shrugged.

'I see,' said Thel. 'How those two selfish people ever produced someone like Sarah is beyond me. They're so lucky and they don't even know it. That makes me so sad.'

'They sent us a cheque,' said Tom.

'I'll bet they did. Selfish bloody people.'

Driving back to Sydney later that night, Tom wondered what *was* his business. What rights did he have to know about his parents' relationship? He couldn't be sure. He would like to discuss it with Sarah. He knew it was a blind spot for him and that he may not see it clearly. He felt he needed clarification.

To Tom it seemed out of character. His relationship with Thel was defined by their absolute honesty. Nothing was taboo. Thel had insisted on it. When the local parish priest had told Tom that touching himself was a sin, Thel had been annoyed and told him that was absolute rubbish and if it felt good, he should do it. She had explained to him about the sticky stuff that he found on his pyjamas some mornings. She hadn't been embarrassed so neither had he.

When he brought Sarah home there was no question that they would share his bedroom. Thel often brought them tea and toast in bed, curling up herself at the foot of the bed for a chat. When he had been younger and Thel had carted him around various artists' colonies, she had happily explained all about the weird and wonderful relationships that were going on around them. Tom had never asked a question of Thel and been denied. Until now.

Tom was surprised at his reaction to Thel's evasiveness. He felt unsettled and he couldn't understand why. All the way home he mulled it over, looking at it from different angles. He looked forward to talking it over with Sarah. He wanted her cool reasoning to help him make sense of it. As he drove, Tom examined his memories of the time when his father had left. He thought of it as his childhood shuddering to a halt. He remembered Thel sitting in the kitchen chair staring blankly at the wall, impenetrable. That was what had scared Tom the most. His wild, gregarious mother sat for hours, not speaking, not crying, not seeing Tom, just staring.

At eight he had had little concept of the future, so the idea of Hal leaving and not returning wasn't the sudden shock for him that it had been for Thel. Tom had no way of knowing what it would mean. Instead, its impact had been felt as a series of hurts and disappointments that Hal wasn't there when Tom expected him to be. He didn't come to footy training that morning, he wasn't in the kitchen boiling Tom's egg the next morning, he wasn't at home after school to admire Tom's science project.

For months Tom had expected Hal to reappear at any second. The realisation that Hal would never again be there to do any-thing with him came to Tom slowly, achingly. He wondered why Hal didn't want to be with him any more. He wondered what he had done wrong. His mother withdrew for a time too. Tom worked very hard at being good after that.

He couldn't retrieve any sad memories before that time. As far as he knew everyone in his little world was happy. But obviously more had been going on with his parents. He saw that now with the logic of an adult. But deep inside he still carried the blame and guilt of that eight-year-old boy.

Tom tried to explain how he felt to Sarah the following night as they sat on the couch, Thel's artwork for their invitations spread on the table in front of them.

'Is it my business? Do I have the right to know why he left?'

Sarah was thoughtful. 'I think that's a conversation you should be having with Hal. He's the one who left.'

Tom considered. 'I know that. And I will, I hope. But what I don't understand is why Thel won't talk about it with me.'

Sarah understood exactly what was upsetting Tom. Thel had always made it clear that her marriage was an area of her life and past that was closed to everyone, including Tom. Sarah could only guess at the depth of pain that would make Thel shut Tom out. She seemed to have closed her mind to her son's own suffering. He needed to know he wasn't to blame. But Thel was unable to help him.

'I don't know,' said Sarah. 'But you are incredibly lucky to have Thel as your mum. We both are.'

Tom smiled. 'I love that you love Thel.'

'Well then, how would you feel if I asked her to give me away at our wedding?'

Tom's face broke into a broad grin. 'That is a great idea.'

Sarah reached for the phone and dialled Thel's number.

Thel was just settling down with a glass of wine in her old leather couch on the porch. Since Tom's visit she had been feeling listless and melancholy. Their conversation had brought up so many painful memories. All day she had skirted around her easel, unable to settle down to work. She listened to Sarah's request.

'I would be honoured, my dear,' she told Sarah.

After the call her house didn't seem so large and empty.

CHAPTER 11

Today we're playing buttons. Press my buttons. Everyone can have a go. Pick a button. You know where they are. Everyone does. It must be written up on a blackboard outside the day room. Or maybe it's tattooed on my forehead. A list of my buttons. Choose well. Then press. Good and hard. The more I react the more you win. If you draw a little blood, extra bonus points for you. It's a team sport, led by Dr Hubert. He's the master. He's so good at it.

Just as dawn broke a summer storm hit, crashing across the city and heading for the sea. Sarah watched its arrival. She had trouble sleeping these days and often found herself standing at the balcony doors, looking aimlessly across the harbour, waiting impatiently for the day to begin. She was restless and uptight, with energy to burn. She felt the temperature drop and walked back to the bedroom.

'It's an awful morning outside,' she said loudly to the mound in the bed that was Tom. 'The sort of morning we should spend in bed. I hope it improves for our picnic this afternoon. You want some breakfast?'

Tom grunted sleepily.

Sarah retrieved the Saturday newspapers from the front door and headed for the kitchen.

Ginny opened her curtains and looked out across the grey, rain-splattered morning.

'You're right, Sarah, it's a bitch of a morning. Or a Sarah of a morning. What do you think of that, Kitty? A Sarah of a day? Hmmm?

'You stay right there, Kitty my dear. I'll be back. It looks like we are all spending the morning in bed. Tee hee.'

Ginny fetched her own morning newspapers from her front door and took them back to bed with a cup of tea and a saucer of cream for Kitty.

She walked back into her bedroom just as Sarah was reading the front-page headlines to Tom. 'Tough policies on homeless. Forty-six dead in Indian train crash. Aussie cricket heroes triumph again.'

She tossed the papers across to Tom and headed back to the kitchen. She loaded up the tray with coffee and toast. When she reappeared Tom still hadn't stirred but Sarah could tell he was awake. It wasn't that he had opened his eyes, or spoken or even wriggled a little finger. As far as Sarah could tell he was in exactly the same position as when she got up. But years of sleeping with the man meant she knew. He was awake.

She picked up the papers and started to read.

'Well, lookie here,' said Sarah. 'A special investigation, by Tom Wilson, in Canberra. You've got the page-three lead, hotshot.'

That got his attention. Tom sat up as Sarah started to read.

Maverick gold-medal winning Olympian Ms Melissa Giles claimed yesterday that the government inquiry into steroid abuse by Olympic athletes will be nothing more than a whitewash when it is tabled in parliament next week.

135

In an exclusive and wide-ranging interview Ms Giles, one-time captain of the Australian basketball team, attacked the Federal Government, three major Australian sporting associations and the International Olympic Committee for not delivering on their promises after the 2000 Sydney games.

Tom listened intently, nodding as Sarah read the twenty-paragraph story.

'Keep going,' he said when she stopped.

'That's all,' she said, putting the newspaper aside.

Tom snatched the newspaper.

'What about the body builder? Where's all the stuff about how he killed his wife?' Tom scanned the article. 'It's not there. They've cut it out. Why would they do that?'

Tom was angry. When he had left work late the day before he had seen the page laid out. And the interview with the body builder had definitely been in then.

As Tom spoke, Sarah peeled off her dressing gown. She had stopped listening, paying attention only to the tingling in her groin. The coffee had hit her bloodstream, giving her a charge, and she felt an overpowering surge of lust.

'I can't believe they cut that out . . .' Tom was saying.

Sarah sidled under the covers, her hands roaming over Tom's bare chest and down his stomach. She nuzzled into his neck, gently nibbling his earlobe.

Tom pushed her away.

'It took me months to get that man to talk to me. He talked about how easy it was to get drugs, how the system almost condoned . . .'

Sarah wasn't listening. She pushed aside the sheets and climbed defiantly onto Tom's lap.

'Sarah, don't,' said Tom.

'Tom,' breathed Sarah. 'I want you.'

Tom saw the naked lust in her eyes and recoiled. He felt bruised and diminished enough by what had been done to his story. Sarah coming at him with all the finesse of a steam train was a further assault on his ego. He felt threatened, under attack. He couldn't just perform on demand, he did not want to. He felt himself shrink further inside.

'No, Sarah,' he said, pushing her off him. 'I'm not in the mood.'

Sarah felt the pent-up energy explode inside her. 'Why not?' she barked angrily, standing naked in front of him, every muscle clenched.

He saw for the first time the new definition of her body. She was tight and muscular. She towered over him as he lay propped against the pillows in bed. Her hands were planted aggressively either side of her taut stomach, her biceps bulging. She looked like a fiery Amazon. Tom looked at her in amazement. She looked magnificent. He could see that. And he had never felt less like making love to her. He felt completely intimidated by her blazing sexuality.

'Oh, it's all right when you're in the mood,' spat Sarah. 'So why isn't it all right when I'm in the mood?'

Tom looked at her in confusion. He didn't understand what was going on here.

There was no love, no tenderness. His beautiful Sarah, loving, warm, kind Sarah, was staring at him with the icy glare of a cold, hard, demanding predator. He rose slowly from the bed and faced her. His towering frame dwarfed her, but it was her explosive energy that filled the room.

'I'm not in the mood, Sarah,' he said quietly. 'Just let it go.'

Wearily, he turned his back and went off to the shower.

Sarah slammed the bedroom door.

'Oh yeah, thank you, Tom,' she muttered, her voice a low deep growl. 'It's always fine when you want to but, oh no, not when I might be in the mood . . . Bastard!' she called out after him.

She was enraged, overwhelmed by her conflicting feelings. She felt strong and virile, ready to burst. She wanted to roar, to bellow, make enough noise to drown out the energy erupting inside her.

★

Sarah ran and ran. Through the park, under the canopy of fig trees. The rain poured down in sheets, heavy and relentless. She ran hard, her heart beating painfully against her chest. Her throat ached with the effort of breathing. She was almost oblivious of the strains on her body. Her mind was screaming. Rushcutters Bay park was deserted. Under the trees the light was sparse and gloomy, droplets of rain finding their way through the dense canopy and landing on her bare head. She focussed on the ground in front of her, leaping over gnarled roots that poked through the concrete. She pushed herself harder. She wanted to hurt. She wanted to feel it. Anything to drown out the screeching inside her head. To blot out that ugly scene, the way Tom had looked at her. The disgust in his eyes. She felt out of control, fighting the hysteria that was rising in her, threatening to overwhelm her.

For Sarah, feeling out of control was the worst thing. It struck at her very core. She thought of Tom. Right now she hated him. It wasn't logical, but she wasn't thinking clearly. She was feeling and reacting. She was a maelstrom of swirling emotions. The pain in her head matched the pain in her heart. She struggled to bring herself back to some sort of equilibrium, trying instinctively to burn off the physical effects of the steroids that, without her knowledge, were coursing through her system, changing the biochemical make-up of her body and playing havoc with her emotions. What was happening to her?

She reached the edge of the park and ran across the road, up the hill. Her calves ached as she powered up the steep incline. Without the trees to block the rain, it fell unchecked on her sweat-soaked back and shoulders. She felt an urgency, an all-encompassing need to keep running, to run from all the intense emotions that were threatening to overpower her.

Her mind was swamped with abstract thoughts and images that she couldn't process. Her whole being was out of kilter. Her body felt like it belonged to someone else. She hardly recognised herself in the mirror any more. Her body felt powerful and strong and she liked that but she felt disconnected from it. Her breasts seemed hard and flat, not like her own at all. She was breaking out on her back, large ugly blind pimples. And she had noticed hair around her nipples – tough, stringy black hair sprouting across her chest. She thought she understood the symptoms. A massive hormonal imbalance brought on by her bulimia. She had been down this path before. When she was in the worst grip of bulimia she had watched her body change. She had developed fine down across her jawline as her body went haywire. Her periods had stopped. She had broken out in pimples.

The bulimia had developed soon after Sarah started boarding school. Her mother's decision to send her away had left the young girl reeling. Everything that had been safe and familiar from her life in the Singapore household was gone in an instant. She had missed the warmth and affection of Mattie, the Malaysian cook, who used to let her sit on the bench and dice the vegetables while around her exotic smells filled the air. And Mr Shiwar, the friendly house driver with the lopsided grin, who picked her up each day from school with a Chinese sweetbread.

But most of all she missed her beloved Amah, the Chinese nanny, who woke her in the mornings and soothed her to sleep at night with interesting stories about people with funny names. She missed Amah's pudgy arms and musty smell.

Her parents had been only distant figures in her life but it didn't matter to Sarah. She was the centre of the little household, completely indulged and adored. And she had been happy. She only realised how happy when she was confronted with her new life, amidst a sea of grey uniforms and new rules that she didn't understand.

She had felt powerless in her new environment. It seemed as if she had suddenly lost control of her world. She lost all sense of who she, Sarah Cowley, was. In a perverse attempt at self-protection, she developed an iron grip on the one thing she could control – her body. Sarah turned inward, focussing all her energy on what went on inside. It gave her back a sense of control that she so desperately needed. The world was too big and unpredictable for her to face. And her emotions were too wild to tame, the depths of her loneliness and alienation too scary. At first it worked well. Eating whatever she wanted, then purging herself, made her feel powerful. Watching her weight drop gave her a deep feeling of satisfaction.

But, ironically, as the bulimia took hold she became powerless against it. It became an addiction. And then she started to feel a deep sense of shame.

Throughout her years at the boarding school Sarah lived on an emotional seesaw, sometimes managing to keep her bulimia under control as she settled into the school and made friends, at other times unable to fight the overwhelming urge to purge.

Starting at university brought up those feelings of isolation. Once again she was just a number in a sea of faces. She started to exercise obsessively, joining many of the outdoor activities. She watched with interest as her body changed. For the first time in her life she developed muscles. Her hip bones started to protrude as her stomach became concave. It was all a novelty to Sarah and she viewed it with abstract interest. She liked the power and strength of her newly toned body. To the outside world she was the life and soul of the party, always ready to try anything. She did her mother proud, ever gay and laughing. But inside she struggled with deep feelings of inadequacy.

Living at university residences it was easy to hide her bulimia. But when she moved in with Thel and Tom it had become harder and she had learned to be secretive. Tom suspected something but never knew exactly what went on during that period. Thel understood a lot more. She recognised the depth of the young girl's pain and ached for her. She accepted Sarah into her home and her family without questions. It was just the space Sarah needed.

Living with Thel and Tom gave Sarah back a sense of belonging. She felt surrounded by love and it went a long way to healing her pain. Tentatively she turned her focus outward and discovered the world wasn't such a scary place after all. She took herself off to see a doctor. Then she saw a therapist.

When finally she understood what was going on inside her own head and why she was doing what she was doing, she sat down and explained it to Tom. She stopped making herself throw up. She lost her obsessive drive to be fit. The knots inside her began to unravel as the tension slowly ebbed from every cell, every nerve. She saw Tom there, patiently loving her and she felt as near to whole as she had felt in her life.

As Sarah ran she recognised all those old feelings of pain and anxiety rising up again inside her. She was back in that dark place, where she was bewildered and angry, and very small. The world seemed malicious and unstable, and nothing could be counted on. And she felt that rage against the world burn inside her again.

But to rage against the whole world, against life itself, was too big, too unworkable. So she focussed her rage on the one person she was closest to in the world. Tom. She directed all her pent-up fury and aggression against him. Where was he when she needed him? Why did he not want her? Why did he shrink from her? Sarah didn't want to go home. She didn't want to see Tom. The intensity of their emotional conflicts exhausted her. She reached the fork at the top of the hill. She had nearly completed the full five-kilometre circuit. The right fork was the final stretch that would take her directly home. With a heavy heart she turned down the road. She had nowhere else to go.

That afternoon Sarah and Tom drove to the northern beaches in silence. Sarah pointedly turned up the radio as soon as they headed off, making conversation virtually impossible. Tom was still mulling over the changes that had been made to his story and was in no mood for another argument. The anger of the morning sat heavily between them.

Tom concentrated on driving, looking steadfastly through the windscreen at the road. There was a little crack in the corner where a stone had hit. He hoped it didn't mean having to get a new windscreen. It reminded him of the registration. He looked across at Sarah's side of the car. It was the same old sticker.

'Did you send the registration cheque?' Tom asked.

Sarah blanched. She hadn't. She had been so distracted this week, what with one thing and another.

'Yes, I sent the cheque,' she replied, feeling guilty, defensive and annoyed, all at the same time.

They pulled into the carpark at Palm Beach and unloaded the car without speaking. As they walked across the grass to the barbecue area Anne rushed over to greet them, her baby in a sling on her stomach. Tom and Sarah smiled the moment she joined them, looking for all the world like a united and happy couple. They cooed at the baby, knowing it was what was expected and Anne would be hurt if they didn't. Neither of them could have felt less like a social afternoon.

'Isn't it a glorious day,' said Sarah, trying to sound enthusiastic. 'And look at little Thomas – hasn't he grown.'

Tom was relieved to see John by the barbecue and bolted towards him. He looked forward to an easy comfortable chat about politics, football, work, anything not related to emotional issues. As head of current affairs for a TV network, John was essentially a business rival. He and Tom sometimes found themselves competing for the same stories. But there was a mutual respect and, away from work, they could relax and swap gossip about the many people they knew in common. They walked a fine line, always talking in generalities and never discussing the details of the stories they were working on. It was an unspoken and mutually understood rule of their working world.

'Oh, just dump me at the first opportunity,' thought Sarah. She was a jumble of nerves. The car ride had been oppressive and she was relieved to be away from Tom but the idea that he might feel the same way irritated her intensely. She tried to stifle her feelings of anger. She was here now and she may as well make the most of it.

It had turned into a perfect summer day. The sun sparkled on the ocean. Surfers dotted the wave break. On the shore children splashed about happily. A group of boys played cricket in the sand. The beach was wide enough to accommodate them all in friendly chaotic camaraderie. Sarah tried to relax, letting the sun warm her through to the bone. Tom stayed with John at the barbecue, leaving Sarah and Anne to play with Thomas. They sat under a tree on a picnic rug, cooing over his chubby little legs and arms.

'Sarah, are you okay?' asked Anne.

Sarah looked surprised.

'You don't seem yourself lately,' Anne ventured.

Sarah looked at her friend. She liked Anne. Trusted her. They had shared many happy and not-so-happy times growing up together in McKenzie's newsroom. She missed her in the office.

'Is everything all right with Tom?' Anne asked, her face furrowed with concern.

Sarah sighed. Everything wasn't all right with Tom, but she wasn't sure where to start. She was at a loss to articulate the whirlpool of emotions swirling about inside her.

'Anne, before you married John, did you have doubts?'

Anne narrowed her eyes. 'What sort of doubts?'

Sarah took a deep breath. 'I love Tom, I'm sure of that. Or I was sure. But lately, I don't know . . .' she trailed off.

'Go on,' urged Anne.

'It's just that we don't seem to be getting on so well. We seem to be fighting constantly. It's like ever since we decided to get married, we have been at each other's throats.' Sarah sighed as it all came tumbling out. 'I feel under so much pressure. At work. From Tom. I'm so wound up. I just want to cry and scream and yell at everybody. I feel like everything always lands on me. I have to do the dinner. I have to clean up. I have to do the shopping and if I don't get what he wants, it's my fault.

'I have to get the car registered. It's like my time isn't as important as Tom's. Why couldn't he take the morning off work to get it registered? It's his car.

'I just feel so scared. Now we have decided to get married I feel suddenly trapped. Is this what my life will always be like? What if we actually aren't right together? Just because we have been together so long, doesn't mean it's right. Maybe we both need to see other people. We've been together since we were twenty.'

Sarah's eyes filled with tears. As she heard herself articulate the words she heard the way they sounded and it scared her even more. Tom was the rock in her life. What was she saying? Life without Tom? It was a thought she hadn't dared allow herself. But out it came.

Anne looked gently at her friend. 'Oh Sarah, honey, we all feel like that at times. Before John and I got married, I nearly called it off three times.'

Sarah raised an eyebrow. This was news to her. They had always seemed so right for each other. From the moment John had joined their network, Anne had single-mindedly set out to get him. He was the brash, hotshot young newshound who the network had proudly poached from a rival station. Anne had fallen for him in a matter of minutes. Or that was how Sarah thought their relationship had been.

'You did?'

'Oh yes,' laughed Anne. 'But he was so good. He just ignored me basically. Put it down to wedding nerves and that was that. Just bulldozed me into it. And I'm glad he did. It *was* just wedding nerves.' Anne looked at Sarah thoughtfully. 'How did you feel when Tom asked you to marry him?'

Sarah smiled at the memory. 'Happy. Like it was right. Like it was inevitable somehow.'

Anne nodded. 'Well, my girl, just hold onto that thought, that feeling. You can't see clearly now. You're all wound up. But when you *were* thinking clearly, that was how you felt. That was the right decision. Honey, just hold onto that and you will be fine.'

Sarah bounced Thomas on her lap, waving her fingers in front of his eyes. He cooed with delight.

'I suppose so,' she said slowly. 'Do you ever feel that you hate John? Actually *hate* him?'

Anne laughed. 'Yep. I reckon I could kill him at least once

a week. But then other times I love him so much I could just die there on the spot. And the rest of the time we just go about living and he's just another regular fixture in my life that I don't think too much about one way or the other. That's the warp and weave of marriage. It goes up and down and everywhere in between.'

Sarah watched as Tom stood at the barbecue, beer in one hand and tongs in the other. He was laughing at something John was saying. His laughter carried across the grass to where she sat. He looked across at her and waved. He pointed to the carpark and Sarah felt a tremor of annoyance. Did he want something from the car? Couldn't he get it himself? She pretended not to understand him. He put down the tongs and started to walk towards the carpark. She looked across and saw Ginny pulling off a bike helmet as Hal steadied his bike. Sarah felt a rush of guilt. What was wrong with her? Why was she so negative? She really needed to snap out of it.

'Here's Hal and Ginny,' she said to Anne. The two women exchanged a little smile.

'Now *this* could be interesting,' said Sarah, happy to have something else to concentrate on. She pushed her own problems aside, popping them into a little compartment where she could retrieve them later, when she was alone.

The two women watched as Ginny stepped off the bike. It was a warm day and she was wearing a leather jacket and leather gloves. She was laughing up at Hal. She looked exhilarated. Tom greeted them. He shook Hal's hand and kissed Ginny on the cheek. Sarah was too far away to see the slow blush that spread up Ginny's throat and across her cheeks. The three of them walked across the grass towards her.

Ginny looked every inch the biker, carrying her helmet under her arm and walking confidently between Hal and Tom. She beamed with happiness.

'That was so much fun,' said Ginny. She was talking to Sarah and Anne but looking at Hal. He was smiling shyly back at her. Ginny breathlessly recounted their trip. Hal interjected occasionally and Ginny was happy to defer to him. Sarah bounced baby Thomas on her lap and smiled encouragingly at her friend. After a few moments Tom returned to the barbecue, taking Hal with him. Ginny's face fell and Sarah noticed how quickly she lost interest in relating to them the rest of her story of their ride.

'So you really enjoyed the ride with Hal?' Sarah prompted.

Ginny didn't seem to hear her. She was watching the men at the barbecue. John was cooking while Tom and Hal stood to one side chatting, a beer in each hand. They were too far away to hear the conversation. Ginny's whole being was focussed on the men at the barbecue. Anne and Sarah exchanged a look.

'I think I'll just see what we're having for lunch,' said Ginny and wandered off towards the men.

'Hmmm. I think we could be onto something here,' said Sarah.

'I think you may be right,' agreed Anne. 'Have you ever seen Ginny so obviously interested in a man?'

'Not since high school,' said Sarah, naively believing it to be true.

Ginny stood between Hal and Tom, enjoying the male banter and basking in the attention of Hal and Tom. She completely ignored John. When the meat was cooked she helped carry it back to the women under the tree and the six sat around on the picnic rug, while baby Thomas gurgled in his bassinette.

Sarah and Tom sat apart and managed to avoid eye contact. Tom passed Sarah a plate of sausages without looking directly at her. Sarah accepted it without a word. Anne noticed their frostiness and so did Hal. John was oblivious of the undercurrents and Ginny was too busy enjoying herself to notice anything but Hal and Tom. She sat opposite them both, looking happily from one to the other.

Ginny held court. She was animated and amusing, continuing the story of her ride with Hal. She laughed as she told how they had pulled up at a petrol station and the woman behind the counter had refused to serve her.

'I still had my helmet on, you see. I didn't realise you were supposed to take them off in the shop. I only wanted a packet of chewing gum. She must have thought I was going to hold up the service station.' Ginny giggled with delight at the thought.

Sarah couldn't remember a time when she had seen Ginny looking so confident. Sarah wasn't in the mood to be bright and bubbly and was relieved her friend was taking the heat off her. Ginny noticed Sarah was uncharacteristically quiet and assumed she was unhappy at being overshadowed.

'Well suffer, baby,' thought Ginny. 'This is my show.' She decided to turn up the heat a little.

'Sarah was telling us all at dinner the other night about the story you are working on, Tom. About steroid abuse,' Ginny said innocently. 'It sounds very interesting.'

The atmosphere changed instantly. John looked alert. Anne looked uncomfortable. Tom stared at Sarah, who stared guiltily at the picnic rug. Hal felt the tension but didn't understand it. Ginny noted it with satisfaction and continued talking into the silence.

'She told us all about it. That body builder who killed his wife. Bashed her to death with a dumbbell. I remember when that happened. It was so awful. And Sarah said you got an exclusive interview with him?'

Tom was quiet and deliberate when he finally spoke. 'I'm afraid my fiancée has been speaking out of school,' he said. 'She shouldn't be talking about such things. I'm sorry, Ginny, but it's not something I can talk about. Particularly in front of John,' he added with a weak laugh.

John cleared his throat.

'Don't worry about it, Tom. We're mates. I saw your piece this morning and I thought it was good. Should stir things up a bit. We're chasing our own story on steroid abuse. I'll just forget that I heard what you are up to.'

'Thanks, mate,' said Tom lamely.

Anne changed the subject but the mood had soured completely. The tension between Tom and Sarah was dense and all-encompassing. It was uncomfortable to be around. Hal suggested to Ginny they ride back early, to avoid the late-afternoon traffic. Anne started to clear away the plates. Sarah was reluctant to leave, knowing she would have to face Tom in the car. She felt the beginnings of a headache. She hoped she wasn't developing a migraine.

Anne understood and was sympathetic. 'It's not that bad, honey,' she said to Sarah as they rinsed the plates under a tap. 'John won't use it. You know that.'

Sarah was unconvinced. 'I'm sure John wouldn't use it. But that's not the point. Tom is furious that I even spoke about it.'

'Bloody Ginny,' said Anne. 'You would think she would know better.'

'It's not her fault,' said Sarah wearily. 'She's not a journalist. Why should she understand what's classified and what's not?'

Anne looked at Sarah in amazement. 'Sarah, I was there when you were telling us. I distinctly remember you saying that it *was* classified. You are so loyal to that girl and I have never understood why.'

Anne seemed to want some sort of response from Sarah. Sarah didn't know what to say. She was tired, emotionally drained. She wasn't thinking about Ginny. She was thinking about the car ride home. She would be trapped in the little hatchback with Tom. She was still angry with him, believing he had let her down. Now she felt the ground had shifted. All the unresolved tension that lay between them would be lost in his self-righteous anger. And she didn't have a leg to stand on. She sighed as she tried to think of Ginny.

'I guess I feel sorry for her. She had a pretty rough time growing up and . . . I don't know. She means well.'

Anne snorted with exasperation. She wasn't sure that was entirely true.

'Anyway, none of that helps me now,' said Sarah. 'Wish me luck. It's going to be a long ride home.'

The four said their goodbyes awkwardly. John once again

tried to reassure Tom that he would never use anything gained through their friendship. Tom waved away John's reassurances, but his face was like thunder. Anne squeezed Sarah's arm.

'You'll be fine,' she whispered.

Sarah offered to drive. She knew Tom had had a few beers and normally, because she drank little, he would have expected her to drive.

'I'll drive,' replied Tom curtly.

Sarah sat meekly in the passenger seat. In her head she went over what she could say, where to start, but Tom gave her no opening. He repelled her with every fibre of his being. He focussed his attention directly on the road ahead, changing gears violently, his knuckles white as he clenched the gearstick. Sarah's head was throbbing. She felt tendrils of pain spreading down the sides of her neck. She longed to be alone in a hot bath.

As they neared the city she could stand the silence and the tension no longer.

'Tom, can we talk about this?' she blurted out.

Tom kept his eyes on the road. 'What would you like to say, Sarah?' he asked coldly.

Sarah felt the icy fingers of dread along her skin. She hated it when Tom was like this. Cold, distant and insufferably controlled.

'Yell at me, scream, lose your temper,' she pleaded quietly. 'Please don't give me the cold treatment.'

'And what would that achieve, Sarah?' he replied. 'I think we have had enough yelling and screaming in the past few weeks, don't you?'

It was a bullseye. The arrow hit its mark, lodging right under Sarah's skin. The implication was clear. She was the one who had been doing the yelling over the past few weeks. She wanted to apologise for breaking his confidence, telling the girls about his story. But that was it. She didn't feel she had anything else to apologise for. Tom was lumping it all together and she bristled.

'I'm talking about your story, Tom,' she said, trying to keep their discussion clearly defined. She didn't trust herself if they moved onto the other problems they had been having.

'I am very sorry that Ginny blurted it out today in front of John. I'm sure he won't use it. You *know* he won't use it.'

'It doesn't matter if he uses it or not. He *knows*. He can't now *not* know. That's just how it is. Whatever he is working on has to be affected by knowing that the body builder has spoken to us. And because I am not privy to what he is working on, I can't assess what that damage might be.

'You know how hard I have been working to get that body builder to talk to me. I am astounded you take my work so lightly that you just chat to all and sundry about it.'

'Tom, it wasn't like that,' said Sarah feebly.

'Oh really?' said Tom. 'You get your friends over, Anne included, and tell them my work secrets. Don't you have enough to talk about without revealing all about my work? What else have you told them?'

His tone was acidic. Sarah had never seen him this angry. The intensity of his anger frightened her.

'I was just explaining why you were in Canberra the night we had dinner. I didn't mean to tell them so much but they were really interested and I don't know why I told them so much. I know I shouldn't have. I was sorry the moment I spoke,' said Sarah, massaging her temples in a vain attempt to quell her throbbing head. 'I am so very sorry it came up today in front of John. I know it couldn't have come up at a worse time. I don't know why Ginny brought it up . . .'

'Don't blame Ginny,' thundered Tom. 'She's not the one *supposedly* marrying a journalist.'

Sarah recoiled at the venom in Tom's words.

'What are you saying, Tom?' she asked quietly.

Tom stared steadfastly at the road. He didn't reply.

'What are you saying?' Sarah repeated, her voice rising.

Tom glared at her, then turned his eyes back to the road.

'Get a grip on yourself, Sarah. I am not in the mood for another one of your tantrums right now, thank you.'

CHAPTER 12

Sarah came back from her run just as Tom was leaving for work. He kissed her awkwardly on the cheek then he was gone. Sarah felt lonely in the empty apartment. Lonely and resentful. She telephoned the station and spoke to McKenzie's secretary, Fay.

'How's his mood?' asked Sarah.

'Fair to middling,' replied Fay.

That sounded promising for a Monday morning.

'Can you tell him I'll be late in? I lost a filling over the weekend and I have a dental appointment at nine,' lied Sarah.

Fay whistled. 'Oh Sarah, I don't think he will be very happy about that.'

Sarah tugged at a strand of hair. 'I know. But I can't help it. I'm in agony. I can't eat or drink anything hot.'

'Oh, you poor thing. Take it easy. I'll tell him. You may be in luck. He's upstairs with the big chiefs and may not be back down here till lunchtime. There's all sorts of heavy shit going down.'

Sarah felt anxious. That usually meant cutbacks. If so, now wasn't the time to be seen to be slacking off on the job.

'Do you know what's going on?'

As long as McKenzie wasn't within earshot Sarah knew she could count on Fay to be indiscreet.

'I can't be sure but I do know the lawyers and the accountants have been called to the same meeting,' said Fay, confirming Sarah's worst fears.

As Sarah drove to the Roads and Traffic Authority at Bondi Junction, she worried about her job. She hated to think what might happen if McKenzie, under pressure from his own bosses, cast an unfavourable eye in her direction.

Sarah was careful to park out of view of the RTA. The car was officially unregistered and she knew she shouldn't be driving it. She didn't want anyone giving her a hard time. She felt close to tears. They welled inside her and she felt ready to burst. She worried that if she let out a little, she wouldn't be able to stop.

The RTA office was like dozens of government offices around the country – grey carpet, grey walls and bored and unhelpful staff milling about behind the counter. Sarah took her number, 42, and sat down. The digital clock showed 27. It was going to be a long wait. She looked at the faces around her. They all looked as bored and hostile as she felt. Everything about the office seemed designed to aggravate. The waiting chairs were uncomfortable, hard plastic, joined in rows of four that made it virtually impossible to separate yourself from your neighbour. The ticket system was dehumanising. The fluorescent lights were harsh and offensive. The carpet smelled like dirty hair. The RTA staff peered out from behind glass screens so you had to yell your business for all to hear. The staff were so used to abuse from the customers they got in first, making clear their indifference. They were inflexible in the face of the bureaucratic lunacy they were paid to administer and forced each day to defend.

Every moment spent waiting heaped more stress on Sarah's already jagged nerves. She fidgeted and tugged at her hair as the morning ground slowly on. She shouldn't be here. She glared at the people behind the counter. *'Hurry up. You're going to make me lose my job,'* she screamed inside. She directed her anger at Tom, railing against him. He should be here, taking some responsibility for the domestic minutiae of their lives.

By the time her number was called Sarah had worked herself into a state. She was near hysterical when the woman behind the counter spoke.

'Yeees,' said the woman, shuffling papers and not deigning to look up.

'I'm here to pay my registration,' said Sarah, pushing the papers under the glass partition.

The woman was in her twenties. Her skin was sallow and she had large bulbous eyes with blobs of congealed mascara on the lashes. She took the papers from Sarah without looking up. Sarah was getting the message. *I'm really too good for this job. You bore me.* It reminded Sarah of the girl in the trendy Paddington dress shop who hadn't seemed to understand the word orange. Sarah hated them both, the tacky little tart with the yellow nail polish and the snooty clerk here with her nose stuck in the air. Sarah hated the inefficient RTA system that had wasted her morning, sucking away time that she should have spent elsewhere. She hated Tom for not being there with her and for a dozen other things that lay in the gulf that was widening dangerously between them.

'I'll have to key these numbers into the other computer,' said the clerk.

Sarah missed the reason why. She was too irritated and impatient to listen.

'I've been waiting for hours and I'm in a hurry,' Sarah said.

The young woman ignored her. As if she had all the time in the world, she swivelled out of her chair and rose, Sarah's papers in her hand. She took them across to a desk where a good-looking young man was staring at a computer screen. The office heart-throb. Sarah thought he looked sleazy. The clerk sidled up to him and spoke. Sarah had a perfect view of her pouting and flirting, giggling suggestively, stroking the young man's shirtcuff, in fact, doing everything but process

Sarah's registration. The clerk didn't seem to care that everybody could see her. The young man leaned back in his chair, clearly enjoying the attention.

Sarah couldn't just stand there and watch patiently. She was way past having such control over her emotions. She tapped her car keys loudly on the glass partition.

'Excuse me,' she called out, then louder. *'Excuse me!'*

The young woman couldn't *not* have heard. Every other RTA employee looked up or across at Sarah, relieved she wasn't their problem. But the clerk steeled herself and ignored Sarah.

'I'm talking to *you*,' yelled Sarah.

The young man looked at Sarah and whispered something into the clerk's ear. She laughed coquettishly, letting Sarah know with the slightest roll of her shoulders that she wasn't about to jump to attention for her.

'Hey, you with the bug eyes,' yelled Sarah.

This seemed to shock the RTA employee and she froze. It shocked everyone else in the offices, the staff and all the customers waiting impatiently on the plastic chairs. Everyone stopped what they were doing – serving other customers, re-reading for the fifth time the road-safety posters on the walls – to pay attention to the angry young woman. She was an anomaly in her surroundings. Designer suit. Expensive shoes. Belligerent and lacking control. Anticipation rippled through the room.

'You tell 'em,' chortled an elderly man in a smelly overcoat.

'Oh get fucked,' snapped Sarah at him.

Something inside Sarah opened up. A gap. A small fissure.

'And you get your fucking fat arse over here and serve me,' she shouted at the young woman, whose mouth was hanging open in stunned disbelief. She looked around for her supervisor. This woman was a nutter. She may not have looked like their normal nutter, but it was pretty obvious to everyone that that's what she was. They had about one a month, a customer who, as they said at the RTA, 'lost it'. This meant the clerk was off the hook. It was over to Mr Singh now. There were procedures in place for such situations.

The atmosphere in the offices changed. It was no longer the employees on one side of the counter and the impatient customers on the other side. Now they were united. Sarah had stepped over that unseen barrier of social niceties and she was on her own.

Mr Singh heard the yelling, it was impossible for him not to, and came out of his glass-walled office, meeting the clerk at the window. His voice was calm when he spoke to Sarah, his face a blank mask of civility. Underneath he was paddling furiously. He was a dedicated civil servant, who had proudly accepted the supervisor's job just two months ago. He knew everyone was looking to him to take charge, to be the boss. He knew he would win. After all, there were rules and procedures. As long as he stuck to those he held the power. That was how bureaucracy worked. But he took his new role very seriously and it was important to him that he do it in the right way. He wanted to be an example to his staff.

'Is there a problem here?'

'Yes, there's a problem,' spat Sarah. 'I've been waiting three hours in that queue and now that I finally get to the front Miss Bug Eyes here is too interested in your office stud to process my registration. I have wasted enough of my life in here. I want some fucking service.'

If only Sarah had not sworn, it could have turned out very differently. She would have been just another angry customer, annoyed by the delay. But swearing and name calling, according to the RTA procedure book, took it to a whole new level. In terms of the law it constituted an assault, a verbal assault. On page thirteen of Mr Singh's procedure book, under the heading 'Customer Disputation', this was a level-three conflict. And Sarah had become 'the Disputant'.

'If madam would just calm down,' said Mr Singh, motioning for his clerk to move aside.

Sarah was incensed by his tone. She knew she was marginalised and on her own because of her own actions, but she was beyond caring. The fissure widened. Her pent-up aggression of the past weeks, her anger at Tom, her fears for her job, the nagging voice inside her head telling her she wasn't good enough, each had been another layer of pressure. The frustration of the morning was that one layer too many. She had let a little of the pressure out and she was powerless now to halt the outpouring of emotion that followed.

She wanted to leap over that counter and smash that polite, insincere smile of Mr Singh. She wanted to grab Miss Bug Eyes on either side of the head and grind her face into the counter. The glass partition blocked her from doing either. In frustration, and with little idea what she was doing, she opened her throat and gave voice to all the rage and pain she had been keeping inside. Oblivious of the shocked faces around her, unaware of everything but her own release, Sarah howled. The sound was so raw and full of such tangible despair that it physically hurt the people closest to Sarah. They recoiled in fear and repulsion. Sarah's agony reverberated around the walls of the RTA offices and out onto the road. She threw herself against the glass partition, pounding it with her fists, the car keys still clenched in her hand. The screen was bulletproof and not likely to break but the sound of the keys and Sarah's fists beating on the glass, made it seem perilously fragile.

What happened next was a blur and the people in the offices gave conflicting accounts to police later that day. One man, customer number 53, grabbed her flailing arms just as James, a young RTA employee, rounded the end of the counter and threw himself on Sarah. Who got to her first was a matter of conjecture and depended on where the observer was standing at the time, but once she was restrained the two men held her tightly on the ground, on her back with her arms pinned to her sides. The man in the smelly overcoat who Sarah had abused, was delighted with the new turn of events and jumped on her feet, sitting triumphantly and smiling back at everyone. In his version of events, he had got to her first.

Sarah, feeling like an animal with a leg caught in a trap and its instinct to run irrevocably blocked, went finally, completely berserk, thrashing wildly, screaming abuse at the men holding her. Most of what she screamed was nonsensical. But there was no mistaking the anger, the rage and the pain in her voice. It was chilling. Women shielded their children and moved as far from the writhing body on the threadbare grey carpet as they could.

Mr Singh, with a shaking hand, dialled the nearby police station.

Sarah was still roaring, her face contorted and unrecognisable, when they arrived to take her away. The policemen tried to be gentle but she fought them every inch of the way, screaming and punching out at them, using her nails, her knees and her elbows. They simply and efficiently overpowered her, putting her into the back of their van. There was no need to turn on the siren. Sarah screamed and raged against them all the way to the police station. Her rage continued as they locked her in a cell and told her once again to calm down. Finally she was left alone with no-one to rage against. She kicked the iron bed, hurting her foot and then burst into tears, great uncontrollable tears that spilled out of her eyes and poured down her cheeks. She howled and howled, giving vent to all the pain and despair she felt.

When a policewoman came to see her half an hour later, Sarah had calmed down. She was completely spent, exhausted. The policewoman looked at her with sympathy.

'How are you doing?' she asked.

'Okay,' said Sarah weakly. 'Am I in big trouble?'

'Not so much,' said the policewoman. 'We were worried you were going to hurt yourself so we put you in here. But you haven't committed murder so I don't suppose it's too bad.'

Sarah considered this perspective. She appreciated the policewoman's sympathy but here she was sitting in a dank cell that reeked so strongly of urine she didn't dare breathe deeply. She was looking at the policewoman through a row of iron bars. She had, through her own actions, put herself on the other side of a line that nicely brought up, middle-class girls like herself, not to mention smart, capable career women with a public profile, weren't supposed to cross. She thought her definition of bad and that of the policewoman must be vastly different. A vision of her mother in one of her smart Chanel suits wafted in front of her.

'Can I go then?' she asked.

'Let me talk to the senior detective. He's the one in charge. You relax and I'll see what needs to be done to get you out of here.'

Sarah was left alone again. She felt miserable. She wanted Tom. No, she realised, she didn't want Tom. She didn't want him to see her like this. She thought about the newsroom and wondered if McKenzie was back from his meeting and looking for her. It seemed a long way away. Sarah couldn't find it in herself to be concerned. She just wanted to go home.

Tom was deep into writing the latest instalment on his steroid abuse series when Linda, the chief of staff, pulled up a chair at his desk. Linda was in her mid-thirties, with neat round glasses and a clipped English accent. She had been Tom's immediate boss for two years and they got on well. She was tough on the reporters, giving them orders each morning and monitoring their productivity throughout the day. But Tom didn't need to be monitored. He was mostly left alone to turn out award-winning ground-breaking stories.

'I'm nearly done,' said Tom, tapping away at the computer.

'Can I talk to you, Tom?' said Linda.

Something about her tone caught Tom mid-thought and he stopped writing immediately. He looked at her and saw she was serious. She was speaking quietly so that the rest of the workers in the open plan office couldn't hear.

'I've just been talking to Bill, the police reporter,' said Linda. 'There has been a bit of a barney at the RTA offices in Bondi Junction.'

Tom wondered what this had to do with him. He could see

Bill standing over by the picture desk, looking at him. He seemed embarrassed when Tom caught his eye.

'I'm afraid it involves Sarah.'

'Sarah? What are you talking about?'

Tom felt the world recede. Everything seemed to slow down.

'There has been an incident at the RTA offices in Bondi Junction involving Sarah.'

Tom had visions of a gunman shooting up the offices and Sarah being caught in the crossfire.

'Is she hurt? Is she all right?'

Linda realised she was being ambiguous but she was trying to be as gentle as she could. She wondered how she would react if she heard bad news about her partner in this way, at work, because it was considered a news story. She felt for Tom.

'No, Tom. Sarah *was* the incident.' Linda frowned. This wasn't coming out at all the way she intended. She tried again. Her words were blunt but her tone was kind. 'It seems, according to police, that she went berserk in the RTA offices this morning. They took her to Bondi Junction Police Station.' Linda watched Tom's face as he processed what she was saying.

He shook his head slowly. 'She went berserk?'

'Yes,' said Linda. She waited for this to sink in.

Tom nodded distractedly. He was thinking of Sarah, his dear sweet lovely Sarah. The past few weeks had been hell. And now this. What was going on? He felt a heaviness as he recalled their parting kiss that morning. Sarah had been so distant. But so had he. When had it got so bad that he didn't kiss her properly and wish her a happy day? That's how it used to be between them. Then they would speak on the phone half-a-dozen times a day. Just to say silly things, to keep in touch, feel connected. When had that stopped? Was it only a few weeks? It seemed so long ago, the gulf between them so wide. He cringed as he recalled the hostility in the car on the drive home from the picnic. His sharp words. The cold silence of their Sunday night. He had been angry then. He didn't feel angry now. He felt foolish and unbearably sad.

Something was really wrong here. He felt the ground underneath him shifting. His past and future with Sarah, which were the cornerstones of his life, had become unstable. Tom was at a loss to understand how it had happened. He had been so determined to pay attention, to keep his eye on the ball. But somehow he had failed.

'Is she still at – the station?' he asked.

'They've let her go,' replied Linda.

'Oh God,' said Tom. He looked again over to where Bill was standing, shuffling about awkwardly. Now he understood his discomfort.

'Is it on the wires?' he asked.

Linda nodded. 'I'm afraid it is,' she said quietly.

Tom took this in. Australian Associated Press monitored the police stations of the city. Then they fed whatever was happening to the newspapers and newsrooms of the television stations. It was over to them whether they used the information or followed the story.

Tom's newspaper wouldn't see it as a big deal. They were a serious broadsheet more interested in issue-based stories and the political and economic machinations of the country. But the rival daily newspaper in Sydney, a tabloid, might be more interested. Sarah was a recognisable face. She was a TV reporter, in people's lounge rooms every other night. That made her news.

'I've go to go home,' said Tom.

'I know,' said Linda.

When Tom arrived home he found Sarah sitting forlornly in the bath. Her eyes were red and puffy. Tom dropped to his knees and took her in his arms. Sarah had no tears left and hugged him back weakly. It was an awkward embrace and Tom's suit coat was quickly drenched. His mobile phone slipped out of his top pocket and landed in the water.

He retrieved it and set it aside while Sarah sat, looking up at him with sad, silent eyes.

'Oh Sarah. Are you all right?' Tom asked.

Sarah shook her head. 'No,' she squeaked in a little voice.

'What happened?'

Sarah shook her head again. She couldn't speak. She had no energy left in her. Tom was desperately worried. She looked crumpled and very small, sitting in the bath, her mass of corkscrew curls a frizzy sodden mess. Her eyes were wide and blank. Her face splotchy from the steam of the hot bath.

'Can I get you something?' asked Tom. 'Why don't I make some coffee while you get dressed?'

Sarah nodded weakly. She was devoid of emotion, devoid of most signs of life. Her eyes were open and her breath was short and shallow, but that was it. She didn't seem to fill the space she occupied.

After a few moments in the kitchen putting on the kettle, Tom returned to check on her. As far as he could tell she hadn't moved. She was in the same spot, sitting staring vacantly at the shampoo bottles at the end of the bath. Her expression was so dead, so blank, it tore at Tom's heart.

He gently helped her out of the bath. He had to take all her weight to get her over the edge. She felt like a child in his arms. Sarah stood, swaying in the middle of the floor, while Tom patted at her body with a towel. He led her to bed and lifted her up, pulling aside the sheets and placing her tenderly underneath.

Sarah didn't say a word. She seemed unaware of what was going on about her. Tom wondered if he should call a doctor. She lay on her side, staring vacantly out of the window at the harbour. Tom stripped off his clothes and climbed in behind her, holding her to him, trying to warm her with his own body heat. He lightly caressed her shoulders and she fell asleep.

The phone rang and Tom carefully disentangled himself from Sarah.

'Could I speak to Sarah Cowley?' said a young man's voice on the end of the line.

'I'm sorry, she's not available right now,' said Tom.

'It's Peter Hatfield from the *Daily News* here. Is that Mr Cowley?'

'No, Peter, it's Tom, Tom Wilson. How are you?'

Peter had worked for a while as a cadet at Tom's newspaper. Tom remembered him as an enthusiastic, confident young kid with a talent for mimicry. He remembered watching in the lunchroom one day as Peter had done an impression of their editor. It had been startlingly good. Peter's powers of observation were impressive and he was clearly not shy. Tom had liked him. He was a good reporter and Tom had told him, the day he left for a two-year stint in the London bureau, that he expected Peter would go a long way.

'Tom Wilson, how the hell are you?' Peter replied.

'I'm fine, mate. I heard you took a job at the *Daily News*. How's it going?'

'Oh, pretty good. I'm working on the Sydney page.'

Tom had assumed as much. It was the most read column in the city, full of juicy titbits about people in the public eye. He knew exactly why Peter was calling.

'I was trying to get in touch with Sarah Cowley. I didn't expect to get you,' said Peter.

'Sarah is my fiancée,' said Tom.

'Oh,' said Peter in a surprised voice. 'I didn't know that.'

There was no reason why he should, thought Tom. That was his private business. There was silence at the other end of the phone and Tom waited for Peter to come to the point.

'I guess you know why I am calling?' said Peter.

'Nope,' Tom lied pleasantly. 'I have no idea.'

'I have a report from Bondi Junction Police Station that Sarah Cowley was arrested this morning on a number of charges arising from an incident at the offices of the RTA.' Peter's voice was friendly but businesslike. He was doing his job. Tom didn't resent it. He understood.

'Uh-huh,' said Tom, noncommittal.

'I was hoping to speak to Sarah. But if she is not available is there something you would like to say?'

'No,' replied Tom.

'Can you confirm that Sarah was arrested?'

Tom knew that Peter didn't need any confirmation from

162

him to know it had happened. The police report would cover that.

'Mate, I've got nothing to say. I don't know what's gone on. How about I tell Sarah that you called and she can call you back if she wants to?'

Both men knew that was unlikely to happen but Peter gave his number anyway and Tom pretended to take it down. There was nothing more to say. Peter wished Tom well and rung off.

A few minutes later the phone rang again. It was McKenzie's secretary, Fay.

'Tom, I've just heard. Is she all right?' said Fay with concern.

'She's asleep,' said Tom, wishing he hadn't answered the phone.

'McKenzie is ropable. He's been shouting and carrying on. It doesn't look good.'

Tom sighed. 'Can you tell him Sarah is not well and won't be in tomorrow?'

'Of course. Give her my love,' said Fay.

As soon as Tom hung up the phone rang again. Tom switched on the answering machine. It was Anne. John had heard and phoned her. Clearly the news was right around Sydney by now. Anne was passing on their concern as Tom turned down the volume on the machine.

Sarah slept deeply and dreamlessly for a couple of hours. When she wandered out of the bedroom Tom was sitting on the floor, working on his laptop. He stopped and smiled gently at her.

'How are you feeling?' he asked.

'Better,' answered Sarah.

She made fresh coffee and sat on the floor opposite Tom.

'How did you hear?' she asked.

'Through our police reporter,' answered Tom.

Sarah winced. 'Will it be in the paper tomorrow?'

'Not in ours,' said Tom.

'And the *Daily News*?'

'I should think so. Peter Hatfield called.'

Sarah looked at him blankly. It would be in tomorrow's paper. The whole world would know she had lost it, big time. She couldn't worry about that now.

'He's a fair man. It could be worse.'

She nodded distractedly.

'I should ring the office,' she said, making no move to do so.

'Fay called. I said you weren't well and would not be in tomorrow.'

Tom watched her. 'Do you want to tell me what happened?'

Sarah looked at him. She didn't hate him any more. She didn't feel great love for him either. She didn't feel anything. Her heart, her mind, everything inside her felt blank.

She thought about the RTA. She thought about the woman behind the counter, the woman with the bug eyes. She thought how she had felt inside, the pressure in her head, how much she hurt, how everything had suddenly exploded, spilled out of her. She felt the faint echo of all the emotions. But she couldn't find the words or the energy to describe any of it to Tom.

'I'm so sorry,' she whispered. 'I'm a mess. I don't know what's going on inside my head any more. I'm so sorry, Tom.'

Tom didn't understand. It made no sense. He wrapped his arms around Sarah and held her. She didn't hug him back but she didn't pull away either. She just sat, neutrally, in the circle of his arms. They sat that way for a long time. Tom gently rocking her backwards and forwards.

'It's okay,' he soothed. 'It will all be just fine.' He wondered if that were true.

CHAPTER 13

*She has such nice blonde hair. Why does she dye her roots black?
Ha! It's a GT stripe. Makes her go faster. Ha! These loons are mad.
Stark raving bonkers. I made a new friend. Hingeman. He thinks
he's a human hinge. Crawls around the floor on all fours, gliding
and sliding along the ground, through the fog. He's cool. Needs oil,
though. Or the floorboards do. Something's creaking. Might be my
brain. Clunking over. The cogs are getting rusty. No need to use it
in here. You sign it in at reception and they look after it for you.
They give you little pills instead. Fog pills.*

Sarah woke early and lay in bed staring at the ceiling. She had
a lot to think about. She knew today would be tough. She would
have to face the repercussions of yesterday. There was no way
around it. She thought of fleeing, getting a taxi to the airport
and flying to the first place she could get a ticket for. That's how
they did it in the movies. It looked so wonderfully carefree and
exciting. She could go to Bali. If she left now, before Tom woke,
she could be sipping cocktails by the pool this evening.

The idea sidetracked her for a few minutes but then the dread that sat heavily in the pit of her stomach took over. She was back in bed, listening to Tom snore, knowing she had to face the day. That meant facing a wakened Tom, an hysterical McKenzie and whatever was in the *Daily News*. She knew a copy of the paper would already be lying on the cream carpet in the corridor outside their front door. It would be there now, waiting for her, and on doorsteps all across Sydney. Her shame laid bare for all the world to read about, comment on, snigger at.

Sarah steeled herself for the day ahead. It was going to be tough, but she'd had tough before. It was going to hurt. But she knew about pain. She was a survivor. She would just take it one step at a time. One day she would look back and laugh. No, that wasn't convincing. She couldn't imagine this ever being funny.

She took a deep breath, then another. In a strange way she felt calm and strong, better than she had felt for weeks. There was nothing she could do to change what she had done yesterday. It was done and there was no going back. All that mattered now was her maintaining her dignity and integrity in the face of whatever was going to follow as a result. She knew it was going to come at her from all directions. And some of it would hurt, really hurt. It was like the ultimate challenge. A TV game show. Test your mettle. Sarah Cowley, come on down.

'All right then,' she said under her breath and slipped quietly out of bed. Without looking at the headlines, she collected the newspapers from the front doorstep. She took them into the kitchen and sat down, preparing herself for the humiliation she knew was coming.

She flicked through the *Daily News* and on page thirteen, under the heading 'Spotlight Sydney', there she was. The top right corner was mostly taken up with a publicity photo of her, just head and shoulders. The photo was beside the heading 'TV scoop turns wildcat'.

She remembered the photo. She was wearing a lavender

suit, neat gold earrings and her mass of curls had been tamed into a sleek shiny ponytail. She had liked the photo when it was taken. She thought it looked professional, businesslike, how she would like to look but couldn't without an hour or so in the make-up chair. She calmed herself, made herself breathe out very slowly, then started to read.

TV reporter Sarah Cowley was arrested yesterday after a violent altercation at the Bondi Junction offices of NSW's Road Traffic Authority.
Witnesses say Cowley, 28, 'turned into a wildcat' and had to be physically restrained by bystanders after a disagreement with an RTA staffer turned violent.
Mr Jason Romash, RTA employee, said of Miss Cowley, 'She went wild, screaming and yelling abuse.'
'She fought us when we tried to stop her attacking one of our staffers. I've never seen anything like it.'
Romash said it took three men to physically hold down the angry woman until police arrived.
According to witnesses the altercation arose as the result of long queues and overcrowding in the RTA offices, something the State Opposition leader has been critical of for the past six months.
RTA supervisor Mr Hari Singh said, 'Monday mornings are our busiest time and we deeply regret that this customer was made to wait. Unfortunately, because of financial cutbacks to our department, we are unable to hire more staff for those busy times and often people are forced to queue for some time.
'However, on this occasion I believe the woman's reaction was entirely inappropriate and caused much distress to our staff.'
While police have confirmed that an incident took place, they cannot say whether charges will be laid against Miss Cowley, who has worked for Channel 8 for the past four years.
Channel 8 news director Bob McKenzie spoke out in

defence of his reporter yesterday, saying, 'I believe this story has been grossly exaggerated. Sarah is one of our best journalists and an integral part of our award-winning news team. She recently won a Logie award for her coverage of the Liverpool bushfires, which confirmed her position as one of the finest TV reporters in the country.'
Miss Cowley was absent from work yesterday and a spokesman said she was unavailable for comment.

Sarah could have been reading about someone else. It was as if it was a familiar story, one that she had heard before and was re-reading some time later, but that was it. She checked how she felt. She was okay. In a strange way the story had crystallised for her what had happened. Until then Sarah had been trying to see it and understand it through the thick red veil of emotional trauma. She had been unable to recall the details of the morning in the RTA office. She remembered only the frustration building up, then the explosion inside her and finally her shame. The newspaper account explained it to her. The event was parcelled up for her into a neat package. And it gave her an inkling about how other people would view it.

She had gone wild, attacked a government employee. Not normal behaviour. Blind Freddy could see that. She had to be 'physically restrained' by three men. She remembered the two men pinning her arms to her sides, leaning over her and breathing their bad breath into her face. She remembered the man in the smelly overcoat sitting on her feet, cruelly twisting her ankles. Being restrained by three men didn't sound at all like the done thing. It wasn't very ladylike. What would her mother say? Actually it didn't sound Sarah-like at all. How bizarre, to know yourself so little, she thought. I have no doubt this will surprise everybody else but, hey, I'm surprised too. *I* didn't know I was capable of this.

She was disconcerted by McKenzie's support of her but knew better than to allow herself the luxury of thinking he meant it. It was the network's approach to dealing with all

168

negative publicity. Deny, deny, deny. No matter what the facts, just keep on denying them. The fact that McKenzie had spoken to the paper at all meant he must have thought it serious. And he would have hated doing it.

Sarah made herself a coffee and considered her options. The newspaper story was out of the way. She didn't think about it in terms of good or bad, just done. Next was Tom.

Ginny had no idea what had gone on for Sarah the day before. She had been at work all day and in the evening when she listened in to Sarah and Tom they said very little. It seemed they had watched a movie and gone to bed so she did too. Reading the *Daily News* over her tea and toast the next morning, it had come as something of a shock to reach page thirteen and see Sarah's photo.

She read every word of the article in a state of growing excitement. When she finished she re-read the story. The photo, showing Sarah looking so neat and professional, contrasted dramatically with the story of the wildcat who had to be restrained by three men. It made it all the more shocking.

Ginny sat for a long time with the newspaper in her hand and her tea growing cold in front of her. She looked through her binoculars at the apartment opposite. The light was on in what Ginny knew was the kitchen but there was no sign of anybody. Ginny made a fresh pot of tea and settled herself into the winged armchair in her bedroom, binoculars to her eyes and waited.

Tom was wearing his dressing gown and a look of concern when he appeared in the kitchen doorway. He took in at a glance the newspapers, the coffee cup and Sarah's face. She smiled at him.

'How's my Sare Bear?' he asked.

'I'm fine,' she replied. 'And you?'

'Oh, I'm okay.'

Tom looked at her closely. She looked a whole lot better

after the night's sleep. The wild staring look had gone from her eyes and they showed life again.

'Did you sleep okay?'

'I slept like a log,' she replied. 'Best sleep I've had in a long time actually.'

Tom poured himself a coffee. On the surface he appeared calm and relaxed. Underneath he was poised like a cat, ready to jump whichever way Sarah seemed to go.

'And how famous are you this morning?' he said, tentatively poking out a paw, attempting some light-hearted humour.

Sarah smiled weakly back at him. So far so good, he thought.

She pushed the newspaper across towards him. 'Read for yourself.'

Sarah watched Tom's face as he read. She saw the bags under his eyes and the pallor of his skin. He didn't look like he had slept so well. Sarah realised she hadn't noticed Tom, really looked at him, for a while. He looked like a man under pressure, a man carrying the weight of the world. Have I done this to him? she thought.

Tom finished reading and looked up. 'Is that what happened?' he asked.

'I guess so, more or less,' Sarah replied.

Tom couldn't help but be shocked. Three men to restrain her. A disagreement that turned violent. What the hell was going on? The Sarah in the newspaper and the Sarah he knew were worlds apart. Until he read the newspaper he assumed that Sarah had screamed at someone in the RTA office, or burst into tears, or that it all had been some dreadful mistake. Tom knew the frustration of dealing with government departments. He did it almost every day of his working life. Sure, it was frustrating. But Sarah's reaction was something he couldn't imagine.

Sarah didn't often lose her temper. When she was angry she would become icy and withdraw. This was something else again. He thought of the tension that had developed between them over the past few weeks. Sarah had been a tight ball of fury, erupting into anger or passion, and Tom had skirted around her. Sarah had been building up to this, he could see that now. But he could never have imagined this to be the outcome. He couldn't imagine her capable of such a thing. And here she was sitting opposite him, looking vulnerable and small, telling him it was true.

Tom always wanted to fix things, make them right. It was his nature, his way of making sense of the world. When Sarah came home after a tough day with McKenzie, he would inevitably offer the advice that she should resign. This would surprise Sarah and the discussion would usually end up with her defending McKenzie. She didn't see it as a problem to be solved but as something to be discussed and shared. He saw every problem as there to be solved.

He had felt impotent in the face of Sarah's emotional exhaustion last night. Her numbness had scared and unnerved him. He was at a loss how to respond. This was a problem way beyond him, Sarah needed professional help. Tom thought he could discuss that with her later. He concerned himself for now with the practicalities. It made him feel better, more in control.

'Are the police going to charge you?'

'No,' said Sarah. 'I received an official warning. And that's it. But the paperwork will go on my file. So if I ever do anything like it again, then this incident may be considered relevant.'

Tom nodded. Sarah felt he deserved some sort of explanation and if she had one she would have gladly given it. At least she could try to offer him some reassurance.

'But I won't be doing it again,' said Sarah firmly.

Tom didn't know what to say to that. He was still in shock that it happened at all. 'What about McKenzie? What do you want to do about work?'

Sarah shuddered. 'I think I will go in and see him,' said Sarah. 'I think I have to, don't you?'

★

171

Ginny was gleeful but she wanted more. She wanted to see the expressions, know what was going on between and around their words. That would be the icing on the cake. She could hardly wait for tonight. Of course she would ring Sarah today, ever the concerned friend, offering sympathy and seeing if there was anything she could do. Perhaps she should drop in after work. She really would like to see Sarah, see how she looked in her worst hour, share it with her. Oh really, this was just too, *too* exciting.

Sarah drove to work listening to the morning radio. It was a pair of comedians who played some music and the news bulletins, and filled in the rest with talkback and chat, usually about Hollywood or what had been on TV the night before. The radio was just background noise as Sarah prepared herself to face McKenzie. She tried to imagine the worst outcome. Perhaps he would sack her on the spot. How bad would that be? Pretty bad, she had to admit. There was the loss of income, the embarrassment, the difficulties of getting another job given the reasons for her sacking. Okay, that's as bad as it could get. She would still have Tom, her health and . . . and she would just find something else to do.

Sarah considered all the angles, trying to paint them as darkly as she could as a form of protection against whatever McKenzie might do. He would yell, sure. So what? He yelled at her every day. She was no longer intimidated by that. The thought cheered her a little. She thought how she could face anyone after working for McKenzie. In fact, she thought, if she lost her job, she would never have to work for McKenzie again, never have to cop it from him again. That thought cheered her considerably.

She thought of all the things she could say to McKenzie before she walked out. How she would love to give him an earful, some of the abuse he so happily dished out but no-one ever served back. Sarah considered it then reluctantly dropped it. No, she would go with dignity, with grace and poise. Satisfying though it may be in the short term, Sydney was too small. And it wasn't really her style.

A phrase on the radio caught her attention. She thought they had said her name. Sarah realised with a start that the radio announcer was relating a more sensationalised version of yesterday's events than had appeared in the *Daily News*. Sarah felt terribly conspicuous to all the other morning drivers. She looked about her in the traffic wondering who else was listening to this.

The male announcer snickered that it had taken three men to hold her down. 'I like the sound of her, a wildcat,' he said.

His female offsider immediately took the opposing view. That was their formula. He would be extreme, prompting outrage and controversy, and she would go as far as possible the other way. When they tapped the right social nerve, which was often, the phones would run hot.

'I reckon that constitutes assault,' she said. 'I feel sorry for this girl. She goes into an RTA office . . . and we all know what they are like . . . she gets annoyed with the slow staff . . . perfectly normal behaviour so far . . . is vocal about her dissatisfaction . . . I'm still on her side . . . and then three wallies jump on her. I'm sorry. If I were her I'd be demanding the police arrest them. Go girl, I say. On ya sister!'

The male DJ guffawed. 'Oh, come on. If that was a man you would say lock him up, the streets aren't safe with the likes of him around.' Sarah listened with disbelief. It seemed surreal that these people were talking about her. That the woman announcer was loudly and publicly championing her supposed 'cause' was too unbelievable. Sarah wondered if the world had gone mad. The announcers invited callers to ring in with their views. Was Sarah's behaviour acceptable or unacceptable? Have your say.

'Go on,' said Sarah. 'Have your say and make my day.' She felt a little lightheaded.

The first caller was a civil servant, angry that he couldn't get a date. No he hadn't read the morning's newspaper, no he had never watched the news on Channel 8, but dammit he was just as good as anybody else and women shouldn't be so rude.

The second caller thought Sarah was awfully pretty and he hoped that the police would let her go because it was only a first offence. How would you know? thought Sarah, bemused at what was unfolding through her radio speaker. She wondered if Tom were listening. She hoped he was. They could have a good laugh about this later on.

The third caller wanted to talk about an anger management workshop he had been on after his wife took out a restraining order against him. He offered to pass on the details to Sarah if she would care to ring him. 'Oh yeah, right,' thought Sarah.

Sarah parked her car in her usual spot, silencing the fourth caller, mid rave. It was an older woman whose car had been stolen. She complained that the RTA had been no help in tracking it down. It was a relief to shut them up. Sarah was surprised to find she was smiling. The world *had* gone mad.

But Sarah's smile didn't last through the carpark, down the corridors and into the newsroom. With each step she felt the dread growing heavier in her stomach. She said hello to the receptionist, who she didn't know well, and her reaction, the merest flash of something in her eyes, confirmed what Sarah feared. Everybody had read the morning's newspaper. She was the talk of the station.

The newsroom was an open plan office with a jumble of desks and computer screens, banks of filing cabinets and people milling about looking busy. Sarah was self-conscious as she made her way between the desks, aware of every eye in the room on her. Dennis Sand, the court reporter whose desk was jammed up against hers, whistled as she sat down.

'Hey there, how's our office wildcat this morning?' he asked.

Sarah flinched inside but smiled back, hoping she looked more confident than she felt. It was going to get worse than this, she told herself.

'I'm fine,' she replied. 'Just fine.'

She put down her handbag and leafed through some telephone messages, turning her shoulders just enough to discourage him. But Dennis was inherently nosy. It was an occupational hazard and Sarah knew everyone in the newsroom also suffered from it.

'What happened yesterday?' It was typical Dennis. Straight to the point.

'You don't know?' said Sarah with mock surprise. 'Dennis, you're losing your touch. You really should keep up. Try the *Daily News*.'

'Ha, ha,' said Dennis.

Sarah picked up her phone to block any further conversation. She dialled Fay. McKenzie's office was only a few metres away. Sarah couldn't see it because of a partition, and she felt too conspicuous and uncomfortable to walk around there.

'Hi, it's Sarah. Is he in?'

'Oh,' gasped Fay. 'Yes he is. I told him you weren't coming in today.'

'Yeah, well I just couldn't stay away from the place,' said Sarah. 'Can I see him?'

Fay didn't bother to cover the mouthpiece as she called out to her boss that Sarah wanted to see him. 'Yes. He's free,' she said.

Sarah steeled herself. At least he would see her. She knew the meeting would be bad but it was better to face him now than spend hours or all day in agony, waiting for the axe to fall. It gave her back some sense of control.

Fay whispered to her as she went past. 'Good luck.'

McKenzie was sitting in the midst of his usual chaos. King of his own domain. He had a perfect line of vision to Fay so he could bark orders, a huge newspaper-covered desk and three television monitors playing with the volume turned down. His purple-veined nose, a legacy of the red wine he consumed in massive quantities, was twitching. Not a good sign. But his expression was calm. Sarah was braced for an onslaught of abuse, but McKenzie was uncharacteristically quiet. He eyed her speculatively. Sarah stumbled in to fill the silence.

'I want to explain about yesterday,' she started. 'The newspaper story is a gross exaggeration of what actually happened. I had a minor disagreement with a member of staff at the RTA. There is no question that the police will press charges. They are in no position to because I committed no offence. However, I realise that as a face of Channel 8 news, I made a shocking error of judgement. I am sincerely sorry if you feel that it has brought the show into disrepute in any way.'

McKenzie didn't respond. Sarah didn't know how to read him. She had not said this many words to him in the two years he had been her news director. Usually he did all the talking. He continued to sit, silently, watching her. Sarah found it unsettling. She tried another tack.

'I appreciate your support of me in the newspaper this morning. I admit to feeling somewhat embarrassed by the story appearing, but I'm sure it will be fish-and-chip wrapping by this afternoon and I have no intention of allowing it to affect my work.'

Still McKenzie didn't respond. Sarah felt herself beginning to babble. It was what she did when she was nervous and faced with an uncomfortable silence. She could see herself doing it but was unable to stop herself.

'It was a momentary lapse of judgement which will not be repeated, I can assure you of that. But, if it's any consolation, I have been listening to talkback radio this morning and it would appear that there is so much hostility against government departments that in some quarters I am being hailed a hero.'

Sarah realised she was sounding stupid and reined herself in. She bit the inside of her cheek to keep herself quiet.

McKenzie watched her, to be sure she had finished.

'Is that it?' he asked finally.

Sarah felt like a child again. She nodded.

'Okay, then close the door.'

Sarah was surprised. McKenzie almost never shut his door. When Sarah was seated again McKenzie did something she never expected to see in her lifetime. He came around from his desk and sat beside her on a chair. His elbow was just inches from her own.

'Sarah, you are a damn fine reporter. There is no question about that. The job you did on the Liverpool fires was first rate.'

Sarah nodded dumbly. She was unnerved by McKenzie sitting so close to her, on this side of his desk. She was unnerved by his serious, almost friendly tone. But she was completely unnerved by what he was saying. This was not what she expected at all.

'I always knew you would be good from the first day I came to Channel 8 and you argued with me. I don't remember what about but I know I was impressed. I thought then that you had spunk.'

Sarah remembered. McKenzie hadn't been interested in covering the court case of a woman who had murdered her abusive husband. Sarah had thought it a strong story and had told him so. The story had resulted in major changes to the law and it was as well that Channel 8 had followed it.

'What I want to say to you I don't want to go outside these walls, at least not for a little while. Pretty soon everyone will know but in the meantime I ask you to respect my confidence.'

Sarah nodded. She didn't feel like such a child any more.

'The network, in all its wisdom, has decided to merge our news program with our current affairs program and make it one hour-long show combining all the elements.'

This wasn't complete news to Sarah. The rumours had been flying around for weeks but she had been so distracted with what was going on in her own world that she had paid little attention.

'There will be one executive producer and it won't be me.'

McKenzie struggled to keep the bitterness out of his voice. For the first time Sarah saw him as a man. Not a tyrant or a boss but an overweight man in his fifties with a long distinguished career behind him, but not much in front of him. He must be very scared, she thought.

'Oh, sir, I'm so sorry,' stammered Sarah.

McKenzie waved away her platitudes. Sarah struggled to think what she could say that would help. Nothing, she realised.

'It's going to get really messy around here for the next few weeks and I suggest you take a few weeks' leave. I know you've got plenty owing, and right now you are a hot potato. The people upstairs read the papers too and they don't like anything that reflects badly on the network. It would be best, for your sake, if you weren't around for the next few weeks while they are looking at who to sack.'

Sarah looked at McKenzie with astonishment. The man she had called tyrant, had railed against and hated, was worrying about her when his own neck was so clearly in the noose. She had misjudged him completely.

'And on the matter of yesterday's little barney at the RTA— my advice to you is just to deny, deny, deny.'

McKenzie smiled, the first time Sarah thought she had ever seen him do so. In the fifteen minutes that had passed since she entered his office, something had shifted. For years she had put McKenzie in a box labelled boss. She had never seen him as a human being with pressures and a life of his own. She was seeing him that way for the first time.

She realised he must have known exactly what she was thinking when he said, 'You think I've been hard on you?' and laughed. 'Sarah, you were worth being hard on. One day you will be a boss. You will run a newsroom somewhere. And I hope you are lucky enough to get a Sarah Cowley working for you.'

It wasn't until an hour later when Sarah was alone in her car and driving home that she realised what that meant. She looked at the past two years through fresh eyes. McKenzie constantly driving her, pushing her, berating her to do better. She remembered how often she had been given the good jobs, the tough assignments, despite her youth. She had been too busy trying to prove herself and not show any fear or inability, to realise what was going on – that she had a mentor, someone looking after her. He may not have been obvious about it but that's what McKenzie had been. She felt humbled. As she crossed the Harbour Bridge, the tears spilled out of her eyes, tumbling down onto her shirt. It wasn't McKenzie she cried for. It was her father. Big sad heavy tears.

CHAPTER 14

Ginny was on tenterhooks all day, unable to keep her mind on the tasks at hand. Dr Black became irritated as she excused herself for the third time to make a phone call.

'Is everything all right?' he asked.

'I'm sorry, Dr Black. My best friend is very sick and I just wanted to reassure myself that she is okay,' replied Ginny, smiling sweetly, as she backed through the swing doors.

Alone in the storeroom she picked up the dusty old phone and dialled the mobile in the roof of Sarah's apartment. Ginny was starting to get frustrated. She had tried Sarah at work and been told she had gone home. Then she had tried the apartment but all was deathly quiet. No-one home there. Where could Sarah be? Ginny couldn't bear to be missing out on all the drama of the moment. The story in the newspaper that morning was the result of her own handiwork. She knew it. She shivered with delight. But how cruel to be denied seeing the ramifications unfold.

Ginny listened to the mobile ringing in her ear, taking a moment to appreciate her own cleverness. She pictured the mobile phone tucked into the ceiling insulation batt, ringing silently. After the phone rang three times, the circuit she had removed from the answering machine picked up the call and the line opened. She was in!

Ginny listened to the television playing. It was *Oprah*. 'Ah, Sarah was home at last.'

Ginny sat listening to the TV show, wondering what Sarah was up to. Had she slit her wrists in despair? Jumped off the balcony? Maybe she was packing up all her belongings ready to disappear, leaving Tom just some pitiful note.

'Don't ever try to contact me . . .'

Ginny let her imagination run free, enjoying the endless variety of possibilities, the more unlikely the better.

She jumped as Annie crept up on her.

'Dr Black wants you in the surgery, now,' said Annie loudly.

Ginny hung up the line, grinning at Annie. Not even she could dampen her happy mood today.

Tom came home early with flowers. All day he had deflected questions about Sarah and her explosion at the RTA so he thought he had some idea of how it must have been for her. And she had the added trauma of facing McKenzie. He had tried to phone Sarah at the office and had spoken to Fay. She had said Sarah seemed okay and had left, taking two weeks' leave effective immediately. Tom didn't think that was a good sign. Fay was sure she said she was going home.

Tom had tried calling her at home and got the answering machine. Her mobile phone had been switched off. He had left messages, hoping she would call him but she hadn't and he had been on tenterhooks all day. He had tried to give her the space she obviously wanted, but he was worried and anxious. Finally he gave up trying to concentrate in the office and came home.

He expected she would be feeling flat, probably depressed, maybe a bit foolish. He was ready for anything. He approached Sarah cautiously, feeling his way and trying to

181

judge her mood. She was pleased with the flowers and she looked relaxed, but her eyelids were red around the rims. They looked painful.

'How was your day?' she asked, cheerfully enough.

She was wearing her bathrobe and her hair was tied back in a messy ponytail with just a few tendrils loose. She was twirling those around her finger. That usually meant she was agitated. She could be either angry or upset, thought Tom.

'Good,' replied Tom. 'I spent some time at the library trying to understand how steroids function. I quite enjoyed it. It's a fascinating topic.'

She nodded.

'How about you? How did it go with McKenzie?'

At the mention of McKenzie's name Sarah's face crumpled and she started to cry again, big sad tears that rolled down her face, sliding unchecked down her cheeks and onto her bathrobe.

It must have been really bad, thought Tom. The bastard. What a bully. For two years Tom had listened to Sarah come home, upset at what McKenzie had said or done to her. Tom thought he knew the type. Newspaper offices were full of them. Aggressive, tough-talking men in positions of authority who loved the sound of their own shouting so much they had forgotten how to speak any other way.

'Oh Sarah,' said Tom, taking her in his arms. 'Was it that bad?'

Sarah was struggling to speak, but her words came out as an incoherent gurgle.

Tom felt his anger rise.

'He said I was the best,' Sarah mumbled into his shirt. 'He said one day I would be running a newsroom and he hoped I would be lucky enough to get a Sarah Cowley working for me.'

Tom did a mental double-take. This didn't sound like the picture he held of Sarah's boss. 'He said that? That's a lovely thing to say.'

Sarah nodded and burst into large howling sobs that

racked her whole body. She was incapable of speaking and Tom held her, till the worst of it passed.

'He said he was hard on me because I was worth being hard on,' wailed Sarah.

Tom was surprised. 'Then, darling, why are you so upset? That sounds like he was nice to you.'

'He was,' wailed Sarah. 'He's always been nice to me. I just didn't see it.' Sarah lost control again, sobbing into Tom's chest.

Tom and Sarah spent the rest of the evening quietly. Sarah didn't want to go out, didn't want to see anyone and didn't want to return any phone calls. She wanted the world to go away. She curled up on one end of the couch and stared mindlessly at the TV. Tom skirted around her, making dinner, bringing her coffee and rubbing her feet. She smiled at him occasionally, but was mostly withdrawn. He wasn't quite sure why McKenzie's reaction had upset her so much. He filed it away as one of those unfathomable things and hoped tomorrow would bring a new day and a new mood.

'What are you going to do today?' Tom asked over breakfast.

'I thought I might dig out all my old photos,' replied Sarah. 'They are loose in a box and I have been meaning to put them into photo albums. It looks like a miserable day outside so that's what I feel like doing.'

'Sounds like the perfect way to spend the first day of your holidays,' said Tom.

'I think so. Do you remember a cardboard box covered in yellow paper going up into the roof when we moved in?'

'Yes, I think so,' said Tom. 'I vaguely remember passing it to Ginny and some photos falling out. Will you be all right getting up there by yourself? Do you want me to help you?'

'No, I'll be fine. I reckon I can get up there with the stepladder.'

Tom looked at Sarah doubtfully. She hated spiders. She hated confined spaces. This was most unlike her. But it sounded like a project for her to get into and he was sure that was better than moping around.

Ginny was getting ready for work and froze as she buttoned up her shirt. Had she heard right? Sarah wanted to get into the roof? What on earth for? *'But you hate spiders,'* she screamed at the speaker in the corner of her bedroom. Ginny panicked. She remembered how professional the junction box had looked. There was just one new wire and Sarah would never notice that. But what about the phone buried in the insulation batts? What if Sarah stumbled across that? She was a clumsy oaf, thought Ginny, and it would be just her luck to stumble onto it.

She dialled Sarah's number. She heard it ring on the loud-speaker, then click onto the answering machine. 'Hi Sarah, it's Ginny, just ringing to see how you are. Sending much love.'

Ginny paced around her bedroom, lifting the binoculars to her face then throwing them back on the bed in frustration because she couldn't see into the kitchen. She heard Tom say goodbye and then the apartment was in silence. Ginny made another call. 'Hi, it's Ginny. I'm suffering from food poisoning. Please tell Dr Black I won't be in today . . .'

Sarah looked at herself in the mirror. She looked how she felt, awful. She decided against a shower. What for? No-one would see her. She fetched her track pants and sweatshirt from the laundry basket and put them on. They probably should be washed but she didn't care. She was feeling grubby and took perverse pleasure in looking it. She wanted to be comfortable and she was.

Outside, the first of the rain landed on the balcony and the glass windows. It made a rhythmic drumming sound that deadened all other noise coming into the apartment. Sarah usually felt hemmed in on days like this. Today she felt cocooned.

She carried the stepladder into the lounge room and placed it under the manhole. She found the torch in the bottom kitchen drawer, checked that it worked and placed it on top of the stepladder. Just as she placed her foot on the bottom step, the intercom buzzed. She swore. She really didn't want to see anyone. She decided to ignore it. She took another step up the ladder, then hesitated. Perhaps it was a delivery of flowers. She wasn't expecting anyone. Everybody would expect her to be at work. She would hate to miss flowers. What if it was the police?

She was surprised when Ginny's voice floated through the intercom. 'Hi Sarah. It's me, Ginny.'

Sarah's first reaction was disappointment. She really did want to be on her own to go through all her old photos. She had thought of it driving home yesterday and it had become something that, suddenly and inexplicably, she felt driven to do. Her second reaction was relief. She was pleased to see Ginny. It meant she may not have to go up into the roof. Sarah felt guilty at the thought. She really shouldn't use her friend in this way. She decided she would wait to see if Ginny offered.

Ginny was all concern and sympathy, worrying that her friend had not returned her call. She looked at Sarah. Her face showed no sign of tears, yet she looked bruised. Her skin was an unhealthy grey and she had black circles under her eyes. Ginny could smell the bitter scent of dried sweat. She saw all this but carefully avoided noticing the stepladder in the centre of the room.

'What happened on Monday? I read the story in the paper. I've been so worried about you.'

Sarah assured her that she was fine. It was all an overreaction. She told Ginny she shouldn't believe everything she read in the newspaper.

'I lost my temper. That's all. I've been a bit . . . over-wrought lately and it all just got on top of me. I'm taking some time off and I plan to just chill out for a while. Read all those books I've been wanting to read, watch *Oprah*, have long lunches and cook proper dinners for Tom.'

Sarah almost convinced herself. She hadn't thought about what she would do for the next two weeks but as she spoke, she started to like the sound of it.

'Hell, I might even clean out the shoe cupboard!'

Ginny seemed to notice the stepladder for the first time.

'What's this then?' she asked.

'I wanted to get my box of photos out and sort them. I've been meaning to for ages. Do you remember a yellow cardboard box full of photos going up there?'

'Yes, I think I do,' replied Ginny. 'I remember putting it up the back, near Tom's scuba gear. Would you like me to get it down for you?'

'Oh Ginny, would you mind? I hate the thought of going up there. I'd be grateful if you would.'

Ginny smiled. It looked genuine enough but the warmth didn't reach her eyes. Sarah was too distracted to notice.

'Why don't you make us coffee and I'll get down the box?' suggested Ginny.

'Oh thanks, Ginny. You have come by just at the right time.'

As Ginny climbed the stepladder, Sarah called out to her from the kitchen. 'Why aren't you at work?'

'Dr Black gave me the day off,' replied Ginny, easing the manhole cover open and laying it carefully down inside. Tossing the torch through first, she hoisted herself into the roof. The air was warm and musty and exactly how Ginny remembered it. Once inside the false ceiling it didn't matter whether it was daylight or not outside. In here it was heavy, cloying blackness. Ginny could hear Sarah's muffled voice as she tried to continue their conversation. Ginny ignored her.

She shone the torchlight around and quickly located the telephone, sitting in its cradle, nestled into the pink insulation batt. Ginny felt the stinging microshards of fibreglass on her hands. It was a prickly, unpleasant feeling and she wiped them on her jeans. The telephone looked exactly as she had left it. She crawled across the crossbeams to the junction box and opened it. Not even the spiders had been interested. There wasn't a single cobweb.

Sarah's voice drifted up to her. 'How are you doing up there?' she called.

'I can't hear you,' yelled Ginny.

Ginny was proud of her handiwork. She would have loved to show Tom how she had rigged this all up. It was so clever. She was so clever. She smiled to herself. It was unbearably stifling above the false ceiling and Ginny wavered between wanting more time to admire her simple but ingenious set-up and wanting to get out. She made her way across to the yellow cardboard box and shuffled it along the beams to the manhole opening. She saw Sarah's head below and passed her the box.

Ginny stepped off the ladder, brushing her jeans and imaginary cobwebs from her hair. 'Oh, there are so many spiders up there,' she said. 'They don't bother me but gee there were some interesting ones, big and hairy.'

Sarah looked horrified.

'None that could hurt you, they just look fierce,' said Ginny. 'Oh, I shouldn't have said that. I'm sorry, Sarah.'

'That's okay, Ginny. I'm just a bit jumpy.'

Sarah sat on the floor and opened the box as she sipped her coffee. It was full of photos, of varying sizes and dimensions. She upended the box on the carpet, laughing as they fell all about her. Images of her life spilled out in front of her in vibrant, living technicolour. Sarah as a baby with her hair standing on end, sitting happily on her father's knee, Sarah and her mother on a rug at some beach, Sarah and Tom during the first year they met, photos of thirty schoolgirls lined up on chairs, saying 'cheese' and 'TV' to the camera, skiing holidays, beach holidays, drinking competitions at uni – silly photos, mad photos, funny photos, poignant photos. It was her life, in a box.

Sarah laughed with delight as she pulled out a colour photo and handed it across to Ginny. Ginny flinched as she recognised it.

The photo showed Ginny and Sarah, arm-in-arm, looking at the camera. Sarah was laughing, her overwide mouth revealing lots of teeth. Her features didn't quite fit her face. But there was already the hint of the beauty she was to become. She looked carefree and confident. Ginny stood beside her, smiling shyly. She was petite and pretty with a neat little turned-up nose and grey-blue eyes. She looked like a little doll. Behind them stood Gus Cowley, one hand on each girl's shoulder. He was smiling broadly while the easy camaraderie between the two young girls was unmistakable. The photographer had perfectly captured their mutual affection. It was palpable and it made Ginny's heart ache.

She remembered that day. Sarah's parents had taken the two girls for Sunday lunch at one of the city's most exclusive restaurants, overlooking the harbour. Ginny always felt awkward around Sarah's impossibly glamorous mother. Sarah and Geraldine had prattled on gaily, keeping a running banter of amusing stories and asides about other diners that had left Ginny in awe. Sarah's father had tried to draw her into conversation, kindly asking about her favourite school subjects. Ginny couldn't believe he would be genuinely interested but she warmed to his attention, talking about the science experiments she was doing. She was uncomfortable around adults, always feeling as if she should be on her best behaviour. And she desperately wanted Sarah's parents to like her.

After lunch they had walked through the park and Geraldine had insisted the three pose for a photo. She remembered the feel of Gus's warm, leathery hand on her bare shoulder, and Sarah tickling her waist to make her smile. An elderly couple enjoying a walk in the park had stopped and told Geraldine what a lovely family she had. Geraldine had beamed proudly and Gus had squeezed her shoulder.

Later that night, when the two girls were sitting on Sarah's bed, Ginny had blurted out to Sarah how lucky she was to have parents who loved her. She was surprised when Sarah had burst into tears.

'I wish they would move to Sydney soon,' Sarah had cried. 'If they really loved me don't you think they would want to be with me?'

Ginny hadn't known what to say, how to comfort her friend. 'Your mother said they would move here next year.'

'She has said that every year for four years,' sniffed Sarah.

Ginny had never heard Sarah speak this way. Nevertheless, the sadness passed in an instant and Sarah brightened as an idea occurred to her.

'But when they do, maybe you could come and live with us.'

Ginny thought that was a lovely idea. The two girls imagined what it would be like, living together outside the high walls of the boarding school.

'We could go to parties all the time,' said Sarah.

'We could go to cafés,' said Ginny.

'We could wear real clothes,' said Sarah. 'Instead of these dull grey things.'

The two girls made plans and giggled until the night-duty nun came and told Ginny it was past lights out and she would have to go back to her own room.

Seeing the photograph of the two of them so young and innocent brought everything back to Ginny. It was around that time they had sliced open the tips of their thumbs with a Stanley knife during a science class and pressed them together as a testament to their friendship and their vow to always be friends, no matter what life brought along. Blood sisters – 'till death us do part'. Ginny's school memories seemed full of Sarah, laughing and talking, always talking.

'Do you remember Sister Conigrave telling us off for talking?' said Ginny.

Sarah remembered. They were constantly in trouble for talking, during class, after lights out, in assembly. It was one long conversation that never seemed to end.

'What did we talk about for so long?' asked Ginny.

Sarah shook her head. 'I have no idea.'

Sarah placed another photo on the coffee table, covering the image of the three in the park. In this one she and Ginny were standing side by side in their school uniforms in front of a huge old fig tree. They must have been about seventeen.

Sarah clearly dominated the photo. She was laughing with one arm around Ginny's shoulders and one leg kicking the air. She radiated energy and vitality. Ginny, by contrast, was perfectly still, with a pensive, closed expression. They were physically alike, both slender and small-boned with even features, but the expressions on their faces and the way they held their bodies, was completely different.

Both women looked at the photo and, in the same instant, recognised that that was who they were. Sarah – confident, happy, in charge. Ginny – quiet, in the background, runner-up. It was a sobering moment as they sat staring at the picture. The hint of warmth Ginny had felt for their shared childhood memories chilled inside her. She felt the bitterness return, squeezing the breath out of her.

Sarah instinctively felt for her friend. Ginny lacked confidence. She always had. Sarah knew that. And Sarah thought it was her role to help Ginny build her confidence and her self-esteem. Sarah's concern pushed her own troubles away. What would help her friend? she wondered. Falling in love would be a good start. Maybe Hal? These were the thoughts that went through Sarah's head as they sat, side by side, looking at the photo.

Ginny's reaction was different. She imagined watching all the photos burn.

Tom came home early. Sarah hadn't been expecting him, which was obvious. The floor of the lounge room was covered in photos. Sarah sat in the middle of them, sobbing. She was unkempt, in her dirty tracksuit, her hair wild and unbrushed.

Tom picked his way carefully to her. She looked at him but didn't seem to see him.

'Why don't we ever realise about people until it's too late?' she said. She didn't seem to expect an answer from him.

'I love you, Tom. Do you know that?' Her tone was urgent and her voice sounded unnatural.

Tom, wearing his best work suit, loosened his tie and sat on the floor facing her.

'Yes, Sarah, I know that,' he said quietly. Tom noticed the photos she was holding. He gently prised them out of her hands. She didn't seem to mind. She didn't seem aware. 'I love you too,' he said.

The photos were a jumble of snaps – one taken of them at a friend's wedding a few years ago, a picture of Sarah and her mother posing at Stonehenge, Ginny and Sarah with Gus, an old photo of her father in an army uniform. They held no clue to this new mood swing. When he left Sarah that morning she had seemed relaxed, a bit subdued perhaps, but he had thought that was to be expected. Now she seemed on the verge of hysteria.

'You *have* to know that I love you,' she said. 'And I love Ginny. And I love Thel. And I love Anne and Kate.'

'Oh darling, and they all love you too. What is this? What's going through your head?'

Sarah didn't appear to hear him. 'I have to tell them how important they are to me. People go away. They leave you or you leave them. It's like McKenzie. I was wrong. I didn't see it. And now it's too late.'

She was off on another tangent. Tom didn't understand where McKenzie came into it. She was babbling. The thoughts tumbled out of her mouth, one after the other.

'Life is all about change. It never stops. As soon as you think you have it figured, whoosh, it changes. Don't get comfortable. That's the message. Because as soon as you do, that's when you'll get hit. Midships.'

Tom listened for a thread, something that he could follow.

'No-one is what they seem. How can you ever really know a person? How well do I know you? How do I really know what you are thinking? If you thought half the thoughts about me that I have about you, I'd be insulted.'

Tom felt himself floundering. 'Sarah, you are scaring me,' he said. 'What is going on?'

It was as if he hadn't spoken. Sarah ignored him, stood up

and went into the bedroom. She reappeared with her runners in her hand.

'I'm going for a run,' she announced.

Tom said nothing. He couldn't think of anything to say. He stayed sitting on the floor, looking at the pile of photos, wondering why his life with Sarah seemed to be spinning further and further out of control.

Tom rang Hal. He desperately needed to talk to his father. He felt emotionally drained by the hysteria that seemed to have become a new fixture in his life. He wanted the cool, calm solidity of a chat with Hal over a few beers, preferably in the public bar of an old hotel, with the races playing on Sky Channel above the bar. Just the thought of it made Tom feel better.

Hal seemed pleased to hear from him.

Hal knew the minute he saw him that Tom was unhappy. He looked like a man under pressure. But Hal wouldn't ask outright. It wasn't his style. Nor was it the nature of their relationship, or it hadn't been, thought Hal. He felt ridiculously pleased that Tom had called.

They talked about bikes, the rugby, Tom's stories on steroid abuse. Hal noticed that Tom didn't once refer to Sarah during the conversation. It was quite a contrast to the last time they had shared a few beers in a pub. Hal remembered the murderous looks that had passed between them at the picnic on the weekend. He figured he knew where the problem lay.

They were on their third beer when he asked, innocently enough, 'And how's Sarah?'

The look on Tom's face was instant confirmation. He looked beaten. 'I don't know. I think . . .' he struggled with the words while Hal waited patiently. 'I think we may be making a mistake.' Tom's voice broke as he spoke, just a little warble on the word mistake, but Hal caught it.

'Why do you think that?'

Tom, who made his living from expressing himself, stumbled to articulate his fears. He felt he was wading through thick treacle. He didn't understand what was going on at home, Sarah's erratic behaviour and his own ineffectuality in the face of it. He was ceasing to like the woman he woke up next to each morning and was feeling angry with the man who stared back at him from the mirror each day.

He was starting to think that together, those two people were not a good combination. But admitting that aloud seemed in itself to be a betrayal. Once those words were out there, he worried what would happen. He felt he may be unleashing something that couldn't be brought back.

'It doesn't feel right,' said Tom. 'Something's not right. Sarah's bitterly unhappy. It's obvious in the way she speaks to me and behaves. I worried at first that I was losing her. But now,' his voice dropped to a whisper, 'I don't think I care. And that's worse, much, much worse.' There, he had said it. It was out. Tom felt he had opened a door that couldn't be closed. He stared forlornly at the bar.

Hal ached for his son. He wanted so badly to be able to help him, to find the right words, to be the wise father that Tom seemed to need. Hal wasn't comfortable talking about intimate relationships. He thought how it was hard enough living through them, without trying to explain them. He thought of his own history and shuddered. It had taken him many years, and much heartbreak, to finally arrive at the point where he understood himself.

'Relationships are tough,' he said. 'They force you to face yourself.'

Tom nodded bitterly. He knew that to be true.

'When everything is going well it's easy. But it's when things aren't going well that the relationship is tested. If it's strong and the foundations are good then it will survive. But if not then it won't. You and Sarah have been together a long time and you seem good together. I would be careful about throwing that away. But also, you are very young. You will both change a lot in the next ten years and perhaps what you want now won't be what you want in the future.'

Tom listened to his father. His words were comforting. The noises and smells of the public bar were comforting. The tight knot in his stomach was starting to unravel. He felt the first whisper of peace he had felt in weeks.

'Is that what happened with you and Thel?' he asked. 'Were you too young? Did you both change?'

Hal sipped his beer slowly and thoughtfully. He had known the day would come when Tom would ask. He had almost prepared what he would say. He wasn't surprised that Thel hadn't told Tom. She had been so badly hurt. He remembered the pain in her voice when he had left. It would be hard for a mother to share that with her son.

But now Tom was asking and Hal wasn't sure it was the right time for his son to hear. He didn't want to bail out on him. He figured he had done enough of that already. But having just found him, he didn't think he could stand the thought of losing him again. And would it help Tom to know the truth now, when his own relationship was in trouble? Hal considered it all before speaking.

'Something like that,' he said. 'I'd like to tell you what happened, but I don't think this is the time. I hope you will understand that. Your mother is the only woman I ever loved. She is the most remarkable lady. I will always love her. But we couldn't live together. When we got married we wanted to build a life together, start a family. Those first few years after you were born we were so happy. But we were such different people. The foundations, I guess, had never been good. Only it took me that long to figure that out. It wasn't your mother's fault. It was mine. Completely mine.'

Tom felt the same overwhelming feeling of confusion, of being lost, that he had felt as a child when his mother explained to him, tears spilling out of her eyes, that his father had to go away and from now on, she said, it would be just Thel and Tom, and they would have to look after each other.

Tom hadn't understood. It made no sense to him. He had looked at his sad, weeping mother and felt scared. He waited for his dad to come home and explain it to him, and it had taken a few days for him to realise that Hal wasn't coming home. To Tom it was like the sun went behind a cloud and stayed there, for many years. He had felt overwhelmed by a world he couldn't understand and standing at the bar next to Hal, he felt that confusion again.

The message from his father, he realised, was that love just may not be enough. He spoke of Thel with such tenderness and Tom remembered the wistfulness in his mother's eyes when she spoke of Hal, before the wall had gone up. They didn't hate each other. That was obvious. So why couldn't they make it work?

It all swirled about in his head. Maybe marriage was an impossible ideal. Maybe it wasn't for him. Maybe he wasn't cut out for it. There were lots of things he wanted to do with his life and maybe marriage would prevent him from doing them.

He couldn't expect Hal to make his decisions for him. Or anyone else. Even Sarah. Especially not Sarah. Tom felt the frustration returning as his thoughts started to rotate around his head, circling back on each other. He changed the subject.

'We were thinking of going along to the Mardi Gras on Saturday night. Would you like to come? We thought of asking Ginny.'

Hal looked embarrassed and Tom felt clumsy. He hadn't meant to put it quite like that.

'Can't, mate,' said Hal. 'I've got something on that night.'

'You're not homophobic, are you?' asked Tom, trying to lighten the mood.

Hal matched him. 'No, mate. Dykes on bikes are some of my best customers,' he said with a laugh.

CHAPTER 15

I've stopped taking them. I'm storing up the fog. In the toilet. I hide them in my cheek, then drop them in the toilet and flush. I've got three already, stored somewhere along those gurgly pipes. I reckon they stop at the S-bend near the wall. That's where they are. My little stash of drugs. Every day I'm going to add to my little stash. No more fog for me, no sirree.

Sarah was asleep when Tom came home and he was relieved. Tom gently pulled back the sheets on his side of the bed, not wanting to wake her, not wanting to talk to her. He wanted to sleep, long and deep and not wake up until the world was back on track and his life started to make sense again.

Sarah stirred slightly as Tom eased his body under the sheets. She turned away from him and backed her bottom toward him. Instinctively he accommodated her, moulding himself around her. Tom lay looking into the dark at the back of Sarah's head. He was aware of her naked bottom, the feel of her soft skin, but his senses were overpowered by her smell. She smelled, he thought, like stale wet nappies. He was consumed by revulsion.

Tom was alone in the bed when he woke, lying precariously close to the edge. He struggled against waking up, trying to linger in the semi-conscious state as long as possible, ignoring the announcer on the clock radio, the feel of the pillow under his head and the sun streaming through the windows onto his face. He didn't want to rejoin the world. It was nicer here, warm and soft. There was a faint, insistent, nagging thought that was trying to rise. Tom didn't want to acknowledge it.

He became aware he was alone before he opened his eyes. Sarah didn't appear to be anywhere in the apartment. She must have gone for her morning run. Tom decided to have breakfast at his favourite café on the way to work. He was showered, shaved, dressed and out of the apartment in less than fifteen minutes.

Ginny fed Kitty some milk and checked on the cockroach still lying at the base of the fish tank. The water was turning milky and the bubble-eyed fish skirted around the dead insect, ignoring it. Ginny took her position at her bedroom chair. She saw Tom walk across the living room floor and pick up his briefcase, then she heard the front door click behind him. Minutes later she watched Sarah walk across the living room, into the bedroom and strip off. She was red-faced, panting and her body was covered in sweat.

She stood naked in front of the mirror, sucking in her stomach and flexing her biceps. She walked around the apartment, still naked, putting on a CD, fixing herself a coffee then sitting down on the couch to read the newspapers.

Ginny had given up any idea of going to work. It had become too much of an interruption. She could feel the tension from Toft Monks, spilling out the speaker with a hiss. She had her notebook on her lap, ready for whatever may happen. Ginny had little patience with people. But if she was studying an animal that interested her she could sit still for hours.

Hal opened his shop, wheeling half-a-dozen bikes onto the sidewalk. He was distracted from the shop, concentrating on the call he planned to make to Thel. He had come very close to contacting her a few times over the years but something had always stopped him. Guilt, fear, cowardice. He had placed money in her account whenever he could. Sometimes it had been a little and at other times it had been a substantial amount. But he had never contacted her. In many ways he felt he had lost that right.

Whenever he felt the overpowering urge to ring he would examine his reasons and every time he felt they fell short. He wanted to hear about Tom, know how his son was doing, check that Thel was okay. The motivation, when he looked at it, was always to make himself feel better. But what would the call do to them? He didn't believe he had the right to cause Thel any further pain. And he believed his son was better off without him. He was not a fit role model. Hal spent years running away from himself, hating himself. When he left Thel and Tom he was a haunted and unhappy man.

Hal had been largely brought up an orphan. His mother struggled on her pension and when it got too hard, she would put him in an orphanage. He never knew when she would come back for him. Sometimes it was weeks, mostly months and once he had not seen her for three years.

Hal had met Thel at the local surf club dance when they were both just sixteen and the attraction had been instant. Thel was like a little dark-haired pixie with her black hair so long she could sit on it and jet black eyes that darted around. She was dainty and feminine and Hal could put his huge hands around her tiny waist. They had married as soon as he left school. They never had any money and they had never cared. There were more important things in life to worry about, like creating the happy family unit that Hal so craved and saving the world from environmental bullies.

Tom's birth had seemed like a miracle to them. Hal loved his son passionately, so much so that it scared him. Watching his son grow, Hal thought he finally had everything he wanted, everything he needed to be a man – a respectable job, a loving wife and a healthy son. But he was wrong. There was a hole inside him that they didn't fill, an ache that wouldn't go away. He didn't understand it. It scared him. So he had left.

He remembered his last conversation with Thel. She hadn't cried. Her face was so blank he wondered if she had understood what he was saying. He remembered every second of that last morning together, sitting in the little kitchen, surrounded by Tom's artwork. That was twenty-two years ago.

Hal knew now the time had come. He wasn't sure what he would say. Mornings in his bike shop were quiet. The bike owners who had jobs were at work and the hard-core bikers hadn't got out of bed yet. He left his assistant to cope with any salespeople or merchandisers that might drop by unannounced and closed the glass door to his office.

Thel was eating breakfast, sitting deep in her favourite leather couch on the verandah, watching the morning surfers paddle their boards out to the first break. She knew Hal would phone. She knew it from the moment Tom had told her he had seen him. And she thought she was ready. She was curious, more than a little scared and quite a bit excited. The telephone sat by her feet. She had been carrying it around with her for days, just in case. She had gone over their life together, meeting at the surf club dance, chaining themselves to trees in some protest or other, riding up the east coast on Hal's new bike, living in that caravan for months before they moved into their first proper little house with its funny crooked doors. And then the miracle of baby Tom. For days she wallowed in the memories, savouring them.

Finally, when she thought she was up to it, she went

through the more painful memories. They were like a pile of photos she had kept face down in her heart for a long time, knowing they were there but avoiding them. She carefully pulled back a corner to see what the image might be, then, when that seemed okay, she gently, nervously, turned it over.

She recalled their final months together. She had known something was wrong, had known it for some time. How lonely she had felt. She remembered the wretched day he left. The discussion they had that morning, sitting in the little kitchen. She remembered the pain as his words sliced through her.

'Thel,' he had said. 'I have to go.'

There was no explanation, no reason given. He had just said it.

She had felt herself separate inside. Part of her had shut down, closed over, while the other part had taken charge. The man she loved so desperately, who had cared for her and created with her a happy little world for the three of them, had, with his words, cut cleanly through it all, leaving her vulnerable and exposed. It was as though she had stood outside herself and watched herself, sitting in the old painted kitchen chair speaking calmly to her husband, as if they were discussing what they should do about dinner.

She showed no emotion as they talked through the details of his leaving and what she would tell Tom. She would grieve later, when she was alone, away from this man who suddenly and inexplicably had become the enemy, deliberately tearing down her world. That part of her that had gone into hiding would come out when she felt it was safe again. So she had been calm. And Hal had left.

Thel would never forget the look on his face or the sadness in his voice when he had turned at the doorway, the last time she had seen him, and said, 'The strange thing is, I'm breaking my own heart.'

His words haunted her for a long time. She never understood them.

★

The phone rang twice and the lilting voice Hal remembered so well said, 'Hi, Thel here.'

'Hello, Thel. It's Hal.'

It took a while for each to adjust to the sound of the other's voice and establish a sense of ease, a comfortable place where they could have a conversation.

'How are you, Hal?' asked Thel.

'I'm fine, just fine,' he replied in that deep baritone that resonated within the walls of her memory.

Thel described her home at Kiama and the work she was doing. Hal told her about his bike dealership. Tom had shared those basic details with both of them but it didn't matter. Gradually their awkwardness receded and they slipped back into being Hal and Thel again.

'Thank you for our son,' said Hal.

'He's great, isn't he?' said Thel.

'Oh, yes. You have done a great job. He is a credit to you. You must be very proud.'

'I am. I think he's wonderful,' said Thel.

They talked of Sarah. Hal was fascinated that she had lived with Thel and Tom and relieved that Thel so obviously adored her. He thought of his conversation with Tom and Tom's unhappiness. He wondered if he should share that with Thel.

'You don't think they are too young?' asked Hal.

'We were younger,' Thel reminded him. 'I don't think that has so much to do with it. I think they are perfect together. They remind me of us in the early days.'

She said it without bitterness. They both paused for a moment, remembering those days at the start of their marriage when they had thought they were the happiest people in the world. Before it had gone inexplicably wrong.

'They were good times,' said Hal.

He waited for a response but Thel said nothing.

'How are you really, Thel?'

What Hal wanted to know was, Are you angry with me? Do you hate me?

Thel was quiet for a moment, knowing exactly what he was asking.

'Are *you* happy?' she asked finally.

'Yes, Thel, I'm happy.'

'Well, okay then,' she said simply.

It wasn't what Hal was expecting. He marvelled at the generosity of this woman. 'Thank you, Thel.'

'When are you coming for dinner? I've got an album full of photos that you must see. Twenty years of our wonderful son.'

'I'd love that,' he said.

When Thel was happy, she whistled. Little ditties that bore no relation to anything on the radio. She whistled that afternoon as she stood at her easel, looking out across the ocean, completely absorbed in the changing colour of the water and the gradations of blue in the sky. She focussed completely on her work, leaving no room for conscious thought. It was how she did her best thinking.

It was twilight when she finished and she looked with satisfaction at the canvas in front of her. It was a mercurial talent she possessed. Sometimes it felt forced, as if she was trying too hard, and at those times inevitably she would end the day feeling frustrated and disappointed. At other times she was able to let go, relax into herself and let it flow. Today had been like that.

She opened her last bottle of Vasse Felix to celebrate and settled down to watch the moon rise. She raised a glass to the canvas. 'Well done, Thel,' she said. She felt lighter than she had for some time.

She decided to spend the weekend in Sydney. She had earned it. She could deliver the canvas to the businessman who commissioned it and it would be an opportunity to catch up with her two favourite people in the world, Tom and Sarah. She was surprised she hadn't heard from Sarah to talk about wedding plans and dresses and all that. Perhaps they could spend an afternoon together, browsing through the dress shops. Thel would enjoy that. She would stay with her old friends Charles and Marilyn. For months they had been inviting her to visit their new art gallery in Surry Hills. And she could deliver the painting she had finished for the foyer of the new city library. And maybe she would drop in on Hal's bike shop.

CHAPTER 16

Sydney was bedlam. For days people from all over the world had poured into the city for the Gay and Lesbian Mardi Gras, the annual celebration of homosexuality. Half of San Francisco had moved residence for the three weeks of festivities, muscular men of all ages in tight white singlets walking hand-in-hand around the streets. Women made way for men as the beauty salons tried to cope with the sudden demand for body waxing, piercing and hair dyeing. The gyms were overflowing as pecs and abs were toned and buffed.

Saturday night's parade was the highlight of the festivities as hundreds of floats meandered around the city streets. The parade culminated in a huge party for 30,000 people. The point of the night was to be as decadent, outrageous and thoroughly wild as you could be without getting arrested. And on that night getting arrested was virtually impossible. Anything goes was the creed. Homophobes stayed indoors while the city celebrated homosexuality in all its cheeky, wanton glory.

For the parade Tom had scored four highly sought-after tickets to a hospitality stand for himself, Sarah, Ginny and

Thel. It should have been a jolly party. But it wasn't. Sarah and Tom had barely spoken for a week, passing each other on the way to the shower, talking curtly if at all. They tried to put on a happy front for the night out but they didn't fool anyone. Ginny was alert to every nuance of their behaviour, secretly revelling in their misery.

Thel was shocked to find them so unhappy. She noticed how strained Tom looked. He was tired about the eyes and his mouth was set in a firm, grim line. He was almost taciturn, grunting if spoken to. Sarah was the exact opposite, speaking at a hundred miles an hour to anyone and everyone, except Tom. She was wired, on edge, her pupils dilated and her movements jerky. Thel wondered if she had been taking drugs. It seemed so unlike the Sarah she knew that Thel dismissed the thought immediately.

But she looked awful. The lustrous long hair that she usually took such pride in was greasy and lank. Her skin was splotchy. Thel had offered to spend the afternoon shopping but Sarah hadn't wanted to. When Thel had mentioned the wedding Sarah had brushed her off, saying she hadn't had a chance to think about it. Very strange behaviour for a bride-to-be, Thel thought.

The four found their seats and Tom and Sarah sat apart with Ginny and Thel sitting awkwardly between them. They were in the front row, and had a perfect unhindered view of the spectacle that was about to unfold before them.

Anticipation of the first float started to build as the master of ceremonies, a radio DJ, announced it had left the starting point. It would take about ten minutes to reach them, he told the cheering crowd.

It was a stinking hot March night, making it impossible to wear anything but the skimpiest of clothing. The crowd lining the roads was a bizarre mix of every facet of Sydney life. Young women wearing Prada shoes and designer handbags jostled for space on upturned milk crates next to mums and dads with their children sitting high on their shoulders. Police officers joked with the crowd, laughing as two men,

205

hand-in-hand and dressed convincingly as policemen turned and flashed bare bottoms, cut out of their uniforms. They were so close Thel was tempted to lean out and pinch those plump bare cheeks. The atmosphere was of one huge happy party.

Transvestites, transsexuals, bisexuals, homosexuals. People with a shared history of being shunned and shamed came out to celebrate their sexuality, openly and proudly. And the rest of Sydney turned out to applaud them. Thel was entranced but could not ignore the heavy mood of Tom beside her.

'You look awful. What's wrong?' she asked.

'Nothing. I'm fine,' said Tom.

'You're not,' said Thel.

'It's just work. Honestly. I've been really busy.'

Thel would have asked more but the first float, dykes on bikes, drew level and the crowd went berserk. The sound of the cheering crashed over them like a wave, blotting out all conversation. One hundred women in leather cruised their Harley Davidsons and BMWs slowly and deliberately down the street. Butch women, feminine women, some in pairs, some solo.

The Qantas flight attendants followed, men of varying ages dressed in skimpy lamé hotpants, mimicking their duties on board the aircraft. They had been rehearsing for months, pirouetting in unison as they offered 'Coffee, tea or me?'.

Thel put her arm around her son and hugged him to her. He looked at her with surprise.

'What was that for?' he asked, leaning close so she could hear him.

'I don't know, but I think you need it,' Thel replied. She looked pointedly at Sarah then back to Tom. He shrugged and looked away.

Sarah was aware of Thel looking at her and talking to Tom. She felt a flash of paranoia then anger. How dare they talk about her! She stared past Ginny to Tom but he was, by all appearances, absorbed in the parade. Sarah didn't believe it for a minute. She was sure he was ignoring her. The gulf between them was growing wider with every minute. She was angry with him, a low simmer that continued to bubble at the back of her consciousness, permeating every interaction she had with him. He was feeling exhausted, emotionally spent.

She felt he had become so distant, so uninterested. When he was home, which wasn't much these days, he was busy working on his laptop, searching the internet for information about steroids. She felt he had emotionally withdrawn from her. She was having so much trouble sleeping she had taken to watching late-night television on the couch, falling asleep in front of the late late movie. Tom no longer said anything when he found her there in the morning.

Around them was a cacophony of colour and sound. Each float played its own loud music, the beat thumping through the ground, surging up through their bodies. The Olympic swimmers' float featured dozens of handsome young lads, sweat dribbling down their hairless, muscular chests, in worship and adoration of the country's gold-medal heroes. The Dame Edna float – a favourite every year – had men in voluminous frocks shouting *'Hello Possums'* and waving gladioli at the crowd. Twenty would-be Kylie Minogues in high heels and miniskirts mimed to 'I Should Be So Lucky'. Every Aussie icon was parodied with high camp humour and the crowd loved it. Different gay minorities carried banners: 'Deaf and Gay', 'Living with HIV' and others.

Sarah watched it all go by feeling edgy. The buzz and energy of the crowd fed her own restless energy. The pulsating beat surged through her, increasing her heart rate. It fed her state of agitation.

A rousing cheer went up as Proud Parents of Gay Children marched by. They were a group of ordinary-looking mums and dads, dressed as if going to the supermarket on a Saturday morning, walking simply behind their banner, dignified and proud. They stood out against the sequined G-strings and giant blow-up phallic symbols that were cavorting playfully in front of them.

Thel was unbearably moved by the sight of them. They

were mostly her age, her era. She didn't know any of them and yet she felt she recognised them. She wondered at the personal dramas they had each survived to be there tonight, normally private people happily sharing the road with such flamboyant, rampant sexual expression. Thel cheered them on. She would always applaud courage.

The four of them – Tom, Thel, Ginny and Sarah – were squeezed closely together, each one's hips and shoulders pressed hard against the hips and shoulders of their neighbour. The still, heavy heat was oppressive, like a warm, moist towel on their skin. They were locked together and yet the noise and energy of the parade kept them apart, each in their own world. Conversation was difficult and each was preoccupied with their own thoughts as the extravagant display continued past them down Oxford Street.

Thel was thinking of Hal. Warm thoughts. She gently prodded her psyche to see where it might be tender. She couldn't find any anger. The pain seemed to have passed. She was left with a lingering, not unpleasant, sense of melancholy and nostalgia.

Tom was thinking of the body builders he had interviewed that week. As hundreds of torsos that would shame a Greek god marched past, Tom wondered if this was a new angle to be investigated. He had been concentrating on sport. He wondered how much steroid abuse went on in the body-conscious gay community.

Ginny was plotting. She was excited and exhilarated. Tom and Sarah's relationship was deteriorating before her. She wondered what else she could do. She had the scent of blood. Now she wanted to close in for the kill. She sat very quietly, her hands loosely in her lap, smiling happily, unseeing, at the parade before her.

Sarah felt uptight and antsy. On the other side of her was a fat woman, taking up more than her share of space. She was loudly and wantonly enjoying herself, forking fistfuls of Twisties into her mouth and spreading herself out for maximum comfort, oblivious of Sarah. Her flabby flesh pressed hard against Sarah's thigh and shoulder. Where the exposed skin met Sarah's skin, the two women sweated and Sarah hated the forced intimacy of their rubbing flesh. Sarah recoiled from her, pushing herself harder against Ginny's thin frame.

Sarah hated the pudgy woman. She resented her selfishness and was repulsed by her gluttony. She wanted to pinch that flabby bare thigh, make it bruise. Every time the fat woman dug her hand into the Twisties packet she jerked her elbow into Sarah's side. It was covered in too many layers of fat to be painful but it was annoying and with each nudge Sarah's blood pressure went up that little bit higher. Usually Sarah would barely notice such a minor annoyance, but with the steroids raging through her system her stress markers had moved. She existed in a state of pent-up aggression.

The four sat watching the parade go by. Together, yet worlds apart.

A loud cheer went up for the leather men. A dozen men on the back of a truck rocked along to a Jimmy Barnes song, 'Working Class Man'. It had become the anthem for the common man. They were dressed all in leather, hotpants, jeans, vests, studded collars, cowboy chaps.

In the middle, facing out to their side of the road, was a tall, middle-aged man in leather jeans and vest with a peaked leather cap sitting rakishly over one eye. He swayed to the music, holding onto a post to steady himself. He looked perfectly at ease with the music, his mates and the cheering crowd.

Tom didn't need a second look. He recognised the man instantly. It was Hal. Unaware of what he was doing, Tom stood up. Thel followed the direction of his stupefied gaze, wondering what was up. She spotted Hal. It had been twenty years since she had seen him but she knew him immediately. The casual way he was leaning, those blue eyes, the blond curly hair, a little less than when she had last seen him and a lot whiter, but she recognised it all the same.

Thel felt the world slip away, the noise and the music

receding in a rush. It gave her the sensation of being alone in a silent tunnel, with Hal gyrating at the other end. Everything else was a blur. Her mind was in shock, trying to make sense of what her eyes were telling her. Twenty years of pain and confusion welled inside her, propelling her to her feet. The look of stunned disbelief on her face mirrored her son's.

Hal rocked to the pounding chorus and his eyes roamed across the cheering thousands in front of him. He was high on adrenaline. This was a significant night for him. It was the first time he had joined in the parade, instead of watching and cheering from the sidelines. He felt liberated, he had finally arrived at a place where he could be who he was. And the cheering crowd were there telling him that was just fine.

He saw Thel and Tom, though he didn't recognise them at first. They stood out in the happy, energetic crowd, conspicuous by their stillness and intensity. He realised with a sharp shock that it was Tom standing there, his mouth agape. He stopped gyrating, too stricken to move. He noticed the short woman with the long braids, standing perfectly still beside Tom, staring at him. She looked familiar and was wearing a look of such pain and confusion that Hal felt his heart break.

The float seemed to hover at the stand, a long slow agonising moment that burned the image of Thel's face onto Hal's brain. His elation evaporated in an instant.

Then the float moved, passing along the road in a roar of thumping bass.

Deep inside Thel, something clicked into place. It was as if everything had transpired to bring the three of them to this spot. She forgot about Sarah and Ginny. She grabbed Tom's hand and dragged him onto the road. Tom didn't resist her. He just had no impetus of his own. He was dazed. Thel, with Tom in tow, pushed her way through people lining the street.

Ginny and Sarah had no idea what was going on. One minute Thel and Tom were watching the parade and the next Thel was waving wildly and they were disappearing into the crowd. Ginny was quick to react, ever alert to Tom. She had seen the look on his face and, without thinking, followed straight after him, catching him just as the crowd swallowed him.

Sarah was bewildered. 'What is going on? What are you doing?' she shouted after them. Ginny, the only one who could have heard her, ignored her. Ginny grabbed Tom's belt loop so she wouldn't lose him. It was the last sight Sarah had of Tom. Without a backward glance in her direction, Tom merged into the crowd, his back rigid with Ginny hooked onto him. The crowd closed behind Ginny and Sarah stared after them, bewildered and indignant. 'What the hell is going on?' she thought.

Sarah felt discarded. It was an increasingly familiar and unpleasant feeling. She pushed her way after them into the crowd, feeling suddenly anxious and a little scared.

Thel pushed on, following the float. She was like a small dynamo, slipping easily between people, carrying Tom and Ginny in her wake. Hal could see them following behind, disappearing behind heads, then popping up again.

Sarah also caught glimpses of them, popping up then disappearing. It made no sense. *Why are they running away from me?* She fought her way through the crowd. Where Thel's emotional energy propelled her forward, oblivious of any discomfort, Sarah struggled. People pressed against her. Everywhere she turned there were sharp elbows, handbags, feet treading on hers. Smelly, sweaty bodies. She stumbled on the uneven footpath.

As the floats reached the final intersection, they unloaded their occupants who milled around in a state of high excitement. Many streamed into the Showground, eager to start the all-night party. Others stood around congratulating each other, rejoicing in the atmosphere, not wanting the parade to end.

Hal leapt off his float, looking for Thel and Tom.

Sarah was determined, her anger spurring her on. She lost all composure in her battle to get to Tom. She saw him and called out his name. He couldn't hear her above the din. Using all her energy she launched herself through the crowd, beating them out of her way, and grabbed his arm. He turned to her, his face a rigid mask.

'How could you run off like that?' she screamed at him.

He looked at her blankly.

More floats banked up, spilling their occupants into the tight crowd. It was chaos. The mob surged forward, pressing harder against each other. Sarah felt herself drowning. She was fighting for air, for space. Her survival instincts took over, unleashing adrenaline into her bloodstream, her body poised for fight or flight. She had to get out of there. It wasn't a conscious decision. Something far more primal took charge.

'I can't breathe,' she screamed at Tom. Then she was turned away, pushing away from him, back through the horde.

Tom recognised the panic on her face. He snapped out of his daze. 'Sarah,' he called after her. But she was gone.

Sarah knew these streets well, but it was all alien to her now. She pushed blindly through the mass of bodies. It seemed to her that there were mad people everywhere, laughing maniacally, leering at her. Her heart pounded painfully in her chest, her blood roared in her ears. She stumbled over the rubbish in the gutter and onto the footpath. The mob pushed her against a wall, bruising her shoulder. She was momentarily winded. Her throat ached. She inched her way along the wall, tears of pain obscuring her vision.

Her hands found the end of the wall. It was an alley. She stumbled into it, gasping for air. Here the crowd was thinner and she pushed her way through, hoping to reach a less crowded street. Tom followed, calling to her, but she couldn't hear above the music and the roar in her own head.

Her foot registered the end of the alley before her brain did and her whole body hit the corrugated-iron fence. A sliver of tin entered her right eye. She jerked her head away. The blood filled the socket and dripped down her face, a warm trickle that seeped into her mouth. She recognised the taste.

Around her people continued to party. A ghettoblaster on

the ground pumped out a pulsating, mindless drumbeat that reverberated inside her head. She couldn't see out of her right eye because of the blood and with only one eye working she lost her sense of distance. Her mind had trouble processing what her left eye saw. The images were overbright, surreal. Anger and frustration spilled out as she jumped about, shifting her weight from one foot to the other, poised like a boxer, ready for the next punch.

Tom was horrified when he reached her. With a glance he took in the blood coursing down her face and her deranged state.

'Sarah,' he called, leaning out to take her arm.

Sarah recoiled. She couldn't hear him and she couldn't make sense of his features. Tom moved forward. It wasn't an aggressive action. He wanted to help.

Sarah was aware of the corrugated iron, cold and hard against her back. She felt trapped. A beer bottle was lying by her foot. She had been dimly aware of it rolling against her shoe as she bounced on the balls of her feet. She grabbed at it and lunged towards her attacker. Her aim was wild and her arms flailed in the air. She should have missed. And had it been anybody other than Tom she probably would have. But he was completely unsuspecting and his natural defences were down. He stood firmly in front of her, his face a mixture of concern and disbelief, as Sarah smashed the bottle hard into his jaw, breaking his skin.

A woman screamed and around them the crowd pushed back. Tom felt the ground rise to meet him and he was aware of the feel of gravel against his cheek.

There was no pain. Not yet. Sarah continued to wave the bottle, now dripping with Tom's blood, as she inched her way along the back wall. The mood of the people in the alley changed as they quickly realised what was happening.

'Get away from me,' she hissed at them.

Two policemen appeared. They saw Sarah, back against the wall, hissing wildly, blood covering half her face and waving a broken bottle at the panicked crowd. They carefully approached Sarah, one policeman distracting her while the other quickly and expertly disarmed her. The last thing Tom saw before he slipped out of consciousness was Sarah struggling against the handcuffs, her face contorted in rage as she spat and swore at the policemen.

CHAPTER 17

They are talking about somebody else. Don't they realise that? That's not me. I scream it. Why don't they listen? Whenever I try to tell them they cart me off again. They tell me not to get upset. They say it like I did something dirty. You got upset. Bzzzz. You lose. Of course I'm upset. I'm stuck in here, aren't I? If that didn't upset you, you should be carted off.

Gotta be careful. The fog is clearing. They wouldn't like that.

Tom was blinded by white when he opened his eyes. White walls. White sheets. Sunlight through the window. He was disoriented. Muffled intermittent clanging noises came from somewhere nearby. It was when Tom registered the smells – astringent, bitter, antiseptic smells – that he knew where he was. In a hospital. He had no recollection of how he got there.

'Hi, honey.'

Tom turned to the voice and felt sharp hot needles shoot up the side of his neck. Thel was standing by his bed, looking down at him, her face soft and smiling. Beside her was Hal, towering over her, frowning with concern.

'Are you in pain?' asked Thel softly.

Tom wasn't sure. If he kept his head still he didn't think there was any pain. But there was something else. He felt like he had forgotten something, something vital. He was late for an appointment. He was supposed to pick something up. What was it? He looked at Thel for help. There was something very wrong and he didn't seem to be able to bring up in his mind what it was.

'Do you remember what happened?' asked Hal gently.

Tom looked at him and something clicked inside the deepest recesses of his brain. The neurons moved back into alignment, and the messages moved along the chemical pathways as Tom's memory returned to full function. It happened almost in an instant. A series of seemingly unrelated images flashed across his mind. Hal on a float . . . A man in a frock on stilts . . . Thel grabbing his hand . . . Sarah's bleeding face . . . Sarah wielding a beer bottle . . . His blood . . . Gravel . . . Sarah fighting the policemen. The anxious feeling that had been nagging at Tom exploded into full-blown panic.

'Sarah?' he said, rising off the bed. The word came out garbled, something like 'shair'. The pain hit him like a machete through his jaw, throwing him back against the pillows. His eyes filled with tears.

'You can't, mate,' said Hal, holding him firmly against the bed. When he was sure Tom was staying put, he released his hold.

Tom tried to speak.

'Wosh app?' he asked. Tom was surprised that the words in his head weren't matching what came out of his mouth. But Hal and Thel understood enough.

'She's being taken care of,' said Thel.

Tom looked at her blankly.

Hal came straight to the point. 'Sarah attacked you with a beer bottle. She got your jaw. It's not broken but it's badly

216

bruised. You've had six stitches in your cheek. You won't be able to eat for a few days but you will be fine.' He spoke slowly and deliberately, his eyes never leaving Tom's. 'Sarah has been put into hospital where doctors will keep an eye on her. It appears she has had some sort of breakdown.'

Thel wasn't sure he needed to know all this. 'But we will worry about that later. Right now you have to get better,' she said, squeezing his hand.

Tom tried to touch his jaw. It was covered in bandages and felt as if it were a few feet out from his face. Another dressing covered his cheek. His whole face felt on fire. But it was nothing compared to the pain in his heart. He looked at his parents, his eyes expressing his bewilderment.

'Eeze Shair okay?'

Thel and Hal hesitated. They didn't know what to tell him. 'We'll have to wait and see about that,' said Hal.

Tom noticed Hal's use of the word 'we'. He saw that Thel and Hal were standing side by side at his bed. He looked from one to the other. Seeing them together, united in their love and concern for him, touched an emotion deep within him. For a moment he was that eight-year-old boy again, safe and secure within the circle of his family.

He saw himself holding tightly onto Hal's and Thel's hands, as they walked along the beach at night dodging the bluebottle jellyfish that had washed ashore. He remembered being wedged comfortably between them on a motorbike. He remembered the feel of the prickly blue blanket on their bed.

Hal was still dressed in leather. He had taken off the leather cap but still wore the leather jeans and vest he wore in the parade.

Tom pointed at Hal and tried to speak. After two attempts finally Hal thought he understood. Whatever Tom was saying included the words 'Hal' and 'float'. Thel held her breath.

'You saw me in the Mardi Gras parade last night,' Hal said.

Tom considered this. It was no longer a shock. It had been when he first recognised Hal, dancing along with the leather men and, while he had not had much of a chance to think about it, somewhere his mind had processed the information.

Tom felt many things had clicked into place but there was still so much to say, so many questions he wanted to ask. But the effort of trying to speak was too great. He put his hand out to Hal as if to shake it. When Tom didn't have the strength Hal just took his hand and held it. There really wasn't any need for words. The tears rolled down Thel's face. A nurse came into the room, all bustle and efficiency, interrupting the poignant family moment. She stopped when she felt the atmosphere in the room.

'I'm sorry,' she said. 'I wondered if Mr Wilson was in pain. He's due for more pain-killers if he requires them.'

Tom nodded feebly. He wanted to sleep. For a long time. Thel and Hal said their goodbyes.

'We'll come and see you later today. Hopefully they'll let me take you home. Get some sleep,' said Thel.

They walked out of Tom's hospital room and down the long corridor. Outside it was dark, just a few hours till dawn. As they walked slowly towards the double glass doors of the entrance Thel caught sight of their reflection. They didn't look much like the young couple she remembered. She saw her voluminous skirt and black hair in messy braids. She looked like an overgrown hippie. The thought almost made her smile. She thought Hal looked like a middle-aged gay man, common enough in inner Sydney. She used to think they looked so good together but now they made an incongruous pair.

She realised they both had become who they really were. It gave her a feeling of life coming full circle. Everything was as it should be. For years she had believed she was somehow to blame. She had taken Hal's rejection personally and her sexual confidence had taken a battering. She recognised the last vestiges of that pain dissolving inside her. She felt lighter and freer. He owed her nothing and she owed him nothing. And yet they shared this beautiful boy. She had paced hospital floors because of Tom on a few occasions. She was glad that tonight Hal was there to pace with her.

'He's going to be okay,' said Hal.

It was a meaningless comment and they both knew it. Tom's bruises would heal but his heart was another matter. Sarah could have killed him. The police made that quite clear. Thel couldn't make sense of it. She thought she knew Sarah nearly as well as she knew her own son.

'I just don't get it,' she said. 'I don't understand Sarah suddenly going berserk. It's out of character.'

Hal looked pensive. 'It happens. It could be a chemical imbalance. She may be short of something or have too much of something in her system and it has caused something like a short circuit in her brain. If that's what it is they can treat it.'

Thel seesawed between empathy for Sarah and anger that she had attacked her beloved son. She didn't want to see Sarah right now. All her emotions were jumbled. She hated Sarah, she was worried for Sarah, she hoped Sarah stayed locked away from her son forever, she hoped it all had been a ghastly mistake and Sarah and Tom could return to normal. It all went around in her head, revolving feelings that she couldn't control. The only one that stood out was worry for her son. That overrode everything else.

Ginny came to see Tom at 8 o'clock that morning. She was horrified at the sight of him. He was almost unrecognisable behind the huge bandage covering his cheek. The icepack on his jaw had been removed but his jaw was still swollen to twice its normal size. Tom couldn't speak so she just sat by the bed. He hardly seemed to be aware that she was there. Ginny didn't mind. She was happy just to sit with him.

She brought the Sunday newspapers and read aloud the stories that she thought would interest him. The newspapers were full of reports on the Mardi Gras. Ginny carefully avoided those. There was no mention of Sarah or her arrest. Ginny was a bit disappointed by that. She wondered if the press didn't know about it. Perhaps someone should tell them, she thought. Something to consider a bit later.

She was reading the stories of the previous day's sporting matches when the head of the department came to check on Tom. It seemed to be such an intimate scene, Ginny sitting by his bed, reading to him, that the doctor assumed she was his girlfriend.

'Would you mind waiting outside while I check on your boyfriend?' Dr Hindson asked politely.

Tom was in no position to correct her and Ginny took it as her due.

'Of course,' she said, smiling sweetly. She leaned over and caressed Tom's forehead. 'I'll be outside,' she told him, behaving for all the world like the loving girlfriend.

Tom accepted it without thought. The world had gone suddenly, inexplicably, mad. So what if Ginny was acting a bit strangely.

Dr Hindson was an imposing presence. She was tall, attractive and robust. In her mid-thirties, she was young to be running the casualty unit but she wore her authority easily. She never raised her voice. She didn't have to. She had a calm, efficient manner. When Dr Hindson asked for something to be done, it was done. Tom found himself being appraised by a pair of cool green eyes. They ranged over his face.

'Did you get into a fight last night?' asked Dr Hindson.

Tom didn't know how to answer.

Dr Hindson continued cheerily on. 'Well, I'd hate to see the other guy,' she said, looking at her clipboard.

Dr Hindson was determinedly cheerful. It was probably the most exhausting part of her job. No matter what new disaster confronted her in the hospital rooms each morning, the battered bodies, the human despair, it was her job to be cheerful.

'You can go. Your jaw will be stiff for a few days and I suggest you keep your talking to a minimum. Try and eat soup. Maybe some mashed vegetables if you feel you are able. You can come back to see us in a few days if you have any concerns or go to your own doctor. The stitches in your cheek will have to come out in a week. We have put a dressing on your cheek and given you antibiotics in case of infection. We also gave you a tetanus shot. That would explain why you are a little tender on your bottom. We'll give you pain-killers to take with you. Do you have any questions?'

Tom had lots. And he felt reasonably sure this woman wouldn't be able to answer any of them. None of them had anything to do with his health. Why had the world gone mad? He'd like someone to answer that for him.

'Right then. I'll tell your girlfriend you're ready to go.'

Ginny reappeared immediately. Dr Hindson was used to that. Relatives always wanted to know exactly what was going on. The nurses used to joke about how you could tell if a consulting doctor was in the room, by the relatives listening at the door.

'He's all yours,' said Dr Hindson cheerfully, then she was gone, off to spread more robust optimism among others who found themselves waking up on Sunday morning in the city hospital.

Tom let Ginny take charge. She assumed the role and he didn't have enough presence of mind to question it. He was beyond caring. She was going to bring the car around to the casualty entrance while he sorted out his paperwork. He guessed he had arrived through these same doors but he didn't remember it. His head thumped and he walked gingerly, placing each foot oh so carefully, to minimise the jarring through his body. He looked like a drunk, unsure of his footing. The two nurses behind the reception counter ignored him as he walked past. They saw more outrageous sights than him every day of their working lives.

Ginny was sitting in her little navy blue car with the engine running. She was smiling and waving. She looked happy, cheerful, much like Dr Hindson. Tom assumed it was an act. Ginny would be just as worried about Sarah as he was. They were all just trying to make him feel better. He looked forward to being alone. He didn't feel cheerful and he didn't want to be around people who were acting so goddamned cheerful.

He would have liked to tell Ginny that she didn't have to

pretend for him. She could relax and be miserable. But he didn't have the energy to fight the pain that he feared a new bout of trying to speak would bring on. So he sat in silence, looking out the window at the sunny morning. Ginny hummed and chattered about anything and everything. The sunny day. She pointed out people just coming home from the night of festivities, and the debris by the sides of the road as they drove along the parade route. Tom leaned back in the seat and closed his eyes. He wanted to block out all evidence of the night before.

He didn't open his eyes until the car stopped. He expected to see Toft Monks before him. Instead, he was in the driveway of an apartment block he hadn't seen before.

'Wewarrrwe?' he tried to say.

If Ginny understood him she gave no indication. Without answering she was out of the car and around helping him out of his seat. He held on tightly to the car door, noticing the plastic covering it, as if it had just rolled off the factory floor. Perhaps it was to protect the door from vomit. God knew it's what he wanted to do. Did Ginny often carry vomiting passengers, he wondered inanely. Ginny chattered on, fussing about him, talking constantly in a stream of soothing sounds that left Tom no place to interrupt, even if he could have.

'You just have to take it easy. You've got a lot of healing to do. We'll get you inside. Get some food into you. I spoke to the nurses and I know exactly what you need.'

The effort of standing up sent new waves of pain through Tom's head and he gasped. He would have sat straight back down again but Ginny had shut and locked the door behind him. She was gently pushing him towards the entrance. Tom could hardly see for the blinding pain in his head. He looked forward to sitting down. He focussed on the thought of the pain-killers in his pocket. Not long now and he could take them. Concentrating on putting one foot in front of the other, he followed Ginny up the stairs and into her apartment. He walked in, dimly aware of baby blue everywhere, and collapsed on the couch by the balcony doors. Ginny opened the doors to let in the breeze.

'Relax, Tom, take off your shoes. I'll get you a drink.'

Tom wasn't fussed about his shoes. He wanted those pain-killers and spilled the bottle on the coffee table in his haste to get to them. He shoved two in his mouth with an unsteady hand and swallowed. He figured it would take about fifteen to twenty minutes for them to work. He would have to work at slowing down his heartbeat till then, to try to stop the throbbing.

Ginny bustled about the kitchen, opening the pantry and removing two heavy-bottomed crystal glasses.

'I think we both need a scotch,' she said. Her eyes were unnaturally bright, the pupils dilated.

She fetched the bottle and splashed it into the glasses. She set one down on the coffee table for Tom and took the other back into the kitchen, placing it on the bench while she rummaged in the fridge.

'Pureed vegetables. Mmmm. Sounds like baby food. The nurses said that was the best thing for you.'

Tom looked at the scotch. It was a bit early in the day for him but then again what better way to ease the pain of his bruises. He took a careful swig. It was awkward, trying to get his teeth far enough apart to tip the scotch into his mouth. Ginny saw the trouble he was having and brought him a straw. Tom took a large sip of the scotch. He felt it warm the back of his throat. It felt good. He took another.

'I'll just change out of these clothes. Make yourself comfortable.'

Ginny's voice floated to Tom from a long way away. He focussed on the pain in his temples and he tried to find the core of it, to go into it. He settled back into the cushions. Kitty eyed Tom with interest from her safe spot under the dining chair. It wasn't often they had visitors.

In the bedroom Ginny opened the cupboard and removed a long black satin sheath. She slipped out of her jeans and top. She unhooked her bra, fumbling clumsily in her excitement,

223

and pulled the sheath over her head. It fell about her body in sensuous folds, lightly skimming her breasts and hips. She had played this scene out many times before. In the bathroom she brushed her hair, smiling seductively in the mirror and pouting at her reflection. She applied bold red lipstick and heavy black mascara. She felt wanton as she floated back into the kitchen, her movements graceful and sensuous.

'Your glass is empty. Let me get you another,' she called, picking up the bottle and gliding across the room.

Tom grunted in response, his eyes still closed against the harshness of the daylight. He hoped the pain-killers would kick in any minute.

Ginny topped up Tom's empty glass, looking out at the view.

'There's Toft Monks. I don't suppose you've ever seen it from this angle?' she said with a laugh.

Toft Monks. The words floated across Tom's consciousness. His home. Where he lived. With Sarah.

Ginny returned to the kitchen. She bustled about happily, boiling vegetables and adding seasoning with a flourish. She climbed the stepladder in the pantry and pulled down the canteen of silver cutlery. She laid two places at the dining table, with two wine glasses of fine-cut crystal. It had just gone midday but in the centre she placed a lighted candle. Onto two large white plates she served mashed pumpkin and potato.

'Please come and sit down,' she said to Tom.

Tom looked up. For the first time since he had entered the apartment he looked at Ginny. She looked different. Very different. For a moment the world slipped. It was the culmination of the alcohol, the pills and the stress of the past twenty-four hours combined with a vision that just didn't make sense. It didn't compute in Tom's brains. He looked at Ginny with complete bewilderment. What the hell was going on?

Ginny saw his expression and interpreted it through her own mad perception of the world. She looked beautiful. She

224

knew it. Tom had never seen her like this. He was clearly overcome. Ginny's angular features softened as she looked at him.

'Your vegetables are ready, Tom, darling. Don't let them get cold.'

Tom's aching mind raced. This was Sarah's best friend. It was the middle of the day. She had candles and wine on the table, she was dressed like she was going to a nightclub and she had a peculiar look on her face that made Tom very uncomfortable. He shook his head. He suddenly understood a lot.

Ginny had looked at him like that before, he realised with a shock. It had made him uncomfortable then too but he had brushed it aside. It had no relevance for him. He recognised it now for what it was. Longing. Yearning. Lust. She wanted him. He was sickened. The scotch, the pain and the look on Ginny's face swirled about inside him and he felt the bile rise in his throat. Before he realised what was happening he was throwing up on Ginny's carpet.

Ginny was all worry and concern as she rushed to his side. The smell of bile filled the small apartment. Ginny didn't seem to notice as she fussed about Tom, wiping the vomit from the carpet, and from where splashes had landed on his shirt and trousers.

'I think you'll have to take those off,' she said, struggling with Tom's shirt.

Tom found Ginny's small hands clutching at his body to be unbearably invasive. They felt like insects, crawling over him, trying to get to him. He brushed her away but she was insistent, pulling his shirt out from the waistband and starting to undo the buttons.

Something snapped inside Tom's throbbing head. He caught both Ginny's hands and held them firmly. She was kneeling in front of him, between his open legs. It hurt Tom too much to speak. He studied her face. She smiled at his scrutiny.

'It's normal, Tom, for you to throw up. After what you

have been through,' she said. Her voice was soft and seductive. She didn't seem to mind Tom holding her wrists.

He was suddenly uncomfortably aware of the physical contact. It was distasteful to him. Ginny sitting so close and looking up at him with that peculiar expression turned his stomach. He dropped her hands and tried to stand up. Ginny thought he wanted to use the bathroom and moved out of the way.

'It's through here. I'm sure I've got something you can put on while we wash your clothes.'

Tom wanted to get out of there. The small apartment. The stuffed cat looking at him wherever he was in the room. The smell of vomit. The baby blue walls and carpet. Ginny in a slinky gown. It was obscene. Tom picked up his bag and started toward the door. Ginny realised what was happening and her voice changed.

'You can't go,' she wailed.

Tom moved towards the door.

'Tom, you aren't well. You need to be looked after.'

Ginny threw her arms around Tom's back and pushed her body into him. He tried to shake her off. She was small but determined while Tom was weak and, under the circumstances, they were an even match. She dug her short nails into Tom's chest. They stayed like that for a moment, swaying together as one.

Ginny couldn't comprehend what was happening. She had played this scene over and over in her head and it always ended up with them making love on the couch, or in the bedroom, or in the shower. Sarah was out of the way and this was how it should it be. Tom and Ginny should always have been this way. Tom couldn't leave. That just wasn't how it was meant to be.

'You can't leave, Tom. No, no, no.' Ginny started to babble, her thoughts pouring out in an almost incoherent stream. 'We can be together now. I love you. You know that. I know you love me. It's taken a while, but now we can be together.'

Tom felt horror, repulsion. What was she saying? Something

very, very wrong, something insidious was going on here that he didn't understand. He just knew he didn't want to be a part of it. He had to get away. 'I've always loved you. We can be together now.'

He gathered his last vestiges of strength and flung Ginny's arms off him. Ginny screamed as Tom propelled himself forward, wrenching himself free of her grip. Ginny kicked out her leg and hooked her foot around Tom's calf. Then she yanked his leg sharply. The movement was so unexpected, Tom was thrown completely off balance. His arms flailed about, trying to find something to hold onto as the room whirled about him. He grabbed vainly at Isabel, knocking her off her perch. She spun in the air, landing upside down, her frozen legs making it look as if she were cycling on her back. Kitty, who had been hiding under the table keeping as far away from the vomit as she could without leaving the room, hissed in fright at the sight of the dead cat staring glassily at her from the floor. Tom hit the floor at the same time, his head landing hard against the table leg with a sickening thud. Tiny slits of iridescent blue light swirled about his peripheral vision and for the second time in two days he passed out.

Ginny stood and looked at him. Poor Tom. He was just exhausted. What had Sarah done to him? She shook her head. Thank God he was here where she could look after him. He looked awkward. He was lying on his side, head jammed against the leg of the dining table and his legs splayed. Ginny tried to straighten him. She pushed him onto his back with his legs out in front of him. He didn't look so good. Fresh blood was oozing from the cheek dressing and his skin was a ghastly grey.

Ginny took both his feet in her hands and tried to haul him across the carpet to the bedroom. Tom was a dead weight that would not budge. Ginny unbuttoned his shirt and eased his arms out of the sleeves. She propped him up to take it off his back. Then she undid his belt and fly, easing his jeans over his hips. He was wearing boxer shorts, big red ones with little Donald Duck cartoons all over them. Ginny hesitated. Should she or shouldn't she? She giggled to herself. Then she removed them too. He had been wearing those clothes for nearly two days now, she reasoned. She was sure he would be happy to wake up to clean clothes.

Ginny threw Tom's clothes into the washing machine on her way to the bedroom. She took her pillow and a blanket off the bed and made a bed around Tom on the floor, gently laying his head on the pillow. Then she peeled off her own clothes and snuggled down next to him, spooning her body around his. She lay one arm across him, delighting in the gentle rise and fall of his chest and the springy hair beneath her palm. She could feel Tom's warmth. With the lightest touch, Ginny gently stroked his chest. It was broad and muscular, firm beneath her fingertips. She nuzzled into his neck, inhaling his scent. He seemed so peaceful, so happy. She imagined he felt safe and protected with her body entwined around his. She moved her leg across his thigh, slowly, sensually rubbing it up and down.

Her hand moved down to his stomach. It was hard and tight, just as she had known it would be. Ginny made little circular movements with her fingertips, tracing the name Tom lightly across his abdomen. She felt a slight stirring against the inside of her thigh. A ripple of pleasure ran through her body. It was all the encouragement she needed. Tom wanted her. He was as filled with desire as she was.

Ginny moved under the blanket and made her way slowly down Tom's body, kissing him gently, lovingly, following with fascination the line of hair from his chest, down to his belly button and into the mass of wiry pubic hair. She took him in her mouth, caressing him with her tongue, loving him. She felt his passion grow and her own rose to meet it. She moved her groin against his ankle and rubbed herself against him. Tom started to convulse and Ginny felt an explosion in her mouth. She savoured his taste and lost herself in her own rolling waves of pleasure.

★

Thel tried to get a couple of hours' sleep but it was useless. She had so much to think about. Tom. Sarah. Hal. The quiet darkness of her friends' apartment magnified her thoughts. She was relieved when morning finally dawned. She watched the sky slowly fade from inky black to purple, to deep blue and then finally to light, cloudless blue. It was going to be a lovely day. She could see that but she couldn't find any room in her heart to appreciate it. She felt heavy and sad as she dressed. How could this ever be made right?

In the hospital's reception area she stood for a moment drawing deep breaths, trying to transform her mood. She would be no help to Tom like this. A mural covered one wall. It was bright and childlike, showing children of all ages, smiling and playing. She focussed on a big balloon that one child held. It was bright bold yellow, cheery, like a fresh daffodil. Yellow always made Thel feel happy. She stood and stared at the balloon, absorbing the cheerful colour. After a few moments she walked into Tom's room.

The bed was empty. She assumed they had moved him out of casualty and went to ask the nurses at reception. Dr Hindson was standing nearby and heard her inquiry.

'He checked out a few hours ago,' Dr Hindson told Thel. 'His girlfriend took him home.'

Thel felt an immediate rush of panic. 'Sarah? Sarah came and took him?'

The way she phrased the question and her manner seemed odd to Dr Hindson.

'I guess so, a dark-haired girl. Late twenties,' she said.

'That's not Sarah.'

'I'm sorry. That's who he left with,' said Dr Hindson. Her beeper rang and she excused herself. When she turned back the woman had gone. Dr Hindson wondered for a moment what family drama might be going on but her beeper rang again and immediately she was absorbed in the next crisis of her day.

Thel walked straight to the public telephone and called Hal.

'He's gone,' she said. 'He left hours ago. But he's not at his flat because I just phoned there.'

Hal heard the panic in Thel's voice. 'Stay where you are. I'll be there in ten minutes.'

Tom felt the naked body beside him and snuggled into it. It was Sarah. Beside him, just like it used to be. He sighed and held her close, drifting off into a dreamless sleep. It was dark when he woke. His head throbbed. He thought he was in his own bed, under the blanket. Then he registered the carpet beneath his back and the sensations didn't add up. He was lying on a strange floor and there was a dark head on his chest that clearly wasn't Sarah's. He wondered where he was and how he had got there.

He had barely moved a muscle but Ginny sensed he was awake. She lifted her head and smiled lovingly at him.

'Hi there,' she said.

Tom's mind reeled. He jolted upright, knocking Ginny aside, as he struggled to get to his feet. He was shocked to find he was naked.

'Wassgoingon?' he slurred.

Ginny laughed with delight. He looked so comical standing there, clutching the blanket to him. After what she felt they had shared she was touched by his modesty.

'You must be starving,' she said happily, moving into the kitchen.

'Wherrmyclose?' asked Tom.

'Oh, don't you worry about that,' said Ginny. 'I'm washing them for you. They will be dry soon. Meanwhile, why don't you put on that dressing gown?'

Tom looked in horror at the fluffy white bathrobe lying over the chair.

'Wohmyclose.'

'Now, Tom, don't argue. Just relax and let me look after you.'

Tom felt horribly vulnerable, physically and emotionally.

He felt he had lost all control of his environment. It was like reading a book where someone had pulled out crucial pages and he couldn't piece together what was going on. Too much information was missing.

Somewhere along the way Ginny had become unhinged. That much was abundantly clear. She was fussing about in the kitchen humming to herself as she tied an apron around her naked waist. That he had to get out of there was blatantly obvious. The rest he just couldn't make sense of. Somehow he had to get his clothes and get past Ginny to the door. Reluctantly he took the bathrobe and put it on. It was way too small. He fought the rising nausea.

'Owlong?'

He meant how long till his clothes were ready but Ginny thought he was talking about food.

'Oh, you do have an appetite,' she twittered. 'Not long. Now just sit down and relax.'

Tom wanted to scream at Ginny, to throttle her, but he knew he didn't have the energy. He remembered her strength when he had tried to leave. How long ago was that? He wasn't wearing his watch. It felt like a long time since he had left the hospital but his memory was jumbled. His head hurt and he was so very tired.

Tom looked longingly at the door, then reluctantly sat down on the couch.

He looked across at Toft Monks. He saw his own empty apartment. The blinds were drawn. The lights were on in the apartment next door and he could see his neighbours, a young married couple, eating dinner at their table. He hadn't realised how close the apartment blocks were and how people in this block were able to see straight in. Ginny must have had a good view of them, he realised with a shudder. She could see right into their home.

The thought unsettled him. It was something else he would think about when he was away from here, safe and alone at home. Ginny offered him another scotch but Tom shook his head. He knew he needed his wits about him.

'Warda,' he said.

Ginny tittered. 'You need more than that, Tom. How about an orange juice?'

Tom nodded weakly.

Ginny bustled about in the kitchen, finding a glass and pouring Tom a juice. While Tom looked across at Toft Monks, she ground two sleeping pills into powder and slipped them into the glass, quickly stirring them about. She presented the glass to Tom, bending forward and brushing her breasts against his arm. Tom shrank from her touch. He was asleep before she served the food.

Hal pulled up outside the casualty entrance on a Harley. Thel was waiting outside scanning each car anxiously, looking for him. He was already standing by her side with two helmets before she noticed him.

'The doctor said a woman with dark hair collected him hours ago. Could that be Ginny?' said Thel. 'Did Ginny come and take him home?'

'Yes, of course. It was Ginny,' said Hal. 'Then I'm sure he's fine.'

Thel wasn't so sure. 'Why wasn't he at home then? I've just come from his apartment and he wasn't there.'

'Perhaps they stopped somewhere on the way . . . for breakfast.' Even Hal didn't think that sounded likely. Tom was in no state to be eating breakfast out. Hal imagined it would be a while before Tom would be enjoying any food at all.

'He may be home by now. Why don't you ring?'

Thel called again. Listening to Sarah's bubbly voice inviting her to leave a message exacerbated her fears.

'No. It's not right. I'm worried,' said Thel.

'Do you know where Ginny lives?' asked Hal.

'Somewhere in Elizabeth Bay. I've got her number.'

They stood by the kerb as Hal dialled Ginny's telephone number. When it started to ring he handed the mobile phone to Thel.

Ginny answered. 'Hello, Thel. How are you?' she said. She sounded relaxed and friendly as if it were perfectly normal for Thel to call for a chat.

'Is Tom with you?' said Thel.

'Yes. He is. Poor baby. He's sleeping.'

Thel nodded to Hal. 'Can I speak to him please?' said Thel.

'Oh no, I don't think I should wake him. He's been through so much. He's a very tired boy.'

It almost sounded reasonable. But Thel didn't like the sound of Ginny's voice, the intimate way she referred to Tom. All her alarm bells started ringing. She wanted to speak to her son.

'Ginny, please put him on. I need to speak to him.'

'I'm sorry, Thel, I can't hear you . . . this is a very bad line.'

The phone went dead. Thel dialled again but the phone was engaged. She repeated the conversation to Hal.

'Well that's okay then. He'll be fine with Ginny.'

The look on Thel's face showed she didn't share his relief. 'No. Something's not right. I can feel it. She didn't sound right.' Thel sat on the bike seat and looked at Hal. 'I've got to see him, Hal. I don't know why but I don't trust her.'

Hal had no reason to distrust Ginny. He was very grateful for how she had cared for Laddie. But he had enormous respect for Thel's intuition. And even if she was wrong and it was just the imaginings of an overwrought mother, he would indulge every one of them.

'Do you know any of their friends?' he asked.

'Yes. I know most of them. Kate and Anne and Marty.'

'Okay then. Let's go back to my place and we'll ring them.' One of them must know where Ginny lives.'

Thel looked at Hal with gratitude. Her expression both pleased and embarrassed him and he looked away.

When Tom woke he thought he was looking at the sky, beautiful faded blue, not a cloud to be seen. But it was a ceiling. He was lying on Ginny's couch and the sun was streaming through the windows. Kitty was curled up on his feet. Everything was quiet. He felt groggy and knew immediately he had been drugged.

Ginny was curled up on the floor beside him. She was sleeping peacefully with a gentle smile on her lips. Tom carefully prised his feet away from Kitty. She barely stirred. With exaggerated slowness and every muscle tensed, Tom lifted himself off the couch. With painstaking effort he placed both feet over Ginny onto the carpet beside her head and then moved his weight across. She sighed in her sleep.

Tom stood up and without daring to breathe, walked quietly to the door. He had his hand on the back of the door when Ginny awoke.

'Tom,' she said startled, jumping to her feet. 'Where are you going?'

Tom wrenched open the door just as Ginny flew at him. He lurched through the opening, then turned and slammed the door hard against Ginny's pleading face. She screamed in pain as the impact struck her, the full force knocking the breath from her body. She slid in a crumpled heap onto the floor as Tom bolted down the stairs, through the lobby and up the driveway.

Tom felt the world was coming to him through layers of cotton wool. The day was just dawning and it was very bright. He winced and stumbled onto the street. He recognised where he was. In his own street. Just a few doors down from his own apartment. A couple of gay guys walking home arm in arm from an all-night party whistled at him and he realised he was still wearing Ginny's bathrobe. He didn't care.

At Toft Monks he buzzed Andy the caretaker to let him in. Andy was far too discreet to comment on Tom's appearance. But he couldn't help a little smile in the lift as they travelled to the second floor. He let him into his silent apartment where Tom collapsed on the bed. For the next fourteen hours he slept. He could have been dead, so deep and dreamless was his sleep.

CHAPTER 18

Thel and Hal sat in the kitchen at Hal's neat terrace house, Laddie at their feet and the phone book between them.

They left a message at the theatre where Thel knew Kate was performing. She wasn't due in for a few more hours but the stage manager promised to pass on Hal's number.

They tried Ginny again at regular intervals but her phone was constantly engaged. They tried Tom also, leaving another message on his answering machine. Leaving the same message felt, momentarily, as if they were doing something.

'Maybe we should call the police,' said Thel.

'And tell them what? That you can't find your son? That he's with a girl you don't trust?'

Thel wavered. She knew Hal made sense but she wasn't used to being sensible. She lived on instinct and intuition. And all her intuition screamed out that something was wrong. Hal watched her. He wanted to be able to help but he wasn't sure how. He poured Thel another cup of tea and pushed it across the table to her. Laddie sensed the sombre

235

mood and sidled up to Thel's leg, licking gently at her open sandal. Thel patted him absently.

'There is another friend, Anne. She used to work with Sarah. But I don't know her last name,' she said. 'Kate would know. Oh I wish she would ring.'

'I think we just have to wait till she does,' he said. 'Thel, it's all going to be fine. Really.'

Thel allowed herself to be comforted. There was something incongruous about sitting in Hal's homely little kitchen, sharing her concern for her son with his father. It was how it should have been, she thought. How she had expected her life to be. But instead, those more than two decades of confusion and pain yawned open behind her.

'I remember the last time I sat with you. That was in a kitchen, a little kitchen not unlike this,' she said.

Hal nodded. 'I remember.'

They hadn't spoken about Hal's homosexuality. Concern for Tom had pushed it to the background. But it was there now, sitting between them. The silence stretched. Thel knew Hal was looking at her but she couldn't raise her eyes to meet his. She felt a profusion of emotions.

When she spoke her voice was soft and controlled. 'Why didn't you tell me?'

Hal looked away. He felt guilt at the pain he had caused this woman, shame for his cowardice in running away and most of all, right now, he was angry at himself that Thel and Tom had found out amongst all the flamboyance and decadence of the Mardi Gras parade. It was not how he wanted them to find out. Tom had said they would be there. But Hal hadn't really taken that in. He had been too preoccupied with his own role in the evening's festivities. Too concerned with himself. Hal wished it could have happened so differently. But they *had* found out that way and he searched for the right words to try to explain himself.

'I'm so sorry, Thel. I didn't know myself. It took me years to figure it out. Many, many wasted years. I didn't want to hurt you. When I left I hated myself. I had everything. You and Tom. Everything a man should want. But it was tearing me up inside. I had to go, to figure it out, figure myself out.'

His anguish was palpable. It touched Thel deeply. She felt the anger seep away as tears filled her eyes and poured down her face. She made no attempt to brush them away.

'I thought it was me,' she said. 'All this time I've thought it was me.'

Her voice was a whisper, plaintive and timid, barely audible. And in it Hal heard the anguish of those years. He felt his own face wet with tears.

'Oh Thel. I am so sorry. It wasn't you. It was never you.' He reached across the table and placed his hand over hers. He could feel her trembling.

Thel sat motionless, her tears falling in one long, soundless stream down her face, spilling onto their joined hands. It was cathartic. All the pent-up hurt of Hal leaving, the blame she took upon herself, her fears about her own womanliness, dissolved in her tears. Hal squeezed her hand and stayed silent, letting her tears shame him further. He had caused this and he felt he deserved it. He wanted it. It was as healing for him to share her grief as it was for Thel to give vent to it. When Thel's tears were spent they sat together, hands clasped, relaxed in the intimate silence.

It was early evening by the time Kate called. She was bright and breezy, fired up for her show that night, and from her manner Hal knew she was unaware of what had happened at the Mardi Gras. He wasn't about to tell her.

'Thel has something she needs to drop off to Ginny. Would you have an address for her?'

He tried to sound casual.

Kate didn't think it was an unusual request but was unable to help. 'I haven't been to Ginny's new flat. Sorry. Sarah would have the address, though. Why don't you ring her?'

'We've tried, she and Tom aren't home.'

Thel listened as Hal spoke. She mouthed the word 'Anne'.

'Would you have a number for Anne?'

Kate did and he wrote it down.

Thel dialled the number but there was no answer. She tried Ginny again. The line was still engaged. Hal thought for a moment.

'I know where Ginny works. We could go around there tomorrow.'

Thel didn't know whether she could wait that long. But she didn't feel as if she had a choice. She was exhausted, emotionally drained. She didn't feel like going back to her friends' place and being with people. She felt her worry for Tom alienated her from the rest of the world. Only Hal shared the space she was in. He understood and invited her to stay.

He made up a bed on the couch for himself and insisted she take his bed.

Thel snuggled under the sheets, looking about her at the male room. It all looked so unfamiliar, stark and bare. Hal stood at the door with his hand on the light switch.

'Good night, Thel.'

'Good night, Hal. And thank you.'

Dr Black was busy with an ailing ginger cat when Hal and Thel arrived at his surgery and Annie wasn't inclined to interrupt him. She was far too interested in Ginny's private life to even think about handing them over to Dr Black. She recognised Hal but wondered what connection Ginny had with the agitated dark-haired woman with the wild black hair and hippie skirt, carrying a bike helmet under her arm.

'I'm sorry,' said Annie. 'I can't give out personal details of our staff members.' She took great satisfaction as she said it to Hal, remembering how disinterested he had been in talking to her during his last visit. 'May I ask what it is regarding?'

Thel thought this young girl needed a good smack. She was tempted to give it to her. Hal placed a restraining hand on her arm.

238

'Our son was in an accident. We think he might be with Ginny so naturally we want to see him.'

'I see,' said Annie doubtfully.

The word 'accident' did put things in a different light.

'I could give you her telephone number. I suppose that would be all right.'

'We have that,' said Thel with obvious impatience. 'Either it's not working or she has been on the phone for the past two days. We need her address.'

Annie decided she might as well hand it over. Hell, she thought, it's not like she owed Ginny any favours.

Ginny was curled up in a foetal position in the corner of her bedroom and sucking her thumb when her intercom buzzed. She was oblivious of the world outside her own head. The carpet was dotted with small piles of cat dung and scratch marks where Kitty, locked inside, had tried to cover over soil that wasn't there. Ginny was unaware of the smell of the excrement mingled with the mouldy food, left untended on the dinner plates on the table.

She felt totally numb, her mind a void, unable to process what was happening. She was unaware of who she was or where she was. She rocked herself backwards and forwards, her head against the speaker, her whole being tuned in vain for sounds of Tom. Tom, who had gone. Tom, who had left her.

The buzzer rang again, loudly and insistently. For one wild moment Ginny thought it might be him returning. Tom, coming back to her. She raced to the intercom.

'Hello?'

'It's Thel. Can I come in please?'

Ginny felt the world swim about her. She was shaky on her feet. 'No, go away.' She hung up the hardset and leaned against the wall.

The intercom rang again, one long constant buzz, that jolted Ginny, the vibration spreading through her body. She snatched the handset off the wall.

'Go away.'

'I want to see Tom.'

'He's not here. Go away.' Ginny switched off the buzzer.

Thel and Hal rang for the caretaker at Toft Monks and in an instant Andy appeared.

'We're looking for Tom Wilson,' explained Hal.

'Have you seen him?' asked Thel.

Andy had a vision of Tom in the short white towelling bathrobe, clearly coming home after one hell of a party, and standing where they were now standing. He smiled to himself.

'Um, yes, I have seen Mr Wilson,' he replied carefully.

'We're his parents,' said Hal.

That was a surprise. They didn't look like what he would expect Mr Wilson's parents to look like, though the man was just as tall as Tom and did resemble him a little, now that he thought about it.

Andy had worked as a caretaker in Sydney for many years and he had witnessed all sorts of wild comings and goings, particularly on Mardi Gras weekend. But he prided himself on being discreet. He doubted whether any hot-blooded young man on a bender wanted his parents to know what he had been up to.

'Uh-huh,' he replied.

'Is he okay? He's not answering his phone or his door. We are worried about him,' said Thel.

Andy looked at her. She reminded him of his own mum. He would hate her to be worried. 'Oh, he was fine when I saw him. He's probably at work.'

'We tried there and they said he wasn't in.'

'Uh-huh,' said Andy again.

'When did you last see him?' asked Hal.

Andy thought for a moment. He knew exactly when it was that he had opened the door to find a dishevelled and disoriented Tom. But he wasn't sure that he should reveal that. He wavered and then decided in favour of the woman with the big sad brown eyes.

'Yesterday morning.'

'And he was fine?' asked Hal.

'Yes, he was fine,' said Andy.

There seemed nothing more to say so reluctantly Thel and Hal turned and walked away.

'Well, he's not being held prisoner by Ginny,' said Hal. 'He's been home and he's fine. You can relax, Thel. He's just gone to ground to lick his wounds. He'll surface when he is up to it.'

Thel had to agree that made sense and knowing that Tom had been home did ease some of her tension. But it didn't stop the acid gurgling in the pit of her stomach. She wouldn't relax till she could see him for herself. Touch him.

It was evening when Tom woke to the insistent ringing of the telephone. He lay in bed ignoring it. After a few minutes the answering machine picked it up. Whoever it was didn't leave a message. He lay listening to the sounds of the silent apartment. The fluffy white bathrobe lay in a heap on the floor by the bed. The sight of it was an abomination to him. He rolled over, facing the empty spot beside him. 'Sarah,' he moaned inwardly.

He got out of bed, aware that his body was stiff and he ached all over. At least his face had stopped throbbing. He smelled stale and sweaty. He wanted to wash, to be clean, to rid himself of all the ugliness of the past few days.

His face stared back at him from the bathroom mirror. He was shocked by his appearance. He looked like a drunk who had been living on the streets.

Blood had seeped through the bandage on his cheek and then dried. His jaw was swollen and the beginnings of a huge bruise, blue, black and yellow, spread across his chin like a birthmark. The other side of his face bore the imprint of the bed sheets, making the skin look like it had been folded.

Tom ran a bath. He didn't think he could stand for very long in the shower.

When he sat in the bath it was painfully hot and the steam

rose off the water in wisps, soaking his face and hair. He stared blankly at his naked knees. He didn't often have a bath. That was Sarah's domain. And everything around him was testament to that. There were bottles of shampoo and conditioner, bath bombs, scrubs, oils and all sorts of things that Tom couldn't identify. He sat perched in the middle of the bath, feeling uncomfortable in the feminine surroundings. Everything around him screamed of Sarah.

Then he cried. Soundlessly. Tears rose from deep within him and he let them run free to pour down his face and drop into the bath where they made soothing little sounds as they hit the water. When he was spent he dried himself carefully, took some pain-killers and went back to bed, crawling between the sheets. He didn't move again until the morning sun had crept across the bedroom floor, tugging at his closed eyelids.

With the new day came a very different world for Tom to face and make sense of. He had dozens of messages on his answering machine. Linda at the newspaper had called repeatedly, looking for him, wondering why he hadn't been at work for the past two days. Thel had called a few times. In the first call she sounded puzzled. In the next five calls she sounded increasingly frantic, then resigned. Each time she left Hal's mobile number. Tom felt a pang of guilt. Detective-Sergeant Paul McCracken from Paddington Police Station wanted him to call back urgently. He had also left a number. Kate and Anne, unaware of what had happened, left cheery messages for Sarah. No calls from Peter Hatfield at the *Daily News*. Tom was surprised. They obviously didn't know about it. Perhaps it hadn't made the wires. Too much else to focus on at the Mardi Gras, he supposed.

Tom's head was clear for the first time in days. He knew exactly what his priorities were. He wanted to know where Sarah was and what the hell had happened. He wanted to see her. And really that was all he could think about. He had some questions, big basic questions, that only she could answer. They went around and around in his head. He felt a kaleidoscope of emotions. He was angry, hurt, worried for her, disbelieving and confused. But mostly he was hurt. It bore down on him like a heavy weight, oppressing him, almost crushing him.

The episode with Ginny disgusted him. It was a surreal memory. He pushed it away.

Tom phoned a mate at police headquarters who told him a police doctor had had Sarah committed for psychiatric evaluation. She was currently under the care of Orchard Park Psychiatric Hospital. The paperwork was still being processed so he could tell Tom little more than that. She hadn't been charged. That would be why it hadn't made the newspapers. He gave Tom the number of the hospital.

'The police want to talk to you, Tom,' he said. 'They have her listed as a possible assault charge.'

Tom wondered how long this nightmare would continue. He dialled Orchard Park Psychiatric Hospital but they would give him no information. He would have to talk to the supervising psychiatrist, Dr Hubert. Tom left his number. Then Tom phoned Thel. She burst into tears at the sound of his voice.

'Where have you been? We have been so worried about you.'

'Sorry, Thel. Ginny picked me up from the hospital. Then I came home and I've just slept for days,' he lied, hoping it sounded plausible. He didn't want to tell Thel about Ginny. He didn't feel he had the stomach for it.

'Oh God, are you okay?'

'Yes, I'm fine.'

Relief washed over Thel like a cool, refreshing wave. 'I'm coming around now.'

Tom knew better than to argue and he didn't want to. He wanted to see Thel. She would provide some sanity in the midst of this madness. She was also the one person who may be able to help him understand what had happened at the Mardi Gras.

Ten minutes later Thel was standing in his kitchen piling plastic containers of soup from the local deli into Tom's fridge.

'You look terrible,' she said.

Tom sat quietly in the kitchen while Thel fussed around him. She alternated between being bossy and being sympathetic. He accepted both patiently.

'We tried everywhere to find Ginny's address. I was so angry that she wouldn't let me speak to you. Why did you go there?'

Tom could tell by Thel's tone she was beginning to relax. He didn't want to start her worrying all over again.

'Oh, stop worrying, Thel. I'm home and I'm fine,' he said vaguely. He wanted to talk to his mother about Sarah. 'What happened?' he asked Thel. 'You were there. The last thing I remember is chasing after Hal's float, seeing Sarah upset in the crowd and then chasing after her. It's all such a blur. I remember her screaming at me . . . then I was on the ground . . . and there were police.'

Thel took a seat opposite him. Tom could see the lines of worry etched into her face.

'I'm sorry, darling. I don't know. I didn't see Sarah after we were sitting watching the parade.'

'How did I get to the hospital?'

'Hal and I took you in the ambulance. We saw police and a lot of commotion and we realised it was you on the stretcher. We didn't see what happened before that.'

Tom shook his head. 'I just don't get it.'

'Neither do I.' Thel looked tenderly at her son. 'Why don't you come down to Kiama for a few days? You need to take some time out. The sun and quiet will do you good.'

Tom shook his head. 'I can't. I need to see Sarah. I need to talk to her.'

Thel understood. She had a few questions of her own for Sarah.

'Sarah didn't seem herself at all on Saturday,' said Thel. 'I noticed it as soon as I arrived. She seemed uptight. On edge. I wondered if she was on drugs.'

Tom looked shocked. The thought hadn't occurred to him. 'Sarah never touches anything like that. She barely takes an aspirin. And as you know she hardly drinks.'

'I know. I figured it was unlikely. But she definitely wasn't herself.'

Tom thought of the past few months and the way their relationship had soured so inexplicably.

'She's been uptight a lot lately,' Tom admitted. 'She's been obsessive. Something has been bothering her, eating away at her. But I don't know what.'

'Could it be the wedding?'asked Thel.

'Why do you say that?'

'Because getting married can add an extra strain to a relationship. It makes you question all sorts of things – about your relationship, about your partner, about yourself.'

Tom considered Thel's suggestion. 'Maybe.'

'Was she upset that her parents couldn't come?'

'Yes, but it wasn't exactly a huge shock.'

Thel remembered the young girl Tom had brought home. She had seemed vivacious and confident but Thel had seen straight through that to the lonely person inside. Now that she could see for herself that her son was okay she turned all her attention to Sarah.

'Had the bulimia returned?'

'I think so. You know how hard it is to tell. She has just been so . . . aggressive. I don't know if that is a sign of bulimia or not. I don't remember that last time. But for the past few weeks, months, she has been like a powder keg, ready to explode. At me or at anyone who gets in her way.'

Tom recalled the incident at the RTA. Thel didn't read the papers and probably wouldn't know about that. Tom didn't feel inclined to bring it up. He felt angry, hurt and confused about Sarah. But he also felt protective. He changed the subject.

'So Hal is gay.'

Thel nodded. They were both quiet for a moment.

'Did you know?' asked Tom. He looked at his mother.

She couldn't meet his gaze. How could she not have

known? She had known gay men. Why had it never occurred to her? She felt so foolish. 'No. I guess maybe I should have, but I didn't.'

'Wow,' said Tom. 'That was some way to find out, seeing him in the parade.'

'On a float with the leather men,' added Thel.

The incongruity of it struck them both at the same time. Thel started to laugh. She laughed and laughed, holding her sides when they started to ache. Tom stared at his mother uncomprehendingly. At that moment she didn't look like his mother. Then before Tom realised what he doing, he was joining in. It felt good.

'My dad, the leather man,' said Tom. 'Didn't you ever suspect he was gay?'

'No,' replied Thel. 'You've got to remember we were very young when we married. We were both so innocent.'

Tom tried to imagine his parents as a young couple, innocent and unaware. He couldn't do it. He saw them through eight-year-old eyes and the memories were too vague and coloured by distance.

Thel tried to explain. 'In those days it wasn't as acceptable as it is now. Homosexuality was considered an aberration, a sickness that you had to be cured of.'

Tom nodded. 'Why did you never remarry?'

Thel looked away. 'I could have, I suppose. There were a couple of possibilities along the way. But it was quite tough on me, as a woman, being rejected in that way. I guess for a long time I lost my faith in myself.'

Tom tried to understand. Thel had always been so open with him about sex and yet he had never seen his mother as a sexual being. He got up and started to move around the room, restless. Thel watched him.

'I don't think any kid wants to imagine his parents having a sex life. You want to change the subject?' she said with a smile.

After Thel left, Tom phoned Dr Hubert again. This time he was in but not very helpful. Tom had dealt with enough doctors in his job to expect that. They were extremely reluctant to discuss patients with anyone but the immediate family and then not normally on the telephone. All Tom learned was that yes, Sarah was there, and yes, she was being treated by Dr Hubert. Tom made an appointment to see him the following day.

He phoned Linda at the newspaper to explain he had been in an accident and would need the rest of the week off. The police he would worry about later. If they wanted him, he thought, they would have to come and get him. He needed to know a lot more before he would help them put Sarah in jail.

He wandered aimlessly about the apartment. It was the home he had made with Sarah and without her in it, it felt oddly empty. Yet it was full of their things: photos, ornaments, paintings they had bought together. Things that on their own didn't mean anything. Everything in it harked back to a happier time.

He found himself standing at the balcony doors looking across at the opposite building. He had never really noticed it before, always looking past it to appreciate the harbour view. He thought he knew which balcony belonged to Ginny's apartment. It looked different from the others. He could see lounge rooms and bedrooms in the other apartments, but Ginny's was a blank. The windows and doors reflected Toft Monks back to him. The apartment looked as if it had no soul of its own.

Tom recalled what it had been like inside. The stuffed cat. Ginny in a sexy gown coming on to him. The bizarre seduction scene she had set up. She had knocked him out and stripped him naked. He remembered the sight of her head on his chest. The two of them naked and entwined under the blanket. He wondered what had happened. She didn't, did she? She couldn't have. But then he wouldn't have. Would he? He had an uncomfortable memory of something happening. He hoped he had dreamed it.

Tom went back over the years, remembering conversations he had with Ginny. He had got on well with Ginny. She was pleasant enough. She was Sarah's best friend. He didn't see her in any light other than that. But now that he analysed his feelings for her, he realised he had never truly liked her. The realisation surprised him. There had always been something unsettling about her, an intensity that made her uncomfortable to be around. He had seen her look at him in a way that seemed odd. But he had assumed she was like that with everyone. He had been too uninterested to give it much thought.

What had she said? That she had always loved him. That they were meant to be together. Tom felt the disgust well up inside him. He shuddered. He didn't want to think about her.

He thought back over his conversation with Thel. She had noticed something wrong with Sarah on Saturday. She had suggested drugs. Tom was sure Sarah didn't take drugs. It was too out of character. She was obsessed with fitness. He tried to imagine her shooting up heroin in the bathroom without him knowing. The image just didn't fit. But there were those mood swings, her aggression.

Tom went into the bathroom. He slid open the mirrored cabinet. It was a sight he looked at every day but never really noticed. His shaving gear. Sarah's hair dryer. Spare toothpaste. Sarah's beauty creams. Suntan lotion. Vitamin pills, C and B complex. He opened each of the vitamin jars and looked inside. He didn't really know what he was looking for but he was satisfied they looked like vitamin pills. He reached up to the shelf and brought down the blue ice-cream container that held their first aid supplies. Bandaids. Throat lozenges that were well past their use-by date. Mercurochrome. Iodine. A bandage. Mouthwash. Pills for period pain. Cotton wool. Everything looked terribly normal.

Tom moved into the bedroom. He opened the drawers beside Sarah's side of the bed. It felt strange to be rifling through her things. He had never looked in here before. There were a couple of books. A bridal magazine. Some bed socks. A couple of photos of him. Hair clips. Chewing gum. A walkman and two tapes.

How well do you really know someone? he thought. How well did Thel know Hal? Not at all as it turned out.

He pulled out a pile of letters buried at the bottom of the drawer and sat on the bed to read them. One was from him when he was in London on a story. He remembered writing it. He had been missing her badly and decided to write and tell her, even though he knew he would be home before she received the letter. It was the only love letter he had ever written. The others were bright and breezy letters from her mother, monologues about their oh-so-fabulous life in Singapore. She signed each of them simply 'Geraldine'. He skimmed them then put them back, feeling guilty for invading her privacy.

There was nothing in there that would suggest she was taking drugs.

Tom sat in the waiting room at Orchard Park. It was a majestic old sandstone building but inside it looked much like any other public hospital, except for the locked cage doors at the end of the corridor. Sarah would be through there, thought Tom. His heart ached for her. How she would hate that. He wondered what she was doing, what she was thinking. Did she hate him? Was that what this was all about? Or was she really mad?

Dr Hubert kept him waiting for half an hour. Every second was agonising for Tom. He rifled through a *National Geographic* that was two years old. He looked blankly at the photo essay of National Fly Swatting Day in China. Hundreds of thousands of Chinese catching flies and presenting them in jars to the judges. That could take off in Australia, he thought idly. Finally a silver-haired man appeared in the doorway.

'Mr Wilson?' Dr Hubert was a grave-faced, short man with a neat silver goatee, steel-rimmed glasses and a jaunty tartan bow tie. 'Sorry to keep you waiting. It's been a rather hectic morning.'

Tom greeted the doctor then followed him down the grey linoleum towards the locked cage doors. He expected they would go through the doors and for a moment thought he was being taken straight to Sarah, but just as they drew close Dr Hubert veered off to the right and motioned him through an open doorway.

It was a basic meeting room, like those in police stations or employment offices. It was bare except for a wooden table and chairs in the centre of the room.

'I'm afraid my office is being painted but we shouldn't be disturbed in here,' the doctor explained.

They took their places opposite each other. Dr Hubert had a manila folder with 'Sarah Cowley' written on it sideways in red capital letters. Seeing her name there made Tom's stomach lurch. The last vestige of hope that Sarah wasn't really here and that it had all been a ghastly mistake disappeared. Dr Hubert placed the file on the table in front of him, his hands clasped on top.

Tom looked into his kindly, intelligent face.

'I am Sarah's fiancé,' said Tom. 'How is she?'

Dr Hubert studied the battered face in front of him, the vivid blue eyes focussed intently on him and the voice thick with concern. He remembered the wildcat who had been brought in on Saturday night, kicking and screaming abuse at the attendants. If this was her fiancé, heaven help him, he thought.

'Did Sarah do this?' he asked, gesturing to Tom's face.

'Yes,' replied Tom reluctantly. He took a deep breath then explained what had happened. How Sarah had looked anxious and stressed, how he had followed her into the alley and how she had attacked him. He was surprised by his own reticence. The account he gave was accurate enough but he was aware he was feeling defensive for Sarah, and trying to play it down. It was instinctive.

'She was cornered. She looked . . . I don't know . . . like a trapped animal. She didn't seem to know where she was or who I was,' said Tom. His voice had a faint pleading quality that the doctor noted. 'I don't believe she attacked me because she wanted to hurt me. She loved me. We were to be married.

Are to be married.' Tom was hoping that was true. If he ignored the recent hell their lives had become, he could almost convince himself.

'Is there a history of violence in your relationship?' asked Dr Hubert.

Tom looked blankly at the doctor. It wasn't just that the question was unexpected, he didn't understand the concept.

'Has she attacked you before? Hit you or been violent in any way?'

'No,' said Tom. 'Never.'

'Have you ever hit her?'

'Good heavens, no.'

'I see,' said Dr Hubert in a flat tone that betrayed nothing. Dr Hubert instinctively believed that Tom hadn't been violent. But he was by profession and by nature a cautious man. He wouldn't rely on his instincts alone. He also wasn't sure he believed that Sarah had not been violent towards him in the past. He considered it a possibility that it may have been a pattern in their relationship. In his twenty-eight years of practice he had encountered battered husbands. They weren't as common as battered wives but nevertheless they were out there. It was just as demeaning to the male psyche and often they would stay in denial, rather than admit to the shame of abuse.

Dr Hubert had read the police report of Sarah's outburst in the RTA office. He had wiped a gob of spit from his arm which Sarah had placed there during her rage while being admitted to his care. He had seen the anger and pain in her wildly staring eyes and felt the force of her demented energy as she raged out of control. He believed he was treating a disturbed young woman, prone to psychotic outbursts. It was too soon for him to make a diagnosis. His approach was to calm her down, settle her into a routine and, when she was back on an even keel, he would work on unravelling her neuroses.

'What do you do for a living, Mr Wilson?'

Tom briefly outlined his job.

'Sarah tells me her parents live overseas,' said Dr Hubert.

'We have been having trouble locating them. The number Sarah gave us is disconnected.'

Tom was surprised. As far as he knew, Sarah had spoken to them just last week. She must have given the hospital staff a wrong number. That gave him some clue to how she felt. She obviously didn't want them knowing she was in here.

'Would you have any idea how we could get in touch with them?'

Tom shook his head.

Dr Hubert assumed he had been given the wrong number. It wouldn't be the first time a patient had done that.

Sarah's reaction when he had started to ask about her parents had also suggested a tender spot. When she revealed she had been sent away at the age of ten he had asked, in his mildest doctor tone, if she minded that.

She had screamed at him.

'What do you fucking think?'

Dr Hubert had written down her response in the file that was now sitting under his clasped hands.

That had seemed to incense Sarah further and she had screamed at him again. *'What the fuck are you writing down? That's* my *life. How dare you?'*

Dr Hubert hadn't been offended. He expected it would be a long process, just to get her to trust him, to work with him not against him. He had made further notes to himself about lines to pursue in future sessions. Issues with authority? Dr Hubert thought of Sarah's blood test results that he had received that day. They had been taken as a matter of course the morning after she was committed. They clearly indicated steroids were present in Sarah's system. He wondered if drugs might be part of her lifestyle.

'As far as you are aware, did Sarah ever take illegal narcotics?'

Tom hesitated. He didn't think so but could he be sure? The idea had been planted in his head by Thel. His eyes betrayed his uncertainty, which Dr Hubert was quick to notice.

'Not as far as I know.' It sounded lame to Tom's own ears. He thought he sounded like he was hiding something. 'She was very health conscious,' he said firmly. 'She wouldn't even take aspirin.'

Dr Hubert watched Tom's eyes sidle off his to somewhere over his left shoulder. He seemed to find something of interest there but Dr Hubert knew, without looking, that it was a blank wall.

'Are you aware she had a high level of synthetic hormone in her system?'

Tom shook his head. A hormone. It sounded like something a gynaecologist might prescribe. Sarah had suffered some problems as a result of the bulimia and had taken different medications but that was years ago. As far as he knew everything had returned to normal.

'No. Could her doctor have prescribed it?' asked Tom.

'Not likely. But can I have the numbers of Sarah's doctor?'

Tom nodded. He wondered if he should tell him about the bulimia. He decided against it. He was surprised and a little intimidated by the doctor's attitude. He wasn't completely sure that they were on the same side. Tom wrote down the name and number of Sarah's doctor and watched Dr Hubert slide it into the file under his hands. Tom glimpsed a stack of papers, then the folder was shut and Dr Hubert placed his hands over it again, almost protectively.

'Does she ever take cocaine, LSD, marijuana or any other recreational drugs?'

'No. Definitely not,' said Tom.

Tom was convincing but Dr Hubert knew a lot about twenty-something lifestyles in inner Sydney. He spent much of his free time sitting in the sparsely furnished backroom of an underfunded Kings Cross halfway house, counselling drug addicts. They didn't all come from disadvantaged, broken homes. Drug abuse cut across all strata of society. Dr Hubert would continue to consider drugs a possibility until he could rule them out definitively.

Dr Hubert looked at his watch and stood to leave. 'Thank you for coming, Mr Wilson. I assure you we will take good care of Sarah.'

Tom felt the situation slipping out of his control. He had come here expecting to see Sarah and somehow make sense of this madness. Instead, he was floundering.

'Can I see her?'

Dr Hubert assumed an expression of caring solicitude. He liked this young man but he was thinking of his patient. She was a young woman in crisis, vulnerable and suffering great emotional pain. He would do everything he could to protect her.

'I'm afraid not, Mr Wilson. Not right now.'

He moved towards the door, Sarah's file tucked under his arm.

'But I'm her fiancé. I have every right to see her. You can't stop me,' sputtered Tom.

Dr Hubert looked over the top of his glasses at Tom. He tried to put it as gently as he could. 'I have every right. Sarah was brought in by the police and turned over to my care. At this stage I don't think it would do her any good. She is . . .' He searched for the right words. 'A little . . . unstable. When she has settled down, perhaps in a few days, we will reconsider the situation. I have your number and we will contact you. Feel free to ring at any time to talk to me. Goodbye, Mr Wilson.'

Tom felt the frustration welling up inside him as Dr Hubert disappeared through the doorway. He thumped the table angrily.

In the hallway Dr Hubert recognised the thud and made a mental note. When he got back to his own office he would record it in the file. He would also add his thoughts about the possibilities of domestic violence and drug use. He wasn't making judgements. They were just new avenues to pursue.

Thel dished the takeaway Thai dinner onto plates and served Tom and Hal. The three of them sat around the kitchen table dissecting what Tom had told them of his visit to the hospital. Tom felt defeated. He had gone to the hospital with some vain hope of sorting it out, whatever 'it' might be, and bringing Sarah home. Instead, he felt as though he had been interrogated. He felt completely powerless in the face of Dr Hubert's authority. It was late when Hal left and Thel moved into the spare bedroom. She wasn't quite ready to let her son out of her sight.

CHAPTER 19

*I'm starting to get it now. It's a game and we're on different teams.
I'm with the Losers. How did that happen? I didn't choose that team.
I shouldn't be here.*

*They've got it all wrong. But they don't listen to the Losers.
What would we know? When you play for the Losers you become
invisible.*

*Well, I quit, resign, give notice, decamp, renounce, haul my arse
out of here. I ain't playing for the Losers. In fact, I ain't playing. Full
stop.*

*Tonight I'm going in. I'm breaking into the whale's chest cavity.
I want to see my innards. They keep having a good look at them,
poking around inside me. I want to know what they think they've
found. After all, they're my innards.*

Tom was glad Thel was staying. The apartment didn't seem
so lonely knowing she was on the other side of the wall. But
he knew he would have trouble sleeping. He wandered into
the kitchen to pour a glass of scotch. His hands were shaky

and he knocked the sugar bowl onto the floor as he was reaching for a glass. The bowl shattered into a dozen pieces, spilling sugar all over the kitchen floor. He stepped through the mess, grinding the broken porcelain under his feet with a satisfying crackling sound. He would clean it up tomorrow, he thought wearily. He took his drink into the lounge room and collapsed onto the couch. The lights from Toft Monks reflected back at him from Ginny's apartment, mocking him. He downed the glass and hurled it at the wall. It didn't break, but left a dent in the plaster, then bounced off, rolling across the carpet. Tom was disappointed. He wanted it to smash into a thousand pieces.

It was nearly 4 am when Tom woke drenched in sweat. He had had a nightmare. Some nameless terror that he couldn't recall. The aftertaste was bitter and he was aware of something horrible looming elusively just outside his grasp.

His mind cranked into gear. *Sarah. Dr Hubert. Synthetic hormone. Unstable. Had he ever hit her?* They were jumbled thoughts, chasing each other like droplets in a waterfall, disconnected, propelled by their own energy. *Ginny. I've always loved you. We can be together now. Now. Now.*

Tom wanted to clear his head. He needed to think. He had to piece this together. Something niggled at the back of his brain but whenever he felt he was getting close to it, other thoughts crowded in on top. He tried to make himself relax. He took his mind back to when he was a child. When he had been stressed, Thel had made him close his eyes, picture a campfire and told him to listen to the smoke. It had always helped him relax and he often used the technique when he had trouble sleeping. He lay like that for about twenty minutes, watching tendrils of smoke swirl into abstract shapes above his imaginary fire. He turned his mind inward to listen to the smoke.

Instead of drifting off to sleep he opened his eyes. He no longer felt tired. He was completely alert. The waterfall of thoughts had slowed to a gently meandering stream. One phrase bubbled to the surface. *Synthetic hormone.* Tom had seen that phrase before, a lot. There were pages and pages about synthetic hormones sitting in his briefcase.

He turned on the kitchen light, shielding his eyes. The sugar bowl lay broken on the polished wood floor, the sugar spilled around it. Tom stared down at it while his eyes grew accustomed to the light. As his focus cleared he realised he was looking at a mass of black dots amongst the spilled sugar. When he looked closer he recognised they were ants, dozens and dozens of dead ants. He frowned. That was odd. He was used to seeing ants in the kitchen. But not dead. Why would they be dead, he wondered. He should clean it up before Thel got up.

Instead, he sat at the table and opened his briefcase. He rummaged through the various papers and pulled out a wad of pages stapled together. He knew what he was looking for. It was a report he had downloaded from the internet, taken from America's National Institute on Drug Abuse and part of their Research Report Series. He looked first under the definition for steroids.

> 'Anabolic steroids' is the familiar name for synthetic sub-stances related to the male sex hormones (androgens). They promote the growth of skeletal muscle (anabolic effects) and the development of male sexual characteristics (androgenic effects), and also have some other effects.

Of course. Steroids was the colloquial name for synthetic hormones. Tom knew the horror side effects of steroid abuse. For months he had been poring over pages of research all about it. He had been immersed in the topic every working moment – talking to doctors, sportspeople and body builders about every facet of it. He flicked to the section of the report titled 'Side Effects'. It was a well-worn page with a dirty coffee stain in the top corner. He had re-read this page at least once a week while writing his series of articles.

The side effects were horrific and he knew them by heart.

He had concentrated only on the effects on men. The incidence of steroid abuse in women was so small he had planned to run it as a sidebar in his final article. He re-read the section with a fresh eye, as if seeing it for the first time.

In the female body anabolic steroids cause masculinisation. Breast size and body fat decrease, the skin becomes coarse, the voice deepens. Women may experience excessive growth of body hair, oily hair and skin, acne and an increase in sexual desire.

Tom turned the page. *Psychiatric effects: Homicidal rage, mania, delusions.*

How could he have been so stupid? Why hadn't he seen this before? Sarah had almost all of those symptoms. He leaned back in the chair, overwhelmed by the torrent of emotions that washed over him. Relief, shame at his own stupidity, sudden blinding understanding.

Sarah was on steroids. He felt like laughing and crying at the same time. Why was she taking them? The reason didn't matter. He didn't care. She would stop and everything would return to normal. They could get back to their life together. He would get his Sare Bear back.

'Oh Sarah,' he said aloud to the empty kitchen. 'Why did you do this?'

He looked at the dead ants on the floor. He didn't register them. He was remembering what Thel had said about marriage bringing up so many fears.

'You're not training for a marathon, my darling. Marriage to me won't be that hard, I promise you.'

Tom thought about the world of body builders and athletes, which he had been immersed in for the past few months. To obtain steroids you had to be part of that world. He had discovered that steroids were readily available through an underground network that was prevalent in the many private gyms in inner Sydney.

But Sarah wasn't a member of a gym. Nor did she know any elite athletes, as far as he knew. She would go for her run

every day, on her own, through the park. Did she meet someone secretly? He didn't like that thought. How much of her
life did he not know? he wondered. How would she have got
hold of steroids? He hadn't found any evidence of them
amongst her things. And why would she do that? She was
obsessive about her body. She bought organic vegetables for
God's sake. She hated artificial substances. That's why she
wouldn't take drugs.

His eyes continued to roam over the papers in front of him,
but he took in little of what they said.

Steroid abusers typically 'stack' the drugs, meaning that
they take two or more different anabolic steroids, mixing
oral and/or injectable types, sometimes even including
compounds that are designed for veterinary use.

Tom stopped at the word 'veterinary'. It jarred for him. It
snagged at his brain. It was like seeing someone in a room
that didn't fit. A homeless drunk in a corporate boardroom.

Veterinary use. A vet. Sarah knew a vet. Ginny. The
thought of Ginny conjured up a new vision. Ginny in a black
satin sheath. Ginny naked, entwined around him. Ginny
wearing just an apron, brushing her breasts against his arm.
Ginny with that mad look of lust in her eyes. Repulsion rose
in him like black vomit. He read the sentence again. '. . .
sometimes even including compounds that are designed for
veterinary use.' Had Sarah got steroids from Ginny?

Tom thought his head would explode. He felt there was
something here, something nearly within his grasp. If only he
could figure it out.

He walked into the lounge room and looked out across the
water at Ginny's apartment.

Did you give her steroids? he thought. Was it you? Have you
been feeding my Sarah with this poison? His loathing for Ginny
had been growing, festering beneath his awareness. He walked
back into the kitchen, his mind racing, filled with possibilities.
They seemed wild and fanciful, unbelievable. But he let them
run, following each tangent until another occurred to him.

He needed a drink. He stepped over the sugar bowl and its splayed contents, noting again the dead ants. Why were they dead? He reached for a fresh glass, his hand stopping, frozen in midair. It hit him like a physical blow. Why were they dead?

'*I've always loved you. We can be together now.*' Ginny's voice rang loudly in his head. He recognised the implication. *Now?* Why now? Now that Sarah was out of the way?

He bent down to inspect the ants. There were dozens of them, dotted through the sugar, each curled up. He poked his finger through the pile, as if sorting the ants from the sugar grains. Carefully, he spread the mound across the wooden floor. He noticed a fine white powder, the colour of sugar, but a different texture. He pulled a magnifying glass out of the junk drawer and peered over the mess. The sugar grains were large in comparison, some bound together where they had come into contact with moisture. But there was also a distinctive white powder. The sugar reflected the light, like small crystals, but the powder was flat. The difference was almost imperceptible. Tom wet his finger and placed it on the fine white powder. He put his finger to his lips. He didn't know what steroids would taste like but he certainly knew the sweetness of sugar. The taste on his tongue wasn't sweet. It was dry, cloying, like the scent of deodorant that clings to your tongue.

Tom sat back on his feet. He barely dared to breathe, his body frozen as his mind took flight. He didn't know how or when but Ginny had planted steroids in their sugar bowl. He was absolutely certain of it. She would have had plenty of opportunity. God, she had a key to their apartment. He had given it to her. When was that? Around Sarah's birthday. Four months ago. Oh God.

Sarah. Oh Sarah. She wouldn't have known why she was feeling so aggressive or why her body was changing. He replayed the past few months over in his head, seeing it all differently. Funny how the same scenes seen with new information had a completely different meaning. He saw the fights, Sarah's manic obsession with exercise, her aggression in bed, her skin breakouts, her sweaty body odour. All of it made sense. How could he not have seen it? He was such a fool. He had let her down. How she must have suffered. How she must be suffering now.

Tom had to get her out. Away from those mad people. Away from that pompous ass in the white coat who wouldn't let him see her. She didn't belong in there.

At that moment Sarah was quietly padding down the corridor of the hospital. For the past few nights she had been storing her sleeping pills in her cheek then slipping them into the toilet. While the women around her spent the night hours passed out in a drug-induced torpor, she had been paying careful attention to what went on in the creaky hospital between midnight and dawn.

There were three heavy security doors, one at the front near the reception desk where two night nurses were stationed, another at the back entrance where the security guard sat and one in the middle to keep the men from wandering into the women's wards at night. Because of fire regulations the wards were kept unlocked.

Sarah's ward was at the front of the building, separated from the dayroom by the main corridor. As long as she kept out of sight of the main desk, she figured she could get to the dayroom unnoticed.

She waited till she heard the cage door lock. That meant the nurse had done her rounds and was safely back at the front desk. Sarah crept out of her room and along the corridor. The only sound was the light swishy noise her bare feet made on the polished linoleum. She reached the section where the two corridors met and listened for a moment. The nurses were watching television and talking in low voices. Sarah crawled along on her stomach past their line of sight. The dayroom was around a bend at the other end of the corridor. She could no longer hear the nurses or the television. The only sound was the fruit bats chattering in the huge Moreton

Bay fig tree outside the window. She quietly closed the door behind her.

At the other end of the room was the nurses' office. It had three glass walls so they could see what everyone was up to and a window that looked outside. Sarah sorted through the pile of games in a bookshelf and selected a heavy wooden pencil box. Wrapping it in a crocheted knee rug which she found on a chair, she smashed a small pane of glass in the office door. The sound of breaking glass seemed loud in the empty room. Sarah crept back and opened the dayroom door to listen. Everything was silent. She expected to hear the security grille being unlocked and see the nurses rushing down the corridor armed with syringes and straitjackets, but no-one came. Relieved, she let herself into the nurses' office.

She knew exactly which drawer she was after in the old grey filing cabinet. She wanted the one marked C–E, where she knew her file was kept. It was an old steel cabinet with warped drawers and Sarah was surprised how easily it opened. One tug brought it flying into her chest. She quickly located her file and moved across to stand beside the window where the security lights outside shone enough light into the room for her to read. It would be dawn soon and she knew she had to hurry.

Sarah opened the folder and started reading. On top was the report of her arrival.

Psychotic rage. Abusive. Her memory of that was sketchy and painful. She quickly moved on.

Parents absent. Patient aggressive when questioned. Sarah remembered that session. Dr Hubert sitting there looking down his beaked nose at her. She had never felt so powerless. They were such personal memories, so painful. Why should she have to talk about them to this stranger? Who the hell was he to ask her such things? She had found his attitude insufferable. He sat there asking the most personal questions, deciding her life for her. Writing it all down.

Stelazine. 5 mg capsules. 4 per day. Yeah right. Not any more, thought Sarah with satisfaction.

Fiancé Tom Wilson. Journalist. Battered partner? Seems to care for patient. Abusive relationship? Tom. He had been here? Sarah felt a rush of warmth. Why didn't they let me see you? Oh Tom, I wish you were here now.

The last page was the results of a blood test. *High presence of synthetic hormone, Limodol.*

Next to it, in a different handwriting, was the query *habitual steroid abuser?*

Sarah gasped. What the hell? No, I'm not. They've made a mistake.

She remembered Tom's stories on steroid abuse, the body builder he had met in Canberra who had beaten his wife in a roid rage. Sarah felt suddenly clammy. She sat heavily in a chair. Her legs felt weak and unable to hold her. Did she have steroids racing through her system? She pictured them as angry red little heads, coursing through her bloodstream, ready to attack.

The idea of them inside her, part of her, was abhorrent. She was repulsed by her own body. How would they have got inside her? She wasn't shooting up steroids into her muscles. It made no sense. But something about it did. She had not been herself. For a while now. She had felt out of control of her emotions and her body. It had frightened her. She had justified it in all sorts of ways. Steroids had never occurred to her. But then, why would it? She closed her eyes and breathed in deeply.

Sarah closed the file. This didn't make sense. It did, but it didn't. She wasn't sure what she would do next. Tell Dr Hubert? He already knew. And it didn't seem to work in her favour as far as he was concerned. Sarah couldn't see that Dr Hubert was on her side, trying to help her. She felt trapped within the system and he was her jailer. He thought she was a loon and that was that. Normal people didn't fly into psychotic rages. She had stepped across a line, the line that separated normal people with all their rights from the rest, the ones who had lost their rights. She was in 'the system' now and normal rules didn't apply. She needed Tom. He would know how to sort this out. She had to get out of here. She had to get to Tom. The thought of Tom made her want to cry. What had she done to him? Would he ever forgive her? Would he even believe her?

Oh Tom. Help me.

Sarah looked outside. It wasn't long till dawn and the sky in the east had started to lighten. The fruit bats in the Moreton Bay fig tree were awake and chattering to each other as they prepared to fly off for the day. She supposed she should go back to bed. It wouldn't help her cause if they found her in here. As it was there would be questions in the morning when they discovered the office door was missing a pane of glass.

But going to bed felt like giving in. She wasn't sure she could face that bed with its scratchy white overstarched sheets and the mad mutterings of the other women. She didn't belong here. She wanted to get out. She looked with longing, through the bars, at the world outside. She felt defeated.

She watched the fruit bats leaving the tree as they started their daily journey back to the Botanic Gardens. How lucky they were, she thought. She wondered how long it would be till she savoured that freedom again.

The huge old hospital building seemed to be asleep.

Sarah felt the frustration well inside her. She picked up the phone and dialled her own number. She heard her own voice inviting her to leave a message.

'Tom,' she whispered as loudly as she dared, 'pick up the phone. It's me. Please help me. They think I'm on steroids. I'm not. They think I'm mad. You've got to get me out of here.' Sarah slumped to the ground, the phone still to her ear. 'Oh Tom,' she sobbed. 'Tom . . .'

Thel was first out of bed. She was cleaning up the sugar when Tom appeared.

'Leave it,' he said sharply.

Thel looked at him.

'It's evidence . . . for the police,' he said.

Thel's eyes widened. Tom showed her the fine powder amongst the grains of sugar.

'I don't believe it,' she said. 'Ginny put steroids in here?'

Tom nodded. He told his mother what he had figured out, telling her about Sarah's rage at the RTA and showing her his notes on steroids. Thel read about the side effects and thought back to Sarah's edgy behaviour at the Mardi Gras.

'Oh, poor Sarah,' she said. 'Why would Ginny do that?'

Tom remembered the episode in Ginny's apartment, the look of crazed lust in her eyes, her mad ravings as she wafted around dressed in just an apron. He shivered with disgust at the memory, unwilling to reveal it to his mother.

'That's for the police to figure out.'

Thel stared at him. 'Poor, poor Sarah. We've got to do something. Get dressed and then let's go to the police.'

On his way to the shower Tom noticed the light flicking on the answering machine. He was surprised there was a message. He had turned down the volume so they could sleep. Had someone called through the night? He turned up the volume and stood frowning at the machine. Sarah's voice was almost unrecognisable. Tom turned it as high as possible. Thel came out of the kitchen and stood listening as Tom played it for the second time.

'*Tom, pick up the phone. It's me . . .*' Sarah's voice was strained and with the effort of whispering it came out of the machine in a high-pitched hiss. There was no mistaking her desperation. Thel, looking small and vulnerable in Tom's oversized bathrobe, put her hand on his arm. '*. . . Tom, oh Tom, I am so sorry. Forgive me. Please.*'

The line went dead and the answering machine tape whirred back to the start. Thel and Tom stood staring at it.

'The police will have to wait. We've got to get her out of there now,' said Tom.

Thel nodded. 'What was their reason for not letting you see her?' she asked.

'I wasn't immediate family. I'm her fiancé but not considered family.'

'Right,' said Thel. 'We'll see about that.'

Ginny cleaned her teeth, brushed her hair and put on clean clothes, her movements focussed and controlled. Tom had gone. He didn't want her. The fictitious world she had created around the two of them had shattered into a thousand tiny, sharp pieces. She felt them slicing through her from inside. They were like little shards of glass working their way through her soft and tender flesh.

He didn't want her. He had pushed her away. Ginny absorbed the pain, savoured its white-hot intensity and directed it towards the person who had made this all happen. Sarah. That vain, self-centred bitch Sarah. Sarah the perfect daughter. Sarah the most popular girl in the class. Sarah with all the boyfriends. Everything that Ginny should have had and should have been, Sarah was. And she had no right to it. It was unfair. And it had gone on for too long. Ginny was going to put a stop to it. Once and for all.

She carefully checked the contents of her handbag as Sarah's voice filled her bedroom.

'Tom, pick up the phone. It's me. Please help me. They think I'm on steroids. I'm not. They think I'm mad . . .' Ginny paused to listen. *'. . . You've got to get me out of here . . .'*

She had heard enough. Ginny was pointing her little blue car out of the driveway just as Sarah's anguished sobs filled her room.

CHAPTER 20

Sarah sat by herself on the bench seat near the pond, watching the family of ducks glide by. The sun warmed her face. She was far enough away from the nurses and other patients with visitors to be able to ignore the steady murmur of their conversations. Every few minutes a nurse would stroll a bit closer, just to let Sarah know she was still being watched. But they didn't speak to her and if she kept her head angled slightly to the left, she could screen out their presence completely. By narrowing her eyes into thin slits, Sarah could make the high brick walls disappear, so she could pretend everything was right with her world and she was enjoying a sunny morning by herself at the Botanic Gardens. Tom would be along later and they would go to the restaurant in the gardens for lunch.

Tom would hold her hand, order her favourite wine and they would talk. Sarah played with the picture in her mind's eye. Tom would tell her how silly she was to worry about hitting him. Of course it didn't matter, he would say. There was nothing she could do that would ever shake his love for her.

Then he would feed her sugar cubes, slowly, placing each one in her mouth and holding it while she nibbled. Then they would slip down their chairs and make love under the table, -screened from onlookers by the crisp white linen tablecloth.

Sarah toyed with her fantasy, touching it up here and there, finally switching the love scene to the idyllic spot by the pond. Forget under the table, they would walk out after lunch and come here, to the willow tree where Tom would take off her clothes piece by piece, kissing her feet until she was unable to bear the delicious sensations any longer and begged him to stop.

The vision lifted Sarah out of her misery, but only for a few moments. As the picture faded of Tom and her entwined on the mossy reed bank, she was left with a large empty hole and such a feeling of sadness that she thought she would drown in it.

Then something caught Sarah's attention and she opened her eyes wider. There was a rustling in the reeds, something moving. Briefly Sarah contemplated screaming 'crocodile!' and running for the gates, but she dismissed the idea as something only a mad person would do. The thought made her smile. Why not? What the hell? Maybe if she ran fast enough she would make it to the gate and, with the grace of an Olympic high-jump champion, could launch herself over the wall.

The rustling continued, spreading further, and Sarah started to become interested. She waited, sitting very still, expecting an animal to waddle out, maybe a duck. But it wasn't an animal that emerged from the reeds. It was a human nose, followed by a head and long hair tied back in a ponytail.

Hingeman, as the patients called him, crawled with cat-like grace out of the bushes and along the ground. He seemed oblivious of Sarah but she knew that wasn't true. He did his hinge act to get attention. It wasn't a coincidence he was crawling out in front of her. He must have gone to great lengths to make his way unseen along the pond bank to where she sat.

Sarah called out, 'Hey, Hingeman . . .' But he wouldn't look up. He kept his eyes firmly on the ground in front of him as he propelled himself soundlessly forward and past her feet. Sarah was disappointed. She would have liked to talk to Hingeman, to get to the bottom of the hinge thing, find out what the neuroses were that inspired this odd performance each day.

She liked Hingeman. Despite his unusual behaviour, he didn't seem as mad as the rest, just interesting. He didn't have that overly intense expression that so many of the patients had. Sarah wondered whether they came in that way or whether they were perfectly normal, like her, and became that way after too long locked up in here. The only way to cope was to go mad too. Go mad on the outside while staying safe and sane on the inside. It would be one way to keep yourself entertained.

Sarah wondered if such an idea was madness itself and was she, in fact, mad? How would she know? Clearly Dr Hubert thought she was. But maybe he was the one who was mad. Who was to say her behaviour wasn't completely sane, given the circumstances? But what were the circumstances? She had steroids in her bloodstream. But how had they got there? Or, she didn't have steroids in her system and someone had made a mistake, swapped her blood test results with another patient. Maybe it was Hingeman's blood.

What did one British cow say to the other? What do you think of this mad cow's disease? The other cow's response: What do I care, I'm a helicopter. Boom, boom. And he's a human hinge. And I'm not mad. Or am I?

Sarah desperately wanted to see Tom. He was her reference point. He would tell her if she was going mad. She didn't trust Dr Hubert with her private musings. If he knew what went on inside her head she would never get out of here. Everything she said or did, even the way she looked at him, went straight onto paper and into her file. And then it became fact. He made her fancies concrete when she wasn't sure that they should be. They were just passing thoughts. She was just as surprised as anybody at what popped into her head. Best to keep it to herself.

Sarah felt, rather than heard, a movement behind her. Ginny was standing by the seat. It looked as though she had been there for a while. Her face was grave and her eyes guarded. She was staring intently past Sarah at the pond.

'Ginny?'

Sarah was so pleased to see a familiar face. She started to rise, expecting a warm, friendly hug, but something about Ginny's manner made her stop halfway. Ginny didn't seem to be able to bring herself to look at Sarah. Sarah wondered if Ginny was nervous about being in a psychiatric hospital. Or perhaps she was nervous of Sarah, now that she had been branded a madwoman. Sarah felt hurt.

'Ginny, it's wonderful to see you. Come and sit down.'

Sarah desperately wanted Ginny to relax, to be normal, her old friend again. She was a reminder that Sarah did exist outside the confines of these walls, that she did have a life.

Ginny sat down next to Sarah, smoothing her navy pleated skirt in a fan around her and patting it with small, jerky movements. When she appeared satisfied with the skirt, splayed neatly about her, she put her handbag on her lap, clasping it tightly with both hands. She looked so prim and compact that Sarah almost wanted to laugh. But there was something very unsettling about her manner. Sarah had not seen her friend like this before.

'Ginny, are you okay?'

For the first time Ginny turned her attention to Sarah, swivelling her eyes slowly across to meet Sarah's. She didn't smile. She looked straight at Sarah with hard, dead eyes. Despite the full sun of the bright autumn morning, Sarah felt a chill run along her nerves just under the skin.

'Are you okay?' she asked again.

Ginny looked straight through her. 'I'm not the one in the madhouse, am I?' she said slowly and deliberately. Her words struck Sarah like a vicious slap.

Ginny's eyes flickered over Sarah's face and slid off. If it had been anyone but her old friend Ginny, Sarah would have interpreted the look as one of contempt. That didn't make sense. Ginny was her friend. But there was something almost sinister about the way she sat, her back rigid, both feet together on the ground. She looked like a schoolgirl posing for a school photo. But she wasn't smiling for the camera. She was staring at her hands. They were perfectly still, tightly clasping her handbag. Sarah noted how tightly she was gripping the handle. Her knuckles showed white and the tension was evident all the way up her arms. Sarah felt the hairs rise on the back of her neck.

Thel and Tom parked in front of the huge sandstone entrance of Orchard Park Psychiatric Hospital. Tom watched his mother march up the stone steps, her black braids swinging behind her. She exuded determination and defiance.

'Go Thel,' he prayed silently.

Tom had a view directly up the steps and watched as Thel disappeared inside. He saw her stand for a moment at the reception desk then disappear from view, he guessed, into the waiting room. He turned on his car radio and settled in for a long wait.

Thel asked for Dr Hubert then sat down. She noticed the old magazines and the locked cage doors at the end of the corridor. All about her was grey linoleum and insipid colourless walls. Maybe they had once been white, or cream, but now they were just dirty. The smells of the hospital stung Thel's nose. She felt her energy start to dissipate in these cold, sterile surroundings.

Finally Dr Hubert appeared. He stood in the doorway, sizing up Sarah's latest visitor.

Thel knew she was being appraised and she was ready for it. She smiled benignly, as if she had not a care in the world, and let the dapper little man with the distinguished-looking silver hair and well-trimmed goatee look her over.

'Dr Hubert,' she said after a moment, graciously extending

her hand. 'How lovely to meet you. I believe you are taking very good care of our Sarah.'

Dr Hubert found himself smiling back into a pair of lively dark brown eyes. The handshake was brisk. He opened his mouth to speak, to ask who this woman might be, but she was ready for him, her words coming out in a steady flow.

'I'm dying to see her. I promised her mother I would look after her. Poor Geraldine, over there in Singapore, not able to be much help. I'll be ringing her the minute I leave here to reassure her that her little girl is being well looked after.'

Thel didn't consider that to be a lie. Although she had never actually met Geraldine, she knew that if she had, she most certainly would have promised to look after Sarah. And it was equally true, as far as Thel was concerned, that Geraldine was of little use to her daughter over there in Singapore. She had said that to Tom on a few occasions. And as for ringing her, as she heard herself saying the words she thought it sounded like a good idea and decided she would. Any mother, even one as uninterested as Geraldine appeared to be, would want to know that her daughter was okay. Thel gave her most winning smile.

'Are you a member of Sarah's family?' asked Dr Hubert, thinking she must be some dotty aunt.

Thel didn't miss a beat.

'Family? Good heavens, what a question. I'm Sarah's other mother. She lived with me for years in Kiama. It's a lovely spot. Beautiful. I paint, you see. The ocean mainly. It's so quiet and peaceful. The perfect spot for Sarah to recuperate, when I get to take her home, after this, um, er, little . . . episode . . .'

Thel's voice trailed off theatrically. Dr Hubert wasn't a tall man but Thel was still shorter. She gazed up at him from under her dark lashes, trying to look concerned and motherly, worried but completely in charge. It was a complex mix and Thel hoped she got it just right.

'I see,' said Dr Hubert. And in fact he did see, rather a lot. He saw straight through Thel. He knew immediately that she was trying to snowball him. But she intrigued him. He guessed she was a shrewd and capable woman, trying to appear as some sort of scatty maiden aunt. He wondered if it was a role she played all the time or if she was putting it on just for his benefit.

Dr Hubert suspected she was deliberately obscuring the exact nature of her relationship with his patient, though he had no idea why, and yet she spoke so confidently he believed she was, to some degree, close to Sarah. She may be able to fill in some of the gaps that Sarah was so reluctant to discuss. Dr Hubert decided that whoever Thel really might be in the scheme of things, she could be of some help to him. He wondered if she knew Sarah's boyfriend and could give some insight into that relationship. She obviously knew the mother so she could at the very least help him work out Sarah's relationship with her parents.

Dr Hubert decided to give Thel a tour of the hospital so he could find out what he wanted to know. Then she could see Sarah. He didn't want to overload Sarah. She already had one visitor. A young woman who said she was family.

Sister Johns was in charge and he knew she would keep an eye on Sarah and notify him immediately if anything or anyone upset her.

He thought it might be good for Sarah to have some company. He still wasn't keen on letting the boyfriend near her, not yet, not until he was sure he wasn't part of the problem. Dr Hubert gestured for Thel to accompany him along the corridor.

Dr Hubert didn't usually conduct tours of his hospital for his patients' relatives. He was just as surprised as Thel when he heard himself saying, in his most charming tone, 'May I show you around the hospital and let you see for yourself how we are looking after your Sarah? Is that Mrs . . . ?'

'Thel. Just call me Thel, everyone does,' she replied, warming to this beak-nosed man with the funny duck's walk.

'All right, Thel, let me be your tour guide.'

Tom's eyes hadn't left the glass doors of the entrance. He had seen Dr Hubert appear at the reception desk, speak to the nurse behind the counter, then disappear from view. Tom could picture the waiting room with its old magazines and grey walls. He tried to imagine Thel greeting the doctor. He wondered what she was going to say. Tom prayed silently, his nerves stretched taut. He expected Thel to reappear at any moment, looking apologetic. She had tried, but they wouldn't let her in, she would say. 'Go Thel, go Thel,' he whispered urgently.

The moments stretched endlessly and finally Tom could stand it no longer. He got out of the car and inched his way around the other cars to get a better view inside the hospital foyer.

Dr Hubert walked into view and Tom ducked behind a tree, feeling guilty and foolish at the same time. When he popped his head out again he saw his mother smiling and chatting with Dr Hubert as he unlocked the cage security grille, holding it open for her to pass. They looked for all the world like a couple of old friends. 'Yes!' said Tom loudly. 'Good on you, Thel.'

He wondered why he had ever doubted his mother. If anyone could talk her way in anywhere it was Thel. Tom watched the security cage close behind them and leaned gratefully against the tree. He stayed for a few minutes, thinking about Thel and about Sarah. It was excruciating being so close to Sarah and not being able to see her. He thought of her voice on the answering machine that morning. She sounded so defeated, so miserable, it broke his heart. He let the emotion pour through him. Thel would sort it out.

Tom looked about the carpark. The day was growing warm and he didn't relish the idea of getting back into his car. He walked aimlessly around, stopping at a navy blue Ford. It looked like it had been parked in a hurry, standing far back from the curb at an odd angle. The car was disturbingly familiar. Tom moved closer and peered in the driver's window. It was neat inside, the plastic still on the inside of the doors. Tucked away in his memory was a vision of his hand on a plastic-covered car door. He remembered how he felt at that moment. Nauseous and disorientated. His head was thumping. That had been in Ginny's car.

Tom sprinted up the stone stairs, taking them two at a time. The medical receptionist was looking up glass repairers in the Yellow Pages when he burst in.

'Sarah Cowley. I have to see her now.'

The receptionist didn't react. She had worked at Orchard Park for enough years not to be fazed by agitated people walking up those steps. Just last week a man had collapsed from an overdose in the waiting room.

'She's in danger. I have to see her – *now*! For God's sake, please. She's in danger.'

The receptionist looked across at the security guard sitting just out of Tom's line of sight. He started to rise from his seat. Feeling more confident, she gave Tom her most reassuring smile.

'What seems to be the problem? Sarah who-did-you-say?'

'Sarah Cowley. She's a patient here. There's a car out the front that belongs to her friend. She's been poisoning her. She's here somewhere. Sarah's in danger. For God's sake . . .'

His words spilled out. Tom could hear the hysteria in his voice but was powerless to control it.

'Let me page Dr Hubert,' said the receptionist gently.

Her placating manner, clearly meant to soothe, only frustrated Tom further.

'No, no, we don't have time. Please, you've got to help . . .'

Tom's tone wavered between hysteria and pleading. The security guard listened to the conversation, ready to step in if he was needed. The receptionist was comforted by his burly presence and the solid desk that blocked her from this handsome but uptight young man.

Tom looked about him wildly. The locked cage doors at the end of the corridor were clearly meant to hold people in, but they were just as effective at keeping him out. He felt cornered, outmanoeuvred. As he watched, the cage doors opened and another nurse walked through. It was Sister Johns doing her rounds. She knew immediately something was amiss. She could see the receptionist was tense. Bill, the security guard, was on his feet. And facing her was a young man, pacing and gesticulating, clearly on edge.

She threw a look to Bill. He moved out from behind the pillar where he could get a clear view of Tom and Tom of him. Broad-shouldered and with a thick neck, Bill stood, feet apart, casually holding his baton, his face completely neutral. Sister Johns walked slowly and calmly toward Tom.

'What's the problem?' she said, careful to keep her distance.

Tom took a deep breath. He knew he had to be convincing, level-headed and above all not sound hysterical. It was his only chance. With supreme effort and fighting the panic that was threatening to overwhelm him, he lowered his voice. He drew on every last ounce of control he could find.

'My fiancée Sarah Cowley is a patient here,' he said, enunciating every word clearly and slowly. 'She has been poisoned. And the person who has been poisoning her is here. Her car is parked outside. Sarah is in great danger. I know this sounds outlandish but it's true. Please help me.'

Sister Johns knew exactly who Tom was talking about. She had just seen Sarah, sitting by the duck pond, chatting to a woman in a navy skirt. His story did sound outlandish but this was a mental hospital and she was used to that. There was something about Tom's earnestness and concern that touched a chord. She nodded to the security guard and he fell in close behind Tom. Sister Johns unlocked the cage door.

Dr Hubert showed Thel the ward upstairs where the patients slept, eight to a room. The room was spartan and sterile. Thel didn't like to think of Sarah here.

'It is very basic I know, but we try to do our best with the funding we receive.' As Dr Hubert looked about him he saw the future, his vision for the hospital when the much-awaited extra money came through from the government. The first project would be to replace the bars with multi-pane windows with special security glass and frames. He fought hard at every level for his patients.

Thel wasn't privy to his vision. She looked about her and hated everything she saw. The whole place screamed to her of pain and suffering. She could feel it in the walls, in the barren greyness.

'We have helped patients here for more than thirty-five years.' Dr Hubert spoke with humble pride. He was clearly passionate about his hospital.

Thel felt the pain of all the patients that must have passed through here during those years. She smiled politely, keeping her thoughts to herself.

Dr Hubert led her along the corridor to the dayroom. It had once been a stylish ballroom, with high ornate ceilings and an elaborate chandelier in the centre of the room, which looked incongruous now the room was filled with unmatched armchairs, a large TV and tables covered with debris – games and paper.

Thel walked across to a massive bay window. It would once have been beautiful. A feature of the room. Now it looked unbearably ugly with huge bars. Thel tried to ignore the bars as she looked out over the garden. Patients were wandering around or sitting with visitors, while nursing staff walked around, chatting to them. It looked a pleasant enough scene. Dr Hubert joined her by the window.

'They're not all mad you know. Some are, of course. But most of the people who come here are just mentally exhausted. Exhausted by life and all its stresses. The human mind is an extraordinary thing and will go to great lengths to accommodate stress, doing whatever it takes to maintain a sense of equilibrium. The manifestation of that can be perceived as mad. Often it is quite bizarre behaviour.'

Thel listened to his voice. It was deep and cultured, soothing. She imagined he would be good at reading bedtime stories to children.

'Is that what is wrong with Sarah?'

Dr Hubert nodded. 'Probably. It is too soon for me to tell

278

what is going on in her mind. She's not being very . . . helpful.'

Thel cheered Sarah silently. Nor would I be, she thought, if I was locked in here and had to share a room with seven others, then spend all day looking out these bars at the world outside.

'Has Sarah been under a lot of stress lately?' asked Dr Hubert.

Thel considered the question. 'She was getting married . . . to my son.'

Thel realised, too late, what she had said. She hadn't meant to reveal that she was Tom's mother. She wanted to imply she was part of Sarah's family. The words had just slipped out. Something about Dr Hubert's kindly eyes and soothing voice had made her trust him, instantly. That, she supposed, was how psychiatrists did their job. Got you to open up. It hadn't worked on Sarah but it seemed to be working just fine on Thel.

Dr Hubert picked it up at once. So she was Tom's mother.

'Please don't misunderstand me. They were very happy. It was just that Sarah did seem to be very stressed over the past few months, just not her normal self, and that is the only thing I can think of that had changed. Getting married can be stressful.'

'What about her parents? I understand they live overseas?'

Thel decided there was no point pretending to know them intimately.

'Well, Doctor, I don't think you can expect much help from them. They haven't shown much interest in Sarah for the past fifteen-or-so years as far as I can tell. When I said I was her other mother, I meant it. She lived with me some years ago and we are very close. I think of her as a daughter.'

Dr Hubert felt he was finally beginning to get somewhere. 'I don't want to upset you, Thel, now that I know you are Tom's mother, but I would like to ask if there was a history of violence in their relationship.'

The look on Thel's face spoke volumes. 'You mean did Tom ever hit her? My God, no.' She glared at him.

Dr Hubert continued, his voice still calm and measured. 'What about Sarah? Did she ever hit your son?'

'Good God, no. Dr Hubert, I am sure you get people in here who do all sorts of violent things like that but Sarah would never ever hurt my son.' As Thel spoke she realised that Sarah had done exactly that and that's why she was here.

Thel looked into Dr Hubert's inquiring eyes, studying her from behind his steel-rimmed glasses. He was quiet, standing very still just watching her. Thel stopped talking. In the silence that followed she realised how agitated and loud she had been, wound up ready to explode, ever since she had arrived at the hospital. She allowed herself to relax, letting her tension dissolve away with a deep outward sigh.

The change in her demeanour was marked and Dr Hubert smiled gently. It was then that Thel really saw the doctor for the first time and felt his kindly, compassionate presence. This man really wasn't the enemy. They stood quietly eyeing each other.

'You care about Sarah, don't you?' she said, voicing her thoughts.

Dr Hubert nodded. 'Of course. She's my patient.'

Thel operated on her instincts. And all her instincts were screaming at her to trust this man. 'Sarah has been fed steroids. By her best friend. She has been poisoned.'

Dr Hubert listened intently, nodding, encouraging her to go on. Thel didn't try to put her thoughts into any order. She blurted out everything that was in her head. She trusted Dr Hubert would be able to make sense of what she was telling him.

'She didn't know. Tom figured it out. She's very upset. She called us last night. She needs me. Please let me see her. I want to see her. Where is she?'

Dr Hubert moved across the room to a side window which looked out across another corner of the garden. He pointed to a neat little duck pond where two women were sitting together on a bench.

'Sarah's fine, she's . . .' Dr Hubert stopped at the look of alarm on Thel's face.

'Oh no,' she said, starting to tremble. 'Oh God. That's Ginny. That's her.' Thel grabbed Dr Hubert's arm. 'How do I get to them?' she screamed.

Ginny was perfectly poised, all her emotions under control, as she looked at Sarah. She gripped the handle of her bag in her lap, holding it tightly to her. Her eyes were cold and hard as she stared Sarah down. They looked at each other and time was suspended. Around them the distant voices of the other patients, mingled with the autumn sounds of birds and whistling trees. It was just Sarah and Ginny, sitting on the park bench, a lifetime of unspoken history between them.

Sarah sensed that something had changed, irrevocably, between them. She didn't understand what but the eyes that bore into hers were filled with such hatred it chilled her to the bone.

'I don't understand,' whispered Sarah. 'What has happened?'

It was as if she hadn't spoken. Ginny continued to stare through her, clutching her bag tightly in her lap.

'You have always had everything, everything,' said Ginny. 'Because you were Sarah Cowley.' Her voice was thin and strained. She bared her teeth as she spoke.

'Ginny, for God's sake, what is going on? You're my friend.'

Ginny's eyes narrowed to thin slits. Her voice dropped to a low hiss. '*I was never your friend.*'

Each word sliced through Sarah. The sentiment was hurtful enough but the malice in Ginny's tone was sharp and shocking. Sarah struggled to make sense of what was happening.

'You had everything, *everything*. Why? Because you were Sarah, beautiful, pampered Sarah. Smart Sarah. Pretty Sarah. Sarah, Sarah, Sarah,' sneered Ginny. 'God, how I *hate* you. Everything about you is by virtue of you being born. That was all you had to do. And you took it all as your due. Your birthright. While what was I? Poor old Ginny. Ginny, the orphan. Ginny, the also-ran.'

Sarah sat mutely through the tirade, too shocked to speak.

'Your life should have been mine.'

Sarah barely recognised the twisted face of the woman sitting beside her, as, for the first time she saw, past the public façade and into the real core of Ginny. It was rotten, putrid, like flyblown meat. The hatred in Ginny's contorted face hit her hard, like a physical blow. Sarah started to tremble in the face of such malevolence. But Ginny was unmoved. She wanted to see Sarah suffer. She knew she was inflicting pain and it delighted her. She moved in for the final blow.

'You have no idea, do you?'

Sarah's head started wobbling uncontrollably.

'I'm your sister.'

Ginny spat it out and Sarah felt a chasm open beneath her. The last vestiges of life as she had known it seeped away, leaving something ugly and deformed in its wake. Sarah felt the air, the garden, everything about her, sullied by its presence.

Ginny threw back her head and laughed. 'Yes, that's right. I'm the bastard child of your father. Your precious Daddy. Couldn't keep it in his pants, could he? Got his secretary pregnant. Oh don't look so pathetic. It's an old, old story. He had his fun then left her with the shame. Left her in Perth and went on to his next glamorous posting. She couldn't tell her parents so I was farmed out, like some shameful secret that could never be exposed. Well, it's time that secret was exposed.'

Sarah recoiled. The images Ginny was painting were obscene. She wanted to run, to get away from this ugliness. Ginny's hand snaked around her wrist, squeezing it tightly, pinning her to the bench.

'You're not going anywhere, precious little Sarah. It's time you knew the ugly truth. What you and your father have done. How you robbed me of my life.'

Sarah looked into the face of madness and braced herself.

She stopped shaking as her strongest, most basic instincts of self-preservation took over. She stared back at Ginny, aware that the woman in front of her was her enemy. And she knew, beyond any doubt, that Ginny was the reason she was locked in here.

'What have you done?' she asked quietly.

Ginny ignored her question.

'Your life should have been my life. Except that your gutless father, our gutless father, wouldn't acknowledge me.'

Sarah kept her eyes fixed on Ginny but was aware of everyone else in the garden. The nurses were too far away to hear their conversation but Sarah knew she could scream and they would be there in an instant. She drew strength from that.

'I don't believe you,' she said.

Ginny laughed contemptuously. 'Oh, it's true. You can believe it. It wasn't my idea of good news either. I rather preferred the story of my parents being killed in a car crash when I was a baby. I wasn't thrilled to discover that ageing Lothario you call Daddy is my father too. At least that vacuous bimbo he's married to isn't my mother. I suppose that's something. My mother died when I was three and I was sent to live with that woman, my so-called aunt.'

'What makes you think he is your father?' asked Sarah.

'You know that trust fund that paid my school fees? Guess who set that up? Mr Augustus Cowley Esquire, retired diplomat, current address Orchard Road, Singapore.'

'How do you know that?'

Ginny laughed with triumph. 'You know my little trip to Perth, to see my aunt and sort out her will? It's all there in her papers. She wasn't my aunt. She was just someone paid to keep me from finding out.

'She wrote me a little letter to be opened after her death. Well, she died and I opened it. And it was full of the whole dirty little secret. How he paid for me, paid for his sins with money, as if that was enough. Guilt money. He wanted me to have every privilege you had. When you were sent to boarding school he wanted me to go to the same school. When you had tennis lessons and piano lessons, I had to have them too. But I wasn't quite as good as his precious little Sarah. While he gave you his name and his love, he gave me his shame. The shame of being born.

'But you know what's even sicker? What our sicko father did?'

Ginny paused for effect.

'It is a condition of the trust fund that if I ever found out, I was to keep the shameful secret of my being born or the payments would stop. If I told his precious little Sarah the truth, the trust fund would be dissolved.'

Sarah reeled from the shock. 'It's not true. It can't be true,' she whispered.

She thought of her father, heard him telling her to invite Ginny along whenever they came to visit, asking after Ginny when he called from Singapore. It couldn't be true. That was just her father being friendly. Her mind grappled with the new information. She tried to reconcile her image of her father, kindly and honourable, with the man Ginny had just described. They were a world apart. Her father wouldn't do that. He just wouldn't. He wasn't like that.

Sarah felt her stomach clutch with the icy tendrils of dread.

Ginny watched Sarah closely, relishing the confusion and anguish that played across her face. Ginny had one more trump card. But she wanted to hold onto it, let Sarah experience this pain completely before she played it. She savoured the moment.

'You thought you could have it all didn't you, little Sare Bear.'

Sarah heard Ginny's voice come to her from a long way off. What did she call her? Sare Bear. Why was she calling her that? Only Tom ever called her that. It was his silly pet name for her. Why was she using it? What did this have to do with Tom?

Ginny giggled with delight. She let go of Sarah's wrist and opened her handbag. She fished around inside and drew out a polaroid photo, brandishing it in the air. Sarah couldn't make out what it was. Ginny dropped it face up in Sarah's lap.

It was a photo of Tom, his eyes closed and with Ginny's arms draped around his neck. The picture was taken at an odd angle, from below the chest and Ginny's naked breast was clearly visible. They appeared to be on a rug. Ginny was smiling dreamily at the camera, while Tom appeared to be asleep. Sarah stared at the image then turned and dry-retched onto the grass.

'Did you think he would still want you after what you did?' hissed Ginny. 'He's mine now.'

Ginny opened her bag again and while Sarah heaved, silently pulled out a syringe. Her hands were perfectly steady as she withdrew the plastic cap.

Sarah stayed bent over, waiting for the nausea to pass. The photo was an abomination. Ginny looked at Sarah's bare arm, eyeing her from wrist to shoulder, then slid silently along the bench. She reached up deftly with one hand, gripping Sarah's bicep, and with the other, raised the syringe ready to jab.

Tom hurled himself across the top of the bench, knocking Ginny to the ground. They landed in a heap on the grass. Ginny struggled but she was no match for Tom. He was stronger and angrier.

The security guard and Sister Johns were seconds behind him. The guard moved Tom away and pinned Ginny to the ground, sitting on her chest. He was a burly man and his weight knocked the breath from her body. When he was sure she had given up the fight, he eased the pressure.

Sarah sat in shock, her arms wrapped about her, staring at the photo on the ground. Tom knelt in front of her. Her face was wretched. She focussed on him and said his name in a small, pained voice. It was as if her face was a mirror shattering in front of him. In her voice he could hear the breaking glass, falling underfoot and being trodden on. He wrapped his arms about her and held her tightly. She didn't respond, just sat mutely in the circle of his arms.

'It's going to be okay,' he soothed. 'It's all over now.' He rocked her gently, patting her hair, trying to absorb her pain and impart his own love and strength.

Thel and Dr Hubert arrived, Thel panting with the effort of running across the lawn.

'Sarah, oh honey,' she said.

While Tom held Sarah, Thel stroked her hair, tears coursing down her face.

Dr Hubert retrieved the syringe from the grass, holding it carefully between two fingers.

'What's this?' he said.

'I think you'll find that contains steroids,' said Tom. 'Or horse tranquilliser. She's a vet and she's been poisoning Sarah.' Tom couldn't bring himself to say Ginny's name.

Sarah heard the words, but they held no meaning. It was as though this was all happening to someone else, somewhere far away, a long time ago.

'And this?' Dr Hubert picked up the polaroid photo. He recognised the people in it. He raised an eyebrow, hesitated, then held it for Tom and Thel to see.

Tom's face drained of colour. 'Oh God. She is sick. She drugged me, kept me in her apartment. She must have taken it then.'

Thel gasped. 'When you came out of hospital . . . I knew it. I knew there was something wrong. I rang but she wouldn't let me speak to you.' She glared at Ginny. Thel had never hated anyone in her life. But she felt an all-consuming black rage against Ginny at that moment. The force of it made her tremble. Dr Hubert noticed and put an arm around her shoulders. Thel leaned gratefully against him.

The small group stood silently looking at Ginny, her small body trapped under the bodyguard, her neat navy skirt, wet and stained with grass.

Ginny kept her head turned away from them all, staring silently out at the pond.

TWO YEARS ON

Sarah peeked through the rhododendron bush, taking care not to be seen by the small group gathered at the water's edge.

'They're all there,' she whispered.

Thel smiled at her. 'Be careful of your dress, honey.'

Sarah stood back and smoothed the loose flowing dress over her bump. She wore a pale pink shift that fell a few inches above her knee. 'Do you think it shows?'

Thel grinned. 'Yep. I'd say it's pretty obvious.'

Sarah giggled with delight. Thel tucked the younger woman's hand into the crook of her arm and patted it.

'You should see Tom,' whispered Sarah. 'He looks so handsome in his tuxedo.'

'All men do, honey,' said Thel.

Sarah was nervous, fidgeting in the small space behind the Toft Monks boatshed. By contrast, Thel was the picture of calm. Her long dark hair was loose, falling softly about her shoulders, a sprig of jasmine pinned behind one ear. She revelled in Sarah's excitement.

It was a vibrant spring afternoon and the waters of Rush-cutters Bay shimmered in the sunlight. The boats moored in the bay jostled with each other, moved by the warm breeze. A sense of anticipation rippled through the small group of people assembled informally by the jetty. Kate, resplendent in figure-hugging leopard skin took a step forward and began to sing.

Never know how much I love you,
Never know how much I care
When you put your arms around me
I get a fever that's so hard to bear.
You give me fever . . .

Sarah and Thel linked arms and stepped out from behind the rhododendron bush. They fell into step together, easily and naturally, walking sedately across the manicured lawns to the water's edge.

. . . when you kiss me
fever when you hold me tight.
Fever
In the morning.
Fever all through the night . . .

Kate belted out the song with all the chutzpah and energy she possessed. Her enthusiasm was infectious. Sarah and Thel sashayed to the beat as they walked.

. . . You give me fever,
Fever when you kiss me, fever when you hold me tight
Fever
In the morning
Fever all through the night . . .

The buoyant mood was contagious and the rest of the group joined in the raunchy ballad. By the time Thel and Sarah reached them they were in full swing, tapping their feet and clapping along.

Sun lights up the daytime
Moon lights up the night
I light up when you call my name
And you know I'm going to treat you right.

The two women walked past Tom, handsome and proud in his tuxedo. Thel winked at her son and he grinned back. They came to a halt in front of the civil celebrant, a neat woman wearing a smart navy suit and the unmistakable air of officialdom. Kate finished singing and everyone clapped.

'Who brings this woman here today?' asked the celebrant.

Hal stepped forward.

'I do,' he said loudly and clearly. He took his place by Thel while Sarah stepped back, slipping her arm through Tom's.

'Do you, Thelma Valda Wilson, take Nicholas Charles Maxwell Hubert . . .'

Dr Hubert looked into Thel's sparkling brown eyes and grinned.

The formal part of the day was over in a matter of minutes. The happy little group reconvened in Tom and Sarah's apartment. Sarah handed around canapés and Tom served champagne.

Sarah had spent days cooking, insisting on doing it all herself despite her advanced state of pregnancy. Thel threw her head back and laughed when she saw the pastry pie Sarah had baked. She noticed Hal's boyfriend David staring at it.

'That's Sarah's specialty,' she said to him.

'What is it . . . a lighthouse?'

Thel chuckled.

'Actually, it's a penis.'

David looked shocked, which amused Thel even further.

'Not like any I've seen,' he said.

Thel raised one eyebrow.

He looked at it again, more critically. 'Mind you, now that you mention it . . .'

They both laughed conspiratorially, like naughty children. Hal joined them by the table, asking what was so funny. They both shook their heads.

'Nothing, Hal.'

Sarah offered a plate of canapés to Dr Hubert, who was standing apart from the rest looking out across the bay.

'How is the nervous groom?'

'I'm doing fine, just fine. How are you?'

'That's such a loaded question coming from a psychiatrist. What can I say? I'm no more neurotic than usual.'

Dr Hubert smiled down his beaked nose. 'Sarah Cowley, you are one of the sanest people I know. To have come through what you did as well as you have is the mark of a very strong character.'

Sarah was thoughtful for a moment. She carried deep and painful wounds from that time, which were still healing. Often in the very early hours of the morning, while Tom slept, she would prowl the apartment, tense and wired, asking herself how it could have happened, going over it all again and again. She relived her school years with Ginny, the horror of the four months when she had lost control of her body, her mind and her life, and the painful showdown she had had with her father.

It had torn apart her relationship with her parents. Her mother had refused to believe any of it while her father had privately admitted it was true, breaking down and sobbing his shame to Sarah. One day the wounds may heal, but Sarah wasn't ready for that yet. Discovering she was pregnant had marked the beginning of her recovery. The anger that had kept her in a holding pattern had started to dissipate. Instead of focussing on what had happened and what could have been, she found herself looking forward to the future and making plans.

'Thank you,' she said softly. 'It is very reassuring to hear you say that.'

Dr Hubert placed a hand on her arm. 'Do you think you will ever stop seeing me as a psychiatrist?'

Sarah laughed. 'That may take more time, I think. But I'm working on it.'

They sipped their champagne, looking out across at the apartment building facing them. Sarah's gaze settled on a balcony. The doors were flung open and she could see inside to a young couple painting the walls. Dr Hubert followed her gaze.

'It doesn't worry you, still living here?' he asked.

'I won't let it,' said Sarah, defiantly.

Tom cleared his throat and tapped a champagne glass to get everyone's attention. 'I would like to toast my mother and the very lucky man who this afternoon married her.'

Thel took her place by her new husband, her dark eyes sparkling.

'My mother is an amazing woman. She has been my best friend all my life. I admire her for her strength, her character, her integrity and most of all her extraordinary compassion. She is mad, of course, everyone here knows that. And that's just one reason that Nicholas is perfect for her. But she is also one gutsy lady. Thel, I pay tribute to you. You light up the world.'

Thel's eyes filled with tears. Everyone raised their glass and toasted her.

'I would like also to pay tribute to Nicholas. I couldn't have picked a finer man for Thel. You share her passion for art, her sense of humour and you have my deepest respect for the way you have come into this unorthodox family and accepted us all exactly as we are. You have seen us at the best and worst of times and yet you are still here. We welcome you with open arms.'

Sarah and Hal shouted, 'Hear, hear!'

Late afternoon turned into early evening and the group moved out onto the balcony, watching the yachts return to their moorings and the sun drop slowly behind the city. The fruit bats started their evening migration, filling the sky as they flew overhead in search of trees, heavy with juicy fat fruit, where they could feast through the night.

As the day slipped away the little party grew noisier. Their voices carried back into the lounge room, drifting up into the ceiling, and along hidden wires to a mobile phone, tucked into the insulation batts.

Two-hundred kilometres away in the dayroom of a women's prison, a young dark-haired woman with stern angular features sat tightly coiled in a broken armchair. She seemed to take up very little space and no-one else noticed her as she sat very quietly, clutching her coins in her hand and waiting for her turn at the telephone.

Jessica Adams
Tom, Dick and Debbie Harry

Richard has a problem. His wife-to-be Sarah has gone missing on their wedding day. His brother Harry's problem is that he only wants one woman in the world – Debbie Harry – but he works in a bank. Richard's best man Tom wonders if it's okay to live with a woman old enough to be his mother.

Meanwhile, far away from sleepy Compton in Tasmania to the mania of a women's magazine in Sydney, Richard's first wife Bronte needs to find a new astrologer for her magazine while working out fifty things to do with bananas.

Will Richard find Sarah? Why is she missing? Will Tom stay with his mother-figure girlfriend? Will Bronte break free of the artificiality of the magazine world? Will Harry ever get to meet his idol?

Welcome to the world of TOM, DICK AND DEBBIE HARRY. Three men, the women they love and a sexually dysfunctional sheepdog.

'Jessica Adams turns her *Single White E-mail* chutzpah loose again in *Tom, Dick and Debbie Harry*. A 90s noir comedy'
AUSTRALIAN

'What Adams does is hit the nerve of everyday life'
PUNCH (UK)

'Who says nothing ever happens in Tasmania? A hilarious romp – perfect for a lazy day in the sun'
ELLE

Beverley Harper
Jackal's Dance

Agony exploded in her knee. She staggered, tried to keep going, then nearly fell as a shocking pain rushed up her leg. Confusion and fear swamped her senses, escape suddenly essential. The tuskless cow turned and hobbled away, each step agonising torture. Her front right knee joint had been shattered by the single copper-jacketed bullet.

Man, her hated enemy, had just handed out a death sentence.

As the rangers and staff of a luxury lodge in Etosha National Park, Namibia welcome the last guests of the season, thoughts are predominantly on the three-month break ahead. Except for Sean, who is fighting his growing attraction for the manager's wife, Thea.

Camping in the park nearby, Professor Eben Kruger has his work cut out keeping the attention of the university students in his charge on the behavioural habits of the cunning jackal.

None of them could ever be prepared for the horrendous events about to take place. Each will be pushed to breaking point as the quest for survival becomes the only thing that matters.

Shocking, gripping, breathtaking. Beverley Harper's outstanding new novel is a guaranteed bestseller.